JUST ONE OF THE GUYS

JUST ONE OF THE GUYS

Kristan Higgins

CHIVERS

British Library Cataloguing in Publication Data available

This Large Print edition published by AudioGO Ltd, Bath, 2011.
Published by arrangement with Harlequin Enterprises BV

| U.K. | Hardcover | ISBN | 978 1 4458 6033 6 |
| U.K. | Softcover | ISBN | 978 1 4458 6034 3 |

Printed and bound in Great Britain by
MPG Books Group Limited

To Terence Keenan—
Husband. Father. Firefighter.
In that order.

ACKNOWLEDGMENTS

As ever, I am grateful to Maria Carvainis, my kind and brilliant agent;

To Tracy Farrell and Keyren Gerlach for their enthusiasm and support of this book;

To fellow writer Rose Morris, my dear friend and perfect reader;

and to Beth Emery, head coach of women's crew at Wesleyan University, who patiently answered my questions about rowing.

And most especially, thanks to Terence Keenan, my dear husband, who advised, laughed and cooked while I wrote this book, and to my two wonderful kids. You three are the loves of my life.

CHAPTER ONE

'I think we should stop seeing each other.'

My jaw drops. I inhale sharply, and the stuffed mushroom I just popped in my mouth is sucked right into my esophagus. Jason continues, unaware of my distress. 'It's run its course, don't you think? I mean, it's not like we've . . .'

Seems like my little old air passage is completely plugged. My eyes are tearing, my chest convulses—*Before you break up with me, Jason, would you mind a little Heimlich?* I slam my hand down on the table, rattling the china and cutlery, but Jason assumes that my distress is heartbreak and not oxygen deprivation. He looks away.

I'm being killed by my appetizer. I knew I shouldn't have ordered it, but Emo makes the little number drenched in butter, with little bits of garlic and parsley and . . . um . . . *Must breathe now. Save food review for later.* The pressure in my neck is building. I make a fist, wedge it just below my sternum, and slam myself into the table. The mushroom shoots out, hits a water glass and comes to a rest on the white tablecloth. I suck in an enormous breath, then begin coughing.

Jason eyes the mushroom with distaste, and without thinking, I grab it, stuff it in a napkin

1

and take another beautiful gulp of air. Breathing. It's so underrated.

'I was choking, you idiot,' I manage to wheeze.

'Oh. Sorry about that. Well, good thing you're okay.'

It's hard for me to believe that I was even dating Jason to begin with, let alone the fact that he's dumping me. Dumping *me!* I should be dumping *him!*

I glance at the wadded-up napkin containing the instrument of my near death. The poor busboy who has to deal with that. Should I warn him? Otherwise, he'll shake it out, innocent, unaware, and the unchewed mushroom will fly across the kitchen, sliding on the floor, maybe getting squashed under a shoe . . .

Focus, Chastity, focus. You're being dumped. At least find out why. 'So, Jason, that's fine. I mean, clearly it wasn't love at first sight. But other than that, do you mind telling me . . . well, why?'

Jason, whom I have been seeing for about three weeks, takes an impervious sip of wine and stares over my head. 'Do we have to dissect this, Chastity?'

'Well, um . . . think of it as my desire to gain information. I *am* a journalist, remember.' I try a friendly smile, but I'm not feeling so chummy right now. Or ever, now that I think of it. At least, not toward Jason.

'Do you really want to know?'

'Yes, actually, I do.' I pause, feeling a flush prickle its way up my chest. Our brief relationship has been tepid at best, but I thought the malaise was emanating from me. More than anything, this is a matter of wounded pride. Jason and I have been on four dates now. He lives in Albany, and it's a bit of a hassle to make the drive, and sometimes neither of us is feeling that inspired. Still, I didn't see this coming.

Jason's tongue is searching for something near a back molar. His mouth contorts as his cheek bulges. I find myself hoping he'll choke, too. Seems only fair. His eyes still don't bother to meet mine. 'Fine,' he acquiesces, leaving whatever morsel lurks at the back of his mouth for later enjoyment. 'You want to hear the reason? I just don't find you attractive enough. Sorry.'

My mouth drops open yet again. 'Not attractive! Not attract— I'm very attractive!'

Jason rolls his eyes. 'Sure. A handsome woman. Whatever. And with shoulders like those, you could find work down on the docks.'

'I row!' I protest. 'I'm strong! That's supposed to be sexy.'

'Yes, well, proving that you could pick me up didn't exactly set my libido on fire.'

'We were horsing around!' I cry. It was, in fact, the one lighthearted moment in our courtship . . . we'd been hiking, he complained

3

that he was tired, I took over. End of story.

'You gave me a piggyback ride for a mile and a half, Chastity. That's something a Sherpa should do, not a girlfriend.'

'It wasn't my fault that you couldn't manage a measly twelve-mile trail!'

'And another thing. You yell.'

'I do not yell!' I yell, then catch myself. 'I have four brothers,' I say primly and much more quietly. 'It's not always easy to make oneself heard.'

'Look. Is there any point in this?' Jason asks. 'I'm sorry. I just don't find you that attractive, Chastity.'

'Fine. For that matter, I think you need to bathe more often, Jason. This whole Seattle-grunge-patchouli thing is so 1990s.' It's not a bad comeback, but my face is burning nonetheless.

'Whatever. Here.' Taking out his wallet, he puts a few bills on the table. 'This should cover my half. Take care of yourself.' He slides out of the booth.

'Jason?' I say.

'What?'

'You throw like a girl.'

He rolls his eyes and walks out.

I don't care, do I? It's not like he was The One. He was just an experiment, just a toe-dip into the dating pool of upstate New York. The good thing is, I don't have to look at his freckled, hairless legs any more. At least I won't have to watch him cut his food into tiny, tiny bites that he chews relentlessly until they are merely flavored saliva. Won't have to hear that funny nose whistle he has all the time and is completely unaware of. He was only five foot ten to boot, almost two inches shorter than my superfox self.

Superfox. Right. I shove my mushrooms away—who's hungry now?—and drain my wineglass. *Not attractive.* Jerk. How dare he say that? It's not like he was George bleeping Clooney, either! Just a skinny, pale, mop-haired dweeb who happened to ask me out. *He* initiated contact! I didn't throw myself at him. I didn't kidnap him. There were no bags over heads, no handcuffs, no long rides in the trunk of my car. I did *not* have to dig a pit in my basement and chain him there. Why am I suddenly not attractive?

This means nothing, I tell myself. Jason meant nothing. It's just that he was the first guy I'd dated since moving back to my hometown. And, now that I think of it, the first guy I've dated in . . . um . . . crap. A long time. So Jason was, well, the frog I was kissing. I want to settle down, sure. Maybe I'm feeling a little under the gun to get married and spawn the four babies I always wanted.

I'm almost thirty-one years old, and these are the ugly years for women like me. What happened to all those guys in my mid-twenties? In grad school? At the paper? There

5

must be some line that we women cross. College, grad school, just starting out in a job . . . we're a blast then. A few years of career under our belt . . . watch out, boys! She's a-wantin' a ring!

I glance furtively around the restaurant, hoping for a distraction. Emo's is packed tonight—families, couples of all ages, friends. My newly dumped status seems broadcast throughout the restaurant. It's better than being with Jason, actually, but still. I'm the only person here alone. Emo's—a place so often visited by my family that we have a booth named after us—is half bar, half restaurant, separated by double French doors. The bar, I can see, is packed. My beloved Yankees are playing at home. They've won their first five games of the season. Why, I wonder, did I agree to go out with Jason when I could be watching Derek Jeter instead?

Without further thought, I leave the booth, the site of my humiliation and near-death episode, wave to the waitress to alert her to the change of venue and go into the bar.

'Hey, Chas!' Several men—Jake, Santo, Paul, George—chorus my name, and my battered ego is mollified somewhat. Having four older brothers, two of whom are Eaton Falls firefighters alongside my father, a captain, ensures that I know just about every local male under the age of fifty. Unfortunately, this has done nothing for me

6

thus far on the boyfriend front, since there seems to be a law against dating the O'Neill girl—me.

'Hello, there, Chastity,' says Stu, the bartender.

'Hi, Stu. How about . . . um . . .'

'Bud Light?' he suggests, my usual drink.

'Nah. How about a Scorpion Bowl? Okay?'

Stu pauses. 'You sure? They're not really just for one person.'

'I'm walking home. It's fine. I need it, Stu. Oh, and some nachos, too, please. Better make it grande.'

I find an empty stool and turn my attention to the Bronx Bombers. The mighty Jeter makes a trademark twisting leap, snags the ball, then tags out the runner who was foolish enough to assume it was safe to leave second base. Double play, thank you, Derek. At least something's going right tonight.

Stu puts my drink in front of me, and I take a large gulp, then grimace. Stupid Jason. I wish I'd dumped him before he dumped me. I knew he wasn't the one I'd end up with, but I was hoping to like him more as time went on. Hoping for some hidden qualities to seep out from his pallid, freckled skin and eradicate the sneaking suspicion that I was dating him because I had no one better to be with.

Didn't happen. Another gulp from the Scorpion Bowl burns down my throat. *Don't worry about that jerk,* the Scorpion Bowl seems

7

to say. *He was icky, anyway.* Yes. True, Scorpion Bowl. But he did beat me to the breakup punch. Damn.

'Here you go, Chastity,' Stu—six feet even—says, setting down the nacho mountain in front of me. Cheese oozes off the sides, jalapeños are glommed on top of a cloud of sour cream, and suddenly, I'm starving, the mushroom mishap forgotten.

'Thanks, Stu.' I pull off a hunk of nachos and take a bite. Heaven. Another swallow of hideous drink. Not so bad this time, not with a nacho chaser, and a pleasant buzz fuzzes my brain. Good old Scorpy. Haven't had one since an ill-advised college drinking party, but I'm starting to remember why they were so popular back then.

The inning is over, and a commercial comes on. Taking another bite and another slug of my drink, I glance back out at the restaurant. Through the French doors at the table nearest the bar sits a good-looking man. Though I can't quite see his companion, her hair is white, making me think she's his mother, possibly his boss. He really is handsome in that perfect and somewhat sterile *New York Times Magazine* way . . . prep school rich, full lips, long, flopping McDreamy-style blond hair, bone structure of the gods. Six-two. Even though he's sitting, I can estimate his height to within centimeters, barring unanticipated leg amputation, of course. Six-two. The perfect

8

male height. Aside from Jeter, and Viggo Mortenson as Aragorn in *Lord of the Rings,* this guy is basically my ideal man.

Watching him, my heart sinks a little further. A man like that is way, way out of my league. Not that I'm a hideous, stooped, wart-ridden hag, but I'm . . . well. Perhaps I'm a bit . . . tall? But isn't tall in? *The fashion designers love tall women,* the Scorpion Bowl tells me. I snort. Maybe women who are thirty or forty pounds lighter than I am, but still. Better five-eleven and three-quarters than four foot nine. And yes, I'm strong. Healthy. Strapping. Muscular. Teamster-esque.

I sigh. No, Mr. *New York Times* Fashion Section would never even notice me. It's a pity, because I'm getting a little turned on just watching him chew. It's sexy. Sexy chewing. Listen to me! And yet it's true. I've never seen sexier chewing.

Someone slides in next to me at the crowded bar. Trevor. Great. He looks at me, does a double take, and one gets the impression that he wouldn't have chosen this particular spot at the bar had he known the O'Neill girl was sitting here.

'Hey, Chas,' he says amiably enough. 'How's it going?'

'Hi, Trevor, I've been dumped,' I announce, regretting it immediately. It was supposed to sound self-deprecating and wry, but it falls flat.

'Who dumped you?' he says. 'Not that

skinny pale guy?'

I nod, not looking at Trevor, who is neither skinny nor pale, but brawny and chocolate-eyed and irresistible.

'Are you kidding? *He* dumped *you?*'

A small smile tugs at my mouth. 'Yes,' I acknowledge. 'And thanks.'

'Well, you're better off without him,' Trevor says. 'He was an idiot.' Trevor met him only once, but his assessment, I must admit, is spot on. I don't answer, and Trevor looks at me carefully. 'You want me to walk you home, Chastity?' He glances around the bar. 'I guess none of the boys are here.' The boys being my brothers and dad, of course.

'No,' I sigh, a bit wetly. 'I'll just sit here and watch the Yanks.'

'Right. Well, I'll hang out with you,' he says, dutiful as ever.

'Thanks, Trev.' I blink back the pathetic tears that his offer—and probably my beloved Scorpion Bowl—invoke, then mentally slap myself. Jason is not worth any angst or woe. It's just that what Jason said . . . it hurt. Even if he was a patchouli-reeking jerk.

'Come on. There's a booth.'

Trevor grabs the nachos, I grab my Bowl.

Trevor—five foot eleven and a half—occupies an odd spot in my heart. On the one hand, he's like my fifth brother. I've known him since I was in third grade, and he's the best friend of both Mark and Matt, two of my four

10

brothers. In fact, Trevor has spent more time with my family than I have in the past ten years. He works with—and reveres—my father, who is Trevor's captain. He's godfather to one of my nephews. He's arguably my mother's favorite child, biology be damned.

On the other hand, and this is probably the hand that matters, he's Trevor. Trevor James Meade. Beautiful name, beautiful man. And though he's a longtime, very close family friend, and though I find him very, very attractive, Trevor is not a possibility. *Don't dwell on it,* Scorpy advises. Scorpy has a point.

I try not to look at Trevor, turn my eyes to Jeter—six-three, God bless him—and the other boys, but the score is, oh, heck, three hundred and twelve to two or something and the Yanks are on their eleventh batter of the inning, so it's not exactly a nail-biter. I glance across the table. Trevor gives me a perfunctory smile, but he looks a little uncomfortable. I can't remember the last time that he and I were alone together. Oh, shit, yes I can. When he came down to New York City and told me he was getting married. How can a girl forget? Another grim, embarrassing memory. I sigh, sip and take another layer of nachos.

Trevor signals effortlessly to the waitress—being female, she noticed Trevor the minute he walked in, and she stumbles to a halt at the joy of being summoned. Typical.

'Is that your first drink, Chas?' Trevor asks.

11

'Yes,' I reply. 'Just one little Scorpion Bowl. They're kind of cute, aren't they?'

Trevor smiles more genuinely. 'Hope you won't mind if I walk you home tonight.'

'Not at all, Firefighter Meade.' I grin back a little sloppily.

'What can I get you?' the waitress breathes in a Marilyn Monroe sex-kitten voice. 'Would you like a beer? The wine list? A few kids and a mortgage?' Actually, she didn't specifically say that last one, but it was clearly implied.

'I'll have a Sam Adams,' Trevor says, smiling up at her.

'I'd like another Scorpion Bowl,' I tell her.

'I'm Lindsey,' she breathes, ignoring me. 'I'm new here.'

'Nice to meet you, Lindsey,' Trevor says. I don't bother to reply, since I'm not part of this conversation anyway. On the television screen, Jeter clips the ball over the first baseman's head and flies off down the first base line, stretching the hit into a double. I get the feeling he knows I'm feeling down and is doing his utmost to cheer me up. Oh, now he's stealing third. Yes, it's clear. Jeter loves me.

The waitress is slipping a piece of paper to Trevor. Her phone number, no doubt. Possibly her bra size and the preferred names of their unborn children. What am I, bleeping invisible? How is a woman who is five foot eleven and three-quarters invisible? And what if Trevor and I were on a date? We're not, but

12

it could happen!

Trev has the grace to look sheepish, and my irritation fades. It's okay. I understand. Trevor is, though not exactly handsome, one of those guys who renders women helpless. His features taken one by one are not so special. Put them together and you have the male equivalent of death by chocolate. An utterly appealing, absolutely luscious man. Damn him.

I eat some more nachos and finish my beloved Scorpy. Maybe I should try being as bold as Lindsey, the sex-kitten waitress. After all, she's been here for a minute and a half and a really nice, good-looking firefighter has her number.

'Sorry about that,' Trevor says.

'Sorry about what?' I say casually, looking out again at the restaurant half of Emo's. There's the *New York Times* model. He is *so* handsome. His bone structure suggests an icy reserve, if such a thing is possible, not like Trev's instantly loveable face.

Another Scorpion Bowl appears before me, as if by magic. No, not magic. Stu, the bartender—who noticed me when Lindsey the waitress did not. Good old Stu. Too bad he's married and sixty years old. Otherwise, I'd be all over him. I take a grateful sip, wince as my taste buds protest, then swallow. I need the booze, frankly. It's not every night that I nearly choke to death *and* get dumped, after all.

13

'So what did your dumb-ass boyfriend say, anyway?' Trevor asks, taking a slab of nachos for himself.

I pause. The Scorpion Bowl demands that I answer honestly. 'He said I'm not attractive enough.'

Trevor stops chewing. 'What an asshole.'

I smile. Another show of loyalty. 'Thanks.' Taking a chip devoid of any cheese or olive, I break it into crumbs and arrange them in a pattern on the table. This is good, because if I look up, the room spins a little. Scorpy the Second suggests that I pick Trevor's brain. After all, Trevor is an expert on women. And, Scorpy continues, hasn't Trev known me long enough to be honest, if nothing else? 'Trevor, tell the truth. Am I . . . pretty?'

His eyebrows rise in surprise. 'Of course you're . . . well, okay, maybe pretty's not the right word. *Striking*. How's that?'

I roll my eyes. 'Kind of crappy, to be honest. Striking. As in striking out, as in "When will A-Rod stop striking out in the post-season?" Or as in a protest, as in "We're striking because conditions suck." '

Trevor grins. 'Let's switch you to some water, what do you say?'

'Come on. Tell me.'

'Tell you what, Chastity?'

'Well, you slept with me. You must have found me attractive, right?'

Trevor freezes, his beer halfway to his

14

mouth.

'Columbus Day weekend, remember?' I continue. 'My freshman year of college. You—'

'Of course I remember, Chastity,' Trevor says, his voice low. 'I just wasn't aware that we were going to discuss it. It's been, what, twelve years? Maybe I could get a little warning next time.'

'Don't get all prissy,' I say, taking another sip of my drink. 'So?' My tone is nonchalant, but my face, I note, feels warm. Scorpy II tells me not to worry.

'So what?' Trevor says, his face stern.

'Well, you must have found me somewhat attractive, right?'

'Of course I found you attractive,' Trevor says carefully, shifting his gaze to a point to the left of my head. 'You're very attractive.'

'But . . .' I prod.

'But nothing. You're attractive, okay? You're unconventionally beautiful. Don't let that scrawny little weenie make you feel insecure.'

'I'm not. Just wondering—if men find me attractive.'

'Well, I'm wondering if you need something a little more substantial than nachos. How about some dinner? Want a burger?'

'I'm not hungry,' I say around the last mouthful of nachos.

Trev runs his hand through his wavy brown hair, hair I've always loved. Thick, rich, wavy

15

and tousled, the color of black coffee, silky smooth . . . I'd better stop. He's looking at me oddly. 'So what do you want from me?' he asks.

Four children. 'Just be honest.'

'About what?'

'About men and me.'

There must be something in my expression that makes Trevor take pity on me. 'Chastity,' he begins. 'Men love you. You're lots of fun. In fact, you've always been one of the—' He breaks off suddenly.

'What? One of the what? One of the *guys?* Is that what you were going to say? That I'm one of the guys?' My voice is shrill. And possibly a little loud.

'Uh, well, in a good way, you know?'

'How is that good?' I demand.

Trevor winces. 'Well, you know a lot about sports, right? And many men enjoy sports.' I groan; Trev grimaces. 'And you play darts and pool and stuff like that. Um, we all had a good time doing that triathlon with you a couple years ago. The MDA thing?'

I sigh and reach for my Scorpy, but Trevor has moved it out of reach. He pushes a glass of water toward me instead. I roll my eyes . . . one seems to get stuck . . . and look once more at Mr. *New York Times.* I wish I was married to him. I wonder if there's a way I can convey this somehow. *Look over here, buddy. Marry me.* He smiles at something his white-haired

16

companion says and continues to be unaware that his soul mate sits just yards away.

Just then, the pretty, slutty, number-giving-out waitress reappears with yet another Scorpion Bowl. Even in my tipsy state, I realize that Trevor is right and I shouldn't drink another drop. Then, realization dawns in a glorious sunburst. Someone is sending me a drink!

'From a potential friend,' Slutty Waitress says, her voice loaded with meaning, and sets the glass in front of me.

Well, this is a change! Someone is interested in me! How thrilling! My cheeks flush in pleasure. Thank God! Talk about the cavalry rushing in just at the right moment! Just when my ego lies twitching in the gutter, someone has sent me a drink! Oh my God, could it be from Mr. *New York Times?* No *wonder* he wouldn't look at me . . . he's waiting to see my reaction! A surge of adrenaline floods my chest, and my eyelids seem to be fluttering. I glance over. He's still not looking. Must be shy. How adorable!

'Is it from the—' *god* '—man at that table?' I ask, gesturing in his general direction.

'No. From the . . . person? Over there,' the waitress says. 'At the bar.'

Heart thumping, I crane my neck to see who it is. Trevor does the same.

Sitting at the bar, looking at me with a smile, is a woman. She lifts her beer glass—I'm

17

guessing Miller—and salutes me. Because I don't know what else to do, I wave back weakly. She's fairly attractive, with short dark hair and a pleasant plumpness to her, and she seems to have a nice face. However, this doesn't erase the fact that I'm not a lesbian. Trevor covers his eyes with one hand. I suspect he is laughing. His mouth twitches. Yes. Bastard.

'Could you . . . could you tell her . . . I . . . it's just that . . .' My face is flaming.

'She's spoken for,' Trevor manages to say somberly. 'Thanks anyway. You can take the drink back.'

The waitress nods, takes the glass away and undulates her ass inches from Trevor's shoulder. I put my head on the table.

'Oh, Chas,' Trevor laughs. Without lifting my head, I give him the finger.

He gets out of his seat and comes to sit next to me, putting a brotherly arm around my shoulders. 'Don't be glum, Chas. Things will work out.'

'Blah blah bleeping blah,' I mutter, resisting the urge to punch him in the kidney. Such platitudes are as about as helpful as tossing a bowling ball to a drowning man. I hate the fact that I put up with the tepid and freckled Jason, even for a few weeks. Hate it that Mr. *New York Times* is miles out of my league. Hate the fact that I've just been mistaken for a lesbian.

It's not fair. Here's Trevor, the vagina

magnet, able to seduce in ninety seconds. My brothers, ranging in age from thirty-eight to thirty-two, have to fight women off with a Taser and a sturdy chair. Yet somehow, at just past thirty, I've become a pariah. Mention my age to a man and he looks stricken, as if I've just told him exactly how many viable eggs I have sitting in my ovaries and how very much I'd like them to be fertilized. It's not fair.

As I sit next to Trevor, the embodiment of everything good in a male, my first love, the first man I slept with, the man who I'm just going to have to get used to seeing with other women, I make a vow.

Things are going to change. I need to fall in love. Fast.

CHAPTER TWO

I always knew I'd move back to Eaton Falls. It was my destiny. The O'Neills go back six generations here, and I want my future children to emulate my own wholesome childhood—fishing on Lake George, hiking the many mountain trails of the Adirondacks, canoeing, kayaking, skiing, skating; breathing pure, clean air; knowing the people at the post office and the town hall; and of course, being near the family.

Granted, I'd imagined that the day I moved

back, it would be because my adoring husband and I were ready to settle down and raise those four kids. Instead, though, I moved on my own. I'd been working at the *Star Ledger,* living in glamorous Newark, when fate intervened. The *Eaton Falls Gazette,* my hometown paper, was looking for an editor—soft news and features. I'd done my time at a big-city paper and was ready for something else. Everything fell into place at once—I took the job, moved back in with Mom, and two weeks later, made an offer on a tiny and adorable house. Because the mortgage was a little steep, I took on my youngest brother as a tenant, slapped on a few coats of paint and moved in.

That was six weeks ago. It's all been a little rushed, but it's really come together.

Today is a soft, beautiful Saturday morning in April, possibly the most perfect day ever made. The sky is pale blue, fog swirls off the mighty Hudson River, and the trees are topped with only the palest green blur of buds. I don't see a soul as I run down Bank Street, my sneakers slapping the pavement. At the end of the lane is a large shed made of corrugated metal. I stop, sucking in a breath of the clean, damp air, simply, utterly, deeply happy to be back in my hometown.

I rent this shed from Old Man McCluskey. It's a far cry from the boathouses I've used in the past, but it will do. I twist the combination on the lock and open the door. There she is,

Rosebud, my magnificent wooden King rowing shell. 'Good morning, sunshine,' I say, my voice echoing off the metal walls. Grabbing my oars, I take them out to the dock, set them down carefully, then go back in the shed, take Rosebud down from her canvas harness and carry her outside. She may be thirty feet long, but she's light as a feather—well, a thirty-five-pound feather. I slip her into the water, set the oars and then, holding her steady against the dock, I climb in, tie my laces and off we go.

I began rowing when my brother Lucky joined the crew in college and needed someone to impress. I was that person . . . what are little sisters for, after all? Lucky let me try out his scull, and we instantly discovered I was born to row. When I went to Binghamton University, I was on the exclusive four with three other brawny, proud girls. While in New Jersey, I belonged to the Passaic River Rowing Club, but now, back home, I row alone, and I think I've discovered the true, Zen-like serenity of the sport. Last week, I saw a V of geese returning, like me, to the Adirondacks from their southern sojourn, flying so low I could see their black feet tucked against their downy bellies. Thursday, it was an otter, and yesterday, I saw a giant blur of brown that may have been a moose. In the fall, our famous glowing foliage will light up the hillsides like yellow and golden flame. Bleeping glorious.

The narrow shell slices through the river,

the only sound the gentle lapping of the water against the hull. I check over my shoulder and pull harder, feather and square, feather and square, gradually increasing the load of the water against my oars, cutting them into the river at precise angles, my body contracting and expanding with each stroke. Little whirlpools mark my progress up the river, and the dripping oars leaving a map of where I've been. Feather and square, feather and square.

It's a good cure for the hangover I woke up with after my night with the Scorpion Bowls, and a good prevention for the headache I'm sure to get at Mom's later today. Family dinner, attendance mandatory. That means Mom and Dad, my four brothers, Matthew, Mark, Luke and John, better known as Matt, Mark, Lucky and Jack, and their spouses and progeny.

Jack is my oldest brother, married to Sarah and the proud father of four kids—Claire, Olivia, Sophie and Graham. Lucky and Tara are in hot pursuit with three—Christopher, Annie and baby Jenny. Sarah and Tara are better known as 'the Starahs.' Mark, the third O'Neill boy, is in the middle of a bitter divorce from my oldest friend, Elaina. They have a son, Dylan. Then comes Matt, single, childless and currently my housemate, and finally me, the baby of the family.

Trevor may also be there, the unofficial O'Neill, practically adopted by my parents when he was a teenager and a frequent guest at family events. Good old Trevor. I pull harder, faster, streaking up the Hudson in a gliding rhythm. My muscles ache with a satisfying burn, sweat darkens my T-shirt, and all I can hear is the slip of the oars into the water and my own hard breath.

An hour later, I finish my row feeling substantially less polluted than when I started. I lift Rosebud into her sling, pat her fondly and jog home. Yes, I'm a jock. All that exercise lets me enjoy every junk food on earth, so if for only that reason, it's worth it. I run up the front porch stairs, open the beautiful oak door and brace myself against the wall. 'Mommy's home!'

And here she comes, my baby, one hundred and twenty pounds of loose muscle, drooping jowls and pure canine love. Buttercup. 'Aaaahhroooorooorooo!' she bays, her giant paws scrabbling for grip on the hardwood floors. I wince as she gathers her sloppy limbs and leaps, crashing against me.

'Hello, Buttercup! Who's a pretty girl, huh? Did you miss me? You did? I missed you, too, beautiful girl!' I pet her vigorously, and she collapses in a grateful heap, snuffling with joy.

Being Buttercup's owner, I feel that maternal obligation to lie to her about her physical appearance. Buttercup is not a pretty dog. As soon as I had my house secured last month, I went to the pound. One look and I

23

had to have her, because it was clear no one else would. Part bloodhound, part Great Dane and part bull mastiff, her coat is red, her ears are long, her tail like razor wire. Bony head, awkward body, massive paws, drooping jowls, doleful yellow eyes . . . Well, she won't be winning any doggy beauty pageants, but I love her, even if her only tricks thus far are sleeping, drooling and eating.

'Okay, dumpling,' I say after Buttercup has lashed me with her tail and slobbered a cup or so of saliva on my sleeve. She wags once more and falls almost instantly asleep. I step over her large body and head for the kitchen, weak with hunger.

As I rip open a package of cinnamon/brown sugar Pop-Tarts, I lean my head fondly against the kitchen cabinet. I love my new house, the first that I've owned. Sure, it has its problems—capricious furnace, tiny hot water tank, unusable master bathroom, but it's pretty much my dream house. A Craftsman bungalow (Eaton Falls is full of them, and I've always coveted their petite charm), the house has sturdy stone columns on the porch, funky lead-paned windows and patterned hardwood floors. I have the bigger bedroom upstairs, Matt has the smaller one off the kitchen. Once we worked out the 'toilet seat goes down' rule, my brother Matt and I have gotten along quite well.

'Hey, Chas.' Said brother emerges from the

bathroom in his ratty blue-plaid bathrobe and a cloud of steam.

'Hey, pal. Want a Pop-Tart?'

'Sure. Thanks.'

'Did you just take a shower?' I ask.

'Yup. All yours.'

'And of course, being the one considerate brother I own, you left me some hot water,' I say with great hope.

'Oops. I did kind of space out in there. Sorry.'

'Selfish, spoiled baby.' I sigh with martyrish suffering.

'Don't talk about yourself that way.' He grins and pours us each a cup of coffee.

'Thanks. Hey, when are you guys going to start the upstairs bathroom?' I ask, taking a grateful sip. 'No offense, but I'm really looking forward to a tub of my own.'

'Right,' Matt answers. 'Hm. Not sure.'

Like most firefighters, Matt has a side job, since the city fathers don't see fit to pay its heroes a livable wage. (This is a tirade I was raised on.) Matt, along with Lucky and a few other guys, do renovations, and so of course I hired them to redo my bathroom. Someday, it will be gorgeous—Jacuzzi tub, new tile floor, a pedestal sink, pretty shelves and all sorts of neat containers to hold my girly stuff. Unfortunately, other jobs from nonrelatives have taken precedence.

'Maybe you can get started before my

death,' I say around a bite of Pop-Tart.

'Yeah, well, that's gonna be tight,' Matt deadpans. From the other room, Buttercup, who has been sleeping soundly, scrabbles from her prone position as if she's just scented a missing child. Matt braces himself against the wall. 'Hi, Buttercup.'

'Aaaahhrooooroooroo!' she bays, rejoicing at the sound of Matt's voice as if she'd been parted from him by war and not her own nap. Tail whipping dangerously with love, she lumbers over to him—jowls quivering, hindquarters swaying—crashes into his pelvis, then collapses with a groan at his feet, heaving herself on her back, softball-sized paws waving in the air.

'My God, you're a whore,' Matt tells her, obligingly rubbing her expansive tummy with his foot.

'Takes one to know one,' I comment, bending down to unlace my sneakers.

'Speaking of whores, how was your night?' Matt asks. 'You went to Emo's, right?'

I sigh, then look at his face. He's trying not to laugh. 'You already know, you bastard. Who told you? Trevor?'

'Santo called. Said you have a new girlfriend.' Matt straightens up, laughing. 'So are you batting for the other side now, Chas?'

'Bite me, Mattie.' I grab my Pop-Tarts and head for the stairs. 'Listen, I'm gonna finish painting my wainscoting. What time is dinner at Mom's?'

Matt grimaces. 'Two.'

'Where do you want to go first?'

'The Dugout?' he suggests. Yes, Mom is cooking dinner. That's the point.

'Sounds great.'

A few hours later, Matt and I hop in my car, Buttercup draped over the backseat, snoring loudly. Leaving her in the car, we drop into the Dugout for buffalo wings and fried calamari, amiably watching *Sports Center* as we eat, then pay our tab and head for the family home.

'Where have you been?' Mom barks as we come through the door. The roar of the family gathering hits me like a truck.

'Gutterbup!' Dylan shrieks, running toward my dog, who collapses on the floor, rolling over so the toddler can scratch her stomach. From the other room, Elaina gives me a wave. I distantly hear my brother Mark speaking sharply to someone from the basement. Uh-oh. Elaina and Mark in the same house . . . not pretty.

'Hi, Mom,' I say, bending to kiss her cheek. 'Nice of you to invite Elaina.'

'It's about time those two got back together,' she announces, yanking the ties of her apron a little tighter.

'And are they falling over each other in love?' I ask.

'Not exactly,' she acknowledges. 'She hasn't forgiven him yet.'

27

'He did cheat on her, Mom.'

'Do we have to discuss this now?'

'No, we do not. Is everyone else here?' I ask.

'Yes, we've been waiting for you two, the roast is almost ready, now shoo! Get out of the kitchen! Take that carcass you call a dog with you. Go!'

'Auntie! Auntie! Play Bucking Bronco with me! Please? Please? Pleasepleaseplease?' my nine-year-old niece Claire begs.

'No! Wild Wild Wolves! You promised, Auntie!' Annie, seven, yanks my hand.

'Okay, okay, wolves and Broncos, coming up. Let me move Buttercup, okay?' Buttercup does not agree to get up, just blinks at me reproachfully. I slide my arms around her belly and heave her to her feet, but, jellylike, she refuses to stand. I'm forced to grab her collar and drag her into the living room, where she lies next to the door, happily allowing Dylan to look in her massive ears.

Dad's sitting in his chair, pretending to be asleep. Sophie and Olivia giggle wildly as he snores. 'Wake up, Grampa!' Sophie orders. 'It's dinnertime!' Dad snuffles and snores some more, then lurches upright.

'I'm starving!' he bellows. 'But not for dinner. For . . . for . . .' He looks at his granddaughters, who wait with breathless joy. 'For children!' He growls and lunges at them, pretending to devour limbs and heads and bellies as the girls scream and pull away, then fling themselves back for more.

'Hey, everyone,' I say.

'Wolves, Auntie!'

'Yup, in a minute, kids. Hi, Lucky,' I say. 'Hi, Tara.' I kiss my sister-in-law's cheek. 'How's it going? Where's Jack?'

'He and Trevor are in the cellar with Chris. Playing Nintendo, I think. Mark's down there, too, avoiding his wife,' Lucky says.

'Ex-wife,' Tara murmurs.

'Not yet,' Lucky corrects.

'I'm right here, so if you're gonna talk about me, could you at least keep it quiet?' Elaina says, doing her inimitable Latina head wiggle. 'Hey, Chas, what's new?' Before I can answer, she picks up Dylan and sniffs his bottom. 'Hold that thought,' she says, hastening off down the hall, her black curls bouncing.

'Are you ready to play Broncos, Auntie?' Claire begs.

'Chastity,' Tara says. 'Listen, before it gets crazy in here, I wanted to ask you a favor. It's our anniversary at the end of the month, and we were wondering . . . we hoped, actually . . .'

'We prayed, Chas,' says Lucky, putting an arm around his wife. 'We prayed on our knees that you would find it in your heart to watch the kids for us. Friday till Sunday, last weekend of April.'

I pause, bending down to pick up Graham, Jack's youngest, who is one and a half and

29

gnawing on my bootlace. 'Are you out of your minds?' I ask Lucky and Tara. 'Come on! You want me—me!—to babysit your little monsters? For an entire weekend?' They have the grace to look ashamed. 'Do you remember what happened last time? The rope burns on my ankles?' Tara grimaces. 'Christopher eating raw pumpkin and throwing up behind the couch? Annie peeing on my bed?'

'I remember that!' Annie exclaims joyfully. 'I peed on Auntie!'

Lucky hangs his head. 'Forget it,' he mumbles. 'Sorry.'

'Oh, lighten up.' I grin. 'Of course I'll do it.'

'Told you,' Lucky murmurs to his wife. I nuzzle Graham's soft, chubby cheek, then imitate a bird to make him smile.

'You're a saint.' Tara sighs happily. 'Name your price.'

I feel a flush creep up my neck. 'Well . . . '

Their eyebrows rise expectantly. The flush prickles hotter, but I can't afford not to ask. 'I'm interested in . . . you know.'

'Becoming a lesbian?' Lucky guesses with a knowing wink.

I punch him in the ribs, gratified to see him wince. 'Aren't you supposed to be kissing up to me right now, Lucky?'

'Yes, yes, of course,' Lucky amends. 'What can we do for you, Chas?'

I heave a sigh and roll my eyes but force myself to continue. 'I'd like to meet a decent

30

guy,' I mutter. 'So if you know anyone . . . '

'Sure!' Tara chirps. 'Slim pickings so far in Eaton Falls?'

'Well,' I say, staring at Graham's creamy skin and translucent pink stick-out ears. 'It's not that I don't meet single men. It's just that they tend to be . . . freaks. No one I'd want to father my children. You know how it is.' Actually, she *doesn't* know. She's thirty-one, married for eight years with three gorgeous kids. 'Anyway. I can use all the help I can get.'

'It takes a village,' Lucky murmurs with false compassion. I narrow my eyes at him, but I need him. All the literature on dating (yes, I've read it) says to tell everyone you know that you're seeking a mate. However mortifying and demeaning that might be.

'I'll keep my eyes open,' she says. Lucky nods. From the bedroom down the hall, Jenny cries out, and they both head down to check on their youngest. Graham squirms to be let down and toddles after them.

I find that my hand is over my abdomen, as if checking for my own baby. Not there, of course. At this moment, it's hard to imagine what it would be like for my stomach, which is as lean and hard as plywood, to swell with a baby. For the pink-cheeked, drowsy-eyed baby to be my little boy or girl.

'Auntie, look!' Olivia says.

I put my hand on her glorious red curls (she takes after her mom and not the black-Irish

O'Neills). 'What is it, Poopyhead?'

'I have a loose tooth!' she announces, opening her mouth. Before I can protest, before I can even get a sound out, her chubby finger shoves a front tooth way, way back to reveal a gaping, crimson crater. A string of blood trickles down, threading through the other teeth. My stomach drops to my knees and all the breath seems to leave my lungs.

'Thee?' Livvy asks, still revealing the pit. A little blood-tinged spittle lands on my hand. 'Thee it? It'th tho looth!'

'Don't . . . I . . . honey . . .' My vision is graying, my hands clammy and cold. I take a staggering step back, bumping into my father, who steadies me.

'Livvy! You know Auntie doesn't like blood! Show Uncle Mark instead.'

I blink, then shake my head in disgust. 'Thanks, Dad.' I sigh.

'My poor little weenie,' he says, patting my shoulder.

The familiar mixture of irritation and self-disgust rolls over me. In a family of alpha-male hero types, not only am I the only girl (*and* single, *and* childless), I am also the only wuss. Just in case I didn't feel different enough. Despite my strapping stature, my ability to run marathons and hike the Appalachian Trail, there's a chink in my armor, and its name is blood. And gore. The twins, Blood and Gore. I am the only O'Neill who missed the 'I'll save you' gene.

As members of the Eaton Falls Fire Department, Dad, Mark and Matt (and Trevor, for that matter) have saved dozens, possibly hundreds, of lives in one way or another, whether it's carrying someone out of a burning building or doing CPR or pulling them out of the river or just installing a free smoke detector. Lucky is a member of the New York State Police bomb squad. Jack is a helicopter paramedic, now with a private company in Albany. He was awarded the Congressional Medal of Honor for a dramatic rescue during his tour in Afghanistan, for crying out loud.

Even my mother, who is five foot two and weighs one hundred and eight pounds, gave birth to five children, none of us under nine pounds, without a drop of painkiller of any kind.

But somehow, I have the embarrassing tendency to faint at the sight of blood. When Elaina invited me to witness Dylan's birth, I nearly peed myself. Once, at the bris of a friend's son in New Jersey, I hyperventilated and staggered into the hors d'oeuvres table, ruining two hundred dollars' worth of deviled eggs, smoked salmon and matzo balls. When we had to dissect a frog in high school, I passed out, hit my head on the lab counter, came to, saw my blood and fainted again.

But I'm taking steps on that front. Though I

33

won't tell my family about this until it's over, I recently enrolled in a course to become an EMT. An emergency medical technician. Me. Surely, I like to imagine, buried beneath my layers of weenie-ness and a massive case of the heebie-jeebies, there lurk the genetics that let my brothers enjoy their adrenaline-soaked lives. Plus, maybe there'll be a cute guy in the class.

'Who wants to play Wild Wild Wolves?' I ask my nieces.

'I do!' shriek Claire, Anne, Livvy and Sophie.

'Who wants to be the hurt bunny?'

'Me! Me!'

I get down on the floor and begin snarling. 'Grr! Oh, man, it's been a hard winter, and I'm so, so hungry! Oh, look! A poor wounded bunny rabbit!' The girls scream with joy and try to crawl away, dragging their legs behind them. I pounce, drag and chew, their screams of joy piercing the air.

'So how's everything else with my little girl?' my father asks as I gnaw on his grandchildren. His black hair, heavily laced with silver, is mussed. 'Did you start work yet?'

'Just the meet and greet. Grr! Gotcha! Delicious! And you're the only man on earth who refers to me as little,' I answer. 'I'm starting Monday, actually.'

'Can't wait to see your byline.' He winks.

'Hey, Chastity.' I turn to see Trevor leaning

in the doorway, smiling, and my knees tingle shamefully.

'How are you, Trev?' I ask briskly.

'Great. How are you?' He smiles in conspiratorial knowledge—ah, yes, the Scorpion Bowls—and my stomach tugs in embarrassment.

'So what's new at the firehouse these days, guys?' I ask both my dad and Trevor, while still chewing on Claire's chubby little foot.

'Oh, the usual,' Dad answers. 'Fifty pounds of shit—'

'In a five-pound bag,' Trevor finishes amiably.

'Porkchop,' Dad says, 'what's this about you wanting a boyfriend?'

My jaw clenches, but I'm saved by my niece, who crashes into my father's knees. 'Grampa, can you eat us again?' Sophie begs. 'Can you pretend to be asleep, and then we'll play with your hair and then you can open your eyes and say you're hungry for children and pretend to eat us? Please? Please?'

'Not now, honey. Grampa wants to eat real food.'

'Should have stopped somewhere first, Dad,' Jack calls. I wave to him.

'I won't have you kids insulting your mother's cooking. It's perfectly wonderful,' Dad states loudly. 'Of course, I stopped at McDonald's, so . . .' he adds much more quietly.

35

Trevor wanders off to get a beer, so I am saved further humiliation as my father picks up the thread of our earlier conversation. 'Anyway, Chastity, why do you want to start dating? Don't you know what schmucks men are?'

I finish chewing on Graham, who's the most recent wounded bunny, and stand up. 'You need to get over that weird Irish idea that it's my destiny to wipe the drool off your chin, Dad. And, yes, of course I know what schmucks men are. Look around! You gave me four brothers.'

He smiles proudly.

'I'm a normal person, Dad,' I say with a sigh. 'Of course I want to get married and have some kids. Don't you want more grandchildren?'

'I have too many grandchildren already,' he answers. 'I think I may have to start eating more!' With that, he pounces on Dylan, who bursts into tears.

'Dad! Come on! I told you he doesn't like that!' Mark yells, scooping his son into his arms. 'Don't cry, buddy. Grampa was just being an idiot.'

He pushes past Elaina without so much as a glance. She hisses at his back, then cuts her eyes to me. 'Come over later. I'm so fricking mad I could spit acid.'

'Sounds like fun,' I answer. 'Eight o'clock?'

'Dinner!' Mom barks.

We file into the dining room—Mom, Dad, Jack, Sarah, Lucky, Tara, Elaina, Matt, Trevor and me jammed around the table. Mark, in order to avoid Elaina, announces with great martyrish resignation that he'll eat in the kitchen and supervise the kids.

Mom leans over and snatches the cover off the platter, unveiling her creation. Calling it dinner would be inaccurate and somehow cruel.

Jack stares at it despondently. 'That pot roast will come out of me the same way it goes in,' he announces. 'Stringy, gray and tough. And with a great deal of effort.'

'John Michael O'Neill! Shame on you!' Mom sputters as the rest of us try unsuccessfully to hide our laughter.

'Thanks for sharing, Jack,' Sarah says with resigned amusement.

'That was really gross, buddy,' Lucky says. 'True, but gross. *If* it comes out, that is. Last time we ate here, I was bound up for a week. Lamb stew that made my legs hurt. I think I actually bled when—'

'Luke!' Mom barks. Lucky ducks just in time to miss her halfhearted slap.

While I understand that Irish cuisine is very popular right now, Mom's Irish cooking is more in the potato-famine style. Large hunk of poor quality beef—boil it. Huge pot of grayish potatoes, bought in twenty pounds sacks and stored indefinitely in the cellar—boil them.

37

Carrots? Boil. Turnips? Boil. Green beans. Boil. Gravy? Burn.

'Mmm,' I say brightly. 'Thanks, Mom.'

'Kiss-ass,' Matt mumbles next to me.

'Bite me,' I mumble back.

We pretend to eat, shoving food around furtively, occasionally risking a bite of something when we can't avoid it. I try slipping some meat to Buttercup, who just stares at me dolefully from her pink-rimmed eyes, then lets her head flop back on the floor with a hopeless thump. From the kitchen, we can hear Mark refereeing the kids. 'Dylan, stop throwing, buddy. Annie, that's not cute, hon. Put it back in your mouth. I know, but Grandma made it. Here, Graham, I'll hold that for you.' He's trying very hard to sound saintlike. Elaina pretends not to notice. I can't really blame her.

'Well, this is as good a time as any,' Mom says, putting her fork down. 'Listen up, people. I've decided to start dating.'

The rest of us freeze, then, as one, look at Dad—except for Elaina, who continues to cut her green beans into tiny molecules that she doesn't eat.

'What are you talking about?' Dad asks.

My parents got divorced about a year ago. It wasn't traumatic or angry—more like a game they play with each other. While Dad now has an apartment downtown, things have remained pretty much the same. If the furnace goes out,

Mom calls Dad. If the car needs fixing, Mom calls Dad. They eat together a couple of times a week, go to all the grandkid events together, and I'm guessing they still sleep together, though this is not something on which I wish to dwell.

'Dating, Mike. We're divorced, remember? For a year now. As I said to you on eighteen thousand occasions, I want certain things. Since you have refused to give them to me, I'm moving on.'

So begins their traditional argument. 'More wine, anyone?' I ask.

'Yes, please,' comes the chorus.

My parents love each other, but it doesn't seem like they can live happily together. It's not easy to be a firefighter's wife. Every time Dad was late coming home, Mom would slap on the TV and sit, grim-faced, in front of the local channel, waiting to hear news of a fire. And if there was a fire, she'd twist her wedding ring and snap at us kids until Dad came home, sooty and tired and buzzed on adrenaline.

In addition to the terror of losing one's spouse to a horrible death, there's the reality of being married to a firefighter. Sure, it's a heroic job. Yes, the spouses are so proud. You bet, those guys are great. But how many Christmases and Thanksgivings and games and school recitals and concerts and lessons and swim meets and dinners took place without Dad? Dozens. Hundreds. Even when he was

39

home, the scanner was on, or Dad was talking on the phone to one of the guys, or going to a union meeting or organizing a training class. On the rare weekend when Dad didn't work, he'd be so antsy by the time Sunday afternoon rolled around that he'd go to the firehouse just to check in.

Then, two years ago, Benny Grzowski, relatively new to the department, fell off the roof of a burning building while cutting a ventilation hole and died. He was twenty-five.

There is no event more somber and spectacular than a firefighter's funeral. The O'Neill clan was there in full, stone-faced (except for me; I was bawling). When we got to the cemetery, we all filed past the headstone, already carved with Benny's name and years and the traditional inscription. *Husband. Father. Firefighter.* I remember Mom looking at the headstone after the service. 'You'd have to reverse the order for your father,' she muttered, turning away. 'Don't ever marry a man who loves his work more than he loves you, Chastity.'

It was after Benny's death that Mom started pressuring Dad to retire. She wanted to go on cruises, play bridge, join the Eaton Falls Senior Club, which sponsors trips to the racetrack and casinos, the outlets and Niagara Falls. She asked, waited, demanded, waited, ordered, waited and finally filed for divorce. I guess she thought he'd cave once she divorced him, but

40

she just waited some more.

Looks like the waiting is over. She stares impassively at my father and takes a bite of her stringy meat.

'This is ridiculous!' Dad pronounces. 'You're not dating anyone!'

'Really? Watch me, old man,' she hisses, then turns to me. 'Chastity, I heard you telling Tara that you want to meet someone.'

'Thank you, Mom! Okay! Can we change the subject?' I exclaim, my face burning.

'I think we should go in on this together,' she announces brightly. 'Double date.'

'Jesus,' I mutter. Matt smirks, and I shoot him the finger.

'You're not dating,' Dad repeats. 'You're just doing this to piss me off, and it's working. Enough.'

Mom continues unfazed. 'We can register at eHarmony, go to singles dances—'

'You're not dating!'

'—speed dating. It'll be fun! Mike, you get no say on this, so shut it.'

Dad's face is bright red. 'You're. Not. Dating.'

'Mom.' Lucky, the peacekeeping, bomb-detonating middle child, gives it a shot. 'Mom, can't you give Dad another chance?'

'I've given your father four "another chances,"' she says, glaring at Lucky. 'He loves that firehouse more than he loves me.'

'That's just stupid,' my father barks,

41

wadding up his napkin.

'Yes, it *is* stupid!' my mother snaps. 'That's my point entirely!'

'You're an idiot, woman! We're not discussing this! You're not dating!' He storms out, stepping over my dog, and slams the back door. A second later, we hear his car start.

Sarah and Tara are staring at each other. As if on cue, they both turn to my mother. 'We brought dessert!' they chorus.

*   *   *

'So, Mom, are you serious about this?' I ask later when everyone else has gone. The house is quiet, while outside the birds call to each other as the sun sets over the mountains. My dog's huge head rests on my mother's foot as if in solidarity.

She sighs. 'I know you love your father best, Chastity—' she begins.

'Untrue,' I respond dutifully.

'—but I don't want to spend the rest of my life alone like this.'

'He will retire, Mom. He'll have to. Aren't there union rules or something? I mean, he's fifty-nine years old, right?'

'Fifty-eight,' Mom says. 'He'll retire whenever he feels like it, honey. Six years? Seven? Ten? Am I supposed to sit around waiting? For thirty-nine years, I've put up with it! It's my turn to decide a thing or two about our life, and he won't accept that, and it's not fair.' She settles back in her chair. 'So I'm finding someone else.'

'Don't you still love him, Mom?'

'Of course I do,' she says. 'That's not the point. It's that I want someone who will put me first, and honestly, your father has never done that. He wasn't a bad husband, but he never put me first.' Her tone is that of a professor announcing historical facts. I nod and pick at the sole of my hiking boot. Who knows? Maybe her plan will work and a little jealousy will get Dad's attention at last. She loves him. She doesn't want anyone else, not really.

'We'll have fun, honey,' Mom proclaims. 'I've already signed us up for singles grocery shopping! Doesn't that sound fun?'

'Um, no,' I answer.

'Oh, come on! You haven't even tried it yet! It's fun!'

'Have you gone?' I ask.

'No, but how can singles grocery shopping not be fun?' She continues to describe the anticipatory thrill of examining produce with other mate-seeking individuals. I grimace and let my head fall back against the arm of the chair.

The truth is, I'll go. I don't have time to waste, do I? I can feel my ovaries sighing in impatience . . . *We're still functioning. For now, at least* . . . The blurry memory of the slutty

43

waitress pops up in my mind. I have no desire to watch Trevor rake in the females as I sit around single and childless, staring at my empty ring finger.

And so I make a pact with the devil, or in this case, my mommy. We'll try it together. Why not? What have I got to lose?

CHAPTER THREE

Because I've begun my story on the night when I was dumped *and* had a woman hit on me, I might've given the impression that I don't have any male admirers. I do . . . just not the males I want.

Case in point—Alan of the Gray Tooth, managing editor at *Eaton Falls Gazette,* where I have just shown up for my first official day of work. Alas, Alan and I are alone in the *Gazette* 'office suite,' which is really just a big room divided into gray burlap cubicles, a conference room and a cramped office for our boss.

'I really hope you'll like it here,' says Alan (5'8" and this is with chunky-heeled Doc Martens), grinning. Like Judas at the Last Supper, the gray tooth is malignantly out of place, sitting ominously in the middle of an otherwise unremarkable row of normal teeth. I try to look away from it, but it's weirdly compelling. Alan raises an eyebrow. Eech.

44

'Sure. Yeah, I'm, uh, I'm sure I will. Thanks.'

'Maybe we can get together for drinks later on at the old watering hole where us journalists like to hang out.'

That should be 'where we *journalists like to hang out,' Al, old buddy.* 'I'm . . . I don't . . .' I can't hear properly. The Tooth has taken control of me.

'Drinks it is, then,' Alan says. 'Awesome.'

Jesus. How did that thing get so gray? Doesn't Alan know his own tooth is rotting away in his mouth? Shouldn't it be pulled? It certainly should be capped. As Alan talks, the gray tooth blinks darkly, Alan's narrow lips moving around the words that I'm ignoring, fascinated by the evil power of The Tooth. Like Tolkien's Ring, it has a hypnotic, undeniable power. *One tooth to rule them, one tooth to find them, one tooth to bring them all, and in the darkness bite them.*

I shudder, then straighten a few books on my desk. 'I should get organized,' I say to Alan with what I hope is an apologetic smile and not a horrified grimace.

'So. Six o'clock?' The Tooth asks.

Yes, Master. 'Excuse me?' I realize I sound like an idiot, but really, someone should tell him. It dawns with sudden horror that he's just asked me out on a date. 'No! No, sorry. I can't. Something . . . some other thing going on.' I flush with the lie, but Alan doesn't seem to care.

'That's okay. How about Friday?'

'You know what?' I blurt. 'I don't date coworkers. Sorry.' There. Great excuse. No hurt feelings, right? Alan doesn't seem like a bad guy. Just physically repulsive on many levels. Oh, no, it's not just The Tooth. There's a paunch that droops over his belt . . . the musty, grandmother's-bedroom smell that floats around him in a geriatric cloud, the Donald Trumpian comb-over . . . but lording over them all, yes, The Tooth.

'No, no, not a date. Just two fellow journalists having a few drinks.' His words are lost as I again find myself gazing into his mouth, swallowing sickly as the sinister power of The Tooth oozes toward me. Perhaps I can fake impending stomach distress. If I don't look away soon, I won't have to fake anything.

'So. That works for you, then?' The Tooth asks.

'You know, Alan, I think I ate something that was off this morning,' I begin.

'I have some Imodium on me,' he offers immediately, groping behind the pocket guard on his breast pocket.

Luckily (or not), Lucia bursts through the door balancing a box of doughnuts in one hand, several newspapers and coffees in the other. 'Good morning!' she trills, then lurches to a halt in front of my desk. 'Oh. Chastity. That's right. It's your first day.' Her nose

46

twitches. 'We have a meeting every Monday and Wednesday. Ten minutes. Have your ideas ready.'

'Nice to see you again,' I say, raising an eyebrow. Lucia is the receptionist here at the *Eaton Falls Gazette* and has worked here since she was eighteen—that is, about half her life. Penelope, the owner and publisher of the *EFG* confided that Lucia applied for my job and was deeply wounded when she didn't get it.

Speaking of Penelope, she wobbles through the door. 'Morning,' she sighs. 'Chastity, can I see you in my office first thing?'

'Sure, Penelope,' I say, rising. Lucia shoots me a glare and sniffs loudly, her eyes running contemptuously up and down my form. Doing my best to ignore her, I go into Penelope's office and close the door.

'So, welcome, of course. It's great to have you here. Listen, Chastity, do you know anything about skin cancer?' She yanks down the collar of her sweater. 'Look at this mole. Is it changing color? I think it looks cancerous.'

'Well, I really don't . . . '

'Do you? Think it looks cancerous?'

I squint at her neck. 'I don't really know what it looked like before, so . . . '

'Doesn't it look cancerous, though?'

'I wouldn't know. Maybe you'd feel better if your doctor took a look,' I suggest.

She sits with a thud in her chair. 'You're right. You're right. Sorry. I was up all night,

47

looking at pictures on the Internet,' she says. 'Melanoma.com. Very ugly.'

'Sorry.'

'It's okay. Welcome! Welcome to the *Eaton Falls Gazette*. Did Lucia give you a hard time?' She smiles and sits up straight.

'Not really.' I smile back.

'All ready for the meeting?' she asks brightly.

'Absolutely. I'm really glad to be here, Pen,' I say.

'We're glad to have you.' She smiles.

I really am relieved to be away from the urban heartbreak of Newark. Here, I'll cover soft news and features: new stores opening, the principal retiring, the daffodils in Memorial Park. Alan will continue to cover the harder stuff: city hall politics, regional affairs, etcetera.

Ten minutes later, we're all assembled in the small conference room. The staff consists of Penelope, Alan, Lucia, Carl, our head photographer, and Angela Davies, the food editor. Suki, a part-time reporter, covers the stories that Alan and I won't be able to get to. Pete handles advertising, and Danielle does the layout. That's it. It's such a change from the legions who worked in Newark, so cozy, almost.

'So!' Penelope chirps, fingering her mole. 'What have you got for me?'

Alan goes first, outlining the stories he

48

believes will be top news this week, ruling out fires, murders and terrorist attacks. He's tied into a few national stories and will try to put a local spin on them—a former resident has been connected with the Mob in Florida, the effect of gas prices on summer rentals in the Adirondacks. He talks about the endless construction to replace the water lines all along Main Street. Then there's the ongoing investigation of our state representative, who seems to have (gasp!) taken illegal campaign contributions. Aside from his tooth and his inability to take a hint, he seems quite competent.

Then it's my turn. 'Okay,' I begin. 'I'd just like to say how happy I am to be h—'

'I had a great idea for a story,' Lucia interrupts, turning a treacle gaze on Penelope. 'A woman in Pottersville knitted the fourth-largest scarf in the world. I thought it could be a wonderful story, about what kind of yarn she used, her pattern, her plans for the scarf, her inspiration! Our readers would love it!' She glares at me, hoping I'll disagree.

'I disagree,' I say. Penelope covers a smile. 'I'd like to see the *Gazette* concentrate on stories with a little more substance.'

My shot across the bow is received with venom.

'Well, maybe you need to understand what our readers like, Chastity!' Lucia snipes. 'You just got here—'

'I grew up here,' I interject.

'—and you might be surprised at how down-homey people here are. Right, Penelope?'

Penelope's smile drops, and she rubs her mole harder. 'Um . . . well, you have a point, Lu, but I think we'll see how Chastity does. It's why we hired her. Lots of experience.'

'But not in Features!' Lucia protests. 'Features is—'

'Master's in journalism from Columbia. Very impressive,' Pen smiles. I acknowledge my stellar education with a modest nod. Where I went to school doesn't matter. Lucia will hate me regardless. Penelope warned me about Lucia at my interview lunch. She said that I was by far the most qualified candidate they'd had, and that Lucia would be fighting mad. Pen went on to confide over her third glass of wine that she'd once made the mistake of letting Lucia write a features article. This was well before my time, and it never actually ran but Penelope showed me the piece . . . ten thousand words, a novella, really, on Mrs. Kent, who won first prize at the county fair for her German chocolate cake.

'Features with substance. I like that.' Alan lifts an eyebrow suggestively, his lip raising enough for me to get a glimpse of The Tooth. I look away.

'What else have you got?' Penelope asks.

Lucia's ruby-red lower lip sticks out obstinately as I continue. 'We need to focus on

50

hyperlocal stories,' I say. 'Papers all across America are watching subscriptions fall. People can get news anywhere—CNN, Internet, even on their phones—so we have to offer Eaton Falls readers stories they can't get anywhere else. I think people want to read more than cutesy features or stuff pulled off the AP wire. And of course, all of this will be on the Web site, too, which I'll be beefing up considerably.'

Lucia snorts.

I smile at her, which makes her scowl even more. 'I know, Lucia,' I say, hoping to placate her. 'It's a paper first and foremost. But if people aren't reading it, then let's get them to go to our Web site, which is sponsored by our advertisers. It only makes fiscal sense.'

'Great, Chastity,' Penelope says. 'This is why we hired you.'

'Obviously, we have to do a piece on the Resurrection for Easter,' Lucia announces, not placated.

'Maybe a piece on the town egg hunt and some local traditions, but no, we're not doing a story on the Resurrection. That's not news, Lucia,' I state firmly. 'That happened almost two thousand years ago.'

Lucia's mouth drops open. 'Penelope!' she protests. 'She can't—'

'I'm going to defer to Chastity here, Lu,' the boss says, lovingly stroking her mole. 'Let's move on. Angela?'

51

Angela, a soft-spoken, gentle-faced woman about my age, has been sitting silently throughout the discussion. 'Well,' she says in a near-whisper, adjusting her glasses, 'Callahan's is opening tomorrow, so I'll review that. I'm doing low-fat Easter favorites for next weekend. The nutritious school-snacks column is featuring ...'

I try to pay attention as Angela details the asparagus bisque recipe she hopes will dazzle our readers. Though I'm not much of a cook, I do love to eat, and all this talk of food is making me hungry. And while Angela carries the title of food editor, she will answer to me, and her recipes and advice will give our readers another reason to check out our food Web page, which can carry more information than the Thursday edition of the paper.

After our meeting is done, I get to work calling the freelancers the *EFG* uses, introducing myself, checking the town calendar for events I should go to, chatting up the nice lady at the chamber of commerce. I edit a piece for our next edition, then, glancing at my watch, decide I have time to extend the old olive branch.

I grab my backpack, check my cell phone and go over to Lucia's desk, where she is busy filing. 'I hear you're engaged, Lucia.' It's my peace offering, and it works.

She is more than happy to rant and rave about the stresses of being engaged for the next ten minutes. 'So anyway, I told the florist that I didn't care what was in season! Teddy—my fiancé?—I call him Teddy Bear, isn't that cute? Anyway, he loves sweet pea. He just loves it! I have to have sweet pea! He wanted it mixed in with baby's breath? So beautiful! In these little bowls? And candles? And here was this stupid florist, telling me I couldn't have sweet pea? I don't think so!'

I force a smile, nod and glance at my watch, wondering if all brides are this psycho, and if all grooms are invested in centerpieces as Ted. Sounds like . . . well. I'm the one who was mistaken for a lesbian, so what do I know?

'Well, I'd love to hear more, but I'm doing an interview. Should be back before five, okay?'

'Fine,' she snaps. Apparently, it will take more than a feigned interest in her wedding for us to become friends.

It's a lovely, warm day. The pale green leaves are just about edible, and I stop for a moment to look to the hills as well, a smile coming to my face. Most of the buildings of the downtown area were built at the turn of the last century and exhibit a grace and attention to detail that would be considered too costly for a design today. Brick or limestone, most are only four or five stories tall, with all sorts of cunning detail and gilt painting. Little alleys run off the main street like tributaries off a river, and a wave of affection washes over me.

53

I love Eaton Falls. I love being a journalist. I'm so glad to be back. This is a new phase of my life, and I'm determined it will be a good one. True adulthood. A home, a dog and soon, hopefully, a boyfriend/fiancé/hubby/father of my strong and attractive children.

I walk the three blocks to the new toy store, conveniently located next to Hudson Roasters. I pop into the coffee shop, order two tall lattes and, as my stomach growls, a cheese danish, then take my bags next door to Marmalade Sky.

'Hello,' I call, pushing open the door. It's very cute inside. Toys . . . well, obviously . . . puzzles, Legos, stuffed animals, all in a cheerful, crowded atmosphere. 'Kim? It's Chastity O'Neill from the *Gazette*.'

A heavyset young woman wearing a brown denim jumper comes out of a door toward the back. 'I'm Kim Robison. It's so nice of you to come!'

Kim's interview had been scheduled by my predecessor, and I'd decided to take it myself. Her toy store opening is just the sort of soft news that I've been looking forward to covering, a far cry from the urban heartbreak of Newark that I'd been immersed in for the past five years.

'I brought you a latte,' I say, holding out the cup.

'Oh, you're so nice,' she smiles. 'Sorry, though. I can't have any.'

Probably one of those green-tea types, I guess, judging by her rather crunchy look. Kim invites me to sit in the reading area at the back, surrounded by glossy picture books, classic Pooh figures, and a mobile shaped like a ship with rainbow sails. I take out my notebook. 'So, Kim, how did you come up with the name Marmalade Sky?' I ask.

'It's from the Beatles' song.' She smiles, shifting in her chair.

I pause. 'The LSD song?'

'No,' she answers. '"Lucy in the Sky with Diamonds."'

I pause. 'Uh . . . that's the LSD song.'

Her face falls. 'Oh, no,' she says. She thinks for a moment. 'Oh, for God's sake. Of course it's the LSD song.'

I laugh. 'Don't worry. I won't put it in the article. Okay, next question. When did you become inspired to own a toy store?'

'I guess when my sister had her first baby,' Kim says. She talks about her love of children and their vast imaginations. I smile and nod as she talks, sometimes mentioning one of my eight nieces and nephews. Kim smiles often, her plump apple cheeks bunching attractively as her glossy hair swings. 'See, Chastity,' she says, leaning forward, 'when you give a child the right toy, you're giving them hours of fun and creativity and imagination, almost giving them the key to . . . their own . . . '

'To their own world?' I suggest, scribbling

away. She doesn't answer. I look up.

Kim rises awkwardly out of her chair and stares down at her ample stomach. 'I think my water just broke.'

My head jerks back, and my stomach drops as if I'm on the express elevator in the Empire State Building. 'You're—you're pregnant?' Not heavyset. Not chubby or plump. Pregnant. Crap. Some journalist I make.

'Yeah, I'm . . . ooh! Yes, that's water breaking.' She lifts the hem of her long dress and examines her ankle. 'Oh! Oh, boy. Yup, it's started.'

In response to those words, my own water breaks—sweat. I am suddenly drenched in sweat, from the soles of my feet right to my scalp. Because even if I've never seen a baby born, I know how it goes. Pain. Screaming. Blood. Gore. 'Uh-oh,' I choke out. My throat slams shut, and I can't seem to breathe. I raise a shaking hand to push my hair off my face, pictures of bloody afterbirth flashing through my mind.

'Um . . . can you . . . can you just call my husband for me?' Kim sinks back into the chair, takes a deep breath and rubs her abdomen.

'Are you . . . um . . . are you . . .' There is a watery stripe of blood on her bare ankle. *Don't look. Too late. Don't look again. Stop looking.* 'You're bleeding,' I say in a hoarse whisper, tearing my gaze off her ankle and pointing in

56

the vague direction of her foot.

Kim glances at her ankle. 'Oh, they say that's normal.'

I swallow repeatedly. 'Oh.'

'Do you mind?'

'What? Do I mind what?' There's a buzzing in my ears, and Kim sounds very far away. *Stay with it, Chastity! She needs help!*

'Can you call my husband? He's number one on speed dial. My cell phone is in my bag behind the counter.' She breathes in deeply and exhales with a long shushing sound, rocks back in her chair.

I force myself to stand, though my knees are buckling. How can they buckle just because of a little bl—red stuff? I can run five miles without breaking a sweat! I lurch over to the counter, fumble for her bag and dump it out. Keys, wallet, sunglasses, tissues . . . 'I can't find it!' I call, my voice rough. I order myself to stay calm. Myself doesn't listen. The panic is rising like icy water, and I do in fact feel close to drowning, my breath coming in labored gasps. 'Your phone! Where's your phone? I can't find the phone!'

'It's right in the . . . oh, man . . .' She takes a deep breath, then releases it slowly. 'Ooh! A contraction! It's in the side pocket.'

'Side pocket, side pocket, side pocket.' I can hear myself distantly. *Easy, Chastity, easy . . . breathe, breathe, breathe.* I can't faint. I want to, apparently, but I can't. I have to help this lady.

57

What if that blood means something bad? Someone will have to help her. Someone like me, for example, since I'm the only person here. Renewed terror zips through my veins. I can't get enough air and I'm hot and cold at the same time and shaking like a leaf in a hurricane. 'Are you sure blood is normal?' I squeak.

Kim straightens up in her chair to look at me as I rifle through her bag. 'It's okay,' she assures me. 'The blood is just from my cervix dilating. Perfectly natural.' She takes a deep breath and lets it out slowly, then smiles at me. 'They say it will take a long time, even from when your water breaks. The baby won't come for hours. Maybe not even until tomorrow.'

They say. Who the hell are *they,* and what do *they* know? And why is Kim so calm? Isn't she worried about her own child? I would be! Babies are born in freaky places all the time! I wouldn't want my baby to be born on the sidewalk or backseat of a cab or on some carnival ride or in a toy store!

The phone! 'I found it!' I announce, but it slips from my sweaty hands and skitters away on the wood floor. I pounce on it, snatch it up and stare at the console. How is anyone supposed to make an emergency call on buttons that are a bleeping millimeter wide? Carefully, as Kim inhales and exhales in the background, I punch in 911 with a violently shaking finger and wait for the dispatcher's voice.

'911 emergency, how can—'

'A woman is having a baby!' I bark. 'A baby! Right now!'

'Is that my husband?' Kim asks.

'Where are you, ma'am?' the dispatcher asks.

'Um, uh, we're um, let's see now, um, the new toy store? In Eaton Falls? On um, let's see, Ridge Street? Next to the coffee place, about eight blocks from the firehouse, okay? So send them, okay? They have an ambulance and everything! Are they on their way yet? I don't see anybody. Where are they? Why aren't they coming?'

'That's not my husband, is it?' Kim demands in the background. 'Did you call 911? What did you do that for?'

'Because you're having a baby and I can't deliver it!' I yell.

'Eaton Falls Fire is on their way,' the dispatcher says. 'Would you like to stay on the phone until they arrive?'

'Yes! Yes! Don't hang up on me! Don't leave me.'

My chest is heaving as I try to suck in enough air, but I stagger over to Kim, who is looking at me disapprovingly over her stomach. 'Don't push,' I tell her. 'They're coming. Do not push. Do you want me to get some towels? How about that coffee, huh? There's a danish, too, but I was going to eat

59

that. But you can have it! Sure! Want the danish? Just don't push. I'm not good at this sort of thing.'

'Really?' she says, and is that a bit of sarcasm? During labor? How can she be so calm? 'Can I have my phone, please?'

I'm still pressing the phone against my ear, hard enough for it to hurt. 'Ma'am?' the dispatcher says. 'What's the situation?'

Sirens go off down the street. 'Finally!' I shout. 'Oh, God, hurry. Don't worry, Kim, don't worry, they're coming.'

Kim stands up—surprising for a woman about to give birth—and pries the phone out of my hand. My watery knees finally give out, and I sink to the floor with a heavy thud, gasping. Winnie the Pooh looks on unblinkingly, and Eeyore frowns with the expected disapproval.

'Hi,' Kim says into her itsy-bitsy cell phone. 'This is the pregnant woman. I'm fine . . . No, you don't need to send them . . . my water broke, but I'm . . . oh, okay. Sure, fine. Thank you.' She hangs up. 'I just wanted you to call my husband,' she tells me, accusation heavy in her tone.

From my place on the floor, I have an all-too-clear view of the smear of blood on her ankle. *Please let the baby be okay,* I pray distantly. *Please, God.* My ears are roaring, black holes are appearing in front of me, and I can't get enough air. I inhale desperately, but my vision is fading. I tip my head between my knees and try to breathe.

I hear the bell over the front door tinkle, and look up to see four men trooping into the store single file, carrying bags of gear. Dad, Trevor, Paul and Jake, turnout gear on, reflective letters catching the light. Thank *God*. The guys lurch to a stop when they see Kim standing calmly over me, her hands on her hips. 'Hi,' she says. 'My water broke. I didn't actually mean for the fire department to come.'

My father looks down at me. 'Get some oxygen, okay, Paul?' he says.

'I don't need any,' Kim says firmly.

'It's not for you.' Trevor smiles. 'How far along are you?'

'I'm due tomorrow,' she says. 'This is my first baby, and they said it will take a while. I'm really fine.'

They are all standing around, looking at me. Paul comes back and kneels next to me. 'Slow down, kid,' he says. I force myself to obey, managing a few normalish breaths before he slips a mask over my mouth. I breathe in gratefully, feeling the slight rush of one hundred percent oxygen.

'Oops, here's a contraction,' Kim says, breathing deeply and exhaling.

'Would you like to sit down?' Trevor offers.

'No, no, I can stand through it . . . there. It's gone.'

'You're a champ,' my father tells her. 'My wife had five kids. Natural childbirth for every one of them. You'll do great.'

Thanks, Dad. And Kim! Can't she ham it up a little for my sake? Standing through contractions—show-off. Now that I'm no longer hyperventilating, my cheeks start to burn. Crap. It's happened again.

'You okay, hon?' Dad asks me.

I don't bother to answer.

'We'd be happy to take you to the hospital,' Trevor offers Kim.

'My husband works at the school,' she says. 'I'll just give him a call and he can come get me. But thank you.' She dials her husband's number and speaks softly into the phone.

Dad radios back to dispatch. Paul picks up a Legos model. 'I think my son has this one,' he murmurs, turning it over. 'Yup. Star Wars Destroyer. Remember this one, guys?' He holds up the box.

'I love that movie,' Jake says dreamily. "May the Force be with you . . . always." So cool.'

Dad asks the woman about name choices, Paul opens a copy of *The Miraculous Journey of Edward Tulane*. I suck oxygen. Three minutes later, the husband arrives and gently escorts his wife to their car. 'Thanks!' she calls, smiling. 'Just turn the lock in the doorknob before you leave, okay?' I wave feebly.

Trevor kneels beside me and takes my pulse. 'How's our little midwife?' he asks, mouth twitching.

Maybe I'd laugh, too, if I didn't feel like such an ass. Maybe I'd feel small and cherished if I weren't two centimeters short of six feet and didn't weigh in well past a hundred and fifty pounds. I inhale deeply once more. 'Chastity?' Trevor asks. 'You okay?'

I sigh, causing the mask to fog, then reluctantly take it off. 'Fine.'

He looks up from his watch. 'Heart rate's down to normal. Do you still feel lightheaded?'

'I'm fine, Trevor! You know how it is. An irrational fear of a harmless object or situation resulting in physical response such as hyperventilation, fainting, accelerated pulse, blah blah bleeping blah.'

'Just asking. Any numbness or tingling in your arms or legs? Chest pain?'

'No.' I sound like a sullen four-year-old. Trevor smiles and keeps looking at me.

'How's my girl?' Dad asks, squatting in front of me. 'Need a ride home, Porkchop?'

'No, Dad. I'll just . . . I'll just go back to work.'

Dad stands up. 'Okay, guys. Let's pack it in.' Paul takes the oxygen tank away and I move to stand up, my legs still shaking. Trev offers his hand. I ignore it and haul myself to my feet solo.

'See you later, sweetie,' Dad says. He smiles a little, pats my shoulder.

'Bye, Chastity,' Trevor says with a grin that curls around my insides. I shove the warmth away.

'Thanks, guys,' I answer. 'Sorry to waste your time.'

'Beats watching *The Tyra Banks Show,*' Paul says.

'You think?' Jake returns. The guys laugh and walk out, and a few minutes later, they're driving off down the road, lights off, sirens quiet. Fighting feelings of embarrassment, humiliation, mortification and general stupidity, I sigh, turn the lock in the doorknob and close the door behind me.

CHAPTER FOUR

When I was in sixth grade, Elaina and her family moved to Eaton Falls, and if there was ever a bigger chip on a shoulder, I'd never seen it. Fascinated by the attitude, the slight accent and the inch of makeup on her adolescent face, I decided instantly that I must have her as a friend. 'Hi,' I'd breathed at recess that first day as she sat on a bench at the edge of the blacktop.

'Whachoo want, townie?' she asked, flipping her hair back in delicious contempt.

'I can do a hundred chin-ups,' I offered.

'So do it,' she instructed, snapping her

fingers. I complied, won her admiration and never looked back. All through high school, college, grad school and beyond, Elaina has been there for me and I for her, and she remains the only living creature I ever told about Trevor.

In high school, Elaina asked Mark to our senior prom and the rest was history. They got married four years ago and had Dylan two years later. Elaina was tired and stressed, Mark was strung even more tightly than usual, and things were tense. And how did my brother deal with the pressures of family life? He had a one-night stand. Granted, it's a move he deeply regrets, which Mark shows in his typical emotionally constipated way—lashing out at those he loves. Suffice it to say, Elaina hasn't forgiven him, because he hasn't apologized. And they remain at a ridiculous standoff—separated, divorce pending, loving each other, hating each other, fighting constantly, bitterly mourning what they've lost.

'That fucking brother of yours,' she begins one night as we sit in front of my computer screen. I'm filling out an online questionnaire, and Elaina is coaching me on the answers. Buttercup snores gently at our feet.

'What now?' I ask with resignation.

'He says he won't pay for Dylan's soccer camp.'

'Dylan's two, Lainey,' I say, glancing from the computer screen to her. Mark has his son this weekend, so Elaina and I are here, drinking chardonnay and registering me on e.Commitment, a humiliating, degrading and shamefully fun process.

'So? The great ones all start young. Don't say yes to that one, sweetie. That's a trick question.' She leans forward to read it aloud. "Do you find a variety of men attractive?" See, they're trying to see if you're a party girl, you know? Group-sex kind of thing.'

'Are you sure?' She nods wisely. 'Okay. I'll just put "not applicable." How's that? And maybe Dylan should be out of diapers before he starts camp,' I add reasonably.

Elaina sighs. 'I know, I'm crazy. I just mentioned it to him, you know, as something Dyllie might do when he's older, okay? And Mark, he's all, "Don't you put my son in camp without discussing it with me!" And I'm right back at him, "Don't you tell me what to do with my son, you miserable cheating bastard!" And we end up screaming at each other and hanging up. You want another glass of wine? And dog, get your big bony head off this foot, or I'm planting it up your ass.'

'Don't be mean to my baby,' I chastise. 'And yes to the wine.' I stretch, rubbing my lower back, which is cramped from hunching over the keyboard, then bend over to pat my poor maligned dog. 'You know, Elaina, a psychiatrist might say something about all that fighting and screaming, you know.'

She does her little head wiggle, something I tried for years to emulate before realizing my Irish genes lacked the Latin disdain required to pull it off. 'And what's that, know-it-all?'

'That you still love him and this kind of fighting is a way of having a passionate relationship, even if it's not the kind of passion you really want.'

'No shit, Dr. Joy Browne. I'll get the wine.'

I grin, finish stroking Buttercup's rough red fur and finish my profile. *Profile.* Sounds like something the FBI has on me. *You fit the profile for the serial killer, Ms. O'Neill.* There's nothing to be ashamed of, of course; lots of people do online dating, let no stone go unturned, blah blah bleeping blah. But still. It's humbling nonetheless, having to check out a Web site for my mate. I never pictured turning thirty, let alone thirty-one, without having an adoring husband and a couple of kids.

The profile includes a personality section of no fewer than one hundred and six questions, a physical description (forty-two questions), my ideal date (choose from twenty-three options) and a new e-mail address and user name. I chose GirlNextDoor.

e.Commitment boasts lots of touching—and possibly even true—stories of people meeting their soul mates here. I pause for a second. Maybe—probably not, but maybe—this is how I will find The One. That Trevor's image

67

instantly leaps to mind is quite irritating. I force him out and stick in another picture. Derek Jeter. Yummy. Well, maybe hoping for the bazillionaire baseball god is a little bit of a stretch. Aragorn, on horseback. Yeah, baby! Okay, okay. That also may be a little unrealistic . . . hm. The guy at the restaurant the other night. There! Mr. *New York Times,* sure. Just as appealing as Trevor. Just as attractive. Let's also assume he's kindhearted. And decent. Also, funny. Strong, yet vulnerable. Quiet, yet expressive. Sensitive, yet stoic.

Elaina returns to the tiny study that's just off the living room. Matt's working tonight, so we have the house to ourselves. 'This house is fantastic, sweetie,' she says, handing me my glass.

'I know. I love it,' I answer. 'I'm thinking of painting this room yellow, what do you think?' Elaina has a great flair for colors.

'Perfect. You done filling that thing out?' she asks, tapping a long fingernail against her wineglass.

'Yes. Not that this is going to pan out, Elaina.' Buttercup groans as if agreeing.

'How do you know? It's better than you mooning—'

'I'm not mooning anyone. Phone's ringing!' Saved. I snatch up the phone. 'Hello?'

'Hello, Chastity, this is your mother speaking.' Her traditional greeting. 'Did you fill out your form?' Mom's the one who told me e.Commitment was ranked higher than the other dating sites, after her exhaustive, fifteen-minute search on the Web. 'Also, I'm taking French. Your father is very jealous, barely speaking to me. Do you want to get our hair colored next week?'

'Hi, Mom.' I grimace and pantomime hanging myself for Elaina's benefit. 'Um, yes, great, no comment, not really. Anything else?'

'Honey! So? Do you have any hits? Your father went through the roof when I told him about this. He said some whack job would strangle me in under a week if this is how I go about dating.'

'What a sweet thought. I just finished filling out the form, Mom. Elaina's here. We're having—'

'So? Check your e-mail! Maybe you have someone already!'

I cover the mouthpiece with my thumb. 'She's on amphetamines, it seems. You talk to her.'

'Hi, Mamí,' Elaina says, winning ten thousand brownie points for calling her mother-in-law that particular moniker. Elaina is revered by my mother—Elaina's quirks being found simply charming while those of her own offspring are cause for torment and dismay. They chat merrily, laughing away. Dutifully, I check my e-mail, and what to my wondering eyes should appear but a message!

Holy crap!

'I got one,' I announce with pride. Buttercup's thin tail lashes my shin.

'She got one,' Elaina translates. 'Oh, sure, Mamí. Here she is.' She passes me the phone and takes a handful of Doritos from the bowl I so thoughtfully put out.

'Yes?' I say.

'So?'

'So what, Mom?'

'So read the damn thing! You only got one, right?'

'Um, well, I just finished my profile about five minutes ago.' I take some Doritos, too. 'When did you do yours?'

'Good! I finished mine a half hour ago.'

'Great. And do you have any hits?' I ask.

'Well . . . um, yes, I do.'

I can tell by her tone, which has become suspiciously gentle and kind, that she's hiding something. 'How many?' I growl.

'Well . . . more than one. Don't take it personally, Chastity. I'm sure you'll have twenty-three pretty soon, too.'

'You have twenty-three hits, Mom?' Buttercup growls in her sleep.

'Holy shit!' Elaina exclaims. 'Let me have the phone! Mamí, are you kidding me? Oh, my God, you know? That is so great! Any keepers?'

While they're talking, I look at my message, blandly entitled 'hi.' What the hell. I click on

70

it.

Dear GirlNextDoor,

I really liked your profile. It seems like we have a lot of interests that are the same. Check out my profile, and if you're interested, drop me a line.

—husbandmaterial.

Well, the name is promising, anyway.

'You're joking!' Elaina squeals. 'Chastity, your mother has four dates lined up already! Can you believe it?'

'I can't believe it,' I mumble. I click on husbandmaterial's profile as instructed, glancing impatiently through the list of attributes. Attractiveness—he's given himself a six-point-five out of ten . . . I wonder what *that* will translate to. Gollum? Freddy Kruger? Jason of the Freckled Legs? Well, moving on . . . *Loves outdoor activities.* Great. *Enjoys good food.* (Honestly, is there anyone alive who doesn't?—*I enjoy bad meals and the intestinal distress that follows . . .*). I forgive him and move on. *Athletic,* great. *Family-oriented,* cool. He sounds pretty good, actually.

Elaina hands the phone back to me. 'Oh, look, here's another one!' my mother crows in my ear. "Dear OlderandWiser, I'd love to meet for coffee. I live in Thurman and would be happy to come into Eaton Falls and see if you can possibly be as great as you sound!" Oh, Chastity, isn't this fun?'

'Oh, yes,' I lie.

71

'I got *another* one! I can't believe I waited this long to dump your father. How many have you got now?' she demands.

I check my listing. 'Um, still just the one.'

'Well, honey, don't worry. All it takes is one, right?'

My phone bleats in my ear. 'Mom, I have another call. I'll call you back, okay?' I push the button for the next call. 'Hell—'

'It's your father. Did you know your mother registered on some crazy Web site? She's going to get herself killed! I mean it, Chastity. You are not to encourage her. Oh, gotta go. We just got a call. Bye.'

Sighing, I hang up. 'I'm hungry,' I tell Elaina. 'Shall we make something for dinner?'

'By we, do you mean me?' she asks, preening.

'Yes, Elaina. Would you care to whip up something fabulous from the meager offerings of my kitchen? Please? Pretty please?'

'Sure, baby. I'd love to.' She ruffles my hair, does a neat leap over Buttercup and sashays into the kitchen. She does love to cook . . . incomprehensible, but convenient for me.

I glance back at husbandmaterial and decide to e-mail him back. Right now. What the heck, right?

Dear husbandmaterial,

You sound really nice. Tell me more about yourself. What do you do for work? Does your family live around here? What kind of sports do

72

you like? You're not a Mets fan, are you?

I hit Send, pleased. I'll let him reveal more about himself before I do. I'm a little wary over the six-point-five, but this is just a trial run. Besides, men have no idea how to rank themselves. Jason, after all, considered himself too attractive for me. I ranked myself a seven, which I felt was quite honest. Once I get my hair cut, I may upgrade to seven-point-five.

The phone rings again. Glancing at the caller ID, I see that it's the Eaton Falls Fire Department. Must be Dad again.

'Hi, Daddy,' I say.

'Hi, Porkchop.' There's a smile in the voice, and the voice is not Dad's.

'Trevor?' I press a hand against my suddenly hot cheek. In the kitchen, Elaina is singing.

'Hi. Sorry. Yes, it's Trevor. How are you?'

'I'm fine.' Is it possible that I, who hold a master's from Columbia University, can think of a wittier response? 'Great, I mean. And you?' I close my eyes. 'I thought you guys went out on a call.'

'Oh, just the engine went. I'm tails on the ladder this week.'

'Oh.' Another captivating response.

He pauses. 'I've been instructed by my captain to find out if Mom is really going on a date,' he says in a low voice. Trev's called my mother 'Mom' since he was about sixteen years old. And his captain is my father, of course.

'Yeah. I guess she is,' I answer. My shoulders

73

drop a little. I should have known he wouldn't call for purely social reasons.

'It's hard to believe she's really looking for a boyfriend,' Trevor says.

'Yeah.'

'Well. Okay, Chas. I better run. See you around.'

'Okay. Thanks for calling. Bye. Take care.' I sound like a jerk.

Luckily, my computer dings softly. *You have one new message, GirlNextDoor.* Hooray! Husbandmaterial is back!

Dear GND (We're on nicknames already—fantastic),

I'm a Yankees fan, not to worry. I have a big family. As far as sports and hobbies, I like to hike, mountain bike, kayak a little. What about you? Hobbies? Pets? What makes you the girl next door?

'Dinner in ten, sweetie!' Elaina calls, rattling some pans. 'Chicken quesadillas!'

'Angels bless you, Elaina! Be right there. Just answering an e-mail.'

Husbandmaterial sounds . . . well, great. Friendly, kind of sweet. I immediately write back. *I also have a big family. I like hiking and rowing (single scull). Have lots of nieces and nephews. Love animals. I have a big dog who slobbers, and I worship the Yanks.* I hit Send and wait.

Thirty seconds later, bing! *You have one new message, GirlNextDoor.* Yippee! I click immediately.

Chastity?

Oh, my God! Husbandmaterial knows me! Shit! Or is it good? *Yes?* I type back.

It's Matt.

Clapping my hand over the shriek of laughter (or is it horror?) that bursts forth, I snatch up the phone, dial Matt's cell. 'Hello?' he chokes. I can barely wheeze back. 'You're disgusting,' he says. 'Checking out your own brother. Gross.'

'You wrote first, pervert.' I wipe my eyes and try to control myself, but it's no use. We laugh in mutual horror for a good two minutes. 'You are to tell no one about this, Matthew.'

'Right back at you, Chastity,' he says, still laughing.

'I find it hard to believe that you have trouble meeting women, Matt,' I tell him when I've calmed down. 'Oh, and you're a ten, by the way. A six and a half? Come on! You look like Mel Gibson!'

'Ew.'

'Well, okay, not the drunken, sun-damaged mug shot Mel. Young, wholesome Mel. Road Warrior Mel. You're a good-looking guy, Mattie.'

'Well, you know, it's weird to fill out all that stuff,' he says. 'I do meet plenty of women, but you know. Haven't met the right one. I figured I could cut through some crap. This single thing's getting old. I don't want to live with my sister for the rest of my life. No offense, Chas.'

'None taken,' I say. 'Well, I'll keep my eye out for you. And you do the same for me, okay?'

'Sure. Not that I know anyone I'd actually fix you up with, Chas. All I know are firefighters, and you don't want to end up like Mom, do you?'

'Mom has twenty-three hits on her profile, Matt. And she just registered an hour ago.'

'Jeez! I only got fourteen all day. How many did you get?'

'Once you upgrade that attractiveness level, you'll have more,' I answer, craftily ignoring his question. 'Gotta go. Elaina's over and she just made dinner.'

'Don't tell her about this! And save some food for me.'

'Okay. Talk to you later.' Checking once more to see if I got any more hits—I don't—I sigh, my humor evaporating. I've been registered for forty minutes now. Mom had twenty-three hits in that time . . . I've had one, and it's from a blood relative.

'Come on. Stop feeling sorry for yourself,' Elaina says from the doorway. 'Everything's better after a quesadilla.'

I sign off the computer, and for the briefest second, I let myself recall Trevor's voice. Then I shake my head and join my friend for dinner.

CHAPTER FIVE

When Trevor's sister died, she and I were both ten years old.

Her family had moved to our town while I was in fourth grade. Michelle was a pale girl with pretty, dark hair. Being a well-dressed new kid had ensured her popularity, and for the first month, she was surrounded by admirers who wanted to hear all about the glamour of Springfield, Massachusetts, where she was from. When we were assigned to the same reading group, we chatted, found that we both wanted to be horse trainers when we grew up, and started eating lunch together. But a week or two later, she became sick—no one knew what she had, just that she was out. She came back after a few weeks, but only for a day or two.

When she'd missed more than a month of school, I went to see her, bringing some cookies that Mom had baked. She only lived three blocks away, and Mom allowed me go all by myself with strict instructions to call if I were going to stay more than a few minutes. I rang the bell, and Michelle's big brother let me into the foyer. Over his shoulder, I could see someone lying on the couch, obscured by a puffy comforter.

'Is Michelle here?' I asked. 'I'm her friend

from school.'

'She's kind of sick,' the brother said. 'She can't play right now.'

'Oh.' Blushing, I handed him the cookies. 'Tell her Chastity said hello,' I said, scuffing my feet. The brother was a seventh-grader, and kind of, well, cute. I peeked again over his shoulder. Michelle lifted her hand. I waved back, not realizing that I would never see her again.

'Okay. Thanks for coming by, Chastity,' he said. 'Thanks for the cookies, too.'

I learned later that Michelle's leukemia was so virulent that her immune system couldn't handle the risk of germs from outside visitors. While I missed her, it was more on the theoretical side—we hadn't really had time to become good friends. My life continued on pretty much the same, basketball, homework, soccer, CCD. Then one night, months after she'd left school, my mom popped into my bedroom, her face unusually grim. 'Say a prayer for Michelle Meade,' she told me. 'She's very sick.'

I obeyed, chanting the hot, fervent prayers of a child. 'Please, please, please don't let anything bad happen to Michelle! Please let her be okay. Please let her get better.'

She didn't get better.

My mother let me stay home from school to go to the funeral, and I cried great gulping sobs as the small white coffin was wheeled down the church aisle. Her parents were limp and pale with grief, her brother standing thin and ignored between them, like something left at the lost and found. At the sight of him, the barefaced knowledge that a child could die, that I might lose Jack or Lucky or Mark or Matt the way that boy had lost his sister—that my brothers could lose *me*—made me almost hysterical. Mom carried me to the car, staggering a little—I was already nearly five feet tall—patting my back and murmuring. When she got behind the wheel, she wiped her eyes with shaking hands. 'I love you so much, Chastity,' she said, her mouth wobbling. 'I love you so, so much.'

A few weeks later, I saw Michelle's brother, alone, dribbling a basketball at the school playground. Mom was inside for Mark's parent-teacher conference, and I was pretending to read *The Hobbit*. Instead, I watched covertly as Michelle's brother shot basket after basket until finally the fates acknowledged me and the ball bounced off his foot and rolled over to me. I picked it up and waited.

'Hi,' I said as he came over to retrieve the ball.

'Hi,' he said.

Being raised by the laundry Nazi, as Jack and Lucky called her, I noticed that the brother's clothes were kind of grubby. His sneakers looked like they were on their last legs, and his hair needed to be cut. There were dark circles under his eyes, and his pants drooped at his waist.

'I'm Chastity O'Neill,' I announced. 'I came to your house once.' Part of me wanted to get a reaction, to somehow state my importance and let him know that I, too, suffered and understood his pain.

He looked at the ground. 'Right,' he said, offering nothing more.

'I'm Matt and Mark's sister. Do you know them?' My youngest brothers flanked him in school, Mark a year ahead of him, Matt a year behind.

'Sort of,' he said, still looking at the ball that was tucked firmly under my arm. We didn't say anything more for a minute.

'I'm sorry your sister died,' I blurted.

The brother looked at me from his dark eyes for a minute, then pinched the bridge of his nose and dropped his head. I'd seen my dad do that sometimes, when he banned us kids from the living room and spoke to Mom in a low voice, telling her about a bad day, a day when someone had been hurt badly . . . or when someone hadn't made it. It seemed like such an adult gesture, and to see Michelle's brother doing it now made my throat ache. I realized I didn't understand squat about his pain, that I wasn't suffering at all compared to him.

'Do you want to have supper at our house?'

80

I whispered.

He hesitated, still looking at the ground, then nodded once. Then I stood up, and to spare him the embarrassment of being caught crying in front of a ten-year-old girl, showed him my excellent layup and jump shot.

Trevor's parents divorced later that same year, as is common with couples who lose a child, I later learned. Things weren't great to begin with, apparently, but after Michelle died, Mr. Meade moved to California, and Mrs. Meade stopped being much of a mother anymore. I gathered from many an eavesdropped conversation between my parents that Mrs. Meade was drinking a lot, and worse, that she was not nice when she drank. Mom called her up, talked in what we called her Father Donnelly voice, the gentle, compassionate one reserved for teachers and clergy members. Trevor started coming to our house more and more, where he was fed and fussed over and made to laugh almost against his will. Before long, he was sleeping in the bottom bunk in Mark's room on weekends, shooting pool with Jack and Lucky in the basement, helping Mom wash the dishes after dinner.

After that first year, he became a lot of fun, a king of practical jokes which often involved wildlife and my bedroom. He complimented Mom's cooking (something none of us ever did) and shadowed Dad in the garage. Once or

81

twice, he helped me with my math homework when a brother wasn't available, and occasionally he would play basketball with me. If he ever noticed that I worshipped him, he was kind enough not to comment. Instead, he treated me like, well, like one of the guys, including me when my own brothers might have ignored me. When I, a mere high school sophomore, came downstairs in a poofy floor-length gown for the senior prom of a boy in Jurgenskill, Matt and Mark howled that I looked like Lucky in drag. Trevor told me I looked pretty.

How could I not love him?

During his senior year of high school, Trevor's mom moved to Idaho to live with her sister. Trevor spent the year with us, carefully perfect as the not-quite son, never sulking like a true O'Neill, never insulting or overly loud, calling my parents Mike and Mom, doing chores without being asked, almost as if he was afraid he'd be kicked out if he was anything less than wonderful.

It was my father he loved the most, I think. Matt and Mark were his best friends, Jack and Lucky the older brothers he never had. I was a substitute, perhaps, for the little sister who would never grow older than ten. Mom's heart ached for him, and she doted on him and spoiled him in a way that she never spoiled us, because after all, we already knew we were loved. But our dad . . . Our dad became the father Trevor desperately needed. Dad taught him to drive, gave him the lecture on safe sex, and let him hang out at the firehouse on weekends, putting him to work polishing the trucks and cooking for the guys. My father was who Trevor wanted to be.

These thoughts all come back to me as I walk into Emo's one night later that week. At the booth in the corner, sit Dad and Trevor, deep in a conversation of considerable gravity, it seems, judging by their expressions. A few other members of the gang are there as well, but clearly Dad is addressing Trevor, barely sparing a glance for Jake or Paul.

In some ways, Trevor is just as much my father's son as the biological O'Neill boys. Trevor has a sense of respect for my dad that's missing from his own biological children, as if with shared DNA comes the entitlement to ignore and mock one's parent. Trev folds his arms just the way Dad does, drinks the same type of beer, uses Dad's mysterious word 'jamoke' to connote a person's idiocy. Now that Dad lives on his own, Trevor often hangs out at Dad's or invites him over for dinner.

'Hi, Chas!' a few of the other members of C Platoon call as they catch sight of me.

I walk over to the booth, which is situated right under a photo of the tragic Lou Gehrig, pride of the Yankees. 'Hey, guys!'

'What are you doing here, pretty girl?' Santo asks.

83

'Dinner,' I tell him, smiling. Dropping in at Emo's for dinner is becoming something of a sacred tradition for me. I hate to cook. Cooking is wasted on one person, and Matt works so much overtime these days that, even if I could manage to create something tasty . . . well, no point in even following that train of thought. I'm my mother's girl when it comes to the kitchen.

'My girl! Just the person I wanted to talk to,' Dad says. An empty shot glass and a pint of Guinness sit in front of him, and he already seems a little tipsy. 'Don't anyone talk about Chastity's little incident at the toy store, okay, boys?' he orders.

'Gee, thanks, Dad. You're a master of subtlety.'

'Have a seat, Chastity,' Trevor says, getting up to grab a chair. I genuflect briefly in front of St. Lou and join the table.

C Platoon consists of my dad, the captain, and Paul, Santo, Jake and Trevor. Also Joey 'Hoser' McGryffe, but he's been out with a knee injury, and today Matt is covering for him.

'How about a Bud and some wings, Stu?' I call to the bartender. He nods agreeably.

'Have you spoken to your mother?' Dad demands.

'Sure,' I say.

'Everyone thinks it's a bad idea, her dating,' he continues. Jake, an ass-kisser, nods

84

emphatically. 'Are you really going to do that singles crap with her, Chastity?' Dad continues. 'Go cruising for seedy men you barely know?'

I sigh audibly and with great exaggeration. My father has called me no fewer than eleven times to discuss this matter. Stu brings me my beer. 'Thanks, Stu, old buddy. Dad, I'm just keeping her company, okay? Trying to make sure she stays safe,' I say, hoping he'll remain silent on my own single state. 'I'll keep an eye on her, don't worry.'

'Good girl, good girl,' Dad nods. 'Listen, Porkchop, why don't you do this? You get the name of any scumbag interested in your mother, and you give it to me. I'll take care of the rest.'

I glance at Trevor, who makes a subtle 'cut him off' sign to Stu. 'I don't think so, Dad.'

'Why? You want your mother attacked by some pervert?' Matt snorts.

'I don't think Betty would go for some pervert,' Trevor murmurs.

'Shut up, you. She's not going for anyone,' Dad snaps.

'Excuse us, we're gonna shoot some pool,' Santo says, rising along with Paul. 'Jake? Want to play?'

'Not really,' Jake says, but Paul grabs him by the collar and drags him up.

Stu delivers my wings and slips my dad a glass of seltzer water.

'Listen, Dad,' I say, trying to keep my voice friendly. 'I'll watch out for Mom, but I'm not spying on her. Sorry. Matt, get your hand away from my plate or draw back a bloody stump.'

'You will be sorry, when you have some lecherous creep for a stepfather.' Dad takes a sip of his water and sulks.

'I'm not getting a stepfather,' I say with great patience, taking a bite of chicken. 'She's just trying to get you to retire. Pulling the jealousy card.'

'Retire!' My father snorts as if I'd just suggested he smother kittens. 'Why would I retire?'

I roll my eyes and slap Matt's hand as he tries to steal another chicken wing. I can't help noticing that Trevor changed before coming here, unlike the rest of his platoon. He's wearing a white T-shirt that makes his eyes look even darker. Molten chocolate, God help me. His hair is tousled—needs a trim, probably—and my hand is twitching to smooth it. The sleeves of his T-shirt stop right on the curve of his brawny biceps. Beautiful arms. Damn. I force my eyes away to the dimples of Lou Gehrig. Trevor and I were together once. Didn't work out. End of story. No point in tormenting myself.

'Chastity!' Jake calls from the pool table, rescuing me. 'Come over here! I need you, babe.' He grins wickedly at me, and I smile back gratefully. Not that Jake means anything by it . . . anything with a pulse and two breasts, that's his motto. I take my beer, leaving Matt the last chicken wing, and join him. 'Atta girl,' Jake says. 'Now, you can see what a mess I've gotten into. Can you sink that little baby over there?'

'Of course I can,' I answer, sucking some sauce off the side of my thumb. 'Stand back and learn, boys. Five ball, center pocket.' I take the cue, bend over and shoot. There's a satisfying smack as the cue ball hits the orange five ball, which bounces off the rail and glides to the center pocket.

'Well done,' Jake murmurs from behind me.

'Don't you be looking at my daughter's ass!' dear old Dad bellows from twenty feet away. 'Jake! You wanna lose some teeth?'

'Sorry, Cap! Force of habit.' Jake grimaces. 'No offense, Chastity.'

'None taken, Jake,' I say, batting my eyelashes.

Trevor joins the four of us by the table to watch. 'You guys may as well pay up now,' he tells Santo and Paul with a grin.

'Six ball in the corner pocket.' I lean, bridge, shoot, sink. Paul grimaces and takes out his wallet.

'I don't want my daughter to end up with some jamoke firefighter!' Dad continues.

'Don't worry, Dad. I won't,' I say. 'Two in the center.' Clack, spin, thunk.

Trevor winks at me. 'Here she goes.'

I squint at my next victim. 'Six ball in the back corner.'

'You'll never make that shot,' Paul says.

'Ten bucks says she can,' Trevor says right back.

'Done.' Paul folds his arm smugly. It is, granted, a tough shot. Mr. Six Ball will have to bank just shy of the eight ball, which is only a couple of centimeters from the pocket, then cross the entire length of the table to the left rear pocket. I'll need to give the cue ball a good bit of English, but I'm not concerned. I've been playing pool with my brothers since I was five. I set up, study my angles, take the shot and, because I'm so incredibly cool, turn away for a sip of my beer before the six ball reaches its destination. It sinks into the pocket with a most satisfying thunk.

'Shit!' Paul exclaims, and I blow my dad a kiss. He's not looking, staring at the table glumly.

'Thanks, Chas,' Trevor calls, taking Paul's ten dollar bill.

'Eight ball, side pocket.' I lean over once more and win the game. 'And I think we're done, here, Jake.'

The guys applaud, and I grin.

'Thank you, gorgeous. I mean, thanks, Chastity.' Jake grins and accepts the five dollars from Paul.

'I earned that, don't you think?' I ask. Jake raises an eyebrow, hands me the five and gives me a lecherous look. Suddenly I feel kind of beautiful. I mean, after all, here I am, surrounded by men, some of whom are nonrelatives *and* single. Being one of the guys has occasional benefits.

'Don't you marry a firefighter,' Dad growls as I return to the table. 'Bunch a' jamokes, if you ask me. You'd just end up all bitter and dried up and angry, like your mother.'

'There's a happy thought,' I murmur. Not that a firefighter would dare ask out the O'Neill girl, mind you. I kiss my dad's bristly cheek, grab my jacket and head for home. Trevor will make sure Dad gets home okay. They only live half a block from each other.

CHAPTER SIX

The next night after work, I take Buttercup on her nightly drag. I suck in a few breaths of the clean mountain air, and admire the neighbors' gardens, which are bursting with daffodils and grape hyacinth. Buttercup stops to sniff a flower, then attempts to collapse upon it. 'Come on, Butterbaby,' I say, tugging at the leash. She flops, just missing the flower, and gives me a mournful look, sighing deeply. A squirrel, correctly assessing her energy level, darts right over her front paw. Buttercup doesn't move, just flops on her side, moaning.

'Come on, Buttercup!' I end up hauling her to her feet and practically carry her home as she moans and wags. I think she kind of likes this form of transportation. 'You're pathetic,' I say laughing. She wags her tail agreeably.

Ten minutes later, I'm showered, changed and on my way out again. Buttercup gives one mournful howl, sounding very much like a werewolf or the hound of the Baskervilles, then doubtlessly flops down for a snooze.

Tonight is my first EMT class, and though I'm quite unsure that I want to attend, I'm also pretty sick of making an idiot of myself every time someone has a boo-boo. My whole life, I've been queasy (putting it gently) around blood. It's time to take charge. I'd really like to be more like . . . well, like Aragorn. Now there's a guy you can count on in times of trouble. After the toy store debacle, after making a fool of myself in front of Kim and Dad *and* Trevor, I've decided that knowledge is power. Desensitization time.

I obediently report to Eaton Falls Hospital, where class will be held once a week. Once again, the notion that I'll meet a friendly guy here pops into my brain. So far, Tara and Sarah, good sisters-in-law though they may be, have turned up squat on the date front. Every man they know seems to be married or related to me. Maybe I should take out my high school yearbook and take a flip through. Give a few guys a ring. I sigh. *Hi, it's Chastity O'Neill! How are you? I'm back in town, thought we could meet for a drink, shoot some hoops . . . and by the way, are you married?*

I walk in the hospital's main doors, lost in thought, and slam into someone coming the opposite way. 'Sorry!' I exclaim.

'My fault,' he says, and holy crap, it's him! It's the guy from Emo's! Mr. *New York Times!* Mr. Cheekbones! The one who didn't send me a drink!

'Hi!' I sound like a breathless teenager upon glimpsing Justin Timberlake. He smiles distantly and continues on his way, as I, open-mouthed, watch him go. Beautiful. He's beautiful, even from behind. Make that *especially* from behind. His hair blows in the evening breeze, his suit jacket ruffling. A suit, but no briefcase. Does he work here? Visiting? Probably visiting his supermodel wife, who just gave birth to perfect twin girls.

'Do you happen to know who that man was?' I ask the elderly woman at the reception desk.

'Which man, dear?' she asks.

'The one who just left?'

'Sorry, I didn't see him.'

Damn. Can't catch a break these days. I head to the meeting room where our class will be held once a week for the next eight weeks. *Maybe I'll meet someone here,* I remind myself.

I don't. Well, not that kind of someone. There are six of us, three men, three women, and I try not to be disappointed that none of the men is going to be my husband, being that two are in their fifties and all are married. Perhaps the teacher is some hunky paramedic or E.R. doctor . . . but no. In strides a brisk-looking middle-aged woman with wiry gray hair and sturdy shoes. She whips out a clipboard and peruses it intently. 'O'Neill?' she barks, looking at the list.

'Here,' I answer.

'I meant, are you one of *the* O'Neills?' She cocks her head, birdlike.

'Um, if you mean one of Mike and Betty's kids, then yes.'

She bursts into a smile. 'I'm Bev Ludevoorsk. I know your dad,' she says. 'And your brothers, let's see . . . Matthew, Mark, Luke and John, right?'

I nod, simultaneously proud and irritated. Proud of my brothers, irritated at being pigeonholed.

'What great guys!' Bev barks.

'I can see you don't know them well,' I joke.

'Hahahaha! You should certainly sail through this class, with the family history you've got!' she booms approvingly. 'And look at you! Just as big and strong as your brothers. Patient lifting won't be a problem for you, now, will it?'

'I guess not,' I mutter, trying to feel flattered.

'What's your first name?' she asks.

'Charity?'

'Chastity,' I correct. One of my classmates smiles. 'My father thought it was funny,' I explain. 'My middle name's Virginia.'

'Ouch,' the woman says.

'Tell me about it.'

'Chastity's whole family works in emergency services,' Bev barks. 'Right, Chastity?'

'Three firefighters, a bomb detonator and a chopper paramedic,' I confirm.

'And isn't Trevor Meade somehow related to you?' she asks.

'No, actually. An honorary O'Neill, but no relation.' I feel my face warm at the thrill of discussing Trevor, loser that I am. For Pete's sake, I've known Trev my whole life. We were together romantically for roughly seventy-two hours. You'd think I'd be over that.

'Right, so anyway, why don't we introduce ourselves and say why we're here. I'm Bev, as I already told you, hahahaha, and I love doing this job because we help people. Simple as that. Got to think on your feet, move fast, keep a cool head. It's a great job. Who's next? O'Neill? How about you?'

I hesitate, unsure of how much truth to parcel out. 'Well, as you just heard, my family is in emergency services, and I thought it was time I joined the herd. Oh, and by the way, I'm, um, kind of surprising them with this class, Bev, so if you see one of them, I'd appreciate it if you didn't mention this.'

93

'No prob, O'Neill. Next?'

The other people in class—Henry, Ernesto, Ursula, Pam and Todd—say basically the same thing as Bev: it seems like a good way to serve the community, maybe work in the field professionally, yadda yadda.

'Okay, people, so this first class is an overview of the kinds of things we're likely to see in the field,' she begins. My toes curl in my shoes. *Relax, Chastity. You can do this. Knowledge is power.* 'Get the lights in back, O'Neill, okay? We're having a little slide show.'

I obey, dreading what's about to come. My stomach feels cold. Bad sign.

'Great. Slide number one—compound fracture, tib/fib. Anyone know what that means?'

My mouth dries up in instant horror. There on the screen is a close-up of bone jutting out of flesh, the white, jagged end bloodstained, the fibrous cartilage torn. *Look away. Look away!* My neck seems to be made of limp spaghetti, my head wobbles, my eyes flutter closed. *Happy thoughts, happy bleeping thoughts . . . uh . . . let's see . . . rowing, that's good . . . Buttercup when I took her home the first time . . . Twinkies . . . um . . . Aragorn . . . Jeter . . .* There. It's working. I swallow against the bile and pull my head back into position, but I stare down at the desk, averting my eyes from the nasty picture on the screen. My skin crawls in

94

revulsion.

'And next, okay, this is what we call a chronic wound or an ulcerating wound. Old folks, diabetics, bed-bound people are prone to these. Pesky little suckers that take months to heal, if they ever do.'

Don't look, Chastity. But I can't help it. My eyes flash to the screen in time to see an open sore on the leg of a very hairy man. Immediately, I slap my gaze back to the desk, but it's too late. *Breathe in, breathe out, slowly, slowly* . . . I can still see the fragile, angry-looking edges, the greenish center of the wound, like some sort of hideous, decaying eye—*Orlando Bloom and Viggo Mortenson, both in leather. German chocolate cake, extra frosting. Yo-Yos at eleven o'clock at night, Buttercup's head in my lap.* There. Urge to vomit suppressed.

'And this is a degloving. My God, these are gross!'

I have the sense to close my eyes, tipping my head forward so Bev won't see, but her voice is inescapable. 'You can see how the skin is just pulled right back down the hand. It looks kind of tidy, doesn't it? Like he just peeled the skin right off, on purpose. Bitch to fix, though. Stitches everywhere. End up looking like Frankenstein's monster. You okay, O'Neill?'

At the sound of my name, my eyes snap open. Damn it! Now I've seen the degloving! Holy crap! Oh, God, this is the worst one yet.

95

A whimper escapes my lips at the sight of those red, red fingers, the yellowish, waxy skin pulled down like fabric, oh, God, she's right, it's an oddly precise and tidy injury, and I can see veins and muscle and the fingernails . . . the fingernails . . . the fingernails are still on.

'I'm fine,' I manage in a strangled voice.

I spend the rest of the class mentally singing Bruce Springsteen's 'Born to Run,' the last song I heard before leaving the house today, and studying the Snicker's wrapper on the floor. It's not easy—I'm still sweaty at the end of class, because despite my best efforts, certain words have trickled through The Boss's lyrics. Patellar dislocation. 'At night, we ride . . .' Arterial spurt. 'Through mansions of glory . . .' Massive head wound. 'In suicide machines.' Bruce's words have never been more heartfelt, at least in my recollection. Born to run, indeed.

I make a quick stop in the bathroom and assess the grayness of my face. This may have been a mistake. Once I splash some water on my face, I feel a little better. I'll stick this class out. I'll try. I even have enough energy to wonder if I'll see Mr. *New York Times* next week.

Next week. Ew. I have to come again, don't I? Maybe it won't be so bad. Maybe I'll get better. I did make it through tonight, after all. It's a start. Sort of.

CHAPTER SEVEN

A few days later, I take a long look in the mirror, the only thing that actually functions in my upstairs bathroom, as the boys still haven't gotten off their asses and done anything about it. I'm going out tonight, and I'm dressed like a girl. *So far, so good.*

I've always been one of those women who takes some pride in my complete dismissal of clothes. My clothes have always been for comfort and survival, not for attracting the opposite sex. For work, it's always been pants and an oxford, maybe a good-quality wool sweater, solid colors. Around home, it's sweats of varying age, usually with a Yankees logo plastered somewhere. I also have a penchant for *Lord of the Rings* T-shirts. Flannel shirts, jeans, those excellent, fleece-lined duck boots from L.L. Bean that come in handy ten months of the year.

However, my clothing philosophy bit me in the ass the other day when I was mistaken for Lucky while Elaina and I were out for dinner. Thus, I was hauled against my will to the mall by my friend, who has a propensity for brightly colored, low-cut blouses that show off her fabulous cleavage. As I dragged my feet, Elaina turned on me. 'Will you stop whining?' she snapped. '*Madre de Dios,* shut up! Wearing a skirt once or twice a year isn't going to kill you, *querida,* but I might, okay?'

So now my closet contains not just my *This Old House* flannels and Levis, but also some flowery print skirts, a couple of sweaters (one is pink, please don't tell anyone), even some skinny little shoes with straps that aren't nearly as comfortable as my favorite shoes, a worn pair of red high-top sneakers. I tell myself it's all for the greater good.

And the greater good could be waiting for me tonight at Singles Grocery Night, however dubious this might sound. Stifling the urge to crawl back into my I ♥ My Preciousss T-shirt and go for a nice long run, I give myself the thumbs up, force a smile and tromp downstairs, where Matt and Trevor sit in front of the Yankees game. 'I'm meeting someone, boys,' I proclaim optimistically.

'See ya,' Matt says just as one of our own scores. 'Yes! Did you see that!'

'Have fun, Chas,' Trevor says. He glances at me with a smile. There is no jaw-drop, no abrupt realization. He just looks . . . happy. Happy and completely unconflicted—possibly even pleased—that I'm going out to meet (perhaps) my future husband. He just smiles, and when Trevor smiles, his eyes do something that I've spent a good part of my twenties analyzing. His face exceeds the sum of its parts or something. Trevor James Meade was simply born to smile, and his appealing, not-quite-

98

handsome face is transformed into utter irresistibility.

I realize I'm staring. 'Thank you!' I chirrup.

At least Buttercup seems distressed. She moans, hauls herself up and collapses on my strappy shoes, imploring me not to leave. Then Trevor makes a clicking sound, she lumbers over to him, her razor-wire tail lashing through the air, and I'm forgotten. Faithless cur.

I drive to the grocery store, imagining some gorgeous, financially secure, emotionally stable man being reduced to Singles Grocery Night. 'Daddy and I met over the ham hocks,' I say aloud. Yup. Just as I thought. Sounds impossible.

I pull into the parking lot and slosh through the puddles to the entrance, where Mom stands in raincoat and clear plastic hat, impatiently waiting for me. 'Come on! They've already started.'

'Started what, Mom? "Attention, all single shoppers. Ass check, aisle nine."'

'Mouth, Chastity. You'll never get a man with the way you talk.'

'Thanks for the encouragement, Mom.' Rolling my eyes, I follow her in. 'I do actually need some groceries,' I tell her, taking out my list.

'Oh, for heaven's sake.' She sighs. 'Well, just don't buy anything that would put a man off.'

'Like what, Mom? A supersize box of condoms? Or would that make me even more

99

popular?' I'm laughing at her back, because she's squeaking off in her little bitty crepe-soled shoes.

I start with the produce aisle. To the naked eye, it seems like a normal night at the grocery store. Are there perhaps more single men here? Hard to tell. There are, as always, more females than males. But yes, my trained journalistic eye notes a furtive tone to the evening. People glance at each other then quickly look away. A woman buying cilantro seems to be taking great pains to inhale appreciatively. *I am a sensuous woman, appreciative of life's little gifts. Ah.* Jeez. I grab a bag of apples, plop it in my cart, then move on to Poultry.

There's a middle-aged man in front of the chicken breasts, holding up package after package, examining each one closely, a thinly veiled metaphor for his true purpose tonight. 'I haven't had a good meal since my wife left me,' he announces loudly. Four women zip over to advise. No one in Chicken Thighs seems to be my age, so I turn down Juices & Bargains. A curly-haired student type darts a look at me, then pushes his carriage quickly past. *Don't bother,* I tell him silently. A grown man who drinks Kool-Aid? Please. I'm more of the Gatorade type myself.

To think I wore my new shoes for this. Down to Cookies & Crackers. I grab a few packages of Double Stuff Oreos. Can't have enough of these around the house. Matt and I eat them like they're Chicklets. The aisle is empty, as no other shopper is willing to publicly admit they eat cookies.

This isn't working. I didn't really imagine it would, of course. Sighing, I turn sharply at the end of the aisle and head up Cereals & Breakfast Treats. I'm out of Choco-Puffs, and Matt ate the last of the Pop-Tarts last night. There, in front of the specially advertised, cholesterol-lowering oatmeal, is dear old Mom, talking to two men. Cripes. Ten minutes in the store, and she's got two potential dates.

'Chastity! Come over here. Right now.' There's a familiar militant note in her voice. I obey and join her, towering over her suitors.

'This is Grant,' Mom says, indicating the five-foot-seven man. 'And this one . . . Donald?'

'That's right!' Donald (five-four) applauds. 'Well done, Betty!'

'Hello,' I say. 'I'm the daughter. Chastity.'

My mother turns to me and puts her hands on her hips. 'Grant and Donald are interested in a threesome,' she announces loudly. 'With me.'

'Good God!' I splutter. 'Not with my mother, you freaks. Get away from her or I will kill both of you and dump your bodies in the river.' They remain frozen in terror, so I slam my size eleven foot into their cart and send it careening down the aisle. 'Go!' I bark.

Terrified, they scuttle down the aisle toward the vegetable oil.

'Thank you, darling,' Mom says briskly. 'Disgusting! People today! I can't believe that.'

'I can't believe you made me come,' I say. 'Aren't you sorry you're torturing Dad this way?'

She glances in my cart. 'Oh, honey. For God's sake. Oreos? You'll never attract a man with Oreos. Put some chocolate chips in there.'

'Why? To pretend I'll bake cookies?'

'Now you're catching on. How about some yeast and flour? Men love a woman who can bake.'

'I'm not that woman,' I inform her. Undaunted, she grabs my bag of Oreos and plops them on the Quaker Oats display.

'Give those back,' I say, rescuing my poor cookies. 'You might be able to live on two thousand calories a day, but I sure as hell can't.'

'Hello, Betty,' comes a voice behind us.

'Hello, Al!' Mom turns to a balding man about her age and gives him a peck on the cheek. 'Al, you remember Chastity, don't you? Chastity, Mr. Peters was an usher with Daddy in church, remember?'

'How you've grown!' Al (five-seven) says, gazing at my chest.

'It's singles night,' Mom announces.

'I know,' he says, staring first at my left breast, then at my right. 'Are you single,

Chastity?'

I glance nervously at Mom. 'Um . . . yes?'

No doubt about it. He gives me a slow once-over. '*Very* nice.'

Thirty seconds later, Al is shoved through the door into the rain by my irate, five foot two, size four, fifty-eight-year-old mom.

'Is there a problem, ladies?' An attractive, portly man in his fifties pushes his cart over to us. 'I'm Louis Tuttle, by the way, widower, age sixty-two, one year shy of retirement from IBM, strong stock portfolio.'

Mom's expression becomes speculative. I smile. 'No problem, Louis. I'm Chastity, by the way, and this is my mother, Betty O'Neill.'

They shake hands. 'So,' I say. 'I think I'll visit Ben & Jerry before I head out, Mom.'

Mom gives me a little flutter of her fingers, already chatting up Louis Tuttle.

It's kind of cute. Men still love my mother. Maybe it will light a fire under Dad, seeing her go on a date or two. As for me, this is a waste of time, aside from the fact that I'm getting my grocery shopping done. I glance at my watch. Nine-fifteen. I wonder how the Yankees are doing. Wish I was home watching them with the boys, eating Oreos.

Well. Can't have everything, but *can* have some Oreos. I tear open a package and idly eat a few, scanning the aisles, occasionally adding something. Rice and beans. Kraft Dinner. Family size Spaghettios, some vodka sauce for

103

when I feel like something fancier. Popcorn. Sun Chips.

'Nutrition Queen rides again, I see.'

I whirl around. 'Trevor!' My knees wobble with the horror of being busted. I'm positive I didn't tell anyone I was going Singles Grocery Shopping. 'What are you doing here?'

'I'm out of coffee.' Sure enough, he's holding a can of coffee in one hand, some half-and-half in the other. His face is doing that smiling thing again. 'So, Chastity, are you in the market for something other than . . . let's see here, deep fried pork rinds? What's the trans fat count on these little death traps?'

I snatch back the bag. 'Have you tried them? They're delicious. And yes, I am aware that it's singles night. Were you?' I raise an eyebrow back.

'Of course. I'm checking up on everyone's favorite sister. Plus, I needed coffee, remember?'

It's now that I notice that there are three slips of paper sticking out of Trevor's shirt pocket. Great. He sees me looking. 'I guess you can never meet enough people,' he acknowledges, grinning again.

My heart stutters. Trevor at Singles Grocery Night. Like shooting fish in a barrel.

Sure enough . . . 'Hi, Trevor!' comes a silky feminine voice. It is attached to a silky feminine body topped off by silky, supermodel face.

'Hey, Sally,' Trev replies easily. 'How's it going?'

'Great!' Sally says, gliding in front of me and stopping firmly. 'Just had to grab a few things.' Note the denial of singles shopping. Liar. Sally is the cilantro sniffer. Her cart is filled with fresh produce, as well as yeast and whole wheat flour. Mother would approve. 'So, Trevor,' she coos. 'What's new?' She sticks out her Pamela Andersons and flips her hair.

I roll my eyes and eat another Oreo.

'I'm just talking to my friend here. Chastity, this is Sally.'

'Hi,' I say with the enthusiasm of a concrete block.

'Hello,' she replies with equal fervor. She turns back to Trevor. 'Well, I hope you find what you're looking for, Trevor,' she breathes, then whispers in his ear, very loudly. 'And if you ever change your mind, you know where I live.' Then she sashays down the aisle, scrawny ass swinging. I could crush her in one fist.

'So. Sally.' I force a smile.

'We dated a few times,' Trev explains. Ah. Trevor is a bit notorious when it comes to dating. Women, as I may have mentioned, love Trevor. *All* women. Five minutes after seeing him for the first time, they fall deeply in love, move heaven and earth to be with him, are incredibly happy for a very short period before he gently breaks up with them, crushing their hearts. Then they fondly recall him as the one

105

guy they never resented, disliked or mistrusted and would strangle their grandmothers for another chance to be with him. Obviously, I know the feeling.

'So, Porkchop,' Trevor says. I narrow my eyes at him. 'Met anyone decent yet?'

I blink in surprise. This is indeed new. Trevor and I may be on great terms, occasionally get each other in the Christmas grab bag and, as of late, see each other at Emo's here and there, but you can bet the farm we have never discussed my quest for a husband.

'Well, you know, uh,' I stammer, 'I'm actually here with Mom.' He nods. What the hell. I decide to tell him the truth. 'But yes, I guess I'm sort of . . . looking.'

He reaches out for an Oreo and nods again. I wait, actually breathless, for him to say something. *What about me, Chas? Would you ever go out with me again?* He remains silent. Tick . . . tick . . . tick . . . I can't stand it anymore. 'You know, I'm back here, plan on staying. So sure, it would be great to meet someone. Settle down. Have some kids. What about you?' There's his opening. *Take it, Trev. Go for it. Ask me to be the mother of your children. You can do it, buddy.* My forehead is a bit damp, and these bleeping shoes are killing me. Should have worn my red high-tops. They're rather dashing, after all.

Trevor glances into my cart, and I definitely

get the impression he's avoiding my gaze. 'Well, I don't know. I guess . . . I don't know.' He looks up suddenly and forces a smile. 'I've already been engaged once, so maybe I'm a little gun shy.'

'Right.' Of course. Perfect Hayden Simms, five foot five, one hundred and twelve pounds, blonde, cute, smart, openly adored by men, secretly hated by me.

Trevor is still looking at me. 'But yeah, I'd love to be a father someday. Have a couple of kids. The whole nine yards.'

If ever there was a time for him to ask me out, it's now. If ever there was a time for me to speak up, it's now. *Say something, Chastity.* 'Well, I . . . um . . . you know, I—' a bead of sweat trickles down my spine '—you know I've always thought you were . . . just . . . you know. Great.' My heart is thudding so hard I may barf up those Oreos. 'And you'll make a great dad, Trev.'

His eyes soften. Hot fudge. They're the color of the best hot fudge on earth. 'Thanks, Chastity. Coming from you, that means a lot.'

I wait for more. I did my part, damn it. *I just gave you an opening, buddy. Speak now or forever hold your peace.* He doesn't say anything else.

For a second, I feel like I might cry. Okay, fine. I'm used to not being with Trevor. Fine. 'So do you want me to be on the lookout for you?' I blurt. Just so he won't guess that I'm

107

still hung up on him. Just so it will seem like we're just pals, like I'm just one of the guys who happens to have boobs and prettier underwear.

He pauses. 'Uh . . . that's not . . . No. That's okay.'

'Hello, Trevor, honey!' Mom bustles up and kisses her favorite child on the cheek. 'Don't tell me you're looking for a girlfriend? Chastity, you must know someone—'

'Trevor needed coffee, Mom,' I explain hastily, desperate to change the subject. 'He's only here for coffee. And half and half. Trev! Did the Yankees win?'

Trevor is grinning, whether at me or my mom or us both is hard to tell. 'The game wasn't over when I left. But it was eight-zip, so I felt pretty comfortable going. They're looking great this year.'

'Please, God, another Pennant.' I relax a little, back on familiar turf.

'From your lips to God's ears,' he says. 'Gotta go, girls. See you soon. Bye, Mom.' He kisses my mother, smiles at me and takes off.

At the end of the aisle, another woman stops him, and I turn away so I won't have to see them standing there together.

CHAPTER EIGHT

When high school ended, I couldn't wait to go off to college. Home had become boring—Jack was married, Lucky was married, Mark was full of himself and Matt was, well, Matt was actually okay, though off at the fire academy fulfilling his destiny. Trevor, too, was away, but at college. I was so bored at home, so tired of the same old classmates, so dismissive of my hometown. I was dying to go somewhere where no one would know me, where I could make my own mark, to be something other than an O'Neill of *the* O'Neills—Mike's daughter, Betty's daughter, MikenBetty's daughter, Jack's sister, Lucky's sister, Mark's sister, Matt's sister, the O'Neill sister, the O'Neill girl. I couldn't wait to be just Chastity O'Neill. No expectations, no legacy, just me and the new college friends I'd make and all those cool professors and fascinating classes. Binghamton University was waiting for me.

Oh, and Trevor. Didn't I mention that? Right. Trevor happened to go to Binghamton University, too. Just a happy coincidence, I told myself. Definitely *not* the reason I'd applied there. He was a junior; he liked it; he was a great family friend, so that was a nice bonus, someone to share rides with. That was all. You betcha.

When we arrived at the beautiful campus, I tried to hide my excitement as Mom morosely made my bed and my father glumly inspected the fire exits and sprinklers. I chatted with other girls on my hall, lugged in the tiny fridge that bore the dents and scratches of three of my four brothers, hung up my Dave Matthews poster on my side of the room.

An hour after we arrived, Trevor popped in to welcome me to college.

'Hey, Chas,' he said, grinning, gorgeous, those hot-fudge eyes causing warm things to happen to me south of the border.

'Trevor!' my mother barked. 'You'll look after her, won't you?'

'Sure, Mom,' he said, slinging his arm around me. I tried not to blush.

'No drinking,' my father growled, angry at the fact that his baby girl dared to leave home (or, for that matter, leave infancy). 'No drugs, no idiot boys. You hear the fire alarm, you get the hell out of this goddamn building, you understand?'

'Yes, Dad. Thanks.'

We walked around campus, bought the requisite sweatshirts at the bookstore, admired the big shade trees and lush flower beds. When they could stall no more, my parents trudged toward the parking lot, Trevor and me trailing behind.

'I'll miss you,' I said. A clamp seemed to

circle my throat, and panic zipped up my legs.

My father stared at the ground. 'Be good,' he muttered.

I burst into tears. So did Mom. Dad, too. We fell into each other's arms, sobbing. 'Have fun.' Dad choked.

'Study hard.' Mom hiccupped.

'I love you, Mom,' I squeaked. 'I love you, Daddy. I'll miss you so much.'

'Okay, okay,' Trevor said, good-naturedly pulling us apart. 'She'll be fine. We'll come home soon. Come on, Chas, let me get you drunk.'

'You think you're funny?' my dad asked, wiping his eyes. 'You're not funny. No drinking, Chastity.'

'And no unprotected sex!' Mom added, buckling herself into the seat, then blowing her nose.

'No sex at all!' Dad yelled. 'And no drugs of any kind, young lady.' He got into the car and pointed at me. 'No drinking, drugs or sex. You understand me? I will personally kill you if I hear anything different. Love you. Call us tonight.'

As they drove off, it started to dawn on me just how alone I was about to be.

'So, Chas,' Trevor said, 'you okay? I have some stuff to do, but I could hang out for a while.'

'I'm fine,' I said, wanting very much for him to hang out for a while but being too much of a tough cookie to actually ask.

'Good girl. Want to have dinner one night?'

'Sure,' I said, still gazing in the direction of my parents' car.

'Great. I'm in the directory. Give me a ring.' He gave me a quick, perfunctory hug, then loped away. I watched as four girls surged toward him. He stopped, chatted, continued, turning to wave at me as he rounded the corner of the building.

Sure, I'd been dying to get away from the irritating, know-it-all attitude of Mark. From Jack and Lucky's constant stream of advice and input. I couldn't wait to go to class, read, write papers, do labs, make friends, have a boyfriend.

But it was surprisingly hard.

I began to realize how much being the O'Neill girl defined me. Here, no one knew why I ate so quickly, showered faster than a Marine, swore with such color and energy. I found out rather quickly that most college boys don't want to be instantly pinned during a friendly little wrestling match, outscored three to one in a basketball game or thrashed during a pool match.

Likewise, it was harder than I'd imagined to make friends with girls. Elaina and I had been best friends for eons already, that kind of tight-knit, unbreachable bond that kept other friends at a distance. Who needed friends when you had a best friend forever, four brothers, their wives and girlfriends, and Trevor? These girly-girls in their capri pants and tiny canvas shoes, their hair-tossing and flirting, were exotic and mysterious to me. On some level, I wanted to be like them; on the other hand, I knew it was impossible for me, five foot eleven and three-quarters, one hundred and fifty-seven pounds with the legendary O'Neill shoulders, to fit in with the cashmere sweater-set clique.

It was lonely.

At least until crew tryouts, that is. Thanks to Lucky's tutelage, I aced the first round. Coach put me on the exclusive four, which meant I had three instant best friends, all of whom happened to be upperclassmen and who quite admired those O'Neill shoulders. Suddenly, I belonged somewhere based on my own accomplishments. I was judged only for myself, not what my brothers had or had not done. It felt fantastic. I had finally come into my own.

I was meant to row. No tiny little shiny-haired girls on crew, no sir. Every day, we prided ourselves on being tireless, strong, ruthless, relentless. Burning muscles and sweat-drenched T-shirts were our status symbols. We ate together, studied together, hung out in each other's rooms.

At the Head of the Charles Regatta in October, the Binghamton women's four creamed the competition, gliding four lengths in front of the second-place crew, soundly

113

beating everyone who mattered: Harvard *and* Yale *and* Penn. Even freakin' Oxford! We were euphoric. Each of us had been perfect, in sync, our every molecule focused on the row—a study in strength, concentration and unity. Such a victory! Binghamton had never placed so high at such a prestigious event, and we found ourselves local celebrities and campus heroes upon return.

To honor the occasion, the entire women's crew team was invited for dinner at the dean's home. It was a posh evening—I even wore a skirt and eye shadow, my teammates assuring me that I did *not* look like I was a drag queen. Dinner at the dean's! It was a huge honor. We were all nervous, especially me. I was the only underclassman on the winning crew, the only first-year on varsity, and yes, a lot of fuss had been made about me. So when Becca, a senior, offered me a vodka and tonic before the big dinner, I accepted. Then I asked for another. Never having had vodka before, not having eaten anything all day due to said nerves, well, let's just say I relaxed quite a bit.

And then it happened. It was one of those stupid and fairly common moves many college students make. Drinking, I was just now learning, seemed to lower my inhibitions and loosen the old tongue, but I was doing okay, being rather charming, in fact, or so *I* thought. When the dean herself asked me—me!—how it felt to have captured first place, beating some of the best crews in the world, what I imagined was a charming and droll answer fell out of my mouth.

'Well, Dean, those candyass Ivy Leaguers should have been drowned at birth by their parents, seeing that they row like spaghetti-armed third graders! I mean, come on! Did you see those weakling rich kid Harvard anorexics?'

I waited for the roar of laughter from my teammates. None came. Glancing around the dean's posh living room, I noted that my classmates were . . . uh-oh . . . frozen in horror.

I had forgotten—oh, so briefly and so critically—that not only had Dean Strothers attended Harvard, but she had rowed while at school. Furthermore, she had a daughter, at Harvard incidentally, who also rowed. Who happened to be on the very crew we so soundly defeated.

I spent the rest of the evening burning in Dean Strothers's hate-filled glare, trying not to move, trying to melt into the background, which is rather hard to do, since no one wanted to stand closer than four feet. Our celebratory dinner was ruined, the dean was pissed, Coach horrified and my teammates embarrassed. I wanted to crawl into the river and drown.

When dinner finally ended, some four years after it had begun, I slunk across campus to my dorm. It was Thursday night, and tomorrow

115

there were no classes as part of the Columbus Day break. My crewmates and I had planned to storm the campus center and continue our celebration, but there was no way I was going to do that now. Chances were that I'd be the main topic of discussion, and all I wanted was to be alone.

My roommate had gone home for the long weekend, thank God, and I flopped on my bed and cried, torn up that I'd been so thoughtless, so tactless, so stupid, stupid, stupid. I couldn't get anything right. I was a bull in a china shop. I had no social graces. I would never ever drink again. I'd finally found friends and now they hated me. I was a blight on the sport. I didn't deserve to row ever again. Etcetera, etcetera, etcetera.

When a knock came on the door an hour later, I didn't bother getting up, still sniveling in self-disgust.

'Chastity, honey, it's me,' said a voice. Trevor.

I hadn't seen much of him since I'd started six weeks earlier, and when I did, he was always surrounded by friends, usually of the female variety, though he was popular with both sexes. He'd wave, come over for a quick chat, pat me on the shoulder and off he'd go, back to the cool kids, to the fabulous upperclassmen, to the throngs of women who seemed to orbit around him.

I'd hoped that we would hang out at college,

walk across the beautiful campus, have dinner as he'd promised. In my eighteen-year-old mind, our longtime friendship would blossom into something more—a deep and abiding love—and we would soon marry and live happily ever after.

However, it was all too apparent that this would not be the case. Trevor was too enmeshed to seek me out on more than a cursory basis, fulfilling his promise to my parents. It hurt, seeing him so close, so happy, so unattainable.

I told myself I didn't care. I had crew. I had my own friends. Once crew was over, I would probably even have time for a boyfriend. So Trevor didn't matter. That's what I told myself.

But when I saw him standing in my doorway, frowning at the sight of my gloopy mascara and wobbly mouth, I threw myself into his arms and sobbed with renewed gusto. 'Stupid . . . vodka . . . dean . . . candyass . . . stupid . . . Harvard,' I bawled, and somehow Trevor strung the story together. He'd already heard several versions, hence his visit to my room. He led me to my bed and sat down, pulling me next to him as I sniveled and blew.

'It's okay, Chas,' he assured me with a smile. 'It'll be legend in another month. It just seems horrible now.'

'No one likes me, Trevor,' I said, wiping my eyes. 'I only had my friends from crew, and now they hate me. I'm nobody here. Just a bigmouth idiot with the O'Neill shoulders.'

'I like you,' Trevor said.

'Right,' I muttered, stealing a glance at his face. His lovely, happy eyes smiled at me. 'You only like me because you have to, to stay in my family.'

'Not true,' he said, tickling the inside of my elbow. Heat crawled up my arm, melting my insides. I opened my mouth to say something, but I couldn't, trapped in the familiar tangle of my crush on Trevor Meade, world's most popular man. 'Not true at all,' he said again.

'It's true,' I grumbled.

'Come on, Chastity,' he said. 'You're great, you know that.'

'Save the pep talk, buddy,' I said, shoving away from him and standing up. Let him go tickle someone else's arm. One of his girlfriend's. Jerk.

'Chas,' he chided. 'You are. You're beautiful and smart and funny, and yes, you do have the O'Neill shoulders and they're gorgeous. Plus, if we need someone to lift a tree off a car, there you are.'

'Bite me,' I said.

He reached out and grabbed the waistband of my skirt and tugged so that I fell (quite gladly, despite my feigned reluctance) back on the bed. 'Sit down and stop feeling sorry for yourself.'

'I don't. I feel sorry for you, having to babysit me in my time of woe,' I answered.

'I like babysitting you,' he murmured.

'How pathetic.'

He didn't answer. I sneaked a look up at him, and he was just looking at me, a little smile making the corner of his mouth pull up. My breath stopped, and I could feel my face grow hot. Those damn happy eyes dropped to my mouth, and Trevor's smile faded.

Then before he could break the moment, before he could turn away, I kissed him, and he didn't stop me. Instead, he pushed my hair out of my face, and he kissed me back, gently, sweetly, his hand slipping behind my head, his lips moving just right against mine, smooth and warm. I gripped his shirt and sighed against his mouth, and knew that as long as I lived, this would be the one perfect kiss that I'd remember forever.

'Chastity,' he said, but I didn't give him time to say anything else. I just kissed him again.

He tasted like mint and coffee, and his mouth was soft and sure at the same time, and we fit together so wonderfully . . . he was solid and warm and strong, and so was I. I leaned back, pulling him with me so that we lay on the bed, and the kiss became deeper, less perfect, more urgent. My fingers slid through the smooth coolness of his thick glossy hair, and I opened my lips for more.

Kissing Trevor felt like summer in June . . . lovely and lazy and hot, what was yet to come stretching out in front of us, filled with possibility. We kissed for ages without doing anything else, tangled in each other's limbs, kissing and nuzzling and touching until the wee hours. My shirt was unbuttoned a few, and so was his, but that was as far as we went, even though we were both panting and flushed and sweaty and above the age of consent.

Finally, Trevor pulled back. He was lying on top of me, my legs were wrapped around his, my skirt up around my thighs. His dark, thick hair was tousled, his eyes were heavy-lidded, and I could feel the hardness of his body pressed against mine. His arms were shaking slightly. 'I should probably stop,' he said quietly, touching my bottom lip with his forefinger. 'I should go.'

'Don't go, Trevor,' I whispered. 'And don't stop.'

He swallowed and gazed at me, serious and quiet. I could see him weighing the intelligence of what we were about to do, what we had already done, could see his hesitation. Because I'd loved him for so long, been crushed by my yearning for Trevor for so damn long, I slid my hands under his shirt and pulled it over his head. 'Please stay,' I said, kissing his beautiful neck.

'Are you sure, Chastity?' he asked, his voice hoarse. I could feel his heart thudding against mine.

'Yes,' I said. Then he was kissing me again, hotter and more urgently than before, his

120

hands in my tangled hair. And I *was* sure, because after all, I'd loved him for years. Wanted him for years. Wondered and wished and longed for him for years, and having him there on the narrow twin bed, on top of me, I felt more right than I'd ever felt in my life, before or since.

The hot shock of his skin, the smoothness of his back, the noise he made deep in his throat when I bit his shoulder . . . it all made me hot and tight and dizzy . . . and so happy. My heart was absolutely certain. When he rolled over so that I lay on top of him, his hands threading through my hair, he smiled at me, and I thought I'd come apart with joy.

He was my first lover, though I knew I wasn't his. And afterward, instead of making some excuse of how he had to go or maybe this was a mistake, he just slid down a little so that his cheek was resting over my heart, his arms still tight around me. 'Are you okay?' he whispered after a few minutes.

'Yes,' I whispered back. 'Are you?'

He laughed and lifted his head to smile into my eyes. 'Never better,' he said, and I knew I'd love him forever.

For two days, we barely left the room. We got hungry, of course, and when my supply of M&Ms, cream cheese and Wheat Thins ran dry, we went to a diner in town, sitting next to each other in the booth, talking about classes and people and even my social gaffe. We avoided mentioning my family, but otherwise, it was like I always imagined it would be. Once, just when it felt like we'd backslid into pure platonics (during a discussion of the Yankees' postseason), Trevor touched my cheek, his voice stopping midsentence, and I could tell that he thought I was beautiful and desirable and lovely. I blushed fiercely, feeling the sudden need to look away. Trev laughed that low, naughty chuckle that I'd always wanted to hear directed at me, and my heart swelled with so much emotion that I thought I might cry from pure happiness.

On Sunday, we reluctantly parted, needing to do some studying. 'Come to the game with me,' Trevor suggested. The Bearcats were playing at home, and what could be more romantic than the two of us snuggled under a blanket in the stands, holding hands at the football game?

'Okay,' I agreed instantly.

In the doorway, he cupped my face in his hands, studying me. 'Chastity, I—' He paused, frowning a little. For a second, my heart stuttered in fear, but then he smiled. 'I'll see you later,' he finished, kissing me softly. He started down the hall, stopped, came back and kissed me again. 'I'm really leaving now,' he said. One more kiss, a nuzzle, a hug, a final kiss. Finally, I shoved him away.

'Get out, you big lug.' I grinned, practically floating with happiness. He smiled back and

122

finally ran down the hall. Then I forced my pheromone-saturated brain to focus on my *Canterbury Tales* paper.

*   *   *

I was a little late going to the appointed telephone pole in the stadium parking lot. Trevor's back was to me, and I broke into a happy run, fully intending to tackle him, nuzzle his neck and possibly cop a feel. But when I saw who he was with, I lurched to a halt.

It was Matt.

'Hey, Sissy!' he bellowed, running to give me a huge hug. I squeezed back hard, realizing just then how much I'd missed him. My boyfriend *and* my youngest brother, my two favorite men in the whole world.

'Hi, Matt! What are you doing here?' I smiled at Trevor. He didn't smile back, his eyes flickering between Matt and me. In his pockets, his fists were clenched. My heart fell to the asphalt with a nearly audible thump.

'I thought I'd come for the game, hang out with Trev, see how you're doing,' Matt said, his face flushed with the cold. A few of the cashmere set circled like vultures, and Matt's gaze bounced toward them. Oh, he would make a killing this weekend, looking the way he looked and now a fireman to boot.

'Great!' I said. 'Trevor and I were gonna catch the game together, too, right Trev?'

'Yup. That's right,' he answered, forcing a smile.

That was all it took. I knew in that instant that Trevor and I were not going to stay together.

We found our cheap seats and sat huddled, me in the middle, for the duration of the game. I cheered for our guys, asked Matt questions about work and the academy, about Mom and Dad, and Trevor did the same. I didn't let myself think about the warm length of Trev's leg against mine, how I already knew and loved his smell, how his unshaven cheek had left beard burn on my chest. I forced myself to be just Matt's sister, the O'Neill girl, just one of the guys.

Trevor relaxed a little at some point, realizing that I wasn't going to announce the fact that he'd deflowered the sister of his two best friends in the world, the girl who happened to be the daughter of his surrogate parents. He didn't speak to me much, though, talking over my head to Matt instead, offering only commentary about the game to me. He couldn't seem to look me in the eye for more than a second.

When the game was over, Matt said, 'Chas, we're gonna hang out at the pub, okay?'

I was not included, I could tell, being underage and, well, the sister. I glanced at Trevor. He looked away, his jaw tight. 'Okay, guys,' I said. 'See you in a couple of weeks,

124

Mattie. Love you.'

'Love you, too,' he said, hugging me.

Trevor managed to make eye contact. 'Bye, Chastity.'

'See you around!' I called brightly, punching him on the shoulder.

As I left them, I heard Matt say, 'Check out that girl in the red jacket. You know her?'

I paused, wanting to hear the answer. 'Not yet,' Trevor answered with a laugh.

I started walking again. Sure, he was probably just shooting the shit with Matt. But he didn't . . . I could tell . . . he wasn't . . .

The tears were coming hot and fast, so I kept my head down and ran to the library, found a deserted bathroom and cried, my heart open and raw, big bellowing sobs that bounced off the walls. When a librarian came in and asked me if I needed to go to the infirmary for a sedative, I got myself under control, splashed some cold water on my face and went back to my room. I changed, went for a ten-mile run and made my decision.

When Trevor came to my room that evening, any doubt I'd had was cleared up by the misery on his face. 'Hey, buddy,' I said with forced cheer. I suggested we go out, because even though I was resolved, I didn't want to break up in the same room where we'd been making love all weekend. We walked to a bench under a particularly beautiful chestnut tree and sat. The branches rose and then curved downward, nearly to the ground, and the golden leaves sheltered us from passersby, and the dark made what I had to say a little easier. Beside me, Trevor sat stock-still, staring straight ahead, tense and quiet as a cat.

'Trevor,' I said, taking his hand, 'I think we might have made a mistake.'

His shoulders dropped. There was no mistaking the utter relief that lightened his expression. 'I was just about to say the same thing,' he admitted.

Funny how pride makes you tough, sometimes. I turned to face him a little better and swallowed hard. 'Look, Trevor, you mean the world to me. But when I saw you with Matt, well . . .' My voice broke, but I coughed to cover. 'We're young and foolish, and our whole lives are ahead of us, all that crap.' I swallowed again. 'We probably shouldn't be doing this.'

I thought I sounded pretty good, given that my heart was in an increasingly tightening vise. I tried to smile, succeeded, and watched as Trevor nodded, jamming his hands in his jacket pockets.

'Chas, I should've . . . I should never have . . .' He swallowed. 'I'm so sorry. This is all my fault,' he said miserably.

'I think it's both our faults, okay?' I whispered. 'You're not to blame. It's just that there's too much to lose, don't you think?'

He looked at me, his face so terribly serious

126

and grim. 'It's not that . . . that I don't care about you, Chas.' He looked down. 'Because I really do.'

The leaves rustled in the breeze, a dozen or so drifting and swirling to the ground. One landed on his hair, and I reached up and took it. 'Oh, me too, Trev. But the last thing I want is to have things be weird between us. So maybe we should just get while the getting's good.'

His face looked so sad. My throat was killing me with unshed tears, my muscles were taut and ready, my pulse was racing. With my whole being, with every corpuscle, I wanted him to object. To say, *No. I can't. I love you, Chastity. I have to be with you.* Instead, he nodded. 'Yeah. You're right, Chas.'

We sat in silence a few more minutes, me trying not to swallow too loudly. Then Trevor put his arm around me, hugged me fiercely, so hard my ribs creaked, and let me go.

Standing up, he looked to his left, the direction of my dorm. 'Want me to walk you back?' he offered, his voice rough.

'No, no. I, um, I'm gonna run to the library for a book. See you around, big guy.'

I waited until he was out of sight to cry, silent, endless tears that dripped off my chin, cursing my own stupidity. In my hand, I still held the leaf from his hair.

Oh, I knew we'd done the right thing. In that first moment when I saw him with Matt, I knew everything. That he was terrified that being with me would cost him the O'Neill family. That things would change if he were Chastity's boyfriend. And what about the future? How many eighteen-year-olds marry their first college boyfriend? Inevitably, we'd break up, and what then? Where would he go at Thanksgiving? Would my mother welcome him if I was sobbing in my room because Trevor Meade dumped me? Would Dad think of him as his fifth son if he knew that Trevor had slept with his little girl?

Trevor had already lost a family. I wouldn't make him an orphan again.

CHAPTER NINE

As part of the *Eaton Falls Gazette*'s community relations, the paper is one of the corporate sponsors of a ten-mile road race to raise money for breast cancer research. For a week now, the paper's banner had been run in pink, and those little ribbons and pink bracelets were everywhere. The idea was to get people to sponsor you, pay your entrance fee and run, walk or otherwise finish the race. It's a lovely tradition. I've run in it a time or two before in college and after, but now, as an employee of the sponsor, my participation was mandatory.

I arrive at the meeting point, clad in my

lycra running shorts and a *Lord of the Rings* T-shirt—Mordor is for Lovers. There's a stage swamped in pink balloons, vendors selling hot dogs and pretzels, and hundreds of people there to watch the start and finish of the race. The course starts on the green, goes down River Street for a couple of miles, crosses the bridge into Jurgenskill, runs parallel the river again and then crosses the Eaton Falls bridge by the energy plant and comes back into town for the finish.

In addition to the *Gazette,* the hospital has a team running, as do the fire department, Hudson Roasters, Adirondack Brewing and the electric company. I look around, full of smug love for the scenic little city I live in. Pink flags are flapping from all the streetlights. Several of the buildings on this block have pink bunting hanging from their windows. The high-school band plays somewhere nearby, and I can hear the brass section bleating, feel the drums reverberating in my stomach. It's quite the event. I'm pleased to see how it's grown.

Then I see *him.* Mr. *New York Times!* The cheekbones, the hair, the six-feet-two-inches of male perfection—shit, where did he go? Craning my neck, standing on tiptoe, I still can't see him. Damn it! Aside from Trev, that man is the first guy who's done it for me in ages. I need to meet him. I *need* to.

'Hey, Chastity!' It's Angela. 'Oh, wow! Love your shirt,' she continues. 'That's my favorite movie. In fact, I have a life-size cutout of Legolas in my office at home.'

'I think that's sad,' I say. 'Because Aragorn is much hotter.'

She laughs. 'No, he's not. And Legolas is so much *cooler.* Remember that flip thing he does onto the horse?'

'Onto Aragorn's horse,' I remind her. 'Aragorn saved Legolas's ass.'

'You guys are such losers,' Pete from advertising says from behind us. 'Really. Do you play Dungeons and Dragons, too?'

'Not anymore!' I say.

'Not for days,' Angela echoes and we laugh.

'Are you girls walking or running today?' Pete asks.

'I'll probably walk,' Angela says.

'If I ran, I'd probably die,' Pete admits affably. 'Walking is bad enough. Ten miles! Crap! What about you, Amazon Queen?' Pete takes a minute to scan my frame and smiles appreciatively. 'I've always been drawn to domineering women.'

'Don't make me hurt you, Pete,' I say.

'I *want* you to hurt me,' he says. 'Oh, there's my wife. Pretend we're just coworkers.'

Pete's wife, whom I've met a couple of times before, rolls her eyes. 'As long as the life insurance is paid up, I don't care what you do, hon. Have fun today, you guys.'

'Where's the rest of the Gazette Gazelles?' I ask.

130

'Over there,' Angela says, gesturing. Sure enough, my coworkers—Penelope, Alan Graytooth (I can't seem to get that nickname out of my head), Danielle and one of our freelancers, whose name escapes me. Lucia, clad in bubblegum pink, stands close to Pen. She's holding hands with a tall, thin man wearing very tight, black running pants and a bright yellow shirt.

'I see Lance Armstrong has joined our group,' I murmur.

'Oh, that's right, you haven't met,' Angela says as we walk over to the group. 'Ted Everly, Lucia's fiancé.'

'Ah,' I breathe. 'At last. The man, the legend, the *bear*.'

'Hello! Hello, everyone!' Penelope calls. She's wearing an oversize T-shirt that says '*Eaton Falls Gazette*—Committed to the Cure' and yoga pants. 'The race starts in about ten minutes, so let's get over there!'

It's a beautiful, clear day, with a light breeze off the river—perfect for running. We walk over to the start line with hundreds of other participants. I do a few stretches to warm up, and Penelope frowns at me. 'Everyone, do what Chastity's doing,' she says. 'Chastity, you're a bit of a jock, aren't you? Show us a few good stretches.'

'I prefer the word "athlete," Pen,' I say. I demonstrate basic runner's stretches, isolating all the major muscle groups of the legs, hips

131

and lower back.

'Teddy Bear and I do Pilates,' Lucia announces. 'We don't need these.'

'Hi, Teddy Bear,' I say as I loosen up my ankles. 'I'm Chastity O'Neill.'

'So I've heard,' he mutters. 'Nice to meet you.' Judging by the expression on his sharp-featured face, it's as nice as, say, drinking poison, or severing one's finger just for the fun of it. Well! He seems perfect for Lucia, whose hair is sprayed into a spun-sugar cloud of Doris Day blond. Her lips are deep red, her mascara visible at twenty paces.

The mayor of Eaton Falls gives a little speech, thanking the sponsors, getting us revved up. I look around for Mr. *New York Times,* but I don't see him. There are hundreds of runners. I do peruse the crowd wearing EF Hospital T-shirts, but I can't make him out. That's okay. I'm still pretty excited. Dad and Matt definitely are running today—it gives me a thrill of pride that my father can still do ten miles—and I think Mark was planning on it, too, and possibly Tara, who ran track in college. But the rest of the O'Neills will be positioned at some point along the course, ready to cheer on the runners and possibly spray us with a hose.

The starting pistol is fired, and off we go with the rest of the crowd. With the walkers. The runners lope up ahead, and my feet itch to join them. The *EFG* staff walks briskly, but it's

132

not the same. I jog almost in place next to my coworkers. 'Anyone feel like running a little?' I ask. Pete shoots me a glare. 'Except for Pete?'

'I may have a slight lung condition,' Penelope says, patting her chest fondly. 'Chronic bronchitis, possibly walking pneumonia. I was worried about TB, but my skin test was clear.'

'Ange? Want to run?' I ask.

'Um . . . not really, Chas,' she admits.

'Okay,' I sigh, circling our group. Lucia and Teddy Bear do not deign to look at me, simply pump their arms in rhythm and heel-toe, heel-toe with vigor.

'Chastity,' Penelope says, 'if you can run this course, go for it! It'll make the paper look good. Go ahead, go ahead.'

Just the words I've been dying to hear. There's something about a race that brings out the competitor in me. 'You sure?' I ask.

'Go!'

That's all it takes. I'm off, my long legs eating up the street. There are times when being built like an Amazon teamster is a plus, and this is one of them. I already rowed this morning, but running uses a different set of muscles, and I love to run. Granted, I won't win, since I started off with the slowpokes, but I'll catch quite a few, no doubt. Sure enough, I see a few T-shirts that began with us in less than half a mile.

My breathing is even and smooth, my stride

133

long and fast. Ten miles is not the longest course I've ever run; I finished the New York City Marathon twice, Boston once. Still, it will take some gumption. 'Looking good, O'Neill!' I turn my head and catch a glimpse of Bev Ludevoorsk, my EMT instructor, and I wave and smile. 'Nice job in class last week!'

Last week was patient lifting, and as Bev predicted, I'm a natural.

I cross the bridge at the three-mile mark. Lots of people have stopped here to catch their breath and admire the view, but I cruise past, into the shopping district of Jurgenskill. The smell of hot dogs and popcorn is rich in the air, and people cheer and wave and offer us sprays with hoses. The area becomes residential and hillier. People are sitting in lawn chairs, playing inspiring songs on the radio. I catch a few bars of 'Chariots of Fire' and grin. There's even a band at one driveway. Of course, they're playing 'Born to Run.'

At the bottom of a rather long, gradual hill, I hear a wonderful sound.

'Go, Auntie, go! Go, Auntie, go!'

The clan! They're camped out about halfway up the hill on the lawn of Sarah's parents' house—and all my nieces and nephews are jumping up and down, screaming for me. 'Go, Auntie, go! You can do it! Go, Auntie, go!'

Just for them, the sweet little bunnies, I step on the gas, flying up the hill, past the laboring

134

runners, past those who've been reduced to trudging. The kids go nuts. Jack rings a cowbell, Mom calls out encouragement, Lucky flips burgers on a gas grill.

'Teeeaam . . . O'Neill!' I yell, sticking my hand out for high fives as I race past. The kids' faces are shining and proud, and I feel such a rush of love for them, cheering me on like this, that a lump comes to my throat.

'Looking good, hottie!' Elaina calls, holding Dylan.

'Chastity, you're ninety-four seconds behind the fire department!' Sarah calls, glancing at her watch. 'Go get 'em, girl!' She raises a drink—looks like a Bloody Mary—and toasts me.

'You got it!' I call back. The fire department. I can definitely catch a bunch of muscle-bound men.

It's pure joy to run today. The people lining the streets become a blur. I'm almost sprinting—I'll have to curb my pace later—but I'm already at the five-mile mark and barely feeling it. The breeze is strong and dry and feels like heaven against my damp forehead. My feet pound out a hard rhythm on the street, my breath keeping time. And then I see them, the dark blue shirts of the Eaton Falls Fire Department, running in a pack, five across, like it's a parade. My dad, Matt, Mark, Santo and Trevor. Another brief sprint and I'm next to them.

'Oh, hello, boys,' I pant. 'I thought that cluster of heterosexuality was you.'

They laugh. 'Keep us company, Chas,' Trevor says.

'You're too slow for me,' I answer. 'Did you hear that, Mark? I'm going to kick your ass.'

Mark shoots me a calculating look and takes the bait. 'You think you have a chance in hell?' he asks. 'That's fine with me.' He lengthens his stride. 'See you, guys.'

'Good luck, Porkchop,' Dad says.

For the next mile, Mark and I stay neck and neck, each of us testing the other. It's been a while since we ran together, and the competition fuels us both, just like when we were kids. Mark was always the one who took winning most seriously—Jack would let me win, Lucky would run at my side, Matt didn't like competing, but Mark made it his life mission to be the victor. And I always had a lot to prove—that I was as good as the boys. That I could do what they did. That they didn't need to look out for me, because I was fine on my own. Better than fine, really. Superior.

'Care to place a little money on this?' I ask my brother, who, damn him, is showing no signs of fatigue.

'What were you thinking?' he asks.

'Finish my upstairs bathroom?' I suggest, trying not to pant.

'Nah,' he says. 'A hundred bucks.'

'Done,' I say instantly.

136

We're at the seven-mile mark, and the crowds seem to know we need them at this point. Three miles to go, most of it uphill, until we get to the bridge. We round a curve and come to the next challenge.

It's a hill so steep it's like climbing a stepladder, and my calves start protesting immediately. There's a grinding sensation in one knee that wasn't there the last time I ran in a race. But I can't slow down, so I dig into the hill with everything I've got, keeping pace next to my brother.

'This is where I get off,' Mark says, and just like that, he's sprinting up the hill. I try to keep up, but he charges up that thing like it's the Battle of the Bulge. He's five paces ahead, eight . . . ten. My step slows. My shins are killing me, my calves sore. The grinding is more pronounced.

'You're not just gonna sit there and take that, are you?'

Trevor is running beside me. He glances over, grinning. 'Come on, Chas, we can catch him. You know Mark. He's all show. This hill will be his last hurrah.'

With Trev next to me, smiling, I can't help feeling invigorated . . . and so bleeping fond of him. Damn it! The man is a prince. We chug solidly up the hill. 'Hi, Trevor!' calls a feminine voice, and Trev waves but doesn't look over. 'You doing okay?' he asks.

'Great,' I say. We're at the top at last. From

here, it's about two miles to the bridge, then just six more blocks to the green.

'Come on, then,' Trevor says. 'I can see Mark up ahead.'

The field of runners is considerably thinner here. We're at the front of the pack . . . well, in the top quarter, anyway, well behind the true cross-country runners who are probably finishing right this instant. We run along, and I feel my second wind, the runner's high, the endorphins. Or maybe it's just Trevor next to me, his hair damp with sweat, face flushed, dark eyes sparkling.

I need to speed up without burning out, to tail Mark to the bridge without letting him know I'm close enough to make a move. But Trevor was right. Flying up the hill was Mark's mistake, and we close the distance to about thirty yards by the time we reach the bridge.

'Here you go, Chas,' Trevor says. 'It's all yours now. Empty the tank.'

'Thanks, Trev. Couldn't have done it without you.' I blow him a kiss and do as instructed.

I'm flying now. There's a slight incline down to the bridge, and by the time I hit the steel grid flooring, I'm flat-out sprinting. When I pass Mark, I don't say a word, too focused on keeping my stride, on finishing the bridge. I turn onto Ridge Street, taking the corner fast and tight onto the last two blocks of the race. The streets are packed with screaming supporters waving pink flags and cheering madly, and the sight of a flat-out sprinter makes them go a bit nuts. I tear down the last block, cross the finish line, legs rubbery and buckling, and collapse onto the green, heart thundering, lungs burning, happy as all hell.

'You okay?' a race organizer asks, helping me up.

'I had to beat my brother,' I gasp, laughing.

'Good for you,' he says. 'Get some water, okay?'

Mark finishes a few seconds later. 'Crap,' he gasps, slowing to a walk. 'I thought that was you.' He doesn't look happy, and I know him well enough not to gloat. 'Well, shit, congratulations.'

'Thanks, buddy.' We shake hands. Mark slaps my shoulder and goes to get some water without further talking. I catch my breath and stretch my calves and wait for Trevor.

When he crosses the finish line, much more gracefully than I did, he runs right to me and envelops me a big sweaty hug, smelling manly and athletic and somehow of fresh cut grass. 'You beat him, of course?' he whispers, making my entire left side tingle.

'Yes, I did,' I whisper back. 'Thanks, Coach.'

'Good for you.' He lets me go—oh, it feels so damn lonely!—and takes a long pull from the water bottle the race people give out. 'That was a very pretty sight,' he says, wiping his forehead. 'You flew over that bridge like you had wings.'

My heart may burst from pride and happiness. 'Well,' I say modestly. 'It's a great day for running.' In a flash, I decide to ask him out for a celebratory beer. Just him and me. Maybe the possibility of being with Trevor is not quite as dead as I pretend. Maybe things will shift, and we'll see that—

'Hi, Trevor.' We both turn. We both freeze.

It's Hayden Simms, Trevor's ex-fiancée.

The blood drains out of Trev's face. 'Hayden,' he breathes.

'Hi, Chastity,' she says, her eyes flicking to me. She's dressed in white jeans and a pink shirt and looks as cool and fresh as a tulip. Her blond hair hangs straight and silky, and she wears several silver rings on various fingers, making her look artsy and cool. Silver bracelets tinkle and slide over her tanned arms. I am suddenly aware that I can smell my own sweat.

'Hi,' I mumble. 'Wow. Fancy meeting you here.'

'My mom is walking today,' she explains, tucking some perfect hair behind her tiny ears. 'She's a cancer survivor, so I wanted to come, of course.'

Trevor still hasn't said anything.

'How've you been, Trevor?' Perfect Hayden asks softly.

'It's good to see you, Hayden,' he murmurs. Then his eyes start with a smile, and the rest of his face follows. A brief flare of hurt fires in

140

my chest.

'Well, I should go,' I blurt. 'Um, thanks, Trevor. Again.'

He drags his eyes off Hayden's blond perfection and looks at me. 'Right. Sure, Chas. See you around. Good run.'

'Thanks,' I mumble.

No beer. No celebration. No revelation. Crap.

CHAPTER TEN

By graduate school, I believed myself to be over Trevor. Time did its work at healing the old broken heart and all that crap. I had a boyfriend or two in college. At Columbia, I was pretty damn popular with the men, being a professional *one of the guys* type, but I was too busy for anything real. I dated a little . . . Jeff, a fellow grad student who was wickedly funny and edgy and snagged a job with CNN our second year. Then there was Xavier, who taught chemistry at PS 109. But nothing serious. It wasn't time. It was New York City, and in Manhattan, marriage isn't something to think about until you're forty or so.

In the six years since our brief fling, Trevor and I had gone back to the friendship we'd always had, back to a casual, fond relationship, not quite family, more than just friends. I made it a point not to moon after him, to be cheerful and friendly when he was around. It helped that he transferred out of Binghamton after my freshman year, finishing up at University of Vermont before going on to paramedic school. I spent my junior year in France, and when I came back, the ache wasn't as noticeable. I was young, I told myself. Everyone had that wistful first love. I'd get over him.

But then one day, while I was in my final year of grad school, working at the *New York Times* as a fact-checker to make ends meet, Trevor called me. 'Chastity,' he said, 'I was wondering if we could get together. Maybe have dinner? I'll come down to the city, what do you say?'

'Sure!' I said. 'That would be great!' The flush on my cheeks, the slight tremor in my hands told me exactly what I was thinking.

He'd been dating some girl named Hayden, someone from Binghamton, actually, one of the cashmere sweater-set gang. She lived about twenty minutes outside of Eaton Falls, and sometime after college, she and Trevor started hanging out. I'd met her, even, hung out with the boys and Hayden at Emo's last summer and been friendly and fun and relaxed as ever, barely even noticing that she was gorgeous, in law school, cool, confident, and seven inches shorter and probably fifty pounds lighter than I was. I thought I'd done a great job not being bothered.

But suddenly . . . suddenly, Trevor was coming all the way into Manhattan, a good three-hour drive, just to have dinner with me. For the very first time since that wonderful, horrible Columbus Day weekend, Trevor wanted to see me alone. Surely this meant something. He and Perfect Hayden had broken up, right? It had to be. And Trevor was coming down here to tell me that he'd never gotten over me. That now that we were adults (I was twenty-four, he was twenty-seven), shouldn't we do something about the fact that we were meant to be together? *Don't get ahead of yourself, Chastity,* a little voice in my brain warned. *Be cool. Aren't we training to become a journalist? Let's get the facts first.* I didn't listen. Screw the little voice. I didn't call home and ask what was new, either. I didn't even call Elaina. I was afraid that I'd curse my luck if I mentioned that Trevor was coming all the way to the city to see me. That a brother would tag along, or worse, a parent.

In a frenzy, I blew two weeks' pay at Long Tall Sally's, the best place in town for us oversize girls, and bought an outfit that said casual, interesting, funky, confident, but not trying too hard. I bought a new pair of bright red high-tops. I got a haircut and a manicure. I interrogated friends and coworkers for the best place to take Trevor, a place that would show him that I was a cool New Yorker, that was

143

comfortable but not sloppy, casual but still charming, an insider's place.

'McSorley's?' suggested a coworker.

'Too grimy,' I said.

'Aquavit?' suggested my boss.

'Too stressful.'

'Gotham Bar & Grille?'

'Too trendy.'

In the end, after four days spent researching restaurants, I found it. A tiny Italian restaurant in the Village where the waiters spoke broken English and the food was to die for. I knew Trev would love it. It was quiet, the staff would let us take our time, and it was so, *so* romantic with its tiny tables overlooking the street, and its brick walls and wood floor. Tony Bennett would play on the stereo. Our knees would bump, we'd stare into each other's eyes, laugh, kiss. God, I'd missed him! Since the moment I'd hung up, wherever I was—in class, at work, in bed, on the subway—I pictured it over and over. When the little voice inside my head warned me to assume nothing, I told her to shut the fuck up and let me enjoy the moment.

When I finally buzzed Trevor up to my minuscule apartment that I had scoured from floor to ceiling, I was shaking. At last. At last, I would be with him again, because I'd never loved anyone else, that was perfectly clear to me. Not the way I loved Trevor. Never.

'Hey, Chastity!' he said, hugging me hard.

'You look great! Wow. This is really cute!' He came into our flea-size living room, shook hands with my roommate, Vita, who gave me an approving nod.

'Well, we can come back here after dinner and hang out,' I suggested oh-so-casually. 'Hey Vi, want to join us for dinner?' As instructed earlier, she declined gracefully, claiming a difficult paper and late date with her boyfriend.

And so Trevor and I walked through the streets of Chelsea, down into the Village. He was impressed with my knowledge of the city, seemed genuinely happy to see me, and when I reached out to tug him across an intersection when he walked too slowly, he didn't remove my hand from his arm.

'It's great to see you, Chas,' he said, smiling, his eyes doing that transforming thing. My heart bucked in my chest. *Notice everything,* I told myself. *Drink it all in. You'll remember this night for as long as you live.*

And I did, but not for the reasons I wanted.

We got to the restaurant, where I was greeted warmly by the maître d' I'd spent an hour interrogating three days before. He seated us at the chosen table overlooking the street, and our knees did indeed bump. We ordered a bottle of wine, chatted casually about work, firefighting, my family.

'So, Chastity, are you seeing anyone?' Trevor asked a little hesitantly, his chocolate

145

eyes intent.

'Well,' I said, tilting my head, 'not really. There are a couple of guys I go out with once in a while, but nothing serious. Just having some fun.' A perfect answer, one I had practiced in the mirror a dozen or so times, demonstrating that I was sought after, but discerning, and still quite available for a more meaningful relationship.

'Good for you.' He smiled, and I grinned back, taking this to mean good because I was free. For *him*. My toes curled in my high-tops. The waiter came over, we ordered and Trevor took a sip of wine, then set the glass down and straightened the cutlery. 'Chastity, you know I've been seeing Hayden, right?' he asked.

'Sure,' I said, tucking some of my newly cut hair behind my ear. My heart rate sped up, my knees tingled. *Here it comes . . . .*

'Well, things have, um, changed a little,' Trevor said, not lifting his gaze from the tablecloth. His smile, I noted, dropped a notch. Still a little sad about breaking up with her, no doubt, whereas my own heart rocketed with joy. *Oh, God, thank You. Finally.*

I was so prepared to hear 'We broke up' that I almost missed what Trevor actually said.

'We're getting married.'

For a moment, my stupid smile, my expectant, hopeful stupid smile, stayed on my face. My eyes widened, and I took a sharp breath, then another, that stupid-ass smile still there, as out of place as kielbasa at a Seder supper. Then I was blinking, because my eyes were stinging with tears. *Don't you dare*, that little voice hissed with sudden, vicious loathing. *Don't you dare cry, you stupid idiot.* 'Holy crap, Trev! Wow!' I squeaked. 'This is great! Wow! Great!'

'You really think so?' His eyes were full of sympathy—or something, and suddenly, my pride galloped onto the scene.

'Yes!' I exclaimed. 'This . . . I'm . . . surprised, you know? I didn't think you were that serious! But congratulations! She's great.'

'Thanks, Chas.' He leaned forward, his elbows on the table. 'I wanted to tell you in person.'

'That was so . . . nice of you!' *Bastard!* 'Yeah! No, really. Thank you, Trevor.' My fists were clenched in my lap, and I had to swallow again and again. 'So, have you set a date?' The roaring in my ears was enough to drown out the happy details for the happy couple, but not enough to silence my little voice. *You bleeping idiot. Didn't I tell you to slow down? Huh? I can't believe this. If you cry, I will kill us both.*

Mario the waiter brought our dinners, and I ate and ate—the antipasto, the salad, oh, the bread, fantastic, and my penne alla vodka, out of this bleeping world, and if my mouth was stuffed, I wouldn't have to talk, now, would I? Just smile and nod at whatever the hell Trevor was saying now.

147

'I was a little worried,' Trevor admitted, wiping his mouth. 'About telling you, I mean.'

'Why?' I asked, stuffing another hunk of olive-oil-drenched bread into my mouth.

His beautiful dark eyes went sad. 'Well, you know. Because of our . . . thing in college. I felt kind of awkward, telling you about being engaged. I was afraid you'd be—'

'Be what? Are you kidding? Come on! You're like a brother to me, Trev. I'm happy for you. Really. She seems like a great person.'

Trevor—whom I really, really hated at this moment—smiled, albeit awkwardly. 'Well, yeah, definitely. She is. Things just got serious kind of fast . . . Anyway. Thanks, Chastity.' He paused, seemed like he was going to say something more, then asked about my classes.

When Mario brought our tiramisu, I excused myself to the bathroom, threw up, then rinsed my mouth and stared into the mirror. 'Idiot,' I hissed with a shocking amount of self-hatred. 'You pathetic, ridiculous, stupid idiot.'

*   *   *

Trevor and Perfect Hayden moved to Washington, D.C., where she had just signed on at a high-powered law firm. Trev picked up work as a paramedic, and they bought a condo and set a date for their wedding. Fortunately for me, they didn't come home for Christmas

148

that year, because even though I was used to treating Trevor like a pal, seeing him in love with his size-six fiancée would have been too much.

Something happened, though, and I never heard firsthand what it was. Matt told me only that it was Perfect Hayden who called things off, that Trev had wanted to work things out. Whatever the case, he moved back to Eaton Falls, resumed his job on the fire department and was a little quieter and more serious after that.

That was six years ago. Since then, to the best of my knowledge, Trevor hasn't been in a real relationship, despite the number of women who would follow him to the ends of the earth. Maybe he has abandonment issues. Maybe he never got over Hayden. Maybe she was the love of his life. Maybe every night as he's falling asleep, he thinks about her and can't help imagining how incredible it would be if they were together again, if they had that love back, if things had taken a different turn.

And now she's back.

CHAPTER ELEVEN

A few days after the road race, Penelope summons me to her office. I can tell by her tone that I'll be examining some part of her

149

body for disease. When she heard that I was taking an EMT class, she'd been nearly overcome with joy. Sure enough . . . 'Does this look like an AVM?' she asks, pointing to the back of her knee.

'What's an AVM?' I ask, bending down for a look.

'Arteriovenous malformation,' she says with ominous relish.

'Hm. Well, it looks like a varicose vein, if that's the same thing,' I tell her, rising. 'Anything else?'

'Yes. There's a self-defense class being taught at the Y tonight, and I want you to go. I had this great idea,' Pen says, settling back into her chair. 'Heroes of Eaton Falls. We can interview this teacher—Ryan something, I have his name somewhere. He's dedicated to women's safety, wants women to be able to protect themselves—' here I snort '—that sort of thing. And then we can move on to the usual firefighter-cop thing, a few Scout leaders, maybe someone who rescues animals. What do you think?'

'Sure,' I say. 'Sounds nice.'

'It'll sell more papers, too. Subscriptions haven't fallen recently, but they sure as hell haven't budged, either.'

'Well, hero stories always do sell more papers,' I acknowledge. 'That and murders.'

'You have a bunch of rescue workers in your family, don't you?' she asks, lurching upright.

150

'Maybe we can do a story just on them! The O'Neills of Eaton Falls. Family of Heroes. Heroes Are a Family Tradition. Heroism Runs in the Family.'

Heroism runs in the family *to a point,* I think, remembering Kim from the toy store. Still, I feel that familiar tingle of pride and irritation. 'Well, obviously, I'd have a conflict of interest, writing about my family for the paper I work for.'

'True enough, true enough. Okay, well, if we go with that one, I'll assign a freelancer. But let's run with the firefighter thing, just not one of your relatives, okay?'

'Sure,' I say. I don't mind. Firefighters certainly deserve their credit, even if they do sit around bickering like a bunch of old women half the time. 'I know a few guys who would probably talk to me for a story. And there are a lot of other heroes we could unearth, not just the usual suspects. We could do people who work with special-needs kids, the good Samaritan who helped you fix your tire in the rain, that kind of thing. What do you think?'

Pen likes it. We talk a little more, then I head back for my desk. Alan is leaning over Angela, and she's as far as she can get from him without actually breaking through her cubicle. 'Ange, can I see you a second?' I ask.

'Yes!' she exclaims, bolting past Alan to my area. I wait a second until Alan returns to the news desk and picks up the phone.

151

'I don't have anything, really,' I say. 'Just thought you could use rescuing. Think of yourself as little Pippin, me as noble, flawed Boromir, killing all the Uruk-hai in a desperate attempt to save you.'

'You girls really need to get out more,' Pete comments as he walks past. We ignore him.

'Thank you,' Angela says. 'Alan's a nice guy, but . . . '

'I know. He's no Aragorn.'

'He's not even Gimli,' she says, referring to the four-foot-tall dwarf from our favorite movie trilogy.

'Do you want to grab lunch today?' I ask.

'Sure!' she answers immediately.

'One o'clock?' I ask.

'Sounds perfect. I should get back to work. I'm putting together a page on make-ahead meals,' Angela says. She pauses. 'Um, just one more thing, Chastity.'

'Sure,' I answer, tipping back in my chair.

'I happened to see you at Singles Grocery Shopping,' she says in a whisper, blushing attractively.

'I'm not gay,' I interject.

'Oh, I know!'

'Just wanted to get that out there.'

'No,' she continues. 'Um, I was wondering if your brother was seeing anyone.'

'Matt? No, he's not, actually!' I lurch upright. 'He's great. Have you met him?'

'I just saw him at the store that night,' she

murmurs, her face fuchsia. 'And I caught a glimpse of him at the race last weekend.'

I pause. 'Matt didn't go to grocery night.' Then realization dawns. 'Do you mean Trevor?'

'The guy who kissed your mom? Brown hair? Great smile, dark eyes?'

My heart stutters. 'Yeah, that's Trevor Meade. He's not my brother. Family friend, that's all.'

Angela's face is hopeful. 'Oh, okay. Well, do you know if he's seeing anyone?'

My sulky inner child protests. *You can't have him. I've loved him since I was ten years old, damn it!* And then there's Perfect Hayden. I haven't heard what went on with that. 'Um . . . I'm not sure, but I don't think he's seeing anyone at the moment, Ange.' She bites her lip and smiles, and my heart sinks even further. 'Want me to put out some feelers?'

'That would be great,' she says. 'He's really gorgeous. I mean, one look and I could feel . . . you know. That tingle.'

'Yes,' I admit, forcing a smile. 'He's . . . very appealing.' There is no reason for me to object to Angela's interest. Trevor and I are dear friends. Have been for years and years and bleeping years. Oh, and the woman he once loved, who broke his heart, is back in town. Truth be told, I'd rather have Angela dating Trevor than Perfect Hayden. At least Angela's nice.

153

At that moment, a shriek splits the air. 'Omigod! Teddy Bear!' Lucia flings herself at Teddy Bear, who has just walked through the door. 'Teddy and I have to interview caterers,' Lucia announces with the same triumph as if she'd just announced that she won the Pulitzer.

'Have fun,' I call amiably.

'The wedding is only sixteen months away! There's so much to do! Omigod! You wouldn't believe it, Chastity! It's like a full-time job!'

'I can imagine,' I say dryly. 'How long have you been engaged?'

'Four years and seven months,' Teddy answers instantly. 'Let's get going, sweetums.' He turns to Lucia, fixes her collar and gives me a fake smile. He has a sharp way of pronouncing the *S* sound that makes it sound like a hiss. 'We can't have the caterers waiting. And then I have to zip back to work for a meeting with our shareholders.'

'Teddy Bear's the vice president of the company,' Lucia brags.

'I see,' I answer. 'Congratulations.'

'Bye, all! Must run.' Lucia, head high, saunters out of the office, Teddy Bear on her heels.

'If that guy is straight, then I'm George Clooney,' Pete announces. Wincing, I can't help but agree.

At the end of the day, I head for home to grab some dinner before the self-defense class.

154

Taking a bite of the cold pizza from last night, I check my e.Commitment e-mail. My mother has had fifty-nine responses to her profile. Fifty-nine. I've had Matt.

Oh, hey, here's something! Setting my pizza aside, I click on the message. *Dear Girl Next Door, wondering if u want 2 get 2gether. Saw ur picture and thought u sounded cute.* I decide to overlook the irritating abbreviations and check out his profile. Hm, not bad-looking. Favorite things to do: *Baseball, rollerblading, eating out.* So far, so good. Three most important things in his life: *My cat, my mom, the Red Sox.*

Sorry, pal. I suppose I could tolerate a Boston fan (as long as the Red Sox agreed never to beat the Yanks again), but combined with his cat and mother, there's just no hope.

I reach for my pizza—at least there's that— only to find that it's gone. Buttercup is feigning sleep next to my desk. She burps softly. 'Shame on you,' I tell her, petting her head with my bare foot. Her tail lashes the floor.

An hour later, Angela meets me at the YMCA, having accepted my invitation to tag along. Elaina couldn't go, claiming that my nephew had worn down her last nerve and the only person she wanted to be with tonight was Robert Mondavi. I'd left a message for the teacher, telling him I'd be covering the story for the *Gazette* and hoped he'd be available to answer questions after the class.

155

'Hello, sweetheart!'

'Mom! What are you doing here?' I ask, eying my mother suspiciously.

'Your father made me come,' she announces. 'He said if I'm going to be dating freaks, scumbags and perverts, then I'd better know how to defend myself. Hello, dear, I'm Chastity's mother, Betty.'

'Hello,' Angela says in her gentle voice.

'Dad made you come?' I ask, taking off my Binghamton Crew sweatshirt to reveal another in my *Lord of the Rings* collection: Elf Wanted: Archery Skills & Leather Pants a Must.

'Well, yes. If something happens to me, after all, who will cook his dinner?'

'It's not your cooking he wants to protect, Mom,' I say.

'Chastity's father and I are divorced, dear,' Mom explains to Angela. 'He's very bitter. Chastity, sweetheart, I had a lovely date with a nice man named Harry the other night. We might be serious.'

Angela cocks an eyebrow at me and then busies herself retying her sneaker.

'Wow, that's great, Mom,' I lie flatly.

The martial-arts room is packed with young women, all of whom, I note, are rather astonishingly attractive. I feel a little grotty in my aging sweats and ragged high-tops when everyone else seems to have these irritating track suits . . . cute little ensembles with cute little stripes down the side, hoodies cropped

156

short to reveal cute little tummies. There's a lot of lip gloss in this room, a lot of highlights.

The door opens, the teacher enters and my mouth falls open in shock.

It's Mr. *New York Times*.

His presence erases all thought from my mind. He's here. Mr. *New York Times* is here. The man I've been dying to meet for weeks is teaching this class!

My brain distantly registers a mass sigh of feminine appreciation that practically causes his hair to flutter. And such hair! Dirty-blond, long enough to curl at the ends, just enough to make him look careless and casual without drifting into unkempt. He's wearing a black karate uniform that wraps in the front, showing a deep V of golden, glowing skin, and my hand twitches at my side, wanting to Touch. That. Chest.

'Wow,' Angela whispers. Her face is pink.

'Holy crap,' I breathe.

'Good evening, ladies,' he says, smiling, and I stop feeling my legs. His hands go to his belt, and for a brief second, I think he's going to untie the knot and take off his shirt—*Yes! Yes, please!*—and a giddy roll of lust rushes through me. But no, no, of course not, he's just tightening his belt. Just as well. I'd probably jump him. 'My name is Ryan Darling, and I'm a fourth degree black belt in kempo karate. I'm also a trauma surgeon'—*Good God!*—'and I'm sorry to say that I've seen firsthand

157

some of the injuries that occur when a woman is attacked.'

My mother tsks next to me. I ignore her, too caught in Ryan's spell to do anything other than close my mouth and swallow. *Look at me,* I will him. He doesn't, continuing on with his spiel. I should be listening more carefully, as I am doing a story on him, but my hearing seems to be obscured by lust, which is actually causing my ears to buzz. No matter. I know from experience that I'll recall his words later . . . trick of the trade. He moves with catlike grace, pacing in front of the class as he discusses the need for every woman to be able to fight the good fight.

Ryan claps his hand, snapping me out of my daze. 'Okay, let's get started. Everyone, grab a partner. We'll start with some basic stances, blocks and punches.'

Blocking and punching is something I learned my first week of life. We form lines and imitate our Adonis-like teacher. It is immediately apparent that I am clearly the best student here. Yes, I acknowledge proudly as I help the woman on my left set her feet the proper way, I am a natural at fighting off men. Perhaps this explains some of my dating history, but there it is. I correct Angela's weak little fist—her thumb wasn't even across her knuckles, poor lamb—and demonstrate the block with great vigor.

I might not be the prettiest one here, or the

tiniest or the one with the cutest ass showcased in designer sweats, but clearly, I am awesome at fighting. Ryan is at the back of the room, helping my mother and a couple of other women back there. His voice carries to me. 'That's right, good, Betty. Great. Legs a little farther apart.' God, if he said that to me, I'd throw him to the floor and have my way with him, the rest of the class be damned. My insides quiver with lust.

We move on to strategic strike zones, and I'm horrified to learn that some women try to pummel their attackers on the chest and shoulders, rather than going for the pathetically vulnerable groin or oh-so-delicate Adam's apple. Angela holds up a pad for me to hammer-fist. Please. I could have aced this class when I was eight. Still, I imitate Ryan's punches with sharp efficiency, smacking the pad with quite a few more pounds of force than anyone else manages, causing Angela to stagger back. Surely Dr. Ryan Darling, black belt and surgeon, will note my supremacy at beating the shit out of the punching bag.

Unfortunately, my strategy isn't working. Ryan sees those who are struggling and moves through the lines to correct a fist here, demonstrate a block there. Because I am so proficient at man-fighting, his glance flickers right over me.

'Okay,' Ryan says about a half hour later. Some of the poor lambs, Angela included, are sweating up a storm. 'You're a great class, so I think we'll move on to something a little harder. Brittany, would you give me a hand on this one?' Brittany, who looks about nineteen, sways to the front of the room, her long, straight blond hair a curtain of perfection, lip gloss thick as an Exxon spill. She cements her bimbo persona with a light and fluttering giggle.

'Great. Thanks,' Ryan says. 'This next move would be useful if someone was rushing you. You grab the arm of the person, pull them toward you, using his own energy against him. Then you just pull the arm down . . . boom. Your attacker would flip right over.' He pantomimes the move in slow motion. 'You grab . . . you pull . . . you flip. See how easy it is?' Then he grabs Brittany's hand and does it again, though of course he doesn't actually flip her. Her face is glowing, and she's clinging to Ryan's hand like he's pulling her out of a pit of molten lava. 'Grab . . . pull . . . flip. Okay, let's give it a try. Get with your partners, decide who's going to go first . . . '

Bouncing on the balls of my feet, I turn to Angela. 'Don't hurt me, Chastity,' she whispers, blinking rapidly.

'I won't!' I exclaim. 'Come on, attack me.'

Other women are already rushing at their partners, including my mom, who makes an adorable attacker, I note. No one is actually flipping, although one teenager stumbles. This

160

is my chance to shine, but Angela wrings her hands, shifting her weight nervously.

'Come on!' I bark. 'You'll be fine.'

She, grimaces, closes her eyes and rushes. I grab. I pull. I flip.

Angela tumbles neatly through the air and lands with a smack on her back. Her breath comes out in a wheeze.

'Shit! Are you okay? Oh, Ange, I'm so sorry.' Honestly, I didn't think she'd be quite so light. Guilt and remorse stain my face with pink. I cover my mouth with one hand. She's just lying there. 'Ange, I'm sorry!'

Angela adjusts her eyeglasses, which were jarred askew, and blinks up at me.

'Great job!' Ryan appears at my side, reaches down and helps Angela to her feet. She rubs the small of her back and stares reproachfully at me.

'I'm so sorry,' I whisper.

'Are you okay?' Ryan asks Angela.

She nods and smiles ruefully. 'My friend here doesn't know her own strength,' she says.

'Sorry,' I say yet again.

Ryan Darling turns to me. 'What's your name?' he asks, cocking his head. 'You're really good at this.'

'I have four older brothers,' I murmur demurely, then smile. 'Hi. I'm Chastity O'Neill.' *About freaking time he noticed me*, I think, then immediately forgive him. His bone structure alone could send the Greeks to war . . . and his eyes! A pure, clear, Derek Jeter green. Man, oh, man. Nice work, God.

He's returning my look just as intently. My knees nearly buckle. 'From the paper?' he asks softly. *Nice* voice, quiet and deep and gentle, and I can just imagine him saying, *Chastity, I've been looking for a woman like you all my life.*

'Mm-hm,' I squeak, unable to form actual words at the moment.

'Great.' He smiles, my girl parts clench, and he turns to the class. 'Chastity here did a perfect job!' Ryan announces. 'In fact,' he continues, 'Chastity, why don't you come up here with me? We can demonstrate how to break a choke hold.'

He takes my hand—*Pause for a moment, Chas, let it sink in*—yes, he takes my hand in his own warm, strong, brilliant surgeon's hand and leads me to the front of the class. There are many sour faces looking back at me, and I smile modestly (I hope. Frankly, I feel as triumphant as Attila the Hun conquering Europe. Take that, you size zeroes!).

This kind of thing just doesn't happen to me. I mean, sure, I've been attracted to men other than Trevor in my lifetime. But does drooling over Derek Jeter and Aragorn really count? The fact that Ryan—Mr. *New York Times* himself!—is holding my hand, even if he's preparing to strangle me, is stunningly wonderful. Aside from the helpless, discouraging love I feel for Trevor, I can easily

162

say that I've never before been so drawn to a man.

'Great, Chastity,' Ryan murmurs. He places his hands on my neck—gently, even reverently, it seems—and then tenderly pushes some of my hair out of the way. Is it my imagination, or are Ryan's beautiful green Jeter-esque eyes filled with that magical combination of wonder and attraction? My face grows warm, my chest expands almost painfully. Whatever we're about to do, I want to do perfectly. I want Ryan Darling to be proud of me. To be in *awe* of me. To fall in love with me, marry me, have babies with me or, at the very minimum, to ask for my phone number.

'Okay,' Ryan says, turning to address the class. *My God! Those cheekbones!* I stare at the beautiful angles he's presented me and register the length and heft of his eyelashes. Unbelievable. 'Obviously, if you're being choked, you have to act immediately. If your airway is compromised, you're going to lose the fight. Chastity, you're young,' he continues, looking down (yes, down from the lofty two and a quarter inches he's got on me), 'you're in great shape'—*Suppress exclamation of joy and triumph*—'and you're obviously strong.'

I smile again. *Young, great shape, strong.* I love these words! More than that, I love these hands on my shoulders, the thumbs resting just on my collarbones as he lectures the class about walking strong, looking strong, etcetera.

163

I can barely hear. All I feel is the heat from those hands pouring into me, filling me with a kind of languid slowness, as if warm honey is flowing into me from this man—my future husband—and I imagine more: imagine him sliding those hands down my arms and back up again, warm against my bare skin, him pulling me against his golden chest, his mouth lowering to mine—

Suddenly, my throat is being squeezed—not hard, but *squeezed,* mind you—and before my brain catches on, my knee goes up. Goes up *hard.*

And Ryan goes down like a bull in the stockyards. My throat is free, but the man I plan on marrying writhes on the floor, clawing at the mat, because it seems I've just seriously compromised his ability to father our children.

CHAPTER TWELVE

'My daughter kicked a black belt's ass!' Dad announces at Emo's the next night. It's happy hour, two and a half platoons are here, three of my four brothers, a cousin or two, and Trevor, who is talking to Lindsey the Kitten Waitress.

'It was his groin,' I mutter into my Scorpion Bowl. Yes, Scorpy and I are back together, which gives you an idea of how good the past

164

twenty-four hours have been.

When Ryan collapsed, the entire class rushed to him, and I was pushed aside in the stampede to administer first aid. Except for calling out mortified apologies as he baby-stepped to his car, I didn't actually speak to him. Furthermore, I didn't get the story and had to throw together an article on James Fennimore Cooper's influence on current fiction. I'm guessing an entire four people will read that one.

I take another slurp of Scorpy and stare at the bar, carving my initials into a solidified puddle of margarita, ignoring the noise of happy hour. My empty social calendar yawns in front of me. Tomorrow night, I'll be editing next week's features from home, since I must cover the Daffodil Festival during the day. The radiator in the kitchen needs to be scraped. Buttercup could use a bath. And on Friday, I head for Lucky and Tara's house to be abused by their children while my brother and his wife head to Saratoga, where they will hold hands and gaze into each other's eyes. It seems about as close to a romantic weekend as I'm going to get.

I sigh with gusto and stuff a handful of pretzels into my mouth. Mr. *New York Times*—that is, Ryan Darling, M.D.—was my great hope. For a moment, however brief, I *knew* that he was attracted to me. I felt it. He checked me out. He was interested. Until, of course, I'd squashed his testicles into pancakes.

Was it so unexpected, honestly? I mean, there he was, choking me. I'd just flipped Angela and acknowledged four older brothers. Ryan had already commented on my strength, my 'great job' at throwing friends through the air. According to my mother and Angela (who have bonded greatly over this incident, by the way), I was supposed to bring my arms down— or up (we all know I wasn't listening)—and break the choke hold. My knee was supposed to stay out of it. But come on! It was a self-defense class for women! What's the first thing they teach? *Go for the groin, girls. Kick him in the balls.* I probably have it on a T-shirt somewhere.

'Tell us again,' my brother Jack prompts, materializing at my side.

'Shut it,' I mutter. Paul whistles the theme to *The Nutcracker.*

'Come on,' Santo wheedles. 'It's the stuff of legend.'

'Do you want to be next, Santo?' I ask.

'It's her way of standing out in a crowd,' Mark states, closer to the truth than he realizes. 'Knock 'em down and drag 'em off to her cave.'

The guys howl with laughter. Only Trevor doesn't join in, but I'm feeling too bleak to feel grateful.

'Oh, and you're such an expert on the

opposite sex, right, Mark?' I say. 'You're still mad that I beat you at the race.'

'So you're a jock, Chas. A lonely, spinster jock,' he returns spitefully.

'Mark, would you like me to share the fact that you once told me you thought Patrick Swayze was much hotter than Luke Perry?' I ask. 'No? Then shut up.'

The men's tenuous attention is successfully diverted. Granted, Mark will have to deal with gay jokes for the next several decades, but I find I don't care a bit. He showed up at Elaina's yesterday to pick a fight about something in the proposed divorce settlement, yelled at Elaina, snapped at Dylan, slammed the door so hard on the way out that a windowpane cracked. Shithead.

'Your mother had three dates last week,' my father whispers fiercely in my ear. 'She has to stop this. It's ridiculous, not to mention—'

'Shut it, Dad! Haven't you heard of keeping the kids out of your ugly divorce? Okay? Can we talk about something other than Mom's amazing social life and me kicking guys in the nuts? Can we? Huh, Dad?'

Dad starts to say something, wisely reconsiders and slides away to a more amiable product of his loins. Can't say that I blame him. Screw it. I'd feel more cheerful if I were home alone watching Tony Soprano beat someone to death. At least I'd have Buttercup . . . and one of the king-sized Snickers bars I bought at CostCo last week. Make that three Snickers bars. Maybe I'll go home, get the bag of Snickers and my dog, and go over to Elaina's, where we can both be cheered by the sight of Tony Soprano beating the shit out of someone.

I drain Scorpy—I've learned that one is my limit—and swivel around on my stool, ready to leave. Trevor is standing right in front of me. 'Hey, Chas,' he says.

'What do you want?' I grunt, in no mood to deal with anyone, let alone The Man I Love.

'I just wanted to say sorry about your, um, incident.' He smiles a little.

My heart leaps, which causes fresh irritation to flood my veins. 'What for? I felled a black belt. I'm so proud.' I glance over his shoulder. Dad is playing darts with Jack, Lucky is shooting pool with Santo and Jake, Mark is ordering another Jameson's. There are no other women in our group. Just good old Chastity, one of the guys.

'Here's your beer, Trevor,' Lindsey the Kitten sighs, squishing her boobs against Trevor's chest as she sets his glass down on the bar. 'Do you need anything else?'

I can't help rolling my eyes. 'No thanks, Linds,' Trevor says. 'See you later.' Sex Kitty wiggles away, practically purring. And yes, Trevor is watching her go.

Since my night is pure, unadulterated, grade-A, made in America crap and not looking to get better, I decide to make it a clean sweep. 'Trevor, are you getting back with Hayden?'

His mouth drops open. 'Uh . . . no. No. I just ran into her at the race, that's all. But, well, she did move back to the area. She's in Albany.'

Shit. 'But you're not seeing each other?'

He shakes his head.

'Well, here's the thing. I know this woman from work. Very nice, very attractive. Want her number?'

Trevor's eyebrows shoot up. 'Excuse me?'

'Do you want to date Angela, the food editor? She thinks you're cute.'

Trev pauses. 'You okay, Chas?'

I roll my eyes. 'For God's sake, Trevor, yes or no?' He's so close that I can smell his soap, can see that he needs a shave, and if I leaned forward just a little, I could rub my own cheek against his, then lower my head to the crook of his warm neck and kiss the skin there. Bastard. 'So?' I snap.

'Sure, I guess so, Chastity,' he answers slowly, frowning.

'Great! I'll e-mail you her name and number and whatever. Look, I have to run. Buttercup needs me.' I slide off the bar stool and shove past Trevor, who hasn't moved an inch.

'Chastity?' a new voice asks.

My head jerks around. 'Shit!' I exclaim.

It's Ryan 'the Groin' Darling. The blood

drains from my face, then floods back. 'Uh, um, hi,' I stammer. 'Um, how are you?'

'A little swollen,' he admits. I can't suppress a grimace.

Trevor is watching us. 'Hi. I'm Trevor Meade.'

'Ryan Darling. Nice to meet you.'

'You work at the hospital, don't you?' Trevor asks.

'Yes,' Ryan answers. 'I'm a trauma surgeon.'

'Okay. I'm on the paramedic unit of Eaton Falls Fire,' Trevor says.

'Right,' Ryan says. 'Hello.' He offers nothing else, and I can tell he doesn't remember Trevor. Well, I guess a surgeon would be concentrating on the patient—one would hope so, at any rate. But still. Not remembering Trevor is something I can't imagine.

'Chas, I'll see you around.' Trevor looks assessingly at Ryan. 'Nice to see you.' He joins the rest of his platoon in the O'Neill booth.

I turn back to face Ryan. 'Again, I'm so, so sorry.' Closing my eyes, I shake my head. 'I guess instinct just took over.'

'It's . . . well, it's a good example of what I try to teach, I suppose.' He attempts a smile, and another wave a dismay washes over me. Why is he here? A lawsuit? Am I being arrested for assault and battery? The burning attraction I felt for him yesterday seems like a thing of the distant past.

170

'So . . . well, would you like to have a seat?' I ask, gesturing to the stool next to me.

'Sure.' He slides gingerly onto the stool.

'Oh, crap, I'm sorry. Would a booth be more comfortable?' I blurt. 'Or some ice? Would you like some ice?'

He grins. 'No, no, that's fine. I'm here. May as well stay.'

My father is eying me suspiciously. He murmurs something to Jack, who looks over, gives me a reassuring chin jerk, then turns Dad back to the dartboard. I make a mental note to babysit Jack and Sarah's kids soon.

'So, um, Ryan, right?' As if his name wasn't burned into the shame section of my soul already. 'What can I do for you?'

'You never did the interview. I was here with a colleague, saw you, thought I'd come over.'

'The inter—oh, right!' I exclaim. 'Of course. Well, sure, I'd still love to do it.' Not that I thought we'd be speaking again, ever, but crap!

'Great. I was hoping that was the case. And it's not often I get to talk with a woman after she beat me up.'

Dear God in heaven, he's flirting. I suck in an audible breath of joy. I wave to Stu, elation bursting in my heart like a bleeping sunrise. 'Well, how about a drink?' I ask Ryan. 'I definitely owe you a drink. Possibly more.'

'A drink will do,' he answers, then smiles.

171

'For now. I'll have a single malt, if you've got it,' he tells Stu as my toes clench in my high-tops.

'Maclaren okay?' Stu asks, taking away my empty Scorpy.

'That would be great.'

'How about you, Chas?' Stu smiles. 'Another Scorp—'

'Water! Water would be perfect, Stu. Thank you.'

A million thoughts are flying through my head. One, God pities me and is giving me another chance with Ryan. Two, must use inside voice. Three, Ryan is *flirting* with me! And four, the one I like the best, every guy I know—including Trevor—is watching me chat with a very attractive man. Very attractive.

Ryan accepts the drink from Stu and turning to give me the full power of the cheekbones. 'So what kind of an angle were you looking for?' he asks.

'Well, you know . . . um . . .' My mind is blank. 'Local people who, uh . . .' He's staring at me with those green eyes. I've always been a sucker for green eyes. 'Local people . . . you know . . . who um . . .'

'Make a difference?' he suggests, a little smile tugging at the corner of his mouth.

'Yes! That's it. Yup. Give of themselves and all that.' I take a few glugs of water to buy some time and get it together. Though I humiliated him in front of his class yesterday,

172

Ryan Darling is still the first man who really grabbed my interest in a long, long time. I want to make the best impression I possibly can. A little forethought (and sobriety) would definitely help.

'You know what, Ryan? I hate to do this, but I'm wondering if we can reschedule this. I don't have a notepad or my questions or anything.' I pause. Scorpy tells me to go for it. 'Since I still feel bad about the um, injury, how about I buy you dinner and we can do the interview then?'

'Sure. I'd love that,' he says instantly, and I nearly fall off the stool. He said yes! Yes to me, the O'Neill girl, one of the guys. Mr. *New York Times* and I are going out for dinner!

'Um, yikes, I have plans this weekend,' I ay regretfully. 'How about Tuesday or Wednesday?'

'That should be fine, barring any emergency surgery. Can I have your cell number?' Seeing him smiling at me, those cheekbones, those green eyes, a surreal cloud envelops me. I haven't been this attracted to a guy in a long, long time. Maybe, just maybe, Trevor isn't the only guy in town.

We exchange numbers, and I tell him I'll call Tuesday morning with the details. Then I decide to get out of Dodge before my father or any of the other guys decides to join us. 'I'm so glad you're feeling better,' I say with absolute sincerity. 'And thanks. I'm really looking

173

forward to the interview.'

I slip a twenty under my water glass, say goodnight and flee before my menfolk realize that he-of-the-battered-scrotum is sitting in their midst.

By the time I get home, my head is clearer and my mood, needless to say, is much improved. 'I have a date, Buttercup,' I tell my dog as she charges me. She leaps, slobbers, collapses and rolls over onto her back. 'Exactly what I'm thinking, girl. Come on. Let's go for a drag.'

The night air clears my head. It's not just Scorpy, but Ryan Darling who is fogging it. I have a date—well, almost a date. An interview-date. I will pump Angela for recommendations on the very coolest, most intimate restaurant around here.

Speaking of Angela, she'll be pleased to hear that Trevor's interested. As Buttercup crumples on the Manleys' lawn, I decide to be really pleased about Trevor and Angela. Better Ange than Perfect freakin' Hayden Simms. Hauling Buttercup to her feet and luring her down the block with a Slim Jim, I make a resolution: Ryan Darling is going to be the new man in my life whether he knows it or not. And he's going to adore me.

CHAPTER THIRTEEN

On Saturday night, when Christopher, Annie and Jenny are finally in bed (I only had to threaten the use of duct tape once), I clean up the devastation and invite Buttercup to join me on the couch. Surely Luke and Tara won't mind my giant dog on their furniture, not after their children have been so lovingly cared for. Stroking my pup's enormous head and thin, floppy ears, I let myself relax, wincing as the new bruise on my thigh twinges.

It was a fun day . . . we played not only Bucking Broncos *and* Wild Wild Wolves, but also a marathon game of Monopoly, which we had to stop because Jenny kept trying to eat the hotels. We went for a hike, had milk shakes and burgers at the diner, made a Lincoln Log zoo and watched *Finding Nemo*. Then I pretended to be a giant baby and staggered around the house bellowing 'Dada! Mama! Feed me!' while the older two clutched themselves and wept with laughter. Supper time (chicken nuggets shaped like dinosaurs, quite delicious), bath time, story time, jump on Auntie time, call Mommy and Daddy time, bedtime for the girls, another game of Monopoly (the speed version), and finally, bedtime for Christopher.

I don't think I was this tired after I ran the

New York City marathon, quite honestly. I hurt in places I didn't know I had. So much for rowing being the ultimate sport. Motherhood has it beat. And I get to do it again tomorrow. But I find that I'm smiling. Jenny looked so cute in her crib, her little rump sticking up in the air. Annie, who is quite a demon child, was downright angelic with exhaustion, clinging to me as I put her to bed. And Chris, well, he's just a great kid in general. No one got so much as a boo-boo, luckily.

Actually, the only time I don't freak out around blood is when a kid is hurt. Last year, Graham fell and cut his lip, and I was quite competent administering ice and Hershey kisses, the O'Neill cure for any injury. Once, Claire scraped her knee pretty badly when we were riding bikes, and if my hands shook a little as I blotted, I certainly didn't pass out. Granted, Olivia reduced me to jelly with that loose tooth of hers, but if she'd actually been hurt and needed me, I think I would've been okay. It's nice to think that my maternal instincts outweigh my blood phobia.

Buttercup sighs, her jowls fluttering. 'Who's a good baby?' I croon, and her tail whips the couch four times. She's only a puppy still, about ten months old, but she acts like she's a hundred and four, if you ask me, lying around all day, her only activity rolling onto her back for a tummy scratch. 'I don't mind,' I tell her, pulling her ears up just for fun. She looks like

176

a cross between a dog and a jackrabbit, very ugly, very science-gone-wrong. 'I think you're fabulous. Unique. One of a kind.' I pull her jowls out from her face. She snuffles happily. 'Who's a pretty girl? Hm, Butterboo-boo?' Drawing her ears together under her chin, I decide she looks like Aunt Jemima.

The phone rings, but I had the presence of mind to bring it with me so as to avoid unnecessary movement. 'Supernanny, good evening,' I say, expecting Lucky.

'Hey, Chastity.' It's Trevor.

I glance at the clock on the mantel—nine forty-five on a Saturday night. I'm surprised he doesn't have a date. 'Hi, Trev. How are you?'

'I'm good. How's it going over there? You still in one piece?'

'Just about sixteen hours to go, and I can check into a clinic, knock back a couple of transfusions and I'll be fine,' I say, gratified to hear him laugh. Buttercup sighs again, and I run my finger down her silky jowls. 'So what's up, Trev?'

He pauses. 'Well, I was wondering if you had that number. For the food lady?'

I release the breath I didn't realize I was holding. 'Right. Let's see. Angela Davies. 555-1066.'

'That's pretty cool,' he says. 'How you remember numbers like that.'

'Battle of Hastings, 1066. William the Conqueror invades Britain.'

He laughs. 'Very impressive. Do you know mine?'

I have never called Trevor directly, so I can't cop to the fact that yes, in fact I do. That in a weak moment—well, a weak month, really—I Googled him, read every *Eaton Falls Gazette* article in the past five years that mentioned his name (there were three), and that I memorized his phone number the very first time I first saw it on Switchboard.com. 555-1021. Ten twenty-one. October twenty-first, which is Sweetheart Day, if you can believe it. Of course I remember. And not only do I know his damn phone number, but also his address, which is permanently burned into my brain.

'Your number? Um, no,' I lie, realizing the pause has gone on too long. 'I don't actually.'

'555-1021. Just for the record.'

'Gotcha.' I don't seem to be able to think of anything else to say.

He pauses, too. 'Are you going out with that guy, Chas?'

'Ryan?' I ask, as if there's more than one to choose from.

'Yeah.'

'Actually, yes. We're having dinner next week,' I answer. 'But it's work related. An interview. You know.' *Just in case you want to jump in here, Trev, and ask me out instead of Angela . . . .*

'Oh,' Trevor says. 'Well, he seemed nice.'

178

'Yeah. You bet. He's nice,' I babble.

'Okay, Chas. Well, thanks for Angela's number.'

'Sure, buddy,' I say, letting my head fall against the back of the couch. 'Knock yourself out.'

'Have a good night, Chas.'

I keep the phone against my ear for a minute, even though he's hung up, then call Elaina.

'What's up, *querida?*' she asks, chewing on something crunchy.

'I'm going out with the doctor I kicked in the nuts,' I say, trying to replace the image of Trevor's face with that of Ryan's.

'Great! Wow, Chas! I've seen him around the hospital.' Elaina is a pediatric nurse. 'He's never even looked at me, you know, and not to toot my own horn, I'm pretty hot, right?'

'*So* hot.' I laugh.

'And he doesn't date anyone in the hospital, that I know, since it's all anyone on that floor can talk about. And he's freakin' gorgeous, you know? This is fantastic.' She pauses in her babbling. 'You still there?'

'Yup.'

She pauses. 'So what's the problem, then?'

I don't answer for a moment. 'There's no problem,' I say firmly.

'Shit, Chastity,' she sighs. 'It's not still Trevor, is it?'

It's like a punch, really, to hear it said out

179

loud like that. 'Well,' I begin. My voice drops to a whisper since it's easier to say these things softly. 'I do sort of still have feelings for him. He's . . . he was my first love, remember?' Buttercup, at least, is sympathetic, stretching out a massive paw and resting it on my shoulder with a groan.

'Yeah, well, Mark was my first love and look how fucking happy we are, you know? Listen, Trevor's great, okay? He's Dylan's godfather, for Pete's sake. But he has issues, you know?' She pauses. 'And he's had chances, too, you know what I'm saying?'

I certainly do. 'Yeah. No, you're right, Lainey, you're right. I guess I've just been seeing him around a lot more than I'm used to.' I swallow. 'Whatever. Anyway, I'm dating Dr. Good-Looking. Well, it's an interview. But I feel like it's a date.'

'So what did he say, this Dr. Delicious? Tell me!'

I tell her. I even work up genuine enthusiasm, because Ryan really is a great prospect. And I don't think of Trevor again. Hardly at all.

CHAPTER FOURTEEN

'This is my third date with Harry. What do you think? Time for sex?'

180

'Mom! Come on! Leave me alone.'

'Chastity, you're such a prude.'

'Mom, you named me Chastity Virginia, okay? If I'm a prude, it's partly your fault.'

'That was your father's choice. I was too busy thanking God you weren't another boy to notice.'

I smile. 'Well, at any rate, don't go to the Blue Moon tonight, okay? Because I'm going there tonight. With the doctor. Please don't come.'

'Oh, that's right!' Mom crows triumphantly. 'That handsome doctor! How's his groin?'

'I—I don't know. I think it's better,' I answer, gritting my teeth. 'Just make sure you and Harry don't go there, okay? Do not come to the Blue Moon tonight. Are we clear?'

'Yes, Chastity. I'm not an idiot.' She sighs. 'Your father is very unhappy, of course.'

I sigh, glancing at the story on my screen that must be edited and chopped by seventy-five percent. The freelancer who wrote it refuses to accept the five-hundred-word limit I've given her, and as fascinating as the church bake sale may be, it's not getting fourteen column inches. 'Dad loves you, Mom.'

'Well, that's not the point.'

'You sure you want to be with someone other than Dad? Have you really thought this through, Mom?' I ask as gently as I can, deleting paragraphs seven through twenty-three of the bake sale story.

181

There's no sound from the other end. Bad sign. 'Mom?'

'He's promised me four times that he'd retire, and each time, something came up that prevented him from doing it. Jimmy Troiano was out with a back injury. The new hires weren't settled. The pension plan was being reworked.' She sighs with gusto. 'I got married when I was twenty-one years old, Chastity. I was changing diapers for more than a decade without a single day's break. Do you know how many times I had to take you kids to the E.R. ? I counted the other day. Twenty-nine times, Chastity. I had grandchildren before my baby was even out of college.'

'I understand, Mom, but—'

But nothing. She's on a roll. 'No! You *don't* understand, Chastity.' Her voice is General Patton–firm. 'I loved being mother to all you kids, I adore my grandchildren, but I'm at the age where I want my life to revolve around something other than my offspring! I have interests! I have desires, Chastity!'

'I'm glad, Mom, but—'

'Is it so wrong to want to do things just because I want to? To travel and have fun and just do things because they sound interesting?'

'It's—'

'Oh, honey, I don't mean to yell at you. At least I can tell you things. The boys don't want to hear it.'

Don't want to hear that our mother is

planning to sleep with her new boyfriend? Can't imagine why not! 'Look, Mom, I love you and you know what? All I want is to be like you.'

'Don't be silly, Chastity.'

'I mean it, Mom,' I tell her. 'You're an incredible mother and except for the cooking, you made a wonderful home. We're all crazy about you. Look at us! Five kids and not one lives more than fifteen miles away.'

'Which I think is pathetic, by the way,' she interrupts.

I laugh. 'Okay. So we never were able to cut the cord. But just make sure you really want what you think you want. That's all.'

'Well. Thank you, dear.' She pauses, mollified. 'So you want us to come to the Blue Moon?'

'No! Listen carefully, Mom. Do not come to the Blue Moon. Don't come. No Blue Moon.'

'Fine, honey! You don't have to treat me like a child, you know.'

Grinding my teeth, I hang up, finish the bake-sale piece, then check the story on the effects of too little snow this past winter and post everything on the Web site. My day is done.

As mentioned to Mommy Dearest, tonight is my big date with Ryan Darling. Angela recommended the Blue Moon, which just opened across the Hudson in Jurgenskill. She reviewed it last month and found it

183

spectacular, cozy, elegant and very pricey. Hopefully, I can put it on my expense account, since this is an interview, after all.

I fly home and take Buttercup out. She seems to have more pep these days. Maybe she just needed to live in the mountains, I muse, watching her trot down the street in front of me. She sniffs the post of a mailbox, crouches to pee and continues on her merry way. 'Come on, sweetie!' I call. 'Mommy has a date. Mascara must be applied.' Her tail slices through the air, and she lumbers toward me, ears flopping. 'Who knows, Buttercup?' I say. 'Maybe you'll be getting a daddy.'

*   *   *

'So have you always done martial arts?' I ask.

'Yes,' Ryan answers with a smile. 'I started when I was six, got my black belt at fourteen and was on the team in college.'

It seems like I'm on the set of a movie. The Blue Moon is everything Angela said it would be . . . cozy, quiet, classy, filled with shiny-haired patrons and soft-spoken staff. Candles flicker on the table, the wine is excellent, the man across from me is gorgeous and when he smiles at me, a warm curl of pleasure wraps around my stomach.

The night is going so well. My hair came out great. I look feminine and appropriate in a low-cut but not slutty white silk blouse and

184

blue-and-white print skirt, one of the items Elaina forced me to buy. Flats, of course, though not my beloved red high-tops. Cute little ballet flats. Ryan is taller than I am, so heels would shatter my illusion of being a delicate flower. When I walked into the restaurant, Ryan was already waiting, looking like the *New York Times* fashion model that I first imagined him to be. He kissed my cheek and held the chair for me. Definitely surreal. I'm pretty sure we have a future.

Focus, Chastity. You do need to interview him before naming the children.

'And where did you go to school?' I ask.

'Harvard undergrad, Yale medical.'

'So you couldn't get into the good schools,' I say deadpan.

'Those are good schools,' he says, frowning. 'Very good schools.'

'I was just . . . well. Yes. The best.' Okay, so he's earnest. A nice quality.

'I'm sorry,' Ryan says. 'You were joking. My fault. I must have left my sense of humor at the hospital. Sorry.'

'Oh, no, not all.' I smile. 'You're a surgeon, correct?'

'Trauma surgeon,' he acknowledges with a modest smile. I feel that I'm supposed to be even more impressed, but hey, he had me at Harvard.

'Why did you decide to teach a self-defense class, Ryan?' I ask, taking a sip of the very lovely wine he ordered.

'Well, you see, Chastity,' he says, his expression becoming very intense, 'I've always been committed to women's safety.'

'Hm,' I say.

'Most women just don't know how to protect themselves,' he continues.

'How's your groin, by the way?' I ask, glancing up from my notebook.

He pauses, then smiles. 'Fine.'

'Good.' I grin and glance back down at my notebook. Just wanted to remind him who he's dealing with.

He goes on, telling me about his desire to give back to the community, share his knowledge, etcetera. Standard enough stuff. I'm more interested in how his eyelashes catch the light. He's very sincere, frowning slightly as he talks, speaking in long, well-formed sentences laced with impressive vocabulary and an excellent grasp of grammatical concepts.

'Do you have sisters?' I ask, wondering if there's something more that drives his desire to empower women. Not that it's a bad desire or anything, but he's coming across as a little bit . . . well, condescending. Of course, he's a surgeon, so this may well just go with the territory. Add Harvard/Yale into the mix, and I suppose it's inevitable.

'Yes, I do. My sister Wendy.'

'Wendy?' I ask with a grin. 'Your sister's

name is Wendy Darling?'

'Yes,' he says, cocking his head. 'Why? Do you know her?'

'Everyone knows Wendy Darling.' He frowns, puzzled. 'From *Peter Pan,*' I explain. 'Wendy Moira Angela Darling.' I sing a snatch of the famous song. ' "Wendy, Michael, John . . . Tinkerbell, come on! I'm flyyyy . . . ing!" Ryan blinks. 'Well. From *Peter Pan.*'

'I didn't know that,' Ryan says, but he chuckles, entertained. 'You have a nice voice, Chastity.'

'That's the first time I've heard that,' I murmur.

'At any rate. Do you have more questions for me?'

'Um . . . I think I've got enough here.'

'So the interview's over?' He seems a little disappointed.

'Unless there's anything else you'd like to tell me,' I offer.

He sits back, studying me. Man, those eyes. 'No. But I hope you don't have to rush off.'

I smile demurely, suppressing a war cry of victory. 'No, not at all. Shall we order dinner?'

We order and exchange the usual information, where we grew up, family, work experience, the like. His life reads like a résumé for husband, honestly. Sports as a kid. Stable family environment. Community service through church. Stellar education. Impressive career. And hey! Let's be honest. He's bleeping beautiful! As I listen to his well-modulated voice, my toes curl in my flats. I can't quite believe I'm sitting across from him.

Ryan asks me about my nieces and nephews, and when I'm done reciting their names, I ask him the same question.

'I'm afraid not. My sister and her husband are childless by choice,' he answers. 'But I'd like to have a family. What about you? Do you want kids someday?'

I blink in surprise. Not the usual first-date talk! I was just about to ask the Yankees-Mets question. 'Well, you know, I come from a big family, and yes, I'd definitely like to have kids someday.'

'Good.' He smiles broadly, showing me perfect white teeth. 'I think it's good to know that we both want the same thing before we get too serious, don't you, Chastity? I wouldn't want to spend three months dating, only to find out that you don't ever want to get married or have a family.'

'Um, right, sure,' I stammer. Then I get a hold of myself and smile back. 'Yes. Very smart.'

'I know this is officially an interview, Chastity,' he says, 'but I have to say, I'd like us to see each other again. On a date. I think there's potential here.'

Daddy and I met when I kneed him in the groin, my little Darlings . . . . 'That's . . . well, that's a very direct approach, Ryan.' I laugh a little, and he smiles back. He has a beautiful smile. And if he's a little straightforward, who cares? He's right. Let's cut to the chase. 'Thank you. That sounds very nice, Ryan.'

'Hi, Chastity,' says a familiar soft voice. I turn to see Angela, the maître d' and Trevor. My stomach drops. Angela and Trevor.

'Hey! Hi, Ange! Hi, Trevor!' I seem to be blinking rapidly. 'Guys, this is Ryan Darling. Ryan, I think you met Angela at the class, and oh, yeah, you met Trevor at Emo's last week.'

'Nice to see you again,' Ryan murmurs to Angela, then shakes hands with Trevor.

'I didn't know you were coming here, too,' I say. It sounds a little rude. 'I mean, it was a great recommendation.' *Calm down, Chastity,* I tell myself. *Your old pal Trevor is on a date. Big deal.* He's not with Perfect Hayden; at least there's that.

'Well, when Trevor heard I'd recommended this place, he thought it sounded great,' Angela murmurs. 'How's your dinner so far?' Her cheeks are flushed.

'We haven't eaten yet. Would you like to join us?' Ryan offers politely. The maître d' frowns ever so slightly.

No! My heart is pounding away at my ribs like a jackhammer.

'Oh, no, that's okay,' Trevor answers smoothly, looking at me. 'We just wanted to say hi.' *We.* 'Enjoy your dinner. See you around, Chastity.'

189

'Yeah! Sure. Bye. Enjoy.' I roll my eyes at myself and take a deep breath.

'Is that one of your brothers?' Ryan asks as they walk away.

'Not exactly,' I say, then force myself to smile at my date. 'Trevor's an old friend. Friend of the family. And me. A friend of mine, too, since childhood.' *Stop talking. Stop. Talking.*

'Oh, I see,' Ryan says. He tilts his head to one side. 'So, Chastity, do you read a lot?'

'I do, Ryan,' I answer, going on to describe the latest book I read, which, lucky for me, happens to be something cool and erudite and not one of my *Lord of the Rings* comic books. Trevor and Angela sit three tables away, just close enough for me to catch an occasional phrase.

Eavesdropping is a prized O'Neill talent. A survival skill, really, since all the important and fascinating things in life—sex, money, crime— were told in whispered voices away from Us Kids. Throw my journalist background in the mix, and I am a master, quite capable of carrying on one conversation while simultaneously tuning in and out of another. I ask Ryan what he likes to read (alas, the answer is 'medical journals,' though that's probably a plus for his patients), but I can't help myself. I'm focusing on Trevor and Angela. They're talking food, with a nice seg into Angela's work as a food reviewer . . .

190

Heck, I didn't know she went to the Culinary Institute!

'Yes, I spent a year in Paris, actually. I loved it,' I say in answer to a Ryan question. And now Trev and Angela have moved on to family . . . kind mention of the O'Neill clan from Trevor, countered by Angela's listing of two sisters . . . oh, and he's telling her about Michelle, really, it's such a personal and painful subject, I'm a little surprised.

'I never did learn to sail, no, but I do love water sports. I row every day, and I go kayaking once in a while. How about you, Ryan?'

Damn it. Trevor is laughing, and I missed the joke. Well. Almost with a vengeance, I turn my full attention to Ryan, who hasn't noticed that it's wavering. As I said, I'm good at this. Trevor is leaning forward to catch whatever Angela is saying, and I lean forward, too.

Just then, Ryan's cell phone buzzes. He glances at it, then frowns. 'Excuse me, Chastity. I'm so sorry. It's the hospital. This will only take a minute.' He stands up, touches my shoulder and walks to the foyer.

The waiter brings the bruschetta we ordered, and, forcing myself not to look in the direction of Trevor and Angela and trying to turn off my eavesdropping skills, I pick up a piece. It's fantastic, and I'm starving. The bread is warm but not too crisp, the tomatoes succulent, the basil fresh. I look at the ceiling, at the table, at my purse. Just not at Trev.

I pick up another piece of bruschetta, and just as I open my mouth for a bite, a chunk of the topping falls off the bread and lands right on my silky white blouse. Right on the left breast. I dash the tomato bit away—it leaves a streak of olive oil and a bit of chopped basil. I swish again, quickly, but the basil, which is about the size of one of those little round watch batteries, stays.

Directly over my nipple.

And the other thing is, it's a little cold in here. You get the idea. I have a blob of green on my chilly nipple.

'Shit,' I mutter, dabbing with my napkin. The basil is stuck as if it's been superglued on. Glancing back, I can see that Ryan is still talking on the phone. Good. Fine. At least he can't see this. I dab again, but the basil fleck doesn't come off.

My cheeks flush with embarrassment. If Trevor—or anyone else within fifty yards—is so inclined, he can have a perfect view of my faux pas. I sneak a glance. Trev is listening intently, his beautiful dark eyes smiling at Angela, but he seems to feel my gaze. As his eyes shift to me, I automatically jerk my arm awkwardly over the offending breast. He looks back at Angela, and I let out a sigh of relief.

'I'm so sorry.' Ryan sits back down.

'Excuse me,' I blurt. 'I'll be back in a flash.' Clearly, I can't sit here across from

192

Harvard/Yale with some basil on my nipple. Keeping my left arm angled awkwardly across my breast, I grab my purse and flee for the bathroom, racing past Trevor and Angela en route.

Safe in the loo, I hold my white blouse—of course, it had to be white—away from my chest and scratch at the tenacious basil. It doesn't move, sitting there like an eye. 'Come on!' I exclaim, scratching harder.

It's a mistake.

Instead of flicking off as I had hoped, the basil has become pulverized. 'Oh, crap,' I moan. Now, instead of a small green leaf fragment, I've got a green stain directly over my nipple, as if I'm lactating pesto.

Grabbing a couple of paper towels, I run them under hot water and dab at my breast. Big mistake. The green remains but is now spreading with help from the water. 'Come on,' I mutter. The white blouse is wet, my bra is beige, it's even chillier here in the bathroom. You get the picture. Looking in the mirror, I see what seems to be a bright green, anatomically correct nipple.

'Damn it,' I say through gritted teeth. Maybe dry, it will be less evident. Is there an air dryer in this bathroom? I look around desperately. No. Of course not. I'm stuck with the grainy brown paper towels. Why didn't I buy that handy little bleach pen I've seen on commercials? I meant to! I really did.

I have two options. One is to cop to the stain and basically order Ryan and every other human in range to stare at my nipple. The other is to get help. I opt for help. Angela, who is organized, smart and thoughtful, will know what to do. Maybe she'll even have the bleach pen. I'll just flag her down and we'll think of something.

Yanking open the bathroom door, I nearly crash into Trevor.

'Hey,' he says. 'Were you trying to tell me something? You looked . . .' His voice trails off as he glances down. 'Oops.'

'Shit, Trevor! I have a stain.'

'Yes, I can see that,' he murmurs, still staring at my breast.

'So? Do you have a bleach pen or something?'

'What's a bleach pen?'

'Stop staring! How about a jacket? Do you have a jacket I can wear?'

'How about if I ask the maître d' if they have something? You said a bleach pencil?' He drags his eyes up to mine and smiles reassuringly.

'Yes! Good idea, Trev. Bleach pen. God bless you. And stop smiling, okay? I'm dying here! Can you tell Ryan I had to take a call? An emergency call? Should we ask Angela to help us?'

Trevor puts his hands on my shoulders. 'Calm down, Chas.' He grins. 'I'll be right

194

back.'

I skulk back into the bathroom and look at myself in the mirror. There's my chilly green nipple. Hello, Eaton Falls!

A minute later, Trevor knocks. 'Here. Is this what you were talking about?' He hands me a bottle of Clorox Clean-Up.

'This will do. Thanks, Trev. You're a lifesaver.' I close the door again, then yank it open. 'Did you tell Ryan that I had to take a call?'

'Yes,' Trevor says, his eyes wandering down to The Stain.

'Great.' I close the door again, aim the spray bottle at my breast and pull the trigger. Nothing comes out. 'Goddamn it!' My voice echoes off the tile walls.

'You okay?' Trevor's still on the other side of the door.

Twisting the nozzle around to the spray position, I try again. Nothing. 'I can't get it to work, Trev.'

'Here,' Trevor says, pushing open the door. 'Let me try.'

He stands in front of me, takes the bottle from my hand and studies it. 'You just have to turn this to unlock it,' he says. He slides his hand under my blouse. 'Sorry,' he mutters as his knuckles brush against me. His glance flicks to mine, then back down. My mouth dries up. Every part of me buzzes with lust. My knees are pudding. I swallow. *Oh, Trevor, do that again.* He pulls the shirt away from me a little and tries the nozzle.

I can feel the warmth from his hand, which is just about an inch from my skin. From the chilly nipple. I lick my lips, wanting to ignore the fact that Trevor's hand is under my shirt— it doesn't mean anything, he's just helping me—but damn it! Trevor's hand is under my shirt!

'Okay. Close your eyes,' he says.

I obey, my eyes fluttering to a close. I can feel my cheeks burning.

Trevor pulls the trigger. Nothing.

'Huh,' Trevor says, frowning first at the nozzle, then the stain.

'You need to squeeze it harder,' I rasp, my knees shaking.

He looks up. 'Squeeze what, exactly?' he asks, grinning.

'The nozzle, Trev!' My voice comes out louder than I expect, bouncing off the tile walls. 'Come on! Squeeze harder!'

'I'm squeezing, Chas!'

'Maybe I should duck in a stall, take off my shirt and we can do it that way,' I suggest, running a hand through my hair.

There's a little squeak from the doorway, which is partially open. An older woman is frozen in horror, staring at us with her mouth open.

'We're a little busy here,' Trevor says. She flees, her pink jacket flapping behind her.

That's it. I'm laughing so hard it just comes out as a breathy wheeze. I stagger back against the sink, clapping a hand over my breast. Trevor covers his eyes with his free hand, laughing too, a wonderful, unabashed, utterly happy sound that makes my heart swell.

'Shit, Trevor,' I choke out. 'Maybe I should just leave through the back door.'

'No, no,' he manages, calming down. He wipes his eyes with his hand, smiling at me. 'We can do this. You're on a date with a nice guy, and we don't want to blow it. Don't worry, Chas. We'll get it.' He unscrews the entire nozzle from the bottle, pours a little Clorox on a paper towel and bends over to dab at my blouse. 'I had no idea stain removal could be so much fun,' he murmurs, his mouth pulling up at the corner.

My grin fades. I want him to say, *Sure, let's go. I'll just tell Angela I had to run, and you and I can get a pizza and go back to my place.* Instead, he wants my date with Ryan to work. Bastard. Jerk. Prince. Does he have to be such a Boy Scout?

'There,' Trevor says. 'See? The green is just about gone. It looks pretty good. Just dry off a little, and you'll be fine.' He straightens up and smiles. I can see into the depths of his eyes, those lovely warm hot-fudge eyes.

'Thanks,' I say, my voice a little strained.

'You're welcome,' he answers, his voice lowering. He doesn't say anything more for

197

three full heartbeats. Then he steps back and the moment is gone.

I clear my throat. 'You're the best, Trevor. If the firefighting thing doesn't work out, you could always open a laundromat or something.'

It's lame, but he smiles. 'Hey, Angela's great, by the way. Really nice.'

'Oh, yeah, she's so nice.'

'Okay. Have a good night.' He turns and leaves the women's room.

I finish up. My breast is damp but no longer green, and after a minute scrubbing with paper towels, my anatomy is no longer quite so obvious. I wash my hands and sigh, looking at myself in the mirror. 'Ryan Darling,' I murmur. 'Ryan. My boyfriend's a doctor, actually. Hello. This is my husband, Ryan. He's great. So thoughtful. So smart. And have you ever seen such cheekbones? You're telling me.'

When I return to my seat, I find that I'm more than able to ignore Trevor, and if I see him smiling in my direction out of the corner of my eye, I hardly even notice.

CHAPTER FIFTEEN

'So what happened here?' Ernesto asks, gazing down at me with concern.

'I was struck by lightning,' I groan. Peeking

198

up from between my lashes, I see Ernesto struggle not to laugh.

'Are you in any pain?' he asks.

'Yes. Incredible pain,' I murmur. 'It hurts all over. And my eyes are bleeding. Please help me.'

Ernesto snorts and inflates the blood pressure cuff so it tightens around my arm. He releases the valve and waits . . . 'A hundred and two over fifty? Is that possible?' he asks, frowning at the dial.

'I row,' I state proudly.

'Really! Is that you I see down on the river every morning? About six o'clock?'

I rip off the cuff and put it around Ernesto's biceps. 'That's me, buddy. You should try it. It's fun.'

'I'd love to.'

'I'll give you a lesson,' I say, squeezing the little bulb. 'Now be quiet so I can do this.' I put the stethoscope in my ears and wait. 'One-thirty-three over eighty-six, pal. Time to drop a few pounds and start exercising. I'll expect you tomorrow morning at five-thirty, the little boathouse at the end of Bank Street.'

'So you're the bossy type, I see,' Ernesto murmurs suggestively.

'And you like bossy?' I ask, grinning.

'I'm married. Of course I like bossy,' he answers, patting my arm. 'You serious about the rowing? My wife's been after me to exercise.'

199

'Sure! It'll be fun.' I rip off the cuff with great flourish.

'Okay, good work, people!' Bev hollers. 'Pack it in and get out of here. O'Neill, can I see you privately?'

My humor evaporates. I suspect I'm in trouble.

I'm right.

Bev waits till Pam shuts the door behind her. 'O'Neill, I heard about your ride-along.'

I cringe, she sighs. 'You sure you want to finish this class?' she asks gently.

'Look, I know the ride-along didn't go that well,' I begin.

'Disastrous, O'Neill. Fucking disastrous.'

'Okay. Yes, disastrous.'

As part of the course, we're required to tag along with an ambulance crew for a few hours. Ernesto went first and did fine. An asthmatic kid who needed to be transported. Come on. Piece of cake. Then Ursula went. Chest pain. Big deal. Then was my turn.

I try to explain now. 'It was a pretty intense call, that's all. My first time, Bev. I'll do better next time.'

'Look, kid, not everyone is cut out for this kind of work. That's all I'm saying.'

'I didn't faint, though. That was good, I thought. Progress.'

Bev narrows her eyes. 'You dropped the bag on her leg, Chastity. Her broken leg.'

I bow my head. 'Right. That . . . that was . . .

200

bad.'

I panicked. It's not hard to understand why. We were summoned to an apartment building. At the bottom of the stairs was a broken plate, the pieces ominous and sinister. Then we saw the blood, a trail that led up the stairs. Apparently, the woman had taken a header down the stairs, ripped open her arm and broken her ankle. Then she *crawled* up the stairs and somehow managed to call 911.

I was hyperventilating before we even got to her. And then, come on! Muscle and tendon were bulging out of her blood-soaked arm, her ankle was turned at an impossible, freakish angle, practically rotated one hundred and eighty degrees. It was like something out of *The Exorcist,* for crying out loud! Of course I panicked! I'm not proud of it . . . I seem to recall saying helpful things like, 'Holy Mary, Mother of God, it's really bad!' and 'Are they going to have to amputate?' And then, yes, the stupid medical bag, my one responsibility . . . it just slipped from my sweaty hands and landed on her leg.

My bank account is now over two hundred dollars lighter, since I've sent the poor woman flowers every day she's been in the hospital, not to mention three boxes of German truffles and a fruit basket.

'I'm really trying,' I say to Bev. 'To be honest, Bev, I've always freaked out at the sight of blood. I just want to be . . .' I pause.

201

'You know my family, Bev,' I say with bleak honesty. 'I just want to be—' *a true O'Neill* '—normal. A normal, helpful person.'

'All right,' Bev acquiesces at last. 'We'll see how it goes. I'm worried about your day in the E.R., though.'

She's not the only one. My mouth goes chalky at the mere mention of it.

Shoulders drooping, I trudge down the hall to the elevators, press the button and wait. She's probably right. It's not like I'm going to do this for a living. I'm not cut out for this, my heroic family aside.

The elevator doors slide open, and there, dressed in scrubs, is Ryan Darling. 'Chastity!' he says, looking up from the chart he's reading. 'How nice to see you!'

'Hi, Ryan,' I say, blushing. The man fills out scrubs nicely, ladies and gentlemen. I step in. 'I guess you're working.'

'Mm-hm,' he says, glancing back down at the chart. 'And you? Are you looking for me?'

I smile. *Ah, surgeons.* 'No. I'm taking an EMT class.'

'Really? That's interesting. Let me know if I can be any help.' He smiles. 'I'm looking forward to Friday.'

'Same here.' Once my nipple stain had been wrestled into submission the other night, Ryan and I had a very nice time. Very pleasant. He'd asked to see me again, dinner at Emo's, and I accepted instantly.

The elevator stops again, and a middle-aged woman gets on. 'My daughter just had a baby,' she announces, glowing.

'Congratulations!' I say. 'Boy or girl?'

'A boy! Patrick! He's so beautiful!' Her eyes fill with joyful tears, and I pat her arm and smile. Ryan says nothing, engrossed in his chart. Must be a tough case. The elevator stops again, and he glances up.

'This is my floor. Please excuse me,' he says formally.

'Have a good night,' I say.

He turns and leans in, planting a quick and gentle kiss right on my lips. 'You, too, Chastity.' He's gone before the blush can finish creeping up my neck. I bite my lip and smile. He kissed me. Ryan Darling kissed me. And it was nice. Quick, but very nice.

The doors slide shut once more. 'Now there's a handsome man,' the new grandmother comments. 'Your husband?'

'No, no,' I tell her. 'We're . . . well, we're dating.' I'm grinning like an idiot.

'Good for you, hon. A doctor *and* gorgeous.' She smiles and sighs. 'Though nothing beats having a grandchild. Patrick is my first, you know.'

My ego, which was kicked in the head by my review with Bev, has been restored by the brief encounter with Ryan. As the woman pointed out, he is an extraordinarily good-looking man, incredibly smart, talented and well-educated

203

and rather charming, actually.

I think about the bathroom incident. The nipple. Trev's hand. Then I give my head a little shake and recite the mantra I've had going for a good long time. Trevor and I are really good friends. We were together once. It didn't work out. If he's the man I'd choose, well, sometimes you don't get what you want. Doesn't mean I can't fall in love again. Find someone else. I don't have to be stuck on Trevor James Meade for the rest of my life.

I go back home, clip the leash on my baby girl and go for a walk. May is such a beautiful month. The cherry trees in front of my neighbor's house are in bloom, and late tulips nod along the sidewalk. I'll have to do some gardening this year, too. Buttercup sniffs a flowerbed with great excitement, practically inhaling a grape hyacinth into her nostril. A lilac tree promises to be glorious in another week or so.

I head for downtown, past the Civil War memorial, past the library with its big elm trees and benches. The streetlights shed a soft pink glow, and I sneak peeks up at the apartment windows above the shops that line Main Street. Someone has a big bookcase. Someone's room is painted red. Someone loves plants. I love these little glimpses into the lives of the residents, love seeing a tiny slice of someone's life.

Buttercup finds religion at a fire hydrant,

putting her bloodhound genes to good work as she sniffs and sniffs and sniffs. She has more energy these days, and it's not such a trial to walk her, though she is breathtakingly slow for such a big animal. She glances back at me and continues to snuffle along the sidewalk, wagging her tail.

I find myself at my dad's apartment, though I hadn't exactly planned on coming. What the heck. I ring the bell.

'Trev?' Dad's voice asks over the intercom.

'It's Chastity, Pop,' I say.

'Hey, Porkchop!' He buzzes me in and I walk up the three flights to his apartment, practically dragging Buttercup behind me.

'You can do it, girl! Almost there!' I urge as she threatens to collapse on the second landing. Finally, we reach Dad's door, which is unlocked.

'Come on in,' he calls from the kitchen.

I've only been here once before, last summer. It doesn't look much different. There's a futon couch, a TV in the corner, and still a lot of boxes yet to be unpacked. A couple of Eaton Falls Fire Department shirts are draped over the radiator.

'I love what you've done with the place,' I say.

'Don't be a smart-ass. Want a drink?' Dad asks. He's wearing his work clothes still, dark blue pants and a polo shirt emblazoned with the Maltese Cross, the symbol of firefighters.

His thick salt-and-pepper hair is rumpled.

'Sure,' I say. 'Got a beer?'

'Coming up.'

Buttercup flops down in front of the couch, and I climb over her to sit, draping my legs over her broad back. Dad brings me a beer, a whiskey for himself, and sits next to me, slinging his arm around my shoulder.

'Are the Yanks on tonight?' I ask.

'No,' he says glumly. 'Travel day.' He looks at me. 'So what brings you here, Porkchop?'

'I was just out for a walk. Thought I'd drop by and see you. How are you, Daddy? Gonna unpack one of these days?'

He sighs. 'Well, I never thought I'd live here this long,' he says, removing his arm. He sits silently for a minute, sipping his whiskey. 'Your mother is seeing someone, you know.'

I nod.

'Is it serious?' he asks. 'She won't talk to me about it.'

'I . . . I don't know, Dad. I really think you should consider retiring, though.'

'Right,' he snorts. 'So I can sit around and scratch my ass? Hang around at the firehouse and wish I was still working?'

Buttercup rises, wagging. Her tail nearly topples my beer bottle, but I catch it and scratch behind her left ear. 'Rooooo,' she moans in doggy delight. Dad gives a reluctant smile, and Buttercup takes this as permission to climb on the couch next to us. She wedges

206

her giant frame on the space that's left, then drapes her front paws and head across my lap.

'You are the ugliest thing I've ever seen,' Dad tells her, stroking one of her thin, floppy ears. Her tail whips in appreciation.

'Getting back to the subject at hand, Dad. There's so much you could do if you retired. Travel, take up golf, spend a day in the city once in a while . . . you know. Be a normal person.'

'I don't want to be normal,' he says, sounding much like one of his toddler grandchildren on a sulk. 'I'm a firefighter.'

I pause. 'What's it like, Dad? Saving someone, I mean.'

He shifts to look at me but doesn't say anything for a minute. 'It's quite a rush,' he admits, reaching over to pet my dog. 'When everything comes together and everyone does their job and you actually make a grab, it's pretty amazing.'

I try to imagine it. To save someone's life, to rescue someone from danger, just to help . . . to be the one who did things right, instead of the one who freaked out and dropped the bag. 'I wish I could do something like that,' I say in a near whisper. 'Save someone.' I look my dad in the eye. 'To be more like you and the boys.'

Dad rolls his eyes. 'Anyway. Back to your mother.'

Of course. 'Back to your retirement, you mean,' I say, taking a swig of beer.

207

Dad scowls, looking a lot like Dylan. 'I don't want to retire just yet. That's all there is to it.'

'You don't want to be divorced, either. You don't want your wife to be with someone else.'

'She won't really go the distance with that guy,' Dad says, oozing alpha-male confidence. 'She's just trying to teach me a lesson. To torture me, Chastity. It's the essence of marriage.' He leans back in his chair and scrubs his face with his hand. 'Speaking of firefighters and their crappy marriages, have you spoken to Mark? He's wound tighter than a piano wire these days.'

'I know. He and Elaina are practicing the essence of marriage, apparently. Lots of good torture back and forth.'

Dad groans, and Buttercup echoes him. 'Well, shit. So what else is new, Porkchop?'

My legs are losing blood flow under Buttercup, so I wrestle myself free, get up and start folding my father's shirts. 'Well, I'm seeing someone. Sort of. We just started dating.'

'So you can be miserable just like the rest of us?'

'Yup. That's always been my goal.'

'He's not a firefighter, is he?' Dad asks, scowling.

'No, Dad,' I say with exaggerated patience. 'No firefighter would dare date your little angel baby, okay? He's a surgeon.'

'Well, good for you, Chastity. A doctor!

Nice.'

I roll my eyes.

'You know what I mean.' Dad stands also, comes over and gives me a hug. 'Hey, look,' he announces, 'a gray! You have a gray hair.' He tugs on a strand, then moves in to separate the gray hair from the normal blacks. 'Quite a few, actually.'

I swat his hand away. 'Gosh, thanks, Pop. They're probably from you and Mom and all your bickering.' He grins. 'I have to go. You have a good night.'

'Keep an eye out on your mother, okay? Let me know about this Harry.'

'No. I'm not playing Spy vs. Spy for you and Mom. Besides, you said it yourself. She's just torturing you. And if you make me pick, I'll pick Mom. Seventeen hours of hard labor, remember?'

'Of course I remember. I was there. Best day of my life.'

'I love you, Dad,' kissing his cheek. 'And no more Jameson's, okay? One's your limit.'

'Yeah, yeah. I love you, too, Porkchop,' he says. 'Don't worry about your mother and me. We'll be fine. We love each other. And I'm not drinking too much, either.'

'Glad to hear it.' I grab my coat and Buttercup's leash, clip it to her collar and begin hauling her off the couch. She doesn't deign to open her eyes, just pretends I'm not there.

'Is that dog still alive?'

'I think so,' I answer. Buttercup finally topples off the couch with a thud and blinks sorrowfully. Since she refuses to stand, I have to slip my arm around her shoulders and try to encourage her into a standing position. With great reluctance, she finally acquiesces.

Dad opens the door for me. 'Be careful. You want me to walk you home? Or ask Trevor. He lives just down the block.'

'I'm fine, Daddy. See you around.'

He waves. 'Keep me up to speed on the doctor. Way to go, honey.' He closes the door, still smiling.

Walking down the stairs, I try not to be irritated with my father. He's old school, after all, and marrying a doctor used to mean a lot back in his day. Back when doctors made more than plumbers and women quit their jobs upon the conception of their first baby. Still, it rankles a little. Twice tonight, I've been congratulated on the accomplishment of dating a doctor. Big deal. Maybe he's the one who should be congratulated on being with me. Didn't anyone ever think about that?

'Settle down,' I tell myself. Buttercup's tail lashes against my thigh. 'Sorry, honey,' I tell her. 'I'm just . . . I don't know.'

I walk down the block, right past Trevor's building, and I'm not even going out of my way. So it's only natural that I look up at his windows, just like I do to everyone else's,

210

right? And sure enough, there's someone standing in front of the window of the fourth floor. Someone blond. Someone like Angela. Or possibly Perfect Hayden. Clearly, Trevor likes blond women.

I look away before I actually start spying, but my heart feels a little heavy just the same.

CHAPTER SIXTEEN

'Get in here!' Penelope barks the next morning with uncharacteristic sharpness.

'What's going on?' I ask, going into her office and dropping my knapsack onto a chair.

She whips her computer monitor toward me. My mouth falls open. 'Oh, shit!' I squeak.

There on the screen, in full color, is one of those moving computer cartoons. Of Aragorn. And Legolas. In a rather compromising position, though Legolas seems to be having a good time.

'What the hell?' I ask. My heart is thumping wildly, my throat dry. 'Someone must have hacked in! I'll . . . I have to . . . I'll get it off.'

'Yes! Do that!' Penelope says.

I fly over to my desk and turn on my computer. While it's booting up, I notice that everyone else is studiously not looking at me. Lucia is answering the phones, which are ringing off the damn hook with angry citizens, no doubt. Carl is talking in a low voice with Danielle in layout. He glances at me in consternation . . . What the hell? Who could have done this? Penelope and I are the only ones with the password that can access the Web site design.

'Nice abs on Aragorn,' Pete murmurs without glancing up.

'Not funny, Pete,' I say. My eyes are burning. God, this is bad, bad, bad.

Alan looks furious. Well, he should! Our Web site has gay porn on it, for heaven's sake! How many people have seen it? How many kids? Oh, shit!

My computer is finally booted. I start up the Web site design program, type in the password—my hands are shaking and I get it wrong twice—and there it is, Aragorn screwing Legolas.

'Bleecch!' I can't help saying. I click on the image and delete it and it's gone, thank God. Then I quickly save the changes and publish the site to the Internet.

'Is it gone?' I ask Pete.

He clicks on his screen. 'Yeah. Too bad. I was getting a little turned on.'

'Not funny. Still.' For the next hour, I check all the pages and links to make sure Aragorn and Legolas aren't getting it on somewhere else. They're not, mercifully. Though I'm adept at setting up a Web site, I know very little about hacking. How someone got in is a mystery. We have firewalls, the password, which is a long series of random numbers and letters . . . I just don't know. Then I call the company that supplies our domain and ask them to change the password, explaining what happened.

'Well, if someone can hack into the Department of Defense, they're gonna be able to get into a little newspaper,' the drone at the other end of the phone says.

'Great. Thanks for your help,' I snap.

Angela cruises in ten minutes later. 'Hi, everyone! I have muffins from a new bakery in Lake George. Help yourselves!' The mood of the office hits her, and she comes over to my desk. 'What's going on?'

'Someone hacked into the Web site and put up porn,' I mutter.

'Oh, no!' she says, her face falling. 'How could that happen?'

'Got me.' I look up at her. *Lord of the Rings* porn. Aragorn and Legolas.'

She goes white. 'Oh, no,' she says again.

'I know,' I whisper.

A few minutes later, Penelope sticks her head out of her office. 'Staff meeting!'

Like penguins, we all toddle into the conference room. The Web site is my responsibility. I'm sweating by the time I sit down. Even Lucia looks nervous.

'As everyone is quite aware, we're in deep shit,' Penelope announces. 'Chastity. Tell us

213

what happened.'

'Um, well, someone obviously hacked into the Web site,' I say, looking around. 'Someone who wants us to look bad.'

'Who would want that?' Lucia asks, nibbling a cuticle.

We all pause. 'I don't know,' I say. 'I'm trying to figure out how they did it, but the truth is, anyone who can hack past the security we have in place is a lot more clever than I am. I've changed the password and ordered another firewall, Pen. If anyone has more suggestions, please speak up.' My cheeks are burning.

'We've had over fifty calls this morning, Chastity,' Pen says, her usually friendly face grim.

'I'll be happy to field them,' I say, swallowing. 'This is my responsibility. I wish I could do more.'

'Maybe you need to check the Web site every night,' Angela suggests.

'Definitely,' I say. 'I know that I'll be checking it not just when I go to bed, but in the middle of the night and first thing in the morning, too.

'Damage control?' Pen asks.

'I'll run a story, of course,' Alan says. 'We can drum up some sympathy, explain about hackers, security, that kind of thing.' He sighs deeply, shaking his head, then looks at me, his angry expression softening. 'Sorry this

214

happened, Chastity.'

'Thanks,' I say.

'Anything else?' Pen asks. No one says a word. 'Chastity, in my office, okay?'

She lets the door close before leaning on her desk. I sit uncomfortably on the edge of the seat. 'This is bad, Chastity. Do you think it's a coincidence, it being *Lord of the Rings* and all? Because it's kind of common knowledge around here that you're a big fan.'

'So is Angela,' I mutter. 'But yes, it seems a little coincidental, doesn't it? Honestly, Pen, is there someone who might do this? Someone who wants the paper to have a black eye? Or just me in particular?'

We look at each other, both of us worried. After a minute, she looks away. 'I know Lucia was really pissed when she didn't get your job,' she begins, 'but I don't think she'd ever do anything to damage the paper's image. She loves the *Gazette.*'

I nod. 'And honestly, if she knows how to hack into a Web site, she's hidden it well. She can't even forward me attachments, even though I've shown her four times.'

'Yeah, she's a bit slow when it comes to computers,' Penelope acknowledges.

'I know, Pen. I can't imagine . . .' My voice trails off.

'What about someone you know, Chastity? Does someone have a vendetta against you or something?'

I shake my head. 'Not that I know of.'

The rest of the day is grim and quiet. We do what damage control we can. The local news station sends a camera crew over, ensuring that every computer geek teenager in town will try his or her hand at hacking in tonight. I spend another hour on the phone with a Web site consultant and download more security. And I constantly check the Web site, all its pages, dreading what I might find. But it's clean.

I've never been in trouble at work before. This feeling of sheepishness, of letting down the team, is new and not at all welcome. I stay late, check the new firewalls and passwords, then head for the river. Though I rowed this morning, I need to burn off the bad karma that's been floating around me all day. Besides, this morning had been Ernesto's lesson, and I didn't get my usual workout.

I keep a change of clothes at Old Man McCluskey's shed. Pulling them on, I lift Rosebud out of her sling and carry her out to the water. A few pulls on the oars and I'm out on the Hudson. Glancing over my shoulder, I see that the river is clear of any traffic, and I dig in. Feather . . . and square. Feather . . . and square. I don't bother warming up today. I need the punishment. The image of Aragorn and Legolas refuses to be deposed, though. Damn it. Was it personal? Who hates me that much? Could it be a brotherly joke? I dismiss

216

the idea as I pull on the oars, leaning back with all my strength. No, the boys wouldn't—and probably couldn't—hack into our system. Lucky might have the technical knowledge, but my brothers would never jeopardize my work. And there's no way this can be seen as anything but sabotage.

Feather . . . and square. Feather . . . and square. Catch and drive . . . catch and drive. I bury the blade of the oar in the water and pull back, but my stroke is off tonight. My movements are jerky, the run of my boat not nearly as long as it usually is. First I'm rushing, then I'm slow, my seat threatens to jump the track. A shitty row, all in all.

Just then, I commit what is referred to as a crab. Because I'm distracted and off tempo, I don't pull my portside blade out of the water in time. It drags, acting as a brake, and my oar jolts back at me. I struggle for a minute, trying to keep the boat from tipping, then wrestle the oar back into position. I pause, catching my breath. Even if this has been a crap outing, I'm panting like a Labrador in August. Glancing at the shore, I can see that I've drifted to about twenty feet from the riverbank, right by the park that runs along the river. Anyone watching me would have seen my graceless gaffe, which doesn't do any more for my self-esteem.

I pause for a few minutes, letting the current pull Rosebud. The park is lovely, one of the town's finest graces. There are benches scattered about, and lots of people are enjoying this beautiful May evening. Couples hold hands, kids run around shrieking. Someone's flying a kite.

I wonder if anyone there saw Legolas and Aragorn this morning.

Someone's waving to me from a bench right alongside the river, a little upstream of where I am. I wave back before I can discern who it is, then pull on my oars and pull a stroke or two, drawing closer. There are two people, actually. Oh, great. Trevor.

He's with Perfect Hayden.

'Hey, guys,' I call gamely.

'Looking good, Chastity,' Trevor calls back.

'Shows what you know, dummy,' I answer.

'Hi, Chastity,' Hayden says mellifluously. 'Beautiful night, isn't it?' And then, yes, she scootches a little closer to Trevor. Not seeing each other, my ass. I'll have to have a little talk with him. Wasn't he out with Angela the other night, after all? And didn't Perfect Hayden walk all over his heart with her tiny high-heeled shoes once already? Here they are, cuddled up on a bench on a gorgeous spring evening, but hey, they're not seeing each other, are they? Of course not.

Without further thought, I turn Rosebud around and row back to the shed. If I'm stomping a little, who can blame me? It's been a piss-poor day. I pat my boat apologetically as

I put her back. 'Sorry, pal,' I say. 'I'll do better next time.'

CHAPTER SEVENTEEN

When I open the door the next night, I find Trevor, Jake and Lucky standing before me.

'Oh, my dear God in heaven!' I cry. 'Thank you!'

'You're welcome, Chas,' Lucky says, shoving his way in. 'Hey, Matt.'

'Hi, Chastity,' Trevor says as he passes me. Without further ado, they fling themselves on various pieces of furniture.

'Wait a minute,' I say. 'You're here to renovate my bathroom. You are. Tell me you are.'

'Oh, shit, that's right. We really need to schedule that in,' Lucky says. 'Matt, you got any beer?'

'Then why are you here?' I ask him. 'Not in an existential sense, because the answer is sheer random perversity, but why are you here in my living room?'

Buttercup launches herself onto Lucky's lap, rendering him momentarily incapable of speech.

'Yanks-Mariners,' Jake answers, giving me a quick, automatic once-over. 'Matt, I'll have a beer, too.'

219

I gaze sternly down upon Jake. 'Since you're already here, boys, how about you take a few tools upstairs and get going? Everything's down cellar. Take the radio upstairs, listen to the game, do a little installation, hook up some plumbing . . . please? Pretty please?'

'We really don't have what we need, Chas. Sorry,' Lucky says, cracking a beer.

'And yet you cashed my check three months ago,' I comment.

'So I did,' he admits. 'And it will be done. Eventually. Can you move? The game is starting.'

'Please, Lucky. You're still my favorite brother. Don't make me keep sharing a bathroom with Matt. He eats a lot of Mexican food.'

'Ouch,' Jake winces.

'Want a beer, Chas?' Matt offers, ignoring my pleas.

I sigh. 'I'm going out,' I say. 'I have a date.' No one seems to care.

On the TV, Michael Kay's familiar voice begins lauding the superiority of the Bronx Bombers. 'A date?' Lucky asks distantly.

'Yes. A date with Ryan. The surgeon.'

'Great,' Lucky says. 'Maybe he can fix the bathroom.'

'Is he picking you up?' Trevor asks.

'No,' I answer a little smugly. 'He had an emergency consultation at the hospital.'

Lucky moves Buttercup and frowns at her.

220

'Shit, Chas, your dog's bleeding on me.'

'What?'

Lucky lowers Buttercup down to the floor, where she immediately offers her stomach for a scratch, her ears spilling out behind her head like wings. Trevor pushes the coffee table back, and the men crowd around her, checking for wounds, running their hands down her legs and gently ruffling her fur.

'It's okay, honey,' I tell my dog, stroking her ears. 'These guys are professionals.'

'Roooroooo,' she croons, her tail whipping Jake in the face.

'Watch the tail,' Matt says. 'It's a lethal weapon.'

'Yeah, thanks,' Jake mutters, rubbing the welt.

'I think I found it,' Trevor says, grinning up at me. 'Looks like your little girl's becoming a woman, Chastity.'

'What are you talking about?' I ask, still petting Buttercup's head.

'She's in heat.'

'Yuck,' Jake offers, rising quickly and resuming his position on the couch.

'But she's spayed!' I protest. 'They said she was spayed!'

'That explains why she's had a little life in her lately,' Matt observes. 'Love is in the air and all that crap. No more dead water buffalo, right, Buttercup?'

The guys take their seats again, but I stay

221

on the floor with my dog. Poor thing. Do dogs get cramps? Should I stay home and offer a hot water bottle, the way my mom used to do for me?

Damn that pound. I'll have to call them in the morning and ask them to check her file. 'What should I do about the bleeding?' I ask. 'Any ideas?'

'I'll take care of it,' Matt says, gazing at our dog. 'You go, Chas. Have fun. Buttercup will be fine.'

Buttercup does seem fine . . . she rouses herself to bury her sizeable snout in Jake's crotch. 'Come on, dog!' he yelps.

'She's looking for a mate, Jake. Just relax and let her finish,' I say, grinning.

'Makes you feel so dirty, doesn't it?' Trevor says, his eyes laughing.

'She's bleeding on me! Come on, guys, this is gross!' As Buttercup attempts to mount Jake's leg, I decide yes, Matt can handle this. Checking my own jeans for blood and finding them clean (thank heavens), I stand up. 'Okay. Thanks. Just make sure she stays inside. The last thing we want is for her to be knocked up.'

*   *   *

'So, Ryan, are you a Yankees fan?' I ask an hour later. My gaze keeps flickering to the TV in the bar half of Emo's, but alas, I can't see the score. Damn.

'No,' he says, smiling pleasantly. 'I don't really watch sports.' *Problem*. 'But my father has season tickets at Yankee Stadium.' *Problem solved!* 'Maybe we can go sometime, since you're obviously a fan.'

'I'd love to,' I murmur demurely, already mentally reviewing the home-game schedule.

We're sitting at a prime table overlooking the street. Emo's is packed, the food is lovely, and Ryan kissed me when I met him here and apologized for not being able to pick me up. He's very polite.

'I really enjoyed the article,' Ryan says.

'Great! I'm glad you liked it,' I reply. The truth is, I'd kind of forgotten about that article, being preoccupied with the hacking incident. So far, nothing else has happened. But Ryan's article was pleasant if I do say so . . . no mention of any groin injuries and a nice picture of Ryan in his (yum) karate uniform. 'It's gotten good reviews.'

'And it's part of a series, correct?' he asks, taking a sip of his wine.

'That's right. We're doing firefighters next.'

'A predictable choice,' he murmurs.

My head jerks back a fraction. 'Well, yes, I suppose you're right, in the sense that everyone identifies firefighters as heroic.' I pause. Ryan doesn't say anything, just smiles a little, encouraging me to continue. 'After that, I'm doing a story on a pediatrician who goes to South America to treat kids down there. She goes every year. Maybe you know her, Dr. Whitman? Jeannie Whitman?'

'I don't really deal with pediatricians unless I'm getting them up to speed on a trauma patient who happens to be a minor. Usually, though, we fly those patients to Children's in Albany.'

'I see. Hey, you must run into my brother Jack from time to time. He's a chopper paramedic. Jack O'Neill, tall, black hair, looks a lot like me . . . '

Ryan shakes his head. 'Can't say that it rings a bell.'

'Oh,' I say. Our dinners arrive, and we eat and smile at each other. I try to think of something witty to say. I come up empty. Probably, I'm just too used to being one of the guys. And of course, I've been avoiding the subject of his career, but I can't dodge it forever. Finishing my wine, I decide to go for it.

'So, Ryan, tell me about your work. Did you always want to be a surgeon?'

'Trauma surgeon,' he corrects, leaning forward. 'Yes, I did, Chastity. My father is also a surgeon, as I believe I told you, so I was lucky to have someone show me the ropes.'

'Is it hard—emotionally, I mean? Obviously, your patients are in pretty bad shape.'

'Emotionally, no, it's not hard,' he replies, taking another bite of his salmon. 'Obviously, there's a high level of skill involved.' He smiles

224

modestly. 'The more common cases are splenectomies, damaged bowel from a GSW . . . gunshot wound, that is . . . oh, bleeding control, muscle repair. And of course—' he leans forward with relish, grinning '—the more severe the traumatic event, the more fascinating the case.'

I swallow.

'I suppose it's the orthopedic trauma that everyone thinks is more glamorous,' Ryan continues, unaware of my rapidly dropping blood pressure. His voice takes on a slightly bitter note. 'Obviously, I have to repair a hemorrhaging organ before the bone doctors can assess reattachment possibilities, right? Who cares if the femur is shattered if the patient's spleen is gushing and we're running out of blood?'

'God!' I blurt. 'Okay, wow! That is impressive!' Wiping my clammy palms on my jeans, I push my plate back. 'Listen, Ryan, I have to tell you, I'm a little squeamish about this kind of thing.'

He smiles kindly. 'Most people are,' he says almost proudly. 'Want to talk about something else?'

'Yes, please,' I breathe. He reaches across the table and takes my hand, which is clutching a roll.

'I like you, Chastity,' he says, grinning.

Nice to know my phobia is charming. Swallowing bile, I grin back. 'Ditto.' He really is . . . well, he's gorgeous, this guy. Nice, too. 'So where did you grow up, Ryan?' I ask, extricating my hand and taking a bite of my roll.

'Long Island,' he says. 'We started out in Huntington, but my parents now have a cottage in the Hamptons. East Hampton, to be precise. Quite pretty. You'll love it.'

I probably will, but his statement gives me pause. You'll love it when you come down to meet the family, and you will, won't you, since I'm so fabulous. *Stop it, Chastity. He's perfectly nice. Get your panties out of the twist.* He's still talking, and I smile and nod and take a sip of water.

And then I hear something . . . something familiar, though too far away to identify. A quiver of foreboding buzzes through my legs. That sound in the distance affects me . . . or is about to.

'Do you hear that?' I ask Ryan, tipping my head toward the window.

'No,' he answers. 'It's pretty loud in here.'

I can't quite make out the dark shape rounding the corner, but my sense of foreboding grows.

'What is it?' Ryan asks.

'I don't . . . I'm not . . . oh, shit! Buttercup!'

'Aaaahhrooooroooroooo!'

And yes, my dog is galloping—galloping!— her huge ears flapping, jowls rising and falling with each stride, enormous paws flopping

226

gracelessly on the pavement as she runs—runs!—right down the middle of the street. This from a dog who has to be dragged to go outside!

And on her hindquarters, in order to prevent little drops of blood from spattering my house, is a pair of Matt's bright white Calvin Klein boxer briefs. Her tail, which is guided through the front slot of the briefs, whips back and forth. I sit frozen in horror as she careens onto the sidewalk right in front of Emo's.

'Why is that doggie wearing underwear?' asks a little girl.

'Oh, my God!' I stand abruptly, bumping the table. Ryan's water sloshes. 'How did she get out? She's never gotten out before! I told the boys—'

My precious puppy, all one hundred and twenty pounds of randy, menstruating she-dog, leaps up against the window, front paws leaving great muddy smears against the glass, baying with joy at having sniffed out her mistress. 'Aahroorooroorooroo!' she sings, head thrown back in ecstasy.

'Dear God,' Ryan says.

I stare open-mouthed. 'Um . . . I think I'd better . . . that's . . . that's my dog.'

'Dear God,' Ryan says again.

I'm already weaving my way through the restaurant toward the bar. People are either laughing or frowning as Buttercup continues to serenade me. The maître d' and two servers are pointing and talking.

'I'll take care of this!' I tell them. 'She's mine. She must have tracked me here. She's part bloodhound. She's in heat.'

'Thanks for sharing,' the maître d' says.

As I burst out of the restaurant, Buttercup decides she's not ready for capture. She leaves the window, tail whipping, and trots away from me, boxers gleaming, and stops to sniff a tire.

'Buttercup . . . here girl!' I call, trying to sound relaxed and happy to see her.

Just then, a pickup truck comes around the corner. Matt's behind the wheel, while Trevor leans out the window, calling my dog's name. Both of them are contorted with laughter. Buttercup trots a few feet farther away. 'Buttercup!' I croon. 'Come on! Cookie! Salami! Want some salami? Huh, girl? Come on, Butterbaby!'

Ryan comes out of the restaurant. 'What is she wearing?' he asks.

'My brother's underwear. Um, let's just try to catch her,' I say.

Matt pulls up to the curb and gets out, wiping his eyes. 'Sorry, Chas. She escaped.'

'Yes, I got that.'

Trevor gets out, too, staggering, wheezing. 'She found you,' he manages. 'She loves her mommy.'

'Oh, shut up,' I say, though I can't help grinning. 'Don't chase her. Just pretend you

228

have a cookie or something.' Buttercup stops twenty feet ahead and stares at us suspiciously from her yellow eyes. Her tail wags tentatively, but her shoulders are tensed for flight, possibly for the first time in her young life. 'Very slow, boys, very casual.'

'Roger that,' Matt says. 'Come to Daddy, sweetheart.' We start creeping down the sidewalk. Quite a crowd has gathered at the window of the restaurant as people watch to see the capture.

'Butterbaby! Come on, honey!' I call. She sniffs the sidewalk and flops down, apparently done for the night. 'I'm so sorry about this,' I say, glancing at Ryan. He's staring in consternation at my dog.

'Not at all,' he murmurs insincerely.

'Who's my pretty puppy?' Matt says, pretending to hold out a treat. 'Do you want a cookie?' She lets him approach. Trev, Ryan and I hold back. Just as Matt reaches out to grab Buttercup's collar, she twists away, lurches to her feet and makes a dash for freedom. 'Aaaahhrooooroooorooo!' She heads toward the three of us, then dodges out into the street.

'Grab her, Chas!' Matt yells, but my dog darts past me with surprising agility, past Ryan, past Trevor, who just misses her, and continues down the street. From behind her, I can see the red splotch of blood on Matt's underwear.

229

'Holy crap!' I blurt, bursting into laughter. 'Come on!' I start running. Buttercup is a half block ahead, and I'm laughing so hard it hurts. 'Buttercup!' I call in between gasps. 'Come to Mommy!'

Matt crosses the street to try to flush our dog toward me, but she's too far ahead. Behind me, Trevor is staggering unhelpfully, laughing so hard he can barely remain upright. A passing car slows down, and Buttercup shifts to Matt's side of the street, stopping to sniff a parking meter. Her big ears prick with sudden alertness, and I glance up ahead. 'Shit! Catch her, Matt!' I yell.

Up ahead is a tiny Yorkshire terrier on a leash, being walked by a rather plump man.

'No, Buttercup!' Trevor calls. 'You'll kill him, girl!'

My laughter goes silent, tears streaming down my face. 'Buttercup! Salami!' I manage, clapping my hands, trying to get my dog's attention. It doesn't work.

The Yorkie owner is peering into the window of an antiques shop and doesn't seem to sense the imminent danger posed to his tiny dog.

'Mister! Hey, buddy!' Matt calls. 'She's in heat! Pick up your dog! Pick him up!'

Puzzled, the man obeys, just in time, then recoils when he sees Buttercup charging.

'Buttercup, no!' I shout.

'Aahroorooroororooo!' she bays, ignoring

me. Intent on her would-be mate, she leaps against his owner.

'Aah!' he cries. 'No, doggy! Bad doggy! Get down! No! Down!'

Trevor glances down the street and runs across, hauling Buttercup off the man and his hapless dog. Buttercup goes limp, glancing back balefully as Trevor drags her away from her true love.

'That dog should be leashed!' the Yorkie owner spits.

'You're absolutely right. We'll tell the owner as soon as we find him,' Trevor says, throwing me a grin. 'Are you all right, sir?' He sticks out his hand. 'Trevor Meade, Eaton Falls Fire.'

'I'm fine,' the man replies. 'Thank you for stopping that hideous animal. Puffy, are you okay?' He drops a kiss on the Yorkie's head and glares at me.

'Ma'am, you say you know this dog's owner?' Trevor asks me with a conspiratorial wink.

I pause. 'Um, yes. Yes, I do. My neighbor's dog. Very naughty beast. Bad, Buttercup.'

'You tell those people there are leash laws in Eaton Falls,' Yorkie Man says.

'I certainly will,' I say. 'You're a disgrace, Buttercup. Your owners will be so ashamed.'

'Thanks for your help, ma'am,' Trevor says to me. I feel his smile right into my bone marrow.

'Come on, Puffy,' the man says, turning

231

around and heading back from whence he came. 'Poor Puffy. You were scared, weren't you?'

'Scared isn't the word I'd use,' Matt comments, joining Trev and me. He eyes the tiny dog, who twists and whines in his master's arms, struggling to return to Buttercup. 'Puffy had it covered.'

'Imagine their children.' Trevor laughs, kneeling to stroke my dog.

Ryan comes over to me and, to my surprise, puts his arm around my shoulders. In all the excitement, I had almost forgotten about him.

'Ryan! Hey, have you met my brother? This is Matt.' They shake hands.

'Sorry about this, Chas,' Matt says. 'Lucky went out to call Tara, and your horny little dog dashed out.'

'Oh, that's okay,' I say. 'Makes for a memorable night, wouldn't you say, Ryan?'

'Absolutely,' Ryan answers, and suddenly, I feel a rush of affection for him. After all, he was a great sport, wasn't he? I take his hand in mine, and he smiles.

'You can get her back, right, boys?' I ask.

'Sure, Chas,' Trevor answers. 'You kids have a nice night.'

*   *   *

After a much-needed second glass of wine back at Emo's, Ryan asks me if I'd like to

232

come back to his place. The surreal feeling of being with him returns as he opens the door to his condo. It's a sleek, stylish place in a renovated mill building. The windows face upriver, away from the energy plant. Dark-stained wood floors gleam, the oriental carpet glows with jewel tones. A fireplace takes up an entire wall, and it's all very modern and clean, just what you'd imagine for a surgeon.

'What a lovely place,' I say.

'Thank you,' Ryan says. 'Can I take your jacket?' He does, then goes in the kitchen and opens a cabinet. 'What kind of wine would you like, Chastity? I've got a very nice pinot, a gorgeous New Zealand chardonnay, some cabernet . . . '

'Oh, um, you pick,' I say. My heart is beating a little fast, and I swallow. The truth is, I'm nervous. I haven't dated much, haven't had a steady boyfriend in a while. Haven't been back to a man's place in an age. I wonder if all my parts still work.

There are some black-and-white photos on the wall, mostly of buildings, though one of a snowy field. 'Did you take these pictures?' I ask.

'Oh, no. My decorator bought them. Glad you like them, though,' he says, handing me a glass of white. 'Would you like to sit down?'

We sit on the sumptuous leather couch. Ryan picks up a remote control, pushes a button, and voilà! We have a fire. 'Very nice,' I say, taking a sip of the wine.

He pushes a lock of my hair behind my ear and smiles. I smile back. My knees tingle. He moves a little closer. More tingling. His arm slides along the back of the couch, his hand moves to the back of my head. Then he leans in and kisses my neck, sending little shivers down my side.

'So, Ryan, okay,' I blurt. 'I have to ask this . . . sorry.' I shift a little so I can better see his face. 'Ryan, you're a gorgeous man, you're a doctor—'

'Surgeon,' he corrects with a smile.

'Right! A surgeon, a trauma surgeon . . . um, why aren't you married?'

He sits back and frowns. 'It's a valid question,' he says. 'Honestly, Chastity, I always felt that work came first. It's not easy to become a surgeon—'

'Oh, I know,' I smile. 'I watch *Grey's Anatomy* every week.' He doesn't deign to respond. 'Sorry. Go on,' I mumble, looking at my high-tops.

He glances at his wine glass, held loosely in his beautiful hands. 'I always felt that a serious relationship wouldn't be advisable while I was so immersed in my residency, or in establishing my career.' He shifts his gaze to me. 'Now that's done.' He raises an eyebrow. 'And I've met you.'

I blush, pleased. 'I guess I'm surprised you didn't meet anyone else at the hospital, from

234

your residency, maybe?' I suggest. 'Like McDreamy and Meredith?'

'I don't know what you're talking about,' he says, but his tone is fond. 'But I wouldn't want to marry another doctor. One in the family is enough.'

'Oh,' I say. 'And why is that?'

'It's a demanding career,' he says simply. 'When it comes to having children, I think it's best to have at least one parent who can devote a lot of time to them.' He pauses, his eyes dropping to my mouth. His voice lowers. 'Any more questions?'

'Um . . . no,' I whisper. The tingling returns.

'Can I kiss you now?'

'Sure,' I whisper, and he does. He kisses me, a very nice, skilled, gentle kiss. I pull back, set my wine glass on the coffee table, and take another look at him. 'Any pets?' I ask.

'No.' He laughs.

'Okay,' I answer, then grab his shirt and pull him against me and kiss him a little less perfectly than he just kissed me.

'Just so you know,' he murmurs against my mouth, 'I'm looking for a serious relationship. Committed and monogamous.'

'Got it,' I say, smiling. Can't say that I've ever known a man to say such things. 'Me, too, Ryan.' And then he kisses me again, and we stop talking for a good long while.

*　　　*　　　*

235

My girl parts still work, I'm happy to report.

We're cuddling. Idly stroking Ryan's satiny shoulder, I remind myself to moisturize more regularly. This guy is much prettier than I am. I stifle a giggle.

'That was great,' he murmurs, kissing my head.

'Yeah,' I agree. 'Very nice.'

But now that the deed is done, well, I'm feeling a little squirrelly. 'Hey, Ryan, would you mind driving me home?'

'Right now?' he asks. His fingers stop playing with my hair.

'Well, no, not exactly now. But I have an early meeting.' It's true.

'Sure,' he says, pulling back to look at me. 'But you're more than welcome to spend the night, Chastity.'

'Thanks,' I say. 'Next time, but, um, I probably should . . . you know.'

Five minutes later, Ryan kisses me again, very sweetly, then rolls out of bed and pulls on his clothes. I smile, grateful for the years of karate and athleticism that have sculpted his body to Matthew McConnaughey perfection.

That perfection aside, I know I wouldn't sleep a wink, and the little voice in my head is waiting to have a talk with me.

The stars burn bright in the sky, and the streets are empty. The hum of Ryan's Mercedes is barely audible, and he holds my

236

hand the whole way back.

'You'd better stay in the car,' I say, looking at my house. 'My brother's home tonight, and if Buttercup hears a stranger, she'll go nuts and wake him up.' Of course, this is not true. If she even woke, I'd be surprised. I'm not sure why I just lied.

'Okay,' he says, looking at me. He leans over and kisses me briefly. 'I'm glad we're together, Chastity.'

My heart squeezes at his earnestness. 'Thanks. Me, too, Ryan.'

'I'll call you tomorrow.'

'Sure. Thanks.' I open the car door and run up the path. He waits at the curb until I go inside, then pulls noiselessly away.

The only light is from the nightlight in the hall, which Matt and I leave on in case he gets called to the firehouse in the middle of the night . . . or if I need a midnight snack. Buttercup groans from her corner, her tail whacking the floor. 'Hi, honey,' I whisper. She doesn't even open her eyes, too exhausted from her flight through Eaton Falls to come over, just thumps her tail a few more times and goes back to sleep.

Going into the kitchen, I open the fridge, blinking at the sudden burst of light, and stare at the contents inside. Not a whole lot to warm a girl's heart or fill her tummy. I take out the milk and grab the Choco-Puffs from the cabinet. Getting a bowl, I turn around and

237

nearly die of fright. Trevor is standing there like a ghost.

'Trevor! Jeez!' I hiss, bobbling the carton of milk.

'Sorry, Chas,' he whispers. 'Here, let me.' He takes the milk from my hands and sets it on the table. 'Sorry. Didn't mean to scare you.'

'Well, creeping up on someone at three in the morning tends to do just that,' I say. 'Just for future reference.' My heart is thudding so hard I can practically see it coming out of my chest.

Trevor smiles and takes a seat at the table, taking care to be quiet. 'I'm crashing here tonight,' he tells me.

'So I see.' He's wearing jeans and a T-shirt, and his feet are bare. I'm sure he wasn't sleeping in jeans—I end the thought right there. 'Want some cereal?'

'No, thanks,' he says with a grin. 'How was your date? After the wee beastie chased you down, that is.'

I take a deep breath. My purpose in having a little late-night snack was to analyze said date. 'It was great,' I say. 'We had a great time. Ryan's a great guy.'

'Great.'

I look at him sharply. 'We did. He is.'

'I'm not saying you didn't, Chas, or that he's not.' He folds his arms across his chest and continues looking at me, muscles bulging, hair rumpled, utterly luscious. I take a hearty bite

238

of Choco-Puffs and chew. *Go away, Trevor,* I say silently. Because sitting in the near dark at three in the morning is far too intimate. 'How's Angela, speaking of dating?'

'She's fine,' he says. 'Nice girl.'

'So are you guys serious?' I blurt, shoveling in another mouthful of cereal.

'We've been on two dates, Chastity.'

'So? Ryan and I have also been on two dates.'

'And are you guys serious?' he asks.

'Yes, as a matter of fact, we are. We are in a committed, monogamous relationship.' My spoon clatters with unnecessary roughness against the bowl.

'Two dates is a little quick for a serious, committed, monogamous relationship, wouldn't you say?'

'Well, we've just begun the committed, serious, monogamous relationship, Trevor. Gotta start somewhere.' My voice is not quite as casual as I'd like.

'Sure,' Trevor agrees. 'And I'm sure he has a lot of nice qualities.'

Why does he defend Ryan? my little voice squawks. *Why doesn't he say, How about a committed, serious, monogamous relationship with me, Chas?*

Because he doesn't want that, Elaina's voice answers firmly. *He's had his chance, okay? He's had plenty.*

'So?' Trevor asks. 'What do you like about

this guy, Chas?'

'What are you, my big sister now?' I ask, and he grins, and my insides lurch.

'Close enough. Answer the question.'

I get up from the table, put my bowl in the sink and stare out the window at the dark backyard. 'He's really smart, obviously.' *Well-educated.* 'And he's got a nice sense of humor . . . you know, kind of quiet.' *Excellent manners.* 'He's hardworking. Treats me really well.' *Good driver.* 'Didn't mind chasing Buttercup.'

'Sounds like there's some potential here, Chas.'

My throat tightens. 'Oh, yeah. Definitely potential. Listen, buddy, I'm going to bed. Do you need anything? Pillow, blanket, anything?'

'I'm all set, thanks. Night, Chastity.'

'Goodnight, Trev.'

Upstairs in my room, Buttercup has taken her usual position, occupying three-quarters of my queen-size bed. I undress, then realize with an impatient sigh that I forgot to brush my bleeping teeth. And since I don't even have a sink in my stupid bathroom, I'd have to go back downstairs and risk seeing Trevor once more.

Well. I get into my tiny sliver of a bed, shove Buttercup over with my feet and sigh.

Surely I've wasted enough time thinking about Trevor over the past couple of decades. Instead of thinking about Trev, I order myself to think of attainable, relationship-minded

240

Ryan Darling.

I think I could probably love Ryan. Like I said to Trevor, he seems like a very nice, serious, hardworking guy. He's not really funny in the way that I'm used to, the lizards in the bed kind of funny, but he's not un-funny, either. And there's some chemistry between us, sure. If my toes didn't exactly curl, well, they twitched, and this was just our first time. He is certainly good-looking. We'd make beautiful, strong, tall children, hopefully. Smart, too. Ivy League Teamsters.

So yes, we'd done it. Moved the relationship forward, and if it was a little fast, as Trevor so irritatingly pointed out, so what? Ryan and I are consenting adults in our thirties. No big deal. I wince as the words echo in my head. *No big deal.*

It's not that sex with Ryan wasn't nice. It was. Very nice. We took our time, he was considerate, assured me of his good health, took care of the needed protection and all that. It was very nice. If I had to grade it, I'd give it a B+. Good, solid, well-supported sex. Like a hearty meat loaf dinner. And if *nice* isn't exactly what a woman dreams of, if instead of meat loaf, she's wishing for filet mignon, if she's wanting earth-shaking instead of solid, a little more wild, a little less smooth, well, she should probably get over it.

CHAPTER EIGHTEEN

'Happy Mother's Day, Mom,' I say, handing over the tulips, truffles and card.

'Oh, honey! How sweet you are!' Mom cries, tearing open the truffles. 'Oooh, very nice, darling! Want one?'

'No, no, they're all for you,' I say.

Mom reads the card, tears up, hugs me. 'I love you, too, sweetheart,' she says. 'Don't tell the boys, but you're my favorite.'

'Don't tell the boys, my ass,' Jack says. 'She tells us every chance she gets.'

I kiss my oldest brother's cheek. 'You poor neglected baby,' I say. 'Doesn't your mommy wuv you anymore?'

'I'll always be her firstborn,' he says, swatting me. 'You were just an accident.'

'What?' I gasp, feigning shock. 'You didn't want two babies in eleven months, Mom?'

'Oh, you two,' she says fondly. 'All children are a blessing, yadda yadda yadda.'

Jack and I laugh. 'Who sent you those, Mom?' I ask, pointing to a huge arrangement of roses and lilies on the dining room table.

'Oh, those are from Harry,' she coos. Jack shoots me a look. 'Jack, I think Graham is stuck in that tree,' Mom adds, and the two of them go outside to rescue various and sundry children and intervene in a spat over who has to retrieve the soccer ball from the mud.

I go into the dining room and check out the bouquet. Very expensive. All the thorns have been taken off the roses, and the lilies are as pink and sexual as Georgia O'Keefe believed. I glance at the card: *To an amazing woman who deserves to be celebrated on this special day. XOX Harry*

'Bleechh,' I say, wondering what Dad would think. I make a face, then go into the living room where my sisters-in-law sit like empresses. Lucky is serving them Bloody Marys, as he should.

'Hi, Tara,' I say, handing my sister-in-law a card. 'You're a fabulous mother.'

'Oh, Chastity! This is so sweet of you!' Tara opens her card as I hand Sarah hers.

'Happy Mother's Day, Sarah. You're a wonderful mom,' I tell her with dutiful honesty.

'Thanks, Chas!' Sarah cries. I move on.

'I hope you brought me more than a card,' Elaina says, accepting her envelope.

'Vodka. In the car. Didn't want to make the others jealous,' I stage-whisper. 'And you're a wonderful mom, too, blah blah bleeping blah.'

Elaina smacks me affectionately. 'Don't worry, *chiquita*,' she says as I flop on the couch next to her. 'You'll have your turn, okay? And then you'll long for these days when you have no little asses to wipe, no spit-up permanently glued to your neck. Am I right, girls?'

243

The Starahs nod wisely.

'I made Tara breakfast in bed today,' Lucky says. 'She has the whole day off. No housework, no kid care.'

'So what are you doing here? Time's a' wastin',' I comment.

Tara laughs and leans her head against Lucky's shoulder. 'Where else would I want to be?' she asks.

'Oh, gack,' I answer, pretending to vomit. 'What about you, Sarah? Did Jack honor you in some way, preferably by spending lots of money?'

'Yes, he did,' she answers. 'Like the well-trained husband he is. See my new earrings?' She pushes her hair behind her ears.

'Beautiful,' I say. I turn to Elaina. 'And Mark? Anything from him?'

'Well, actually, you know, the bastard did come through,' Elaina admits, toying with her hair. 'Dylan had a card and some nice bath stuff for me this morning, and he said Daddy told him to give it to me.' Her dark eyes soften. 'So that was nice, you know?'

I really am surrounded by women who are wonderful, caring, selfless mothers. Smart, wise, funny, loving, patient. And my uterus is begging for the chance to join the crowd.

As if reading my mind, Elaina turns to me. 'I'm thinking a girl, first, you know? With blond hair like her daddy, okay? And then a boy. Dr. Darling Junior.'

244

'Why can't the girl be Dr. Darling Junior?' I ask, trying to picture Ryan next to me in the delivery room.

'Oh, that's right!' Sarah squeals. 'We heard you had a new boyfriend! Tell all, Chastity!'

At that moment, Trevor sticks his head in the living room. 'Hi, girls,' he grins. 'Happy Mother's Day, you gorgeous creatures.' And then he looks at me. 'Hey, Chas.'

'Bite me, Trev,' I answer agreeably. 'I note that I'm not lumped in with the gorgeous creatures.'

'You know I think you're beautiful. Striking.' He winks and my insides give an unwilling twist. Then he comes in, several bouquets in his arms, and goes first to Sarah. 'Thank you for sharing your kids with me,' he says, kissing her on the cheek. He repeats the gesture and the words with Tara, then Elaina. Each of my sisters-in-law hugs him, exclaims over his thoughtfulness, wipes away a tear.

'Kiss-ass,' I murmur as he approaches me. I'm hoping he won't notice that my eyes are wet, too.

'I was thinking more along the lines of "prince among men,"' he answers. He holds out the last bouquet to me. 'For you, Chas. Just so you don't have a tantrum.'

My heart aches with, um, let's see . . . affection. Yes. 'Consolation prize, huh?'

'Not exactly,' he murmurs.

The image of him and Perfect Hayden leaps

unbidden to my mind, and just in the nick of time. I wonder if he did something sweet for Hayden. Or Angela. Or any of the other women he may or may not be seeing.

'Trev, thank you, sweetie,' Elaina says. 'Your ass looks great in those jeans, by the way. Carhartt, mm-mm!' The Starahs murmur in agreement. Lucky rolls his eyes. 'But we were talking about Chastity's love life,' Elaina continues, giving me a sharp glance. 'So, Chas? Have you done it yet?'

'We've been on just two dates,' I say demurely.

'Answer the question,' Tara instructs.

'I'll just bow out here,' Trevor murmurs.

'You do that,' Elaina says, making a shooing gesture with her hand. 'We want to talk sex, okay? You too, Lucky. Out.'

I shoot her a look that could cut metal, but she's undeterred. Trevor and Lucky obey, as do most men when Elaina gives an order.

'Yes to the sex,' I answer. My sisters-in-law shriek and I grin, pleased to be the center of all this feminine attention for once.

*   *   *

Later that day, in order to counter the effects of too many cheese danishes at Mom's, I pull on my running shoes and clip the leash to Buttercup's collar. 'We're going for a run, you harlot,' I tell her.

246

'Aaaahhroooorooorooo!' she answers.

'No sex with anything under fifty pounds, you hear?' She wags agreeably. 'Let's go, then.'

Then I see the light blinking on the answering machine. 'Hello, Chastity, it's Ryan Darling,' comes Ryan Darling's voice. 'Just wanted to let you know that I'll be on Long Island to visit my mother today, but I hope to get together soon. I had a really nice time the other night. Tell Buttercup I said hello. Speak to you soon.'

Well! That's pretty damn sweet, isn't it? I smile. There was also an attempt at humor at the end. *Good job, Ryan.* Granted, he didn't need to use his last name—we were having sex two nights ago, so yes, I do remember him. I wince a little. Very enjoyable sex. Pleasant. Reliably satisfying. Meat loaf.

'I'll shut up now,' I tell my dog, who is snuffling at the door. 'Let's go for that run.'

Buttercup lopes at my side, surprising me with her energy level. Next week, we have an appointment to get her spayed, so she may well return to her prepubescent level of malaise. But for now, her ears flop and her jowls undulate. We head for the cemetery. My ulterior motive is firmly in place, and my timing is perfect.

Trevor's pickup truck is there. He's kneeling in the dirt next to his sister's grave and looks up in surprise when he hears Buttercup's tags jingling.

247

'Hi,' he says, rising. His jeans are muddy at the knees. 'What are you doing here?'

My dog and I slow to a walk, then stop. 'Well, now that I know Buttercup is capable of forward movement, I thought I'd take her with me when I run. She could use some exercise. I saw your truck and here we are.'

If he doesn't buy my story, he also doesn't let on. Blushing, I unclip Buttercup and let her go snuffling amid the gravestones, her tail slicing audibly through the air, nose glued to the ground like her bloodhound ancestors. She woofs softly and continues, happy as the proverbial clam. Trevor watches her go.

I glance down at his sister's grave, the girl who was briefly my friend. As is typical on the graves of children, there is an ocean of pain expressed. *Michelle Anne Meade, our beautiful girl, forever in our broken hearts. We miss you, little angel.* My eyes fill. Had she had the chance to grow up, we might still have been friends. She might have made Trevor an official uncle, instead of having that title be honorary. Her parents might not have divorced, and Trevor might not have been so alone.

I knew he'd be here. Michelle died on Mother's Day. I can't imagine the pain her mother must have felt, must still feel. What an awful holiday for someone who's lost a child!

'Want some help?' I ask huskily. There are still six or eight plants left in the tray.

248

'Sure,' he answers. 'You can loosen the roots, okay?'

'Loosening the roots, roger that,' I answer, kneeling next to him. 'And thanks for the flowers, Trevor. You didn't have to.'

'My pleasure,' he says, digging into the dirt with his trowel.

We work in silence—well, he works, I hand—until the plants are in the ground. In another month, they'll be beautiful, but right now, they look a little forlorn, small and far-spaced in the brown soil.

'How's your mom?' I ask.

He sighs and sits back on his heels, wiping his dirty hands on his jeans. 'She's okay,' he answers.

'Do you talk to her much?'

'About once a month,' he answers.

It's hard to imagine—Trevor, the perfect son to both my mother and father, phoning his own mom only once a month. He sees Dad probably five days a week, drops in on Mom frequently, helped Jack put on a new roof on her house last month, went camping with Lucky and Matt last fall . . . but his own family is like bits of milkweed, blown to the wind.

'Where's your father these days?' I ask.

'Last I heard from him, he was in Sacramento,' Trevor answers. 'You got any more questions?'

I shake my head. 'Sorry, buddy. I didn't mean to pry.'

'You can ask whatever you want, Chastity,' he says. He sticks out his hand to help me rise, and I take it, the dirt on both our hands mingling for a brief, warm moment.

'Do you still miss her?' I whisper. Those pesky tears are back. For such a tough guy, you'd think I'd cry less.

'Yes,' he answers, brushing some stray bits of dirt from her gravestone. 'Every day.' He pauses, then looks off across the other headstones. Somewhere, wind chimes clink and clang. 'Every day, I imagine if she was here, grown up, maybe married. How we'd have dinner at each other's houses. Stuff like that.' His eyes are sad and soft.

I swallow the fist-size lump in my throat. 'She'd have been crazy about you, Trev.'

Trevor smiles. 'Thanks.'

'And you're like our real brother, you know,' I say. I regret the words immediately.

The smile falters. 'Thanks again.' He puts the tray in his truck. 'You want a ride home?'

'Sure. That'd be great.' I whistle for Buttercup, who comes bounding back, her ears flopping joyfully.

'Do you want to ride in Trevor's truck?' I ask her. She barks once.

'Genius,' Trevor says, hoisting her into the back of the truck. Buttercup collapses like her legs were shot out from underneath her. His laugh is soft, practically edible, like a river of chocolate.

I climb into the passenger's seat, noting that my legs are now streaked with dirt. Also, I really should shave more often. And my T-shirt is damp with sweat, gluing Aragorn's face to my left breast, God bless him. The words None But The King Of Gondor May Command Me are faded with age.

'Did I tell you someone hacked into the *Gazette*'s Web site?' I ask as Trevor gets in behind the wheel.

'No,' he answers, turning the key. 'What happened?'

I fill him in and tell him about the feeling that this was something done to me personally. 'Yesterday when I came into work, my little— um, never mind.'

Trevor glances at me as he turns out of the cemetery. 'What, Chas?'

I sigh and look out the window. 'Well, I have these little figurines on my desk, you know? From . . . well, from *Lord of the Rings,* okay, and don't say anything about it because I already know I'm a hopeless nerd and don't need you to point that out.'

'As long as you're aware,' he says, his eyes crinkling.

'So anyway,' I continue, 'I always have them in a certain order, right? But yesterday, they were in a little circle. It was weird.'

'Maybe the cleaning people knocked them off by accident and just put them back that way,' Trev suggests.

251

'Maybe. I don't know. It's just that they had . . . oh, crap, it sounds so dumb.'

Trevor laughs. 'Please tell me.'

I roll my eyes at myself and obey. 'Aragorn was lying in the middle of the circle, facedown, and all the other characters in this particular series have weapons. So it looked like all of Aragorn's little friends were killing him. Sort of.'

'You need to get out more,' Trevor states.

'You asked, you jerk.'

Before I realize it, we're on my street, pulling up in front of my sweet little house. 'Do you want to come in?' I ask. 'Have a beer, maybe watch the game?'

'Thanks but no, Chastity,' he answers. 'I've got . . . um . . . plans.'

I pause, my hand on the door handle. 'Are you back with Hayden, Trevor?'

He doesn't answer right away. 'Not exactly.'

'Not yet, you mean?' My voice is tight.

He sighs. 'She's mentioned that she'd like that, yes.'

'What about Angela? I thought you were dating Angela.' I'm gripping the door handle so hard it hurts.

'Well, I've been out with Angela. I wouldn't say we're dating,' he says.

'Would she say that?' Trevor doesn't answer. 'Don't lead her on, Trevor.'

'I wouldn't do that, Chas,' he says quietly, staring straight ahead.

252

'You wouldn't mean to, but you might.'

He looks me straight in the eye. 'No. I wouldn't mean to.'

'Make sure you don't,' I snap. Then I take a deep breath. 'Look, Trev, I know you're a good guy and you can be with whomever you want. Just do it right, okay? Sorry if I sounded like a shrew. Thanks for the flowers, thanks for the ride. I'll see you around.'

He nods. I jump out of the truck and haul Buttercup out of the back. 'See you!' I call, running into the house, my dog flopping beside me.

CHAPTER NINETEEN

As I leave EMT class later that week, I'm accompanied by an unfamiliar sense of pride. Yes, pride. I've always been a good student, and suddenly, I'm acing all the checklists on taking a patient's history, remembering what order to assess which systems, knowing the physiology we have to memorize in order to pass our written test. Suddenly, people are asking me for help, leaping at the chance to be my partner, much to Ernesto's annoyance, since he considers me his exclusive property.

Maybe dating Ryan Darling has caused some medical savvy to rub off on me. More likely it's just that I don't have to see real

253

injuries just yet. Don't actually have to help someone who's writhing in pain. Smell the smells that go along with injury and illness. See the twins, Blood and Gore. I swallow. Soon, our practicals in the emergency room will come up, when we have to spend an entire shift in the E.R. I'm hoping my nurse will just tell me to stay out of the way, coward that I am.

I unchain my mountain bike from the rack and shoulder my backpack. I need to run home and grab Buttercup, then head out again. I'm babysitting Dylan because Elaina has a date. I feel a little guilty about enabling my friend to go out with someone who's not my brother. But Mark has brought his problems on himself, and I love Dylan, his tendency to bite me notwithstanding.

Several pain and shriek-filled hours later, I gaze down upon my nephew as he sleeps in his crib, his mouth open, eyelashes feathered on his pink cheeks, snoring just a little. He looks like an angel. I know better.

'I love you, Dylan,' I whisper, stroking the delicious cluster of curls at the back of his head. He is a breathtakingly beautiful child—black hair, dark blue eyes, dimples like Mark, curls like Elaina. Of all us good-looking O'Neills, I'd have to say that Dylan is probably our most stunning, an Irish–Puerto Rican specimen of pure beauty. Of course, then there's Claire, whose apricot cheeks are a

254

study in poreless perfection. And Olivia of the coppery curls. And let's not forget Graham's giant eyes and infectious laugh . . . or Christopher's elfin smile . . . or pink-and-cream Jenny. Okay, so I'm a doting aunt.

I hear Elaina's car in the garage, give Dylan a final kiss and trot downstairs.

'How was your date?' I ask as she puts her keys and purse down.

She bursts into tears.

'Lainey! What happened? Come on, sit down.' I lead her to the living room. She sits down, grabbing a tissue off the coffee table first.

'Did you clean up in here? It looks nice,' she weeps.

'Honey, what happened?' I ask.

Elaina blows her nose and wipes her eyes. 'Oh, Chastity, it was fine. Nice guy, all that crap. I'm never seeing him again.'

'Why?' I ask. 'Was he a jerk? Did he do something?'

'Well, no, Chastity! He just wasn't your brother!'

'I guess it's too soon, huh?' I suggest.

She starts sobbing in earnest. 'Your brother . . . he's . . . I still . . . I just wish . . . '

I move over to the couch and put my arm around my friend, tears in my own eyes at the sight of her heartbreak. 'It's okay, Elaina. Go ahead and cry.'

Buttercup, who has been sleeping in front of

255

the fireplace, clambers up and approaches Elaina, putting her big head on Elaina's lap. This elicits a sloppy laugh from my friend. 'Even your dog feels sorry for me.' She hiccups. 'How pathetic is that?'

'Very,' I say, grabbing a few more tissues.

'So,' Elaina says, sagging back on the couch. 'I still love Mark. I want to forgive the rat bastard, but . . .' Her voice trails off, and she looks so sad.

'Has he apologized, Lainey?'

'Oh, sure. Like, "I said I'm sorry! What do I have to do for you to believe me?" Then he storms out or something. Pretty crappy apology if you ask me.' She sniffs.

'Well, what *would* he have to do, Lainey?' I ask. Buttercup wags her tail, knocking over an empty cup, then woofs softly and collapses, her legs buckling in her trademark flop.

Elaina blows her nose again. 'I don't know,' she says honestly. 'He can't ever cheat on me again, and how can I be sure of that, you know? I mean, it's one thing to be rejected once. Twice, that's another thing altogether. Fool me once, shame on you. Fool me twice, I'm a stupid idiot . . . You know?'

I nod. 'Has he gotten any counseling or anything?' I ask. Mark is the brother to whom I speak the least. Living with Matt gives me an insider's view on his life, obviously, and Lucky is the brother most like me, and we talk a couple of times a week. Jack checks in every

256

Sunday night, doing the eldest child shtick, which I think is kind of cute.

But Mark is the highest strung. Tense, jumpy, too much energy . . . but he also has the biggest heart. No one tries harder than Mark, and no one screws up more, either.

'How was Dylan?' Elaina asks, managing a watery smile.

'Oh, he was great!' I say, deciding against telling her about my nephew's twenty-seven-minute scream fest when I took him out of the tub. Or the bite marks on my shoulder. 'An angel. I was just worshipping him when you came up.'

'And so when are you and Doctor Good-Looking gonna pop some of your own?' Elaina asks.

I smile. 'I don't know.'

'But things are good?'

I nod. 'Yup. Very good. He's a wonderful boyfriend.'

'How is he wonderful? Tell me. I need to hear what wonderful is like.' She wipes her eyes once more and toys with a lock of her curly hair.

'Oh, he sent me flowers yesterday. He took me to a nice restaurant on Tuesday, and yesterday, when he was stuck in surgery, he had a nurse call me and let me know.'

'He had a nurse call? Like she's his answering service or something?' Elaina snaps.

'Well, you know, he was elbow deep in

257

someone's abdomen or something, Lainey. Some gruesome ripping injury thing.'

She sniffs. 'And are you crazy about him?' Her eyes are too knowing.

'Yes. Yes, I am.' I pause. 'I'm getting there.'

'Speaking of boyfriends, have you met Harry? Your mom's guy?' Elaina asks, kindly changing the subject.

'No,' I answer. 'But I don't think it's the real thing. She's just playing with Dad.'

'I don't know about that, Chas.' Elaina blows her nose. 'They've been seeing each other a lot.'

'Dad and Mom?'

'No, dummy. Your mom and Harry.'

A little trickle of dismay wriggles through my stomach, but I dismiss it with a shake of my head. 'Well, whatever. She wouldn't really leave my father.'

Elaina doesn't answer.

'At any rate,' I announce heartily, 'try not to feel bad, sweetie. Mark will come around. You keep your chin up, okay? True love conquers all, blah blah bleeping blah.'

'Such a way with words. No wonder you're a journalist.'

I give her a gentle punch on the shoulder and find my jacket. 'Come on, Buttercup,' I call to my dog. Several minutes later, when I've hauled her to her feet and forcibly walked her out the door, I clip the leash to her collar and mount my bike. I love riding at night, and

258

Buttercup gallumphs along beside me, sloppy and joyous, as we cruise through the dark streets, the pinkish glow of the streetlamps lighting our way. Up ahead are two men, heads close together, shoulders bumping. *Love is in the air,* I think with a smile. As I approach, they thoughtfully step onto the strip of grass between the sidewalk and the street.

'Thanks, guys,' I call, glancing back. Holy crap! I suck in a quick breath and whip my head around, swerving slightly.

One of the men is Teddy Bear, Lucia's fiancé of the past four years.

CHAPTER TWENTY

Since the initial hacking, the *Eaton Falls Gazette*'s Web site has been unsullied. Granted, I check it at least ten times a day and have become obsessed with online security. But I haven't returned to my status as golden girl. Penelope is cordial but not nearly as friendly as before. I'm afraid to ask if subscriptions have fallen. Instead, I just keep my head down and work diligently.

I ask Angela if she's free for lunch and, at noon, we take our sandwiches down to the park alongside the river, sitting on the very bench where I saw Trevor with Perfect Hayden. He's one of the many things I need to talk about today.

'So, Ange, how's it going with Trevor?' I ask, taking a bite of my meatball sub.

'He's so sweet,' she says. 'Really. Such a nice guy. And just so damn cute.'

'Mm,' I say, chewing. 'Do you think it might get serious?'

She tips her head to one side and adjusts her glasses. 'Well, right now we're at the "just friends" stage. Honestly, I'm not sure if there's any real chemistry.'

I choke on a meatball but quickly recover. 'Really? No chemistry? With Trevor?'

She grins. 'It's not that he's not . . . you know. Delicious. He is. It's just . . . well. We'll see.'

I glug some lemonade, torn between loyalties. Should I mention Perfect Hayden? Should I keep my mouth shut? 'You know, he was with someone a long time ago,' I say, hoping for middle ground. 'I'm not sure he ever got over her.'

Angela nods. 'Hm. Yeah. That's the thing. He's perfectly nice and funny and all that, but I get the feeling that he's phoning it in.'

A shameful sense of satisfaction leaps in my chest, and I give my head a disgusted shake. If he's phoning it in, it's because Perfect Hayden is back in town. She who broke his heart. The girl he wanted to marry.

'Any more problems on the Web site?' Angela asks.

260

'No,' I answer, grateful for the new subject. 'But Angela, you know those little *Lord of the Rings* figures I have on my desk?'

'Sure,' she says, taking a bite of her salad.

'Well, someone's been messing with them. Last week, they were rearranged kind of strangely. Then this morning, when I came in, Aragorn's head was missing. Snapped off.'

Angela frowns. 'That's creepy, Chastity.'

'I know it. I feel like I'm being stalked or something.'

'Should you tell the police?' she asks.

I sigh. 'I don't know. The thing is, only staff has keys to the building, right? So I get the feeling that it's just kind of a mean prank.'

'Who would do that?' Angela says. 'Lucia?'

I close my eyes. 'She's the only one who seems to really dislike me. That doesn't mean she did anything, but still.' We're both quiet for a minute, the wind rustling through the maple and cherry trees. A teenager blades by, apparently playing hooky. 'Listen, Ange, on another subject,' I say awkwardly. 'I have to ask you something, just between the two of us.'

'Sure,' she says.

'I have this, um, friend, okay? And I saw her . . . um . . . boyfriend with someone else. Should I say something?' I wince. 'I mean, it's none of my business, but if one of my friends knew something about my boyfriend . . . Crap. I don't know. Probably not, huh?'

'Dear Abby would say you'd just be blamed,'

261

Angela murmurs. 'Shoot the messenger and all that.'

'Yeah,' I agree. 'I guess. Damned if you do, damned if you don't.'

'If it was me, I wouldn't say anything,' she says.

Upon returning to the office, Angela and I are greeted with a scowl from Lucia, who doesn't like the fact that Angela and I are friends. 'Staff meeting in ten,' she snaps, pecking away on her computer.

I zip over to my desk to check the Web site, just in case it's been corrupted again. No. It's clear. And the mood of the office is light. Carl, our fearless photographer, is grinning, and Penelope is laughing on the phone in her office.

'Have you heard?' Alan asks, leaning on my cubicle, smiling broadly. His tooth hardly bothers me these days.

'No. What's up?' I ask.

'You haven't heard?' he repeats.

'No.'

'I'll let Penelope tell you, then,' he says, ambling away. He gives his pants a tug and stops to chat with Angela.

When we're all settled in the conference room, Penelope sways in, grinning from ear to ear. 'This morning, as some of you know,' she says grandly, 'there was a fire at the Graystone Apartments.'

I lurch up in my seat. If any one of my

262

family was hurt—why didn't anyone call me? Is my dad okay? Mattie? Trevor?

'No one was hurt,' Pen says, correctly reading my face. I sag back, my heart rate slowing. Angela pats my hand.

'At any rate,' Pen continues, 'our fearless photographer drove to the scene just in time to snap a few shots. Carl? Would you like to do the honors?'

Carl is practically bursting. 'Thanks, Pen,' he says. 'Ladies and gents, picture number one.' He holds up a dry-mounted color photo about three feet square. I suck in a breath. 'That's an O'Neill, isn't it, Chastity?' he asks.

'Yes,' I say, flushing with pride. 'My brother Mark.'

In the photo, Mark's wearing his gear and yellow helmet, the eye shield pushed up. His face is sooty and serious, and in his gloved hands, he's holding a tabby cat. Behind them, black smoke pours out of a brick apartment building. The cat's mouth is hanging open, its eyes wide and somehow sightless. It looks dead.

'Oh, the poor kitty!' Lucia exclaims.

'Any humans in that building?' Pete asks. 'Not that we don't care about Puss 'n Boots there.'

'No humans,' Alan says. 'Carl, show them the next shot.'

'The family was out of state, thank God,' Carl says. 'Fire broke out about six this

263

morning.' He picks up another photo, clearly enjoying the moment.

This one shows Mark lying the cat down on the pavement. Hose snakes around on the damp ground, and firefighters' boots are in the background. The cat's mouth is wide open; its eyes stare at the sky.

'But wait . . . there's more!' Pen crows.

'These are fantastic, Carl,' Danielle says, coming in for a closer look. She's right—the detail is crisp, the background well framed.

'Thanks,' he says, that shit-eating grin still firmly in place. 'And on to picture number three.'

This one shows Mark holding a small oxygen cone over the cat's mouth, its paws stiff in the air. Mark's face is intent, his hand behind the cat's neck.

'Oh, no!' Lucia says. There are tears in her eyes.

'Don't worry, Lu,' Carl says.

'I think I know what's coming,' Angela says, smiling.

Carl holds up the fourth picture in triumph. There's Mark, laughing, blue eyes glowing, face sooty, looking just so dang handsome as the cat rubs its head against its savior's chin.

'Your brother resuscitated that cat, Chastity!' Penelope announces, in case we missed it. 'And Carl got it on film!'

We all burst into cheers and applause. I'm glowing with pride and affection for my brother—he may have his flaws, but today he saved a life. A cat's life, but a life nonetheless.

'Congratulations, Carl! Beautiful job!' I say, shaking his hand.

'There's more, people!' Penelope calls over our noise. 'Attention, please! Not only are you looking at tomorrow's front page—you're looking at Yahoo's pictures of the day!'

Our cheers turn to shrieks of amazement and joy. We hug and laugh, Lucia is crying, Penelope is practically floating, and Carl is aglow. 'Champagne, everyone!' Pen calls out.

'I want to get these on the Web site right this minute,' I say as she pours.

'Good idea, Chas,' she returns, handing me a glass of champers. 'And please tell your brother that we're very proud of him.'

'I will. Thanks. Hey, Carl, can I have copies of those pictures for my nephew? Mark's son?'

'Of course,' he says grandly. 'I'll e-mail you the files.'

I give him another hug. 'Great job, Carl. Again. Well done.'

'I know it.' He beams. 'This may be the best day of my life.'

I'm so happy for the *Gazette*. It's huge, being on Yahoo! Tomorrow's paper will sell out, even though we'll print extra copies. Carl's career has just enjoyed a huge rush; and the thrill of these pictures being seen *worldwide* must be indescribable.

I get to my computer, extract the files and

open the Web site. No porn, thank goodness. I make the pictures as big as possible, placing them two over two. 'Alan, do you have a headline?' I call.

He sticks his head out of the conference room. ' "No Life Too Small For Eaton Falls Firefighters," ' he says. 'Subhead should read "EFFD battles apartment fire. Family pet saved." ' Alan smiles. 'You must be so proud, Chas.'

'I am, Alan. Thanks.' I type in his headers and update the Web site, then dial Mark's cell. His voice mail picks up. 'Hey, Mark, you big strong hero, you! Congratulations! I'll see you later, okay? Love you.' Then I click on my e-mail to send him a message, just on the off chance that he's home.

I have a new message. From me, apparently. Sure, I send myself messages from time to time—*Don't forget to pick up Elaina*—or something like that, but to the best of my recollection, I haven't sent myself anything today. With a cold sense of trepidation, I click on the message, which is entitled 'chastity.'

You're an egotistical bitch, you know that? Take a look in the mirror, Hulk. You look like a man.

CHAPTER TWENTY-ONE

Two hours later, Angela and I are on our way to the firehouse in her car.

I didn't say anything about the e-mail, not wanting to take the moment away from Carl. But I'm a little scared. Kind of a lot, actually. I'll probably call the police later on and ask if there's anything they can do. Someone is trying to creep me out, and that someone is doing a great job.

I shove my dark thoughts away and try to focus on Mark and the fire, Carl and his pictures. I can think about my cyberstalker later on.

Penelope instructed us to interview a few firefighters. Angela, being the food editor, is obviously going to focus on food—firehouse favorites, cooking for the crowd, heroes' recipes, etcetera. I get to do another in the Hometown Heroes series. Alan has already interviewed the chief, the fire marshal and several of the guys at the call. Suki has called the family, who was on vacation in Florida and is now headed home. Tomorrow's edition of the *Eaton Falls Gazette* will be almost entirely focused on firefighters.

I don't have time to call Elaina, but I can't wait to talk to her. Maybe this will be a turning point for Mark, this excellent publicity. Maybe he'll come out of his angry phase and start feeling good about himself for a change. God, I hope so.

Angela pulls into the parking lot of the firehouse. It's hard to find a space. As is true after most fires, there are several platoons present, hanging around, dissecting the fire, talking to the guys who saw flame, picking apart the performances of their peers. We get out, grab the pictures (on loan, since Carl wants to gaze upon them some more) and go inside. Mark is in the truck bay, at the center of a knot of firefighters—Dad, Matt, Jake, Santo, George and Helen, Eaton Falls's only female firefighter.

'Nice save, Mark,' I say as we approach.

'Hey, Sis,' Mark says with a grin. I see now that he's holding a toy cat, a gift from one of the guys, no doubt. He waves its paw at me. 'It was only a cat.' The stuffed animal meows and we all laugh.

'Well, we all know how much you love pussies,' Jake announces.

Mark's smile drops like lead, and silence falls over the group.

'Jake, keep your mouth shut, asshole,' Santo says.

'Go clean hose,' my father orders tersely. Jake skulks off. Dad scowls after him, then comes over to me. 'Hi, Porkchop. Your brother saved a kitty-cat.'

'So I saw,' I answer. 'Check it out, Mark.'

Angela and I show him the pictures. His cheeks redden in pleasure.

'You're blushing, you sexy beast,' Santo coos, and all the guys crack up.

'These pictures are on Yahoo already,' Angela says. Silence falls.

'Wow,' Helen says. 'Fame for little old Eaton Falls.'

'Your mother will love these,' Dad murmurs. 'I'm gonna call her right now. Yahoo, you say, Porkchop?'

'Dad, this is Angela,' I say. 'Angela, my father, Captain Mike O'Neill, and my heroic brother Mark, and my other heroic brother, Matt, and Santo and Helen and the rest of the gang.'

'Hi,' Matt says, smiling.

'Hello,' she says, blushing. How cute.

'Dad,' I say, 'we're doing a feature on local heroes—' Dad rolls his eyes '—and the chief already cleared it, so don't bother complaining. Angela is our food editor, and she'd like to talk to some of you about firehouse food.'

'This is where I go home,' Helen says.

I grin. 'And I'm supposed to interview some guys about saving lives.'

'Chief okayed this?' Dad says with a pained look. I nod firmly. 'Fine.' He sighs. 'Let's see, who's the best cook around here . . . hm. Matt! You do it, son.'

'Sure,' Matt says. 'Want to see the kitchen?'

269

he asks Angela, whose face is bright red. 'You're Trevor's Angela, right?'

'Um . . . I . . . we . . .' she stammers, and I try not to laugh. My brothers are a handsome lot, but I can't say that I've ever seen a woman quite so affected before. Perhaps now I should tell her about the time Matt dressed up in my pink Easter dress and matching hat when he was six . . . but no, they're already off to the kitchen.

'And what else do you need, Porkchop?' Dad asks me.

'Just to talk to some of you about being heroic, manly alpha dogs who risk their lives to save the rest of us poor slobs. Or, in Mark's case, poor kitty-cats.'

Dad makes a face. 'I don't know, honey. We all kind of hate that crap.'

'That crap is my bread and butter, Daddy. I'm under orders from my editor.'

He sighs. 'Fine. You owe me. Who do you want to talk to? Mark?'

'Well, no, since Alan already got him. Plus there's the family connection, so no O'Neills.'

'Would Jake do?' Dad asks.

'I need someone who can speak in full sentences.'

'Right. Santo? How about you?' Dad asks. 'Care to talk to Chastity for the paper?'

'Sorry, Chas. No. How about Helen?' Santo smiles apologetically.

'Helen has left the building,' George offers.

270

'How about you, then, George?' I ask.

'Yeah . . . no. Sorry, kid. I gotta go, too. Been here all day.' He pats my shoulder and heads out.

I sigh. I knew it would be like this. Firefighters are a modest bunch. They love what they do, talk about it endlessly with each other. But when it comes to public adulation, they clam up and credit everyone but themselves.

'Sorry, sweetie,' Dad says.

Just then, Trevor appears from the truck bay. 'Trevor!' Dad barks. 'You're busted, son. Come over here.'

'Hey, Chastity,' he says. He still smells of smoke, and my stomach lurches at the thought of him in a burning building.

'Were you on the call?' I ask.

'Yeah,' he answers. 'I was in for Dave. Mark made a real nice grab.' He grins, and I look away quickly.

'Chastity needs to interview someone for her paper, and no one wants to do it. How about it?'

Trevor makes the same face of pain my father made.

'Come on!' I say. 'Please, Trev? My editor won't believe that no one would talk to me. I'll probably be fired.' Not true at all. 'You don't want that on your head, do you?'

'Fine.' He sighs. 'Where do you want to go?'

'Somewhere quiet,' I say.

271

'Want to sit outside? It's a beautiful day.'

We go to the back of the firehouse, where there's a picnic table and a few plastic chairs. The sky glimmers bright blue with creamy cumulus clouds piled on top of each other. Birdies sing in the trees, and the mountains glow green in the background. Even at the edge of the parking lot, it's bleeping gorgeous.

Trev sits down and folds his arms across his chest in textbook 'I don't want to talk' body language.

'I really appreciate this,' I say, taking out my notebook. 'I'll make it fun, okay?'

'Make it quick, how's that?' He smiles to take the edge out of his words.

'So, Trev, have you always wanted to be a firefighter?' I ask, giving him a smile.

His own smile drops into a frown, and he just stares at me intently.

'Is there a bee on me?' I ask.

'What's wrong, Chas?'

'Nothing,' I protest. 'I'm . . . I'm fine. Why?'

'You look . . . something happened, didn't it?' he asks gently, leaning forward.

I take a breath, hold it, then let it go. 'Don't tell my dad,' I begin.

'Shit. Is it that doctor?' His face darkens suddenly.

'No! No, Ryan's fine. He's . . . he's great.' I sigh. 'Remember I told you that I thought someone was bothering me at work, messing up my stuff?' He nods. 'Well, someone sent me a mean e-mail today.'

'Who?' he asks.

'I don't know. It said it was from me, so go figure.'

'What did it say?' he asks.

I glance away from his dark, dark eyes. 'Oh, nothing too scary. That I was, um, a bitch. And ugly. He called me Hulk. Like Hulk Hogan, I guess, or the Incredible Hulk. Either way, less than flattering, you know?'

It's when he takes my hand that my eyes fill. His hand is warm and smooth and calloused, and it feels so good and reassuring and perfect. Embarrassed, I wipe my eyes with my free hand.

'Are you going to the police?' he asks.

'Yeah, maybe.'

'You are. And I'm coming with you.'

'No, you're not. I'll—'

'I'm coming, Chas.' He squeezes my hand, then lets it go, and for a minute, my hand just doesn't know what to do, like its purpose in life has been taken away. 'You saved the e-mail, right?' Trev asks.

'Right,' I answer.

'Good girl.'

I swallow, then look down at my notebook. 'Well, I still have to do this little profile, okay? So if you don't mind . . . '

'Sure. Fire away.'

We're back to normal, that strange state of just a little more than friends. 'Okay. Trev, why did you become a firefighter?' I ask.

'To be like your dad.' The answer is immediate.

I smile a little at that, even though I knew the answer. 'And do you love it?'

'Yup. So are we done?' He grins.

I laugh. 'These questions are designed to put you at ease, Trevor, and I can see that they're working just great. Take a breath, relax. We're just getting started.'

'I just don't really like this sort of thing.'

'Why not? You guys are the bomb! Everyone loves firemen. You know that.'

He rolls his eyes. 'Well, I don't want to make myself out to be a hero. Nobody does.'

'But you *are* heroes and we *do* love you. So shut up and get over it, bub.' He smiles and my cheeks feel a little hot. 'So, Firefighter Meade, what's the best part of this job?'

'Serving the community of Eaton Falls.'

I wait, but he seems finished. 'Trevor,' I say through gritted teeth, 'cooperate.'

'Fine. It beats being a garbage man, okay?'

I throw my pen down in disgust. 'My father said you'd help me, okay? So do it, or I'm telling.'

Finally, he laughs. 'Okay, you big baby.'

'Don't make me hurt you.' I pick up my pen again. 'If I were to quote you as saying something like, 'I'm proud to serve the people of Eaton Falls . . . it's good to know that my job lets me help those in need' . . . would that be

274

okay?'

'As long as you make it sound better than that, then sure, I guess.'

I let that one pass. 'Tell me what it's like to work at saving lives.' I give him my best interview smile.

'It beats not saving lives.'

'You know, you were so nice before, and yet now I want to hit you.'

'Come on, Chas!' he says. 'Who can answer this stuff?' I glare. He shifts in the chair. 'Okay.' He sighs. 'Well, of course we don't get to save lives every day, or even save buildings. Most of our work, as you already know, is medicals, automatic alarms, car accidents. But yeah, once in a while, we get to save a life.'

'Can you give me some examples?' I ask.

He thinks. 'A couple days ago, we had this guy about fifty, fifty-five years old. He had a heart attack, and we did CPR, shocked him, got a rhythm back.'

'Did he make it?' I ask.

'No,' Trevor says. 'He died the next day. Most people who get CPR don't make it.' He's quiet for a minute. 'But he died with his family around him, and they had a little time to prepare themselves, to say things to him, even if he couldn't hear it.'

My chest aches. 'That's a gift, Trevor,' I whisper. 'You gave them a chance to say goodbye.'

He shrugs, looking uncomfortable. 'It
275

would've been nicer to give them back their father. Husband.'

'But still.' He says nothing. 'Any others leap to mind?'

He sighs. 'Well, last summer there was a kid who fell in the river, and we pulled her out. She lived. A little brain damage, but she's doing okay.'

'Do you ever see her?'

His looks at me sharply. 'Don't print this, okay?' I nod. 'Yeah, I still see her. I was on dive team that day, and I'm the one who pulled her out. She walks with a limp now, but she's doing fine.'

'God, Trev! You saved a child's life.' Somehow, that story wasn't passed down to me in Newark. I can hardly stand to picture it, the image is so terrifying and heroic . . . Trevor pulling a child from the water, loading her into the ambulance, visiting her in the hospital. I clear my throat. Trevor is staring at the ground.

'Okay, Trev, let's talk about the feelings, because readers love to get all touchy-feely. How does it feel, knowing you saved a life? Knowing that you're a hero?'

Trevor doesn't look up from the pavement. 'I don't think I'm any different from anyone else. I just have a better job than most people.'

'You're wrong,' I say without thinking. 'I'd give anything to save somebody. To really make a difference.'

276

He looks up, stares at me for a beat. 'You do, Chastity. And you have.'

There's something in his eyes that I can't discern, something sad and intent, and I wish I could crawl onto his lap and hug him. Then he looks away, glances at his watch, and the moment is over.

I swallow. 'Well, I meant making a difference in the big scheme of things. "He who saves one life saves the world" and all that.'

'What's that from? The Bible?'

'*Schindler's List* is where I heard it.'

Trevor laughs. 'Chastity, you're so funny. Hey, speaking of heroes, here comes Cat-Man.'

I look up to see my brother coming toward us from the back door of the fire department. 'And then a hero comes along,' I sing. 'With the strength to carry a kitty-cat . . .'

'What the fuck were you thinking?' Mark demands, lurching to a halt in front of me.

I blink. 'Excuse me?'

'You fucking babysit while my wife goes on a date?' he yells, planting himself two feet in front of me. 'What the fuck is that about, you stupid idiot?'

'Easy, Mark,' Trevor says, standing. 'Calm down.'

'Stay out of this, Trevor. I just got off the phone with Elaina and she said you were over there last night while she was off with some fucking moron doing God knows what! You

277

stay out of my business, Chastity, and leave my family alone.'

A hot, slow wave of anger rolls up through me. 'Mark,' I grind out, standing up and taking a step toward him. 'Your family, you ass, also happens to be my family. You're the one who screwed things up with Elaina, so don't go blaming me if she goes on a date, okay?'

'You think you know everything, Chastity?' By now, several other firefighters are gathered at the back door, reluctant to become involved in a family squabble, but not about to ignore it, either. 'Don't you ever babysit for my son again!'

'Oh, for pete's sake!' I say.

'Not when my wife is screwing around on me!'

'Mark, settle down,' Trevor says again.

'Fuck off, Trevor!' Mark bellows. Trevor steps in front of me, but I shove past him.

'You're making an idiot of yourself, Mark O'Neill,' I hiss. 'Again. Okay? Just shut up and get some counseling.'

Mark's fists clench. 'You little bitch,' he snarls.

'Mark!' Trevor barks. 'Enough!'

Mark turns on him. 'Whose side are you on, anyway?' he demands.

'Chastity's,' Trevor answers instantly.

'Why? Are you fucking her?'

Trevor's mouth clamps into a hard line. His arm goes back to hit my brother, but I'm

278

faster. My fist connects with Mark's jaw with a satisfying thunk. Pain shoots up my arm like a knife, and Mark staggers back, stunned. Then my father is there, grabbing Mark.

'What the hell is going on here?' he snaps.

'Get him home, Mike,' Trevor says. 'Chastity, you okay?'

My knuckles are killing me, my arm throbs, but I won't give Mark the satisfaction of seeing me wince. I haven't punched a brother since I was twelve, but you know what? Mark had it coming.

'Chas?' Trevor says, putting his hand on my shoulder.

'I'm fine,' I say tightly, shrugging him off.

'What happened?' Dad asks. Mark is rubbing his jaw and glaring at me. 'Did you threaten your sister, Mark?'

'Jesus, Dad, stay out of it. She overreacted, as usual,' Mark grumbles.

'*I* overreacted,' I repeat. 'That's rich, Mark.'

'Mark, get off firehouse property,' Dad says in captain mode. 'Go home and cool off, whatever the hell it is you're mad about this time. I'll be over when I'm done here.'

Mark obeys, muttering, shoving his way past the guys who just watched his sister slug him.

'Chastity.' Dad sighs. 'Maybe you should go.'

'Okay,' I whisper, my throat suddenly tight. Dad walks toward the firehouse, says something to the guys and disappears inside.

279

'I was planning on hitting him, you know,' Trevor says, and there's a smile in his voice. 'You didn't have to. But thanks for defending my honor.'

'It's not funny,' I say. In fact, my eyes are stinging with tears. 'Don't let them make fun of Mark, okay? This should've been a great day for him.'

'I'll take care of it,' Trevor says. He takes my hand and looks at it, then looks back into my eyes. 'Let's get you an ice pack.' His voice is gentle.

'Remind me never to pick a fight with the O'Neill girl,' Santo says admiringly as Trevor and I go inside.

Angela and Matt are in the kitchen, laughing at the stove. They both start when we come in. Trevor grabs an ice pack, wraps it in a paper towel and puts it on my hand. 'I got it,' I say, holding it in place. My heart feels sore and too big for my chest, and any more sweetness from Trevor and I'll start bawling.

'You okay, Chas?' Matt asks.

'I'll fill you in later,' Trev says quietly. 'Hi, Angela. I didn't know you were here.' He smiles, but it's forced.

'Hi, Trevor,' she answers. 'Um, sorry, I was interviewing Matt. For an article. Firehouse pizza.'

'We need to go, Ange,' I say. My throat is still constricted with anger and sorrow.

'Okay,' she says, frowning at the look on my

face. 'Matt, thank you so much. This was great. I'll e-mail you if I have any questions.'

'Sure. Nice meeting you.'

Angela blushes and grabs her things. Trevor and Matt say goodbye and we walk out to the parking lot.

'Is everything okay?' she asks, opening the driver's door.

'Yup. Just a little spat with my brother,' I answer.

'Oh,' she murmurs. 'I'm sorry, Chastity.' We get into the car, and Angela starts the engine. 'Matt is really nice, at any rate.'

'He's great,' I agree, then turn my face away and rest my forehead against the window.

CHAPTER TWENTY-TWO

The rest of the day is so busy—the Yahoo pictures cause all sorts of coverage, including me interviewing Carl himself—that I don't have a chance to tell Penelope about the nasty e-mail. I call her when I get home that night and fill her in, tell her about Aragorn's beheading. It sounds so bleeping dumb when I say it aloud.

'Call the police,' she says. 'See if there's anything they can do. This sucks, Chastity.'

'It's not a huge deal,' I say, stroking Buttercup's sensitive ears. 'But yeah, I'd feel better.' And so I call the computer crimes specialist at the police department, who seems to take a lot of notes and says they'll send someone in to run some diagnostics on my computer.

'Nothing's happening anywhere but work?' the cop asks.

'Correct,' I answer. 'I feel dumb bothering you with something so small.'

'Better to report it than not,' she says. 'You never know what whackos are out there, prowling on innocent people.'

Gee, thanks, lady. 'Right,' I say.

Matt is working that night, so Buttercup and I are alone. I stick *The Fellowship of the Ring* in the DVD player. Just as I'm settling in, a pint of Ben & Jerry's in one hand, the phone rings.

'Hello, there,' Ryan says. 'How are you?'

'Oh, hey, Ryan,' I say. 'I'm okay. I had kind of a crappy day, actually.'

'Sorry to hear that,' he says. 'What—damn. Chastity, I'm being paged. Can I call you later? I'm really sorry. You're all right, aren't you?'

'Yes, I'm fine. You go. I understand.'

'Love you,' he says and hangs up.

I squinch my right eye shut and grit my teeth. He loves me? Since when? *That* didn't sound very convincing. We've been on five dates. Slept together three times. He loves me?

'Shut it, Chastity,' I say aloud. It's not impossible that a man could fall in love with me in the space of a few weeks. 'I guess I'm a very loveable person, Buttercup,' I say. 'Don't you agree?'

She does. She licks my face and lays her head back in my lap with a sigh.

I'm just at the Prancing Pony scene where we first meet the dark and delicious Aragorn when a knock interrupts me. It's Mark, a box of Twinkies under his arm, a bouquet of irises in his hand. 'Hi. I'm sorry,' he says, thrusting the gifts at me. Any residual anger I might have had melts away at the sight of his tormented face.

'Come in, pal,' I tell him, putting his offerings on the hall table.

He takes off his coat, stopping to let Buttercup sniff his shoes before sitting on the couch. 'What are you watching?' he asks, gesturing at the TV.

'*Lord of the Rings,*' I answer. Turning off the DVD player and TV, I turn to face my difficult brother. 'Are you okay?'

He takes a deep breath. 'No.'

'Can I do anything?'

'You should be mad at me, Chas. Shit, I really fucked up, didn't I?'

'Well, I'm not mad, Mark. Glad I punched you, yes, but not mad. I'm just worried about you, that's all.'

He gives a bitter laugh. 'Why? Isn't my life going great? Come on, dog. Sit with me.' Buttercup lunges on the couch next to him, settling her head on his lap with a groan.

'Mark,' I begin tentatively, 'what do you want to happen next? With Elaina and Dylan and everything?'

'I want everything to go back to where it was,' he answers thickly, petting Buttercup and not looking at me.

'That can't happen.'

'I know. So I'm stuck. She won't forgive me.' A tear plops onto Buttercup's head, but Mark keeps petting.

'She wants to, you know.'

'She says she can't trust me.' His voice is heavy. Mark doesn't cry. Me, I blubber an ocean. Mark . . . he's a desert.

'Honey,' I say gently, 'it takes time. You have to keep trying, show her that you can be trusted.' He shrugs. 'And Mark, you're a mess. You're so angry and bitter, and the thing is, you should be kissing Elaina's feet. You should do whatever it takes to get her back. She's the best thing that ever happened to you, and you're going to lose her.'

My brother puts his hand over his eyes. 'I don't know what to do, Chas. I want to do the right thing, and I just keep getting further and further away from where I need to be. I'm lost.' He shakes his head, this big, handsome, cat-saving brother of mine, tears dripping out from underneath his hand, and my heart aches.

'Okay. Here's what to do. Buttercup, down,

girl.' I drag my dog off the couch and sit next to Mark, putting my arm around him. 'First, you need to get some anger management or something. A psychiatrist, a therapist, something. Would you do that?' He nods. 'Then ask Elaina if she'll go to marriage counseling.'

'That's a lot of shrinks, Chas.'

'So? You just said you're lost. This is a way to get found.'

'What else?' he asks.

'You tell Elaina that nothing is more important than her and Dylan, and you want them back. Simple as that, Mark. Don't tell her that she's bitter or how she should be feeling, don't put conditions on it, just tell her. She still loves you, honey.'

'Did she tell you that?' he asks.

'Yes.' His shoulders jerk. 'She misses the man you used to be, Mark.'

With that, my brother puts both arms around me and bawls into my shoulder like a one hundred and eighty-five pound baby. After a minute, Buttercup joins in, baying sympathetically, and Mark gives a shaky laugh. I pat his back and tell him he's going to be just fine.

CHAPTER TWENTY-THREE

Over the weekend, we are summoned for a family dinner at Mom's. Dad won't be coming. Harry will. Mom wants us to meet him. It's giving me a stomachache.

'So you're going?' my father demands over the phone. I've just returned from a row, need to shower, check the Web site from my home computer, make sure I haven't received any more creepy e-mails and generally don't want to talk to my dad about his problems with Mom.

'Yes, Dad. I'm going.'

'I wish you wouldn't,' he mutters.

'Well, look. If you don't want Mom dating other men, then get off your scrawny Irish butt and do something, okay? You know what she wants. You know her conditions. Make your choice, Dad. I'm hanging up now.'

I shower and dress with care, because not only will we be meeting Harry, Ryan is coming to his first official O'Neill family gathering. He picks me up at the stroke of two, gives Buttercup a tentative pat, and walks me to the car. There's a bouquet of yellow roses in the backseat.

'For your mom,' Ryan says, smiling, and I feel a rush of affection for him.

'She'll just love you, Ryan,' I say sincerely.

'I'm sure the feeling will be mutual,' he says, leaning over to kiss me. Then he starts the car and backs out of my driveway.

My mother is buzzing with energy as she yanks open the door when Ryan and I arrive.

'Hello!' she cries. 'I'm so happy to see you, Ryan! I loved your class! You're a wonderful teacher! Hello! Welcome!'

'Down, girl,' I say, leaning down the eight necessary inches to kiss her cheek.

'So nice to see you again, Mrs. O'Neill,' Ryan says, handing her the flowers.

Mom prepares to faint with joy. 'Flowers! Oh! How thoughtful! Aren't you wonderful!'

I roll my eyes. 'It smells good in here, Mom,' I say suspiciously. 'Did you have it catered?'

'Oh, Chastity! She's joking, of course, Ryan. I love to cook.' Mom zips to the stove. 'No, I've been taking a few classes, that's all.'

I glance in the oven to see a beautiful crown roast, golden and succulent. My mouth waters. 'I feel like I'm in a science fiction movie. Mom's house. Good food. So weird,' I murmur. Mom gives me a swat.

'Auntie! Wild Wild Wolves! Please! Please!'

'Hi, Sophie! Not right now, sweetheart.' I gather my niece up for a quick kiss, then set her down. 'Ryan, prepare to meet the rest of the family. Gird your loins, pal.' I lead him into the living room, where the rest of the family is crowded.

287

For a second, I see them as Ryan might . . . the tall, good-looking men, their attractive wives, the beautiful kids . . . the noise, the bickering, the shrieking, the running, the biting. Well, that's just who we are.

'Guys, let me do this all at once,' I say loudly. 'This is my boyfriend, Ryan Darling. Ryan, don't even try to get everyone's names, but here they are, my brothers, Matthew—you've already met him—there's Mark, that one's Luke, aka Lucky, and John, better known as Jack. My sisters-in-law, Sarah and Tara, also known as the Starahs, and Elaina, whom you may know from the hospital.'

'Of course,' Ryan says. Elaina gives me her Latin head-wiggle—she's already told me that she's never met Ryan personally, just seen him around and listened to the gossip on him.

'And these are my nieces and nephews,' I continue, pointing out the kids as I list them. 'Christopher, Graham, Claire, Olivia, Dylan, Sophie, Annie and Jenny. Questions? Comments? No? Good. How about a Bloody Mary?'

'Very nice to meet you all,' Ryan says rather grandly.

The Starahs descend upon Ryan, eager to screen him as my potential mate. The kids swarm me, their voices blending into one giant request. 'Auntie! Auntie! Can we play Giant Baby/Wild Wild Wolves/hide-and-seek/push me on the swings? Can we? Can we? Huh?

Please? Auntie! I'm talking to you!' I pick up Graham in one arm, Annie in the other, and nibble on their tasty little necks, causing them to squirm and giggle and demand more.

My mother joins the knot of appreciative women around Ryan, making sure everyone knows that Chastity's Boyfriend brought her roses. Jack reminds Ryan of when his chopper delivered a trauma patient to the hospital last week, and they're discussing the victim's prognosis.

The doorbell rings, and, being closest to the door, I open it. It's Trevor. And with him, Perfect Hayden.

'Holy crap,' I blurt, ever gracious. 'Per— Wow! Hayden! How are you? Hi! Come on in!'

'Hi, Chastity,' she says, smiling coolly. 'Nice to see you.' Her straight, silky blond hair is cut into interesting layers and her clothes look expensive, classic and cool . . . and small. She's a size six. Maybe a four.

'Hey, Chas,' Trevor says quietly, following her in.

The crowd grows quiet upon sighting the new arrivals. Whether she knows it or not, Perfect Hayden's in enemy territory. She dumped our Trevor, and we haven't forgiven her for breaking his valiant heart. The bitch.

But still. We're not mean people at heart, and within a few minutes, she's holding Jenny and talking to Sarah about life in Albany. She

289

glances at me, her eyes sliding away just as I force a smile.

It's so crowded in Mom's living room, and so bleeping loud, kids everywhere, Perfect Hayden right in the middle of things. 'Who wants to see *Finding Nemo?*' I ask, opening the door to the basement. The kids swarm after me like bees and drape themselves over the battered couch and LazyBoy chair that make up the seating choices down there.

'Okay, kids, there you go,' I say as the movie comes on. They don't answer, slack-jawed and hypnotized already over this movie they've all seen a dozen times. Good. I need a moment.

My eyes feel hot. My heart is roaring in my ears. I note that my hands are shaking a little.

Matt comes galumphing down the stairs. 'Hey. I'll hang out with the kids. You go up to your boyfriend.'

I force a smile. 'Sure. Thanks, Mattie.'

'You bet. The privilege of being single is that I don't have to schmooze.'

'Lucky boy,' I say. 'Hey, what's Hayden doing here? Did Trev say?' I make sure my voice stays light.

'Yeah, actually. They were hanging out this morning, I guess, and when she heard he was coming here, she asked if she could tag along. Said it would be nice to get to know us again.'

Without quite meaning to, I make a rude snorting noise.

'She's not bad, Chas,' Matt says.

'I thought he was seeing Angela,' I remind him. 'My friend. Also, I thought we hated her, since she ditched Trevor.'

'Whatever.' Matt shrugs. 'Kids, make room for Uncle Matt, okay?'

I trudge upstairs into the warm scent of pork and gravy. There's Hayden, standing oh-so-close to Trevor, holding my niece, looking quite the nuclear family. What a sweet bleeping picture, dark-haired Trev, blond Perfect Hayden and one attractive baby. Freaking adorable. Matt said they were hanging out this morning. Which means she slept over. Which means—

'I love your family,' Ryan says into my ear, making me jump.

'Great!' I say. 'Well, I told you they'd be crazy about you, too.'

Ryan smiles his perfect smile and slips me a quick kiss. I can't help but notice that Trevor is watching, and sure, it's stupid, but I turn to Ryan and kiss him back.

'Ryan!' cries my mother, bustling out of the kitchen. 'I remember you saying that you're a surgeon! How lovely! Your parents must be so proud!'

'She's using the Father Donnelly voice,' Jack comments.

'She doesn't want Chas to blow it. She's always wanted a doctor in the family,' Lucky answers.

291

I shoot my brothers a glance that promises pain and humiliation as my mother continues to babble.

'Thank you,' Ryan says. 'They're quite proud, yes.' He squeezes my hand. 'And eager to meet Chastity, of course. You've raised a wonderful daughter, Mrs. O'Neill.' Lucky makes a choking noise.

'Oh! Call me Betty!' Mom cries merrily. 'I've got to stir the gravy!' Another car pulls up in front of the house, and Mom peers out the window. Her voice drops out of the Father Donnelly range into the General Patton baritone we're more accustomed to hearing. 'Harry's here,' she announces. 'Boys. Behave. Do you understand me?' Her voice pitches up and she bustles to the kitchen door. 'Harry! Hello! Come meet my children!'

Harry Thomaston is a handsome man, shorter than my father but robust, with silver hair and dark eyes. He kisses my mother on the cheek. 'Hello everyone.'

We all shake hands and exchange pleasantries, albeit with a considerable lack of sincerity. Harry looks at my mother with adoration plain in his eyes. It doesn't feel good. None of us really believes that Mom and Dad will actually split up, despite their divorce. They're too embedded with each other. But here she is, clucking and cooing like a pigeon, fluttering about Harry in an all too cheery way.

292

Ryan knows my parents are divorced, but he doesn't know the details or personalities involved. 'Ryan Darling,' he says, shaking Harry's hand. 'I'm Chastity's significant other.'

'Lucky man,' Harry says gallantly.

I can't help but notice that Hayden is whispering into Trevor's ear and smiling. Without thinking, I slip my arm around Ryan's waist.

And so it begins. My one-sided contest of who makes a cuter couple.

My mother forces the kids to come upstairs and meet Harry. More introductions are made. Trevor swoops Dylan up in his arms, introduces him to Hayden as his godson, allows Sophie to climb on his back and mess up his hair. Clearly, Trevor is winning the 'best with children' title.

To strike back, I summon Claire. 'What do you think of my boyfriend?' I whisper loudly enough for all to hear. 'Isn't he so handsome?' Claire bursts into giggles, as I thought she would, and Ryan smiles gamely. Graham pleads with Trevor to be held, and Trev obliges. Therefore, I grab Christopher. 'Guess what, Chris? Ryan reattaches limbs for a living.'

'Awesome!' Christopher breathes with admiration.

'That's not actually true,' Ryan says. 'I'm not an orthopedist, though I assist with reattachments here and there.'

293

'He's more of a blood and guts man,' I say to my nephew. Ryan frowns. Yes, he's a little stiff around the kids. He asks Chris about school, a subject guaranteed to suck the life out of any ten-year-old. But who can blame poor Ryan? My nieces and nephews are like a school of dolphins, leaping, diving, shrieking, eating. They must be overwhelming to a man from a small, quiet family.

'They're all savages,' I whisper in Ryan's ear, having to stand on tiptoe to do it. Well, I don't really *need* to, but I do, just to reinforce the point that Ryan is taller than Trevor. I see Trev looking and take the opportunity to stroke Ryan's neck. *See? He's a great guy, good-looking and smart, and I'm crazy about him. And the feeling is mutual.* I'm well aware of my immaturity, but damn it! I can't help it. I hate Perfect Hayden. She has yet to speak to me, except for the initial required hello. I feel like slugging her.

Jack and Sarah offer to supervise the kids in the kitchen. I envy them. Today's a day I'd really like to be with the kids. It's so awkward—Ryan being so bleeping polite, Perfect Hayden flipping her well-behaved hair, another man touching my mother.

Nonetheless, I wedge myself around the table with the other adults. Mark, I notice, sits next to Elaina, who doesn't protest, shoot daggers at him or make that cool hissing noise. Ryan's next to me—he holds my chair with the

294

manners of a prince—and Perfect Hayden scoots around Tara to make sure she gets the place next to Trev. There's an awkward moment when Mom ushers Harry to the head of the table. My brothers freeze, and Harry takes the hint. 'I'll sit next to you, Betty. Matthew, here, take this seat,' he offers. I give him points for grace under pressure. Mom shoots the boys her 'I'll beat you later' glare.

'So, Harry,' I say gamely, 'Mom says you're retired?'

'I am, Chastity,' he says, turning my way with a smile. 'I recently sold my company, which made a tiny part of a computer chip. Not the most interesting work in the world to talk about, but I liked it. And now I'm trying to do more traveling.'

'Great,' I say, stifling a sigh. A rich retiree who likes to travel. Dad is really blowing it. I take a bite of the tender pork. It's fantastic. Unbelievable.

'Do you have any children?' Ryan asks.

'I have two daughters,' he says. 'Martha, who's forty-three and has a twelve-year-old son, and Greta, who's thirty-seven and has three children, two boys and a girl. And you, Ryan? Any children?'

Ryan smiles crookedly, his eyes crinkling. I believe Tara sighs. 'Not yet, Harry. But when the time comes, I'd love to have a couple.' He looks at me meaningfully. My jaw clenches. Why do I feel I've just been given a mandate for motherhood? No one else says anything for a moment.

'So!' Mom announces as she shoves a platter toward Jack. 'Trevor's here with Hayden, Chastity's got her nice doctor, and Harry is here! Isn't this nice!'

Mark rolls his eyes, and Matt smirks, but no one contradicts her.

'Harry,' Mom goes on in the vacuum of conversation, 'Hayden and Trevor were engaged once. Isn't it nice to see you two back together!'

Hayden smiles demurely. 'Thanks, Mrs. O'Neill.' My grip on my fork tightens.

'And why was it that you two broke up in the first place?' Mom asks.

'Mom! None of your business!' I blurt.

'No, that's a natural question, Mrs. O.,' Hayden says. Oh, I hate her. Trevor concentrates on his plate. 'I think the timing was just wrong, that's all.' She smiles at Trevor, who doesn't contradict her. Doesn't actually agree, but doesn't contradict, either.

My stomach aches. Angela was one thing, Perfect Hayden another thing altogether. She's not worthy of Trevor. She's had her chance. She blew it. Why is it that women like her have everything? The good guys, the smooth hair, the poreless skin, the cute little figure? Why? Huh?

Mom turns the crosshairs on Ryan next. 'And Ryan? What about your people?'

296

'Your people?' Lucky's snort turns into a grunt as Tara elbows him in the ribs.

'My parents live on Long Island,' he says. 'I have a sister who lives in the city. And I hope to introduce Chastity to them soon.' He looks at me seriously. 'Very soon.'

'I can't wait to meet them,' I say, slipping my hand onto his thigh. He smiles. I smile back. My head hurts.

'So things are serious?' my mom asks, scooping more scalloped potatoes onto her plate.

'Absolutely,' Ryan answers.

I open my mouth to say something—what, I don't know—but there's a crash in the kitchen, where the kids are eating under the not so watchful eyes of Jack and Sarah.

'I'll go see if they need help,' I offer, bolting from the table.

'What's going on?' Sarah whispers, nodding toward the dining room.

'Auntie!' the kids chorus. A blob of chewed up green bean falls out of Dylan's mouth, but he just shoves it back in, unconcerned.

'Mom's interrogating Trevor and me about our intentions,' I answer, then realizing how that sounds, backpedal furiously. 'I mean, she asked Trevor if he's serious with Hayden, and the same about Ryan and me.'

'I know what you meant.' She smiles.

'Will you eat with us, Auntie?' Olivia asks. She's now missing her two front teeth and looks cuter than ever. Plus, I get a great view of her chewed up food.

'Chastity has her special friend visiting today, honey,' Jack answers. 'And *are* you serious, Chas? He seems like a pretty good guy.'

'Gorgeous,' Sarah murmurs. 'Absolutely gorgeous.'

'Yeah. Sure. He's great,' I say. 'We're serious. Or getting there.' I pause. 'Jack, do you know him from around the hospital?'

Jack hesitates. 'Yeah, I've seen him here and there.'

'And how is he in action?'

Jack takes a sip of his beer. 'Well, you know, Chas . . . he's a surgeon. All business, not the type to be buddies with us lowly paramedics.' He raises an eyebrow. 'But if he's treating you well, then I won't care about that.'

The if-only's are trying to make themselves heard in my brain. If only Trevor . . . If only Hayden . . . If only . . . 'You guys need anything?' I ask as Claire torments Annie by showing her the contents of her mouth. 'Wine? Sedatives for the children?'

Jack shifts Jenny to his other arm and catches Christopher's glass just before it falls. 'We're fine, Chas. Thanks, kiddo.'

Without anything holding me in the kitchen, I go back to my place. Hayden murmurs something to Trevor, and he grins reluctantly, and it is with a private vengeance that I

298

scootch my chair that much closer to Ryan's.

'I know what you were doing today,' Elaina states later that night. We're sprawled in her living room, both of us disgustingly full from the unexpected feast at Mom's, both of us wearing sweats, both of us contemplating some Ben & Jerry's. Dylan is sleeping, exhausted from the cousins.

'What?' I ask.

'Give it up, Chas. I saw you watching Trevor, comparing him to Ryan, doing that lovey-dovey thing every time Hayden said boo to Trev.'

Crap. I didn't know I was so bleeping transparent. 'Oh,' I mumble.

'Let it go, Chas. That ship sailed, right? Let it go. You have a great thing going on with Ryan. Do you know how many women at the hospital would kill their grandmothers to have a chance with that guy?'

'I know, and I like him! He's great.'

'So why are you still hooked on Trevor?'

'I am not hooked on Trevor!' She snorts. 'I'm not!' I protest. 'I was, but I'm not anymore! I have a boyfriend and we're having a marvelous time, okay?'

'Right.'

I sigh, deflating. 'So what should I do, Lainey? Huh? Every time I see Trevor . . . shit. I don't even want to follow that train of thought.'

Elaina shifts in her chair. 'Yeah, yeah.

299

Maybe you could just . . .' Her voice trails off. 'You have to have a better attitude, okay? Stop looking at Ryan as second best. He's got a lot of good things about him, doesn't he? And he really likes you, Chas.'

I swallow. 'I know. He's a good guy.'

'So what is it?'

'I guess I feel like he was looking for a candidate for wife, and I sort of fit the bill.'

'Maybe you just need to spend more time together. Shift your attitude, *querida*. Trevor was your first love, but he doesn't have to be the gold standard of men.'

Except he is. Elaina reads my thoughts correctly and throws a pillow at my head. 'At least give Ryan a real chance, Chas,' she says. 'You said you thought you could love this guy, didn't you?'

'You're right, you pain in the ass. Let's hit the ice cream.'

'Sounds good.' Elaina pushes experimentally on her abdomen. 'I think I gained five pounds today. Who knew Mamí could cook like that? Fantastic.'

I go to the kitchen and return with bowls of Coffee Heath Bar Crunch topped with billows of whipped cream. Elaina takes a bite, moans and gives me the head wiggle. 'How's the sex? Is the sex good?'

I roll my eyes. 'Yes, Elaina, the sex is fine. It's very good.' Not a lie. Ryan is very pleasing in bed. Very pleasing. Jeesh, listen to me.

'Let's talk about your love life. You and Mark were quite civil today. Very unusual. So, how's it going? Any progress?'

She chews solemnly. 'Yes. And that's all I'm talking about. One of the things he brought up in counseling is that I tell you everything. Oh, and by the way, you're not supposed to know we're going to counseling.'

I smile. 'Who do you think told him to go, dummy?'

*   *   *

Lying awake in bed that night, I come to the realization that Elaina *is* right. Seeing Trevor and Hayden together again made something click into place. That ship sailed. Train left the station. Airplane has taken off. And Ryan really is a wonderful guy, despite his surgeon-arrogance thing. I'll listen with a more sincere heart when he calls, let myself be charmed by his precisely considerate, almost courtly ways. I can make things work with him. I will have a wonderful, full, happy life. I will. I already do.

CHAPTER TWENTY-FOUR

The police department's computer specialist is named, of all things, Chip. As in Computer Chip. He has evicted me from my desk and is presently combing through my files, checking to see if he can find out who hacked into my system. I haven't had any more nasty e-mails, and no one has gotten through the new firewalls. No one has further hurt my little toys, either. Right now, I wish I hadn't called the coppers, since it seems to have blown over. And because my cubicle is too small for two (unless I sit on Computer Chip's lap, which I think he'd like very much), and because Alan is using the conference room for an interview, I'm forced to work on a laptop in the reception area, directly in front of Lucia.

'Computers are such trouble,' she announces in her tight, judgmental voice. 'I don't even have one at home.'

'Teddy Bear doesn't need one?' I ask.

'Teddy and I don't live together yet,' she answers. 'We're waiting until we're married. Saving ourselves till the wedding night.'

Is that what he's telling you? I want to ask. I don't wish to picture Lucia's love life with Teddy Bear, but come on! Does she think it's normal for a man in his late thirties to be engaged for almost five years and not have sex? Come on!

'Well, I told Penelope,' she continues. 'I knew the paper shouldn't have started a Web site. "It'll stop people from buying the paper," I said.'

I roll my eyes, bite my tongue, clench my toes, but nothing works. 'That's just naive,

Lucia,' I tell her. 'We need a Web site. In ten years, there might not be a paper anymore, but there will still be a Web site.'

'You don't know that,' she says. 'We were supposed to be taking a bus to the moon by now, too.'

I open my mouth to protest, but heck, she's right. She flips open her compact and checks her man-in-the-iron-mask style makeup. Today's lipstick is a blood-red matte, which I've never once seen smeared or on her teeth. She's one of those.

As if reading my mind, she says, 'You should wear more makeup, Chastity.'

'I tend to look like a drag queen in more makeup,' I say, glancing at my watch.

'Well, I happen to think a woman should care about her appearance,' she says with a disdainful glance at my chinos, perfectly acceptable blue oxford and snazzy red high-tops. 'I happen to think a woman should look her best at all times.'

'And I happen to think you'd look a lot prettier if you chiseled off some of that Kabuki makeup and returned to the land of the living,' I return with a big fake smile. She merely gives me a pitying look and answers the phone with her trademark song. 'Eaton Falls Gaze-ette! Lucia Downs speaking!'

'I can't find anything,' Computer Chip says as he approaches me. 'Whoever did it hid his route and hid it well. With the number of hits

303

you get on the Web site, it would take weeks, possibly months, to find out. And your case isn't exactly a big priority right now.'

'But it would be if I were, say, murdered?' I ask.

'Definitely.' He grins. 'You wanna go out sometime, Chastity?'

I smile. 'Thanks, but no. I'm seeing someone.'

'And it's serious?' he asks.

'Mm-hm.'

'Too bad for me. Okay. See you around.'

'Bye, Chip,' I call.

Lucia has on her 'I stepped in fecal matter' look. 'I didn't know you were seeing someone, Chastity,' she says.

'I'm dating Ryan Darling,' I say, and for the first time, it feels great to drop his credentials. 'Do you know him? He's a doctor. Trauma surgeon. Black belt in karate. Blond hair, green eyes, six foot two, body like Matthew McConnaughey. I'm going down to the Hamptons this weekend to meet his parents. Well. Must talk to Pen. See you, Lucia.'

*   *   *

Three days later, I've never been so happy to be back home.

The trip to Long Island was a mixed bag. The bad thing . . . well, we'll get to that. The good thing: We got to see a Yankees game and they won. Oh, and our sex life has made the leap to hyperspace, and not just because I was within spitting distance of Derek Jeter (though that couldn't have hurt).

Dr. and Mrs. Darling (whom I was urged to call Dr. and Mrs. Darling) . . . well, they're the kind of people I've read about. Live in the Hamptons, golf, lunch, redecorate their sixteen-room 'cottage.' Their last vacation was spent in Brazil having 'some work done.' Both of them were quite keen on the newest laser face-lift/Botox treatment and urged me to give it a go. *Me.* Thirty-one years old, being urged by my potential in-laws to have a face-lift, twenty minutes after walking through the impressive front door. I stifled my urge to run, and tried to be open-minded.

Meanwhile, Bubbles, the much adored Chihuahua of the elder Darlings, snapped and snarled at my luggage from Mrs. Darling's arms. 'Yi! Yi! Yiyiyiyi!' he barked, the shrill noise like small-caliber bullets.

Mrs. Darling set him down, where he promptly attacked my overnight bag. 'Oh, Bubbles, you naughty wittle darling!' she said in a hideous falsetto voice as he gnawed with his batlike teeth on the handle. 'Don't you wuv Chastity? Hm? Don't you just wuv Chastity?' She scooped the angry rodent up, where he continued to snarl at me, flecks of spittle landing in Mrs. Darling's hair.

Then I was a bit surprised to find that I was

supposed to stay in a separate wing (yes, wing) from Ryan. Ryan is, after all, thirty-six years old, and one would assume that his parents wouldn't feel the need to segregate us. But they did. We had cocktails—martinis, a family tradition—then an awkward, stilted dinner. Glances of concern were exchanged over my large family, Irish surname and profession, though the word 'Columbia' brought a twitch of frozen lips to both parent faces. Mrs. Darling barely ate, which explained why she looked as bony and unappetizing as the pale and doomed Gollum.

Self-conscious of my strapping physique, I picked and nibbled as well, irritated with myself even as I did so, and tried to find neutral topics of conversation. 'So, Dr. Darling, do you—'

'Yi! Yi! Yi! Yiyiyiyi!'

'Oh, no! You naughty wittle thing!' Mrs. Darling jerked up the damask tablecloth and peered underneath. 'Chastity, don't feel bad, but Bubbles just had a wittle accident next to you. He doesn't like strangers.'

Ryan continued to eat his salmon, grinning vacantly as Mrs. Darling sent the grim-faced housekeeper in to clean up Bubbles's wittle accident.

I wasn't expecting it to be fun, exactly . . . I've met parents before, after all, but this was something else altogether. Some awkwardness is to be expected. But my jaw ached from all that smiling, and my shoulders were tight. When our endless dinner finally ended, Ryan walked me to my bedroom door, professed exhaustion and kissed me on the cheek. And I was more than happy to flop into the king-size bed and fall instantly asleep.

The next day, we drove to Yankee Stadium, sitting in traffic for an hour because rich people don't take the subway, however superior public transportation may be in getting one to the Bronx. I was wearing my Lou Gehrig T-shirt to show how old school and classy I was, and I hadn't pinstriped my face, though it is a bit of a family tradition when going to the Stadium. Our seats were twelve rows off the third-base line, and I was a little overcome with the thrill of seeing my boys up close. I may have screamed a few names out, sure. But that's normal, isn't it? Did I perhaps eat a lot of hot dogs? Well, if you think four is a lot, then yes, I did. Remember, though, I hadn't had much to eat the night before, and breakfast consisted of muffins and cappuccino, while, though delicious, is not my usual three bowls of Choco-Puffs or the lumberjack special at Minnie's Diner.

But I did have a great time at the game. It was hard not to scream out my usual encouragement, but I was on my best behavior (except when Jeter hit a line drive double in the eighth to put my boys in the lead. Needless to say, Jeter did not accept my marriage

307

proposal, but I like to think he was flattered, and I definitely know he heard me).

When we got back, we went for dinner at a high-pressure French restaurant in town, where the Darlings schmoozed with fellow Hamptonites, introducing me as 'Ryan's little friend.' Little. Honestly. I'm five foot eleven and three-quarters. I'd like some respect. Ryan smiled and chatted and held my hand, but he had taken on that zombie affect that many men get in the presence of their parents . . . distant and lifeless. I pinched him once or twice, just to make sure he was still with me, and he jumped and asked if my meal was okay. Which it was. Small, expensive, delicious, but *small*, you know?

Finally, though, Ryan snapped out of it. He thought it would be fun to sneak me into his room à la college days, giving a forbidden thrill to our nooky. I sneaked, we were doing it more or less happily (I couldn't seem to stop thinking about how hungry I was and how I might wrangle a snack), when we heard a little sound.

'Darling?' Mrs. D. crooned, tap-tap-tapping on the door with her manicured fingernails.

'Yi! Yi! Yiyiyiyi!' Bubbles. Great.

'Uh, um, hang on a second, Mother!' blurted the devoted son, hauling his now-naked, apparently illicit girlfriend out of his bed. 'Chastity, quick! Get in there!' he whispered, and if I wasn't being shoved into the closet, I'd have thought his panicked expression was kind of cute. But I *was* being shoved into the closet, along with my bra and panties—but no other clothes.

'Ryan!' I squawked.

'Be quiet! Please, Chastity!' he begged. 'I'll explain later.' He slammed the door shut.

Being as tall as I am, I couldn't stand up straight, due to the presence of a shelf that was exactly three inches shorter than I was. Thus, I had to crouch on some ancient lacrosse gear (by the feel of it), which I found a bit uncomfortable. Clenching my jaw, I now found the game of Illicit Girlfriend less than fun. I understood (sort of) Ryan not wanting to get caught in the act, but come on! Hiding me in a closet?

The sound of pants being hastily zipped was heard over the ricocheting yaps of the dog.

'Darling?' Mother called. Illicit Girlfriend wondered why Mother couldn't find a term of endearment for Devoted Son other than their mutual last name.

'Be right there, Mother!' There was a pause, then the sound of the door opening. 'Hi, Mom!'

Illicit Girlfriend heard the scrabbling of tiny toenails as Bubbles the Chihuahua rushed into room and began a frenzied yapping at the closet door. 'Yi! Yiyiyiyi!'

'Darling! I thought we'd have a chat and catch up. We think your . . . er . . . little friend

. . . is quite . . . er . . . '

'She's great, isn't she?' *Good man, Ryan,* Illicit Girlfriend thought, trying to shift so the lacrosse gear wasn't quite so intrusive.

'Yiyiyiyiyi! Yi! Yi!'

'Oh, yes,' Mrs. Darling said. 'She's quite . . . well . . . Bubbles! Stop your barking, darling! You're giving Mummy a migraine!'

The minuscule black nose of the batlike 'dog' appeared in the inch-high gap between the closet door and the parquet floor. Illicit Girlfriend tried to remain frozen and silent. Bubbles was not fooled. Snuffles and frenzied whining ensued. Then tiny black toenails began digging furiously under the door. 'Yiyiyiyi!' The minuscule, snuffling nose returned with Gestapo ruthlessness.

Girlfriend, fearful of discovery, gave said nose a shove with her big toe. A second later, tiny, razor sharp teeth had sunk into aforementioned toe. Suppressing her yelp of pain, Girlfriend jerked foot away, causing precarious balance on the aging lacrosse gear to surrender. Girlfriend fell, thudding against the wall of closet, hitting her head on old cleats, judging from the feeling of spikes in her scalp.

'Yi! Yi! Yiyiyiyi! Yi! Yiyi! '

'What was that?' Mrs. Darling asked.

'What?' Stupid Boyfriend replied, making Illicit Girlfriend wonder just what Harvard/ Yale had imparted on this supposedly brilliant

310

mind.

'What made that thumping noise?' Mrs. Darling queried.

'What thumping noise?'

'Is there something in that closet?'

'What closet?'

Due to fear of making more noise, Girlfriend remained splayed in said closet, still clutching underwear to naked bosom. Girlfriend was very aware that, should closet door be opened, her female anatomy would be quite inappropriately and widely visible.

Luckily, Bubbles, having made the transition from enraged to hysterical, now began the telltale sounds of dog vomiting.

'Roouh! Rooah! Roouh! Rooaaaaaack!'

'Oh! Oh, no! Bubbles! Ryan! Darling! Call the vet! Bubbles is sick! Darling!'

Illicit Girlfriend couldn't see the rest, but there came the sounds of rushing. Bubbles's tiny paws disappeared from the limited view provided by the crack under the door.

'Bubbles! Poor baby! You poor poor poor darling! Did you have a wittle accident?'

Over the baby talk of my hostess and the gacking of her dog, I believe I heard the words 'Be right back' from my boyfriend.

A welcome silence ensued. After a few deep breaths, I decided it was safe to take a look. With a clatter of hangers, disentangling hair from the cleats, I stood up, lingerie still clenched in my fist. Then I tried the door. It didn't open.

Running my fingertips over the doorknob, I ascertained that there was no lock, mercifully. The door was simply stuck. I gave a tentative knock. 'Ryan?' I whispered loudly. There was no answer. Sighing, I assumed that my boyfriend had enlisted the aid of the other Dr. Darling in ministering to the nasty little canine. How I missed Buttercup! She could eat that yipping rat-dog in one gulp.

I tried the door again, which resisted firmly. Gritting my teeth, I pushed again. Nothing. It was one thing to hide in a closet for five minutes—it was even possible that we'd laugh about this someday—but come on! This was getting ridiculous.

Taking a step back for some leverage, I pushed harder, ensnaring my hair on some wooden hangers. 'Crap!' I exclaimed. My back was cramped, my toe throbbed. Finally, I yanked my hair free, losing a few strands. Enough was enough, damn it! I dropped the underwear and, using the famed O'Neill shoulders, rammed the bleeping door like an enraged Brahma bull.

The door, no match for my strength, burst open. I staggered into the room, stepping right into the puddle of dog vomit, naked as the day I was born.

'Oh, there you are, Chastity,' came a voice. 'We were looking for you.'

Dr. Darling Senior stood in the doorway.

312

The blood drained from my face. I remained frozen in the puddle of vomit, horrified, dismayed, unclothed, uncovered, unshielded. 'Ryan and Mrs. Darling took Bubbles to the vet,' Dr. Darling Senior said, giving me the old once-over. 'Care for a drink?'

*   *   *

Ryan came to my room later on to check in on me. Which moves us along to the joys of post-argument sex.

See, Ryan and I hadn't had a fight yet. No, things had been really smooth for the month or so that we'd been seeing each other. There had simply been nothing to fight about. However, being shoved into a closet, abandoned and trapped, having one's potential father-in-law see one breaking down the door, buck naked . . . well, it was a pretty good fight. And let's face it . . . it was kind of fun to be fighting.

'Honey, you're exaggerating,' Ryan said calmly after I chewed him out. 'I'm sorry you're upset, but it's not like I knew the closet door would stick like that. I fail to see what I did wrong here.'

A series of enraged squeaks came out of my mouth. 'Ryan! I—naked—closet—your father!'

'My mother's dog was sick, Chastity. I had to help.' He looked so earnest that I wanted to

313

clock him one.

I took a deep breath. 'You know what, Ry? You're a jerk,' I finally managed.

'I'm not a jerk,' he protested. 'An animal was sick, Chastity. I had to help. It's in the Hippocratic oath.'

'Okay, fine! So you were nice to the dog! But the dog wasn't sick. It was hysterical because it knew I was in the bleeping closet, Ryan! Because you put me there!'

'Chastity, my parents are very strict about house rules, and I wanted to respect that—'

'By sneaking me into your room for a quicky?'

'—so I put you in the closet to avoid upsetting Mother.'

'That scares me,' I snapped.

'And then the dog was sick,' he continued, unfazed. 'I didn't know you'd be stuck. I thought you'd be fine for five minutes. Okay? No harm done.' He had the audacity to smile. 'Why don't you just take a breath and calm down?'

'Calm—calm! I won't calm down! Get out of my room!'

'Fine!' he snapped. 'Be that way!' He strode over to where I stood, still hissing, took hold of my shoulders. 'Good night!' Then he kissed me. Hard.

I looked at him for a heartbeat—the old blood was flowing, you know what I mean? Then I grabbed his hair and shoved my tongue in his mouth and then we were rolling around on the bed, then the floor, then shoving each other against the wall. It was the best sex we'd had yet.

'I'm really sorry,' he said when we were done and flushed and panting. 'I should never have put you in the closet.'

'Oh, no problem. All's forgiven.' I smiled. He smiled. Ten minutes later, we were at it again.

For the rest of the weekend, Ryan kept shooting me newly appreciative glances, slipping me a kiss when his parents weren't looking.

Then, on the way back from Long Island, I asked to drive. 'Well, this isn't a Subaru, Chastity,' Ryan lectured, glancing at me. 'This is a highly sophisticated example of superior German engineering.'

'I see. So my potato-picking Irish paws aren't equipped to hold the steering wheel of the master race?'

'Did I say anything about potato-picking Irish paws, Chastity?' he snapped. 'No. You're exaggerating. Again. But this car does require a subtle touch, if that's what you're asking.'

'Pull over!' I barked.

'Fine!' he barked back. And so, at the Malden rest stop in Saugerties, conveniently located just off Interstate 87, we had boisterous make-up sex in the highly sophisticated example of superior German

315

engineering.

And I did get to drive the rest of the way home.

Which brings us back to where I am now, lying on my bed with Buttercup, wondering if this relationship is working out or failing miserably.

CHAPTER TWENTY-FIVE

Today is my session at the Emergency Room of Eaton Falls Hospital. Without passing it, I won't pass my EMT course. Exactly what I have to do is a mystery. According to Bev, I just check in with the head nurse and do what she says. Stay out of the way and be helpful. No swearing. No hurting the already injured.

I give Rosebud a final pat and head home to shower and eat breakfast. Penelope wants me to write an article about my experiences, God help me. *Then, I dropped a bag on the broken leg of an elderly woman who was bleeding profusely* . . . I cringe. Have I gotten better, I wonder? Am I desensitizing myself? I sure as hell hope so.

I have a little time to kill before reporting to the E.R., so I take out my EMT course book. Sitting on my bed, Buttercup glued to my side, I take a deep breath. Today I may see some of the very things listed inside, not in a glossy photograph, but writhing on a gurney. It occurs to me that Ryan may be called to the E.R. while I'm there today. That he'll see me. I'd like to be at my best. I can't marry a trauma surgeon and not be able to hear about his work, can I? No.

'So how was work, honey?' I imagine saying, offering him a martini.

'Oh, some jogger was attacked by a mountain lion,' my handsome husband will say, nuzzling my neck as he gratefully accepts his martini and slides his hand along my tiny waist. 'Lots of tearing. Limbs hanging by threads. Major organ damage. It was fun.'

Instead of fainting or barfing, I will nod compassionately and ask an intelligent question . . . like . . . like . . . well, I'm feeling a little sweaty right now, but all the more reason to stick with EMT class.

I put my finger on the tab of the atlas of the course book. Very helpful, that tab, for anyone wishing to flip directly to the gruesome photos. 'Here we go,' I say to Buttercup, who does not open her odd-colored eyes. Smart dog. I have new appreciation for her after the weekend with Bubbles.

Taking a deep breath, I open the book and glance down at the first page. *Abrasion, Road. Also called road burn. See page—*

I slam the book shut, causing Buttercup to fly off the bed. 'Aaarrarrrooo!' she howls in dismay. I feel like howling myself. Crap! My stomach clenches, bile burns my throat. The photo showed a ribcage, shredded and flaked with bits of torn skin that looked like pink coconut, black bits of gravel, angry red welts, merciless scrapes . . . Okay! No need to dwell! We saw it. Let's move on.

I seem to be swallowing an awful lot, but I haven't fainted. Not even close. Just a little nausea. My hands are clammy, but that's it. Progress. 'Buttercup!' I call, my voice squeaky. 'Mommy needs you!' She returns warily, blinking suspiciously at me before clambering back onto the bed. Taking a deep breath, squaring my shoulders, I open the atlas again.

Laceration, tendons still intact. Youch! Christ! Again, I snap the book shut. Buttercup startles and blinks, her jowls quivering in disapproval as she moans. 'Can we do one more, Buttercup? Hm, Butterbaby? I think we can, don't you?'

Who do you think you're fooling? she seems to say. I tend to agree, but I open the book again.

Facial avulsion. Slam! I shove the book away from me. 'Okay! We're done, Buttercup! Lesson over.' I curl against her, sliding my arm around her tummy and scratching her chest. 'Good puppy, good puppy,' I croon. It's not enough. The image of the woman who gave new meaning to 'facial peel' is imprinted on my brain. I close my eyes and breathe through my mouth. *Baby, we were born to run.*

'Hey, Chas.' Matt stands in my doorway, just returning from work. 'What are you doing?'

'Oh, just a little, um . . . reading,' I say, opening my eyes and smiling gratefully. 'How are you, Matt? I've hardly seen you the past week or so.'

Matt sighs and comes in. He sits on the floor next to my bed. Buttercup heaves herself off and goes to him, butting her massive head against his chest.

'I was covering for Paul,' my brother says. 'Taking whatever overtime I can get.' He scratches Buttercup's neck vigorously, causing her to moan in ecstasy.

'Are you saving up for something?' I ask.

He doesn't look up, just continues petting our dog. 'I was thinking I might go back to college,' he mutters.

I shift so I can see him better. 'Wow. College. That's great, Matt. What for? Emergency management or something?'

'No,' he says, still not looking at me. 'I was thinking . . . English lit.'

I pause a little too long, apparently, because Matt suddenly pushes Buttercup down and looks at me, almost angry. 'So? What's the big deal? Can't I do something other than firefighting? Just because everyone else in this family is out there saving lives, does it mean that everyone has to?'

'Well, uh, no, Matt. I mean, I don't,' I point out.

'Yeah. Well, you're a girl.'

'Oh, that's right. I forgot.'

He glares at me, ignoring my sarcasm, looking more like Mark than the gentle Matthew. 'Matt,' I continue, 'you can do whatever you want with your life. You don't have to be a firefighter.'

'Yeah, right,' he says, daring me to disagree. 'I'm Mike O'Neill's kid and Jack and Lucky and Mark's little brother. It pretty much feels like I *do* have to be a firefighter. Can you imagine what they'd say if I became an English teacher?'

'Who cares? They'd be surprised, that's all.' I pause. 'So. An English teacher. Is that what you really want?'

'I don't know, Chas. Maybe. Shit. I wish I hadn't brought it up.' He concentrates on scratching Buttercup's left ear as she licks her chops and wags, turning so he can reach her belly, the trashy hound.

Obviously, I've felt on the outside many times in my family, but it's a bit of a revelation that Matt could feel that way, too. 'Matt,' I say carefully, 'I thought you liked being a firefighter.'

'I do,' he admits more calmly. 'Just . . . I don't know, Chas. I don't want to do this forever. That's all. Guys like Trevor and Dad—and Mark, God knows—it's like their destiny. Like they were put on Earth to do this. I don't think of it that way.'

320

I nod, tracing the satin edge of my duvet cover. 'So teaching might be your destiny?'

He shrugs, embarrassed. 'We were at the middle school in March, you know? Fire prevention and all that. And it was great. The kids were asking all these questions, and . . . well, I've been thinking about maybe becoming a teacher. I was talking to Angela about books and stuff the other day when you guys were at the firehouse, and . . .' his voice trails off ' . . . I kind of loved it,' he admits. 'Shit, Chas, don't tell anyone, okay?'

'I won't. I think it's great, Matt,' I say earnestly. 'You shouldn't feel stuck in a career when you're thirty-three years old, buddy. Going back to school would be great, however you do it. Part-time, full-time, whatever. Good for you, Matt!'

'Really?' he asks, and I love him so much just then, not because he's the most considerate of my brothers, or the closest in age, or someone who shares his food, but because he trusts me to give him a good answer.

'Really,' I say. 'But now I've got to run, buddy. Help yourself to my books.' I gesture to the long, low bookshelf that carries seven years' worth of higher education.

'I already have.' He grins.

*   *   *

I arrive at the E.R. and check in with the triage nurse, a tight-faced woman named Gabrielle Downs. She sighs dramatically when I present myself. 'Just what I need today,' she mutters. 'Fine. Stay out of the way. If I'm not totally swamped the way I am now, I'll see if I can find something for you to do.'

'Are you any relation to Lucia Downs?' I ask.

Another dramatic sigh. 'Yes. My sister.'

Of course. Melodrama like this can only come through genetics. 'I work with Lucia at the *Eaton Falls Gazette*.'

Gabrielle raises an eyebrow disdainfully. 'Where she's the receptionist?'

There is such contempt dripping from that word that I can't help feeling defensive of Lucia, however much she doesn't deserve it. 'Lucia is much more than the receptionist,' I return coolly. 'The paper wouldn't run without her.'

'So she tells me every single time I talk to her.'

Gabrielle walks away, leaving me to wonder just what I'm supposed to do. Well, no harm in looking around, I suppose. In the first curtained-off area, optimistically named Evaluation Room 1, an elderly man is sleeping. In the second, a little boy, about seven, is sniffling on the bed, his mom sitting next to him, holding his hand. There's a nearly palpable bond between them, and an unexpected wave of maternal envy and admiration surges through me.

'Hi,' I say, smiling.

'Hi,' the mom answers. 'Are you the doctor?'

'No. I'm an EMT,' I say. 'Well, I'm becoming an EMT. Can I ask your son a few questions?'

'Sure,' the mom says. 'He has a really bad sore throat.'

And clearly, no health insurance, or they'd be at the pediatrician's right now, instead of forced to spend half the day or more here. 'Sorry to hear that, buddy,' I say. 'You feel yucky?'

The boy's name is Nate, he tells me, he's six and three-quarters years old and wants to be a firefighter when he grows up. Perfect. I tell him about my brothers and dad, smiling as his eyes grow wide with awe. 'Do you like the Yankees?' I ask.

'Of course,' he answers, swallowing with a grimace.

'I got to go to a game last week,' I tell him. 'They won. Who's your favorite player?'

We chat amiably until a nurse (not Lucia's sister) comes in to do a strep test, and I'm shooed out of the cubicle.

'Bye, pal,' I say. He waves and smiles, then gags as the nurse sticks a swab in his throat for a culture.

'Thanks. You really helped pass the time,' the mom says.

323

Flushed with pride, I turn away and bump squarely into Ryan Darling, trauma surgeon.

'Uh-oh,' I say. There's only one reason Ryan would be here.

'Hello, Chastity,' he says. 'What are you doing here?'

'It's my E.R. day, remember?' I answer.

'Oh, of course. How's it going?' He smiles, causing a nearby conversation to halt. Imagining that they're admiring my extremely handsome boyfriend, I smile back.

'It's going okay, Ryan,' I say. 'I just got started, really. I don't think I get to do anything much. What about you? Are you here on a consult?'

'Just waiting for the ambulance,' he says nonchalantly. 'Bike versus motorcycle. Possible splenic rupture. Stick around. You can see me in action. When I'm called down, the excitement starts.' One of the orderlies overhears and rolls his eyes.

I raise an eyebrow. 'How humble you are, dear,' I murmur. He shrugs as if to say, *Can't help it if it's true.* 'Anyway,' I continue, 'I'm not sure if I'm supposed to hang around watching trauma surgeons.'

'Oh, if I say you can, you can.' He smiles reassuringly, but I cringe inwardly, for two reasons. One, I don't want to see someone who's really hurt. My palms are already slick. Second, Ryan is being really arrogant, even for a surgeon.

'Well?' he asks.

'Um . . . sure,' I mutter.

'Great!' Ryan turns to Gabrielle, who is approaching with a clipboard. 'Nurse, where the hell is that ambulance? I was paged five minutes ago and they're not even here. I have better things to do than come down here and watch paint dry.'

'Yes, Doctor. I'm sorry.' Gabrielle shoots me a resentful look.

'You'd better get it through your head that a surgeon doesn't have time to burn. I'm not some baby catcher, you know.'

Gabrielle bows her head and scurries away.

'Jesus, Ryan. That was harsh, don't you think?' I ask Ryan in consternation.

He grunts. 'It's all true, Chastity. And there are some people you have to deal with in a certain way if you want to get results. It's just part of the job.'

Another doctor approaches Ryan, describing something about the case in medical shorthand. Ryan gives a slight nod, but doesn't say anything else. Several other staff members are wheeling carts and bustling around in anticipation for this case. My knees buzz with adrenaline and fear.

Just then, the doors to the trauma bay burst open. A gurney is wheeled in, the patient so covered that I can't even tell if it's a man or a woman. Bev Ludevoorsk is the EMT on duty. She's running alongside the gurney, holding an

IV bag.

'Thirty-four-year-old male bicyclist, hit by motorcyclist. Helmeted. A and O on the scene, but fading fast en route. Abdominal pain, right upper quadrant. Breath sounds equal. Road burn on arms and legs, possible broken collarbone and facial fracture. On insulin for Type I diabetes.'

Her voice is its usual brisk, all-business tone. To my untrained eye, it seems like she's done a fantastic job. Ryan doesn't even look at her, just strides over to the patient's side. He palpates the guy's abdomen, causing the guy to scream in pain. Unfazed, Ryan makes his pronouncement. 'CT scan and chest X-rays, stat. Type and cross, and start four units. Call the OR. It's the spleen, all right.' He whips out his stethoscope and listens to the patient's chest. 'Possible punctured lung. Breath sounds are *not* equal. Call Pulmonology.'

Then the patient is being moved again, literally run down the hall, Ryan following behind.

'Hey, there, O'Neill,' Bev booms, slapping my shoulder. 'Your shift?'

'Hi, Bev,' I answer. 'That was great! You were amazing!'

'Well, thanks, kid. How's it going? Was that doctor chewing you out? He's a prick, that one. Stay out of his way if you see him again.'

'Um . . . well, okay, I will. But he's my boyfriend.'

326

Bev's grimace is comical. 'Shit! Sorry!'

I laugh. 'That's okay, Bev. I guess he's a different person in the hospital, because he's really sweet, actually.'

'Hard to believe, O'Neill, hard to believe. Hey, here come paramedics from the fire department. They'll have the motorcyclist from this accident. Isn't that your brother?'

The Eaton Falls Fire Department ambulance pulls up outside the doors. Another patient is unloaded, but not by my brother. By Trevor. He's laughing, talking to the patient, who clearly isn't that bad off.

'Hey, Chas,' he says, his eyebrows rising in surprise. But he doesn't stop, just helps Jake wheel the patient into a treatment area.

Gabrielle appears at my side. 'If you need to do something, go take that guy's blood pressure, and then I'll have to do it again to make sure you did it right. Okay? God, I hate these stupid EMT days.'

'Thank you,' I say sweetly. 'See you, Bev.' I go to the cubicle where the motorcyclist was just taken.

'What's up, Chastity?' Jake asks, giving me his customary once-over.

'Hey, guys. Um . . . well, I'm doing a shift here. I'm in an EMT class. Hi,' I say to the patient. He's about sixty, five foot nine, with a grizzled beard and bald head. His left arm is in a splint. 'I'm Chastity. Can I practice on you?'

'You can do whatever you want on me,' the

327

man says, grinning to reveal gold-capped teeth.

'A little respect, Jeff,' Trevor says. 'She's one of ours.'

'Cool,' the guy says with a lecherous wiggle of his eyebrows.

'So what happened here?' I ask.

Jeff tells me about how the bicyclist veered out from behind a parked car and how they both went ass over handlebars. 'I think I broke my arm,' he says, frowning.

'Oh, you broke you arm, all right,' Trevor says. 'Compound fracture, pal.'

'Which means I'm one brave sonofabitch,' Jeff comments.

I smile and take his blood pressure on the good arm. The wounded arm is packed with ice, and if Jeff is a little pale, he does seem quite brave.

'Could you bend a little lower so I can see down your shirt, honey?' he asks.

'Is it all right if I smack him, Trev?' I ask.

'Of course,' Trevor answers. Jeff smiles and I grin back. Jake checks messages on his cell phone.

'One-sixty-three over ninety,' I announce. 'But that might be from the pain. Do you have a history of high blood pressure, Jeff?'

'Only when I'm looking down your shirt, honey,' he answers. We all laugh, just as Gabrielle bustles up.

'What's going on here? Chastity, flirting with the patients is something you can do on your own time. In the E.R., we don't have time for things like that! Did you even manage to do what you were told?'

'Hi, Gabby,' Trevor says.

She melts. 'Trevor! I didn't see you! What are you doing here? How are you?'

'Just bringing in a patient,' he says. 'I see you know my friend Chastity.'

She shoots me a suspicious glare, looking so much like Lucia that it's spooky. 'Yes. Well? What's his BP?'

'One-sixty-three over ninety,' I say.

'And his temperature?'

'Um . . . I didn't take that,' I answer.

'Why?'

'Because you didn't tell me to?' I suggest.

She sighs. 'Oh, this is such a waste of time.' She bustles to the cabinet, whips out one of those little paper strips that pass as thermometers and sticks it under Jeff's tongue. I notice that he doesn't flirt with her. Instead, he makes a pained face and looks at me for sympathy. Then Gabby takes his blood pressure. 'One-sixty-two over ninety-one,' she announces. Rather brusquely, she whips off the ice pack and looks at Jeff's arm. It's swollen and clearly deformed, an odd lump sticking up between his wrist and elbow. My mouth goes instantly dry, my legs are tapioca, my vision starts that graying thing it does so well.

If I faint now, I'm done. I'll fail my class. I

329

swallow, take a small step back and hit something solid. Trevor.

'Hang in there, Chas.' His voice is so low that I can barely hear it, but there's warmth there, and reassurance. He knows. He thinks I can make it. I take a deep breath and stand a little straighter.

'Fuck me, woman!' Jeff yelps. I blink. Gabrielle is feeling his arm, not tenderly, then slaps the ice pack back on.

'Broken!' she crows. 'I'll schedule an X-ray.' With that, she leaves a considerably grayer Jeff lying on the bed.

'You okay, Jeff?' I ask, feeling less than well myself.

'Yeah,' he says. 'Show me a little cleavage and I'll be as good as new.'

I pat his leg instead.

'Higher, please,' he says with a wink.

'Jake, finish the report, okay?' Trevor asks.

'Sure,' Jake answers agreeably. 'See you, Chastity.'

An orderly comes in and goes to the head of Jeff's gurney. 'How'd you like to take a ride, my friend?' he asks.

'Thanks for everything, sweetheart,' Jeff calls as he's wheeled away.

'It was nothing,' I answer truthfully. But it feels good, anyway.

'So you're taking the EMT class?' Trevor asks, adjusting something on his belt.

I look at him straight in the face for the first

time today. His hair is rumpled, as ever, and eyes are smiling a little.

'Yes,' I answer quietly. 'I'm trying to get the blood phobia under control.'

'How's it going?'

I shrug. 'Not too great. You can see that I almost passed out there.'

'A lot of people would have done the same, Chas.'

'Yes, my child, but not an O'Neill,' I say, heavy on the grandiosity.

'Not everyone is good at this kind of thing. Doesn't mean you're not . . . gifted . . . in other ways.' He smiles.

'Thanks. I think. Listen, Trev, I'd appreciate it if you and Jake didn't say anything to the boys or my dad.'

'Sure,' he says. 'Well, you know Jake's not the sharpest knife in the drawer, but I'll see what I can do.'

'Thanks, buddy.' I pause, then glance out to the nurse's station. Gabrielle is busily writing something on a chart. 'Trevor, are you and Hayden back together?'

Trev's gaze drops to the floor. With every second that he doesn't answer, my heart sinks lower. 'We're . . . we're spending time together.'

'Cheesy answer,' I comment lightly.

He shrugs. 'I don't know, Chas. Sometimes . . .' He shakes his head. 'I gotta run. Good luck here. You want me to put in a good word with Gabby?'

'No, that's okay. I'll sink or swim on my own.'

To my surprise, he leans in and kisses my cheek. 'You'll swim. See you around.'

And then he's gone. A nurse or tech of some kind leans out to check out his ass.

The rest of my day is uneventful. I take sixteen more blood pressures, eleven temperatures, apply ice to a swollen finger and watch as Gabrielle must cut off a wedding ring. I wheel four people in for X-rays and chat with a few not-too-sick people. When my shift is done, I find Gabrielle.

'I guess I'm done, Gabby,' I say.

'Fine! So? What's keeping you?'

'Would you mind signing my form?'

'Fine, fine, fine. Like I don't have a million other things to do.' She signs and hands it back to me.

'Does this mean I pass?' I ask.

'Yes! You passed. Okay? You didn't screw up that badly, so congratulations. Now do you mind? I have work to do.'

'Thank you,' I say, my heart lifting. I passed!

I stop in the lobby and use an in-house phone to call the surgical floor, wanting to share my news with someone. 'I'm sorry, Dr. Darling is in surgery,' says the person who answers.

'No problem,' I say.

'Are you a patient or a family member?' she

332

asks.

'Nope,' I answer. 'I'm his girlfriend.'

'Really?' she says. 'I wasn't aware that he had one. Well, good luck to you, hon.' And she hangs up.

CHAPTER TWENTY-SIX

'Where's Lucia?' Angela asks. 'I didn't think cyborgs missed work.'

'I do not know, Miss Davies, but I did get you a present.' I've become so fond of Angela . . . she's quietly funny, consistently good at her job, and always seems open to doing something after work. Just last weekend, when Ryan had to cancel due to an emergency surgery (branch versus bowel), she came over and we watched *Return of the King,* both of us commenting on the sexist slant of the movie as we ogled the men. Now, I reach in my desk and hand her a bumper sticker.

' "What Would Aragorn Do?" I love it!' she cries. 'Where do you find these?'

'She spends way too much time on geek sites on the Internet, right Chas?' Pete from advertising says, taking a bite of a bagel.

'That's right, Pete. Hey, do you know where Lucia is? Are we having the staff meeting without her?'

'That would be a first,' Pete comments,

turning on his computer.

'Chastity? I need to see you, please,' Penelope calls, sticking her head out of her office.

Oh, crap. This can't be good. Alan is already seated, and both their faces are grave. My heart bucks—has someone broken through my firewalls? More porn on the Web site? Am I about to be fired?

'Hi,' I say tentatively.

'Have a seat, Chastity,' Penelope says. I glance at Alan, who stares at the floor.

'What's going on?' I ask, my heart thudding with dread.

'Look at this,' Pen says, shoving a piece of paper at me.

It's the police blotter, the report of crimes committed over the past week. The *Eaton Falls Gazette* runs it regularly; it's public information, after all, and a guilty pleasure for people to check out the misadventures of their fellow citizens. I scan it, but nothing leaps out. I'm relieved. I thought maybe there was something about an O'Neill in there.

'Fourth one down,' Alan mutters.

I look. *Theodore Everly, 42, solicitation of a prostitute.* 'Who's Theodore—oh. Oh, crap.'

'Teddy Bear,' Alan confirms.

'Oh, crap,' I repeat.

'A male prostitute,' Penelope whispers.

My heart sinks. 'Poor Lucia. No wonder she's not in.'

'The question is, should we run it?' Penelope asks both Alan and me. 'It *is* public record. We've never edited the police blotter before, but . . . '

'It's really your call, Alan,' I say, gratefully passing the buck. 'Crap. I don't know.'

'Great,' Alan says. He makes a face at me, flashing the tooth, but I've grown used to it and it barely freaks me out anymore.

At that moment, the door opens, and Lucia sticks her head in, her face its usual funeral mask of makeup. Her eyes are red. 'Staff meeting in ten,' she announces.

'Lucia! Hi! How are you?' Penelope stands up. 'Come in! Sit down! Um, uh, would you like coffee?'

Lucia enters, and with four of us in Pen's cramped office, I'm close enough to get a contact high off Lucia's hairspray and perfume. I get out of my chair and offer it to her. 'Have a seat, Lucia,' I say. She narrows her eyes at me and remains standing. Penelope and Alan exchange an uneasy glance. Alan begins.

'Um, Lucia, are you aware that . . . see, this morning's police blot—'

'Am I aware that my fiancé was arrested for buying sex from a man? Yes, Alan, I'm aware.'

Okay, well, that settles the question of if she knew. 'We were just discussing whether or not to—' Pen starts.

'Run it. I don't care. It's not my problem, is

it?'

'Lucia,' Penelope says gently, 'we're all really sorry about this.'

'Save it, okay?' Lucia snaps. 'Are we having a staff meeting or not?'

'Um, yes, sure, we will. Sure. Okay.' Penelope tips her head to one side. 'Lu, are you sure you don't want to take the day off or anything?'

'Why? So I can sell my wedding dress on eBay?'

Pen takes a deep breath. 'Okay. Staff meeting in ten.'

Lucia turns a hateful glare on me. 'Chastity, can I see you privately?'

'Um, sure,' I say.

'Use my office,' Pen says, leaping for the door. 'Alan, let's discuss the story on the garbage strike, okay?'

They abandon me with breathtaking speed. 'I'm sorry for your . . . situation, Lucia,' I say tentatively.

'You knew, didn't you?' she hisses. 'You knew Teddy Bear was gay.'

My face grows hot. 'Well, you know, I—I don't really know Teddy Bear, so—'

'He said you saw him! When he was with a man one night. You rode your bike right past them!'

I run a hand through my hair. 'Yeah. I did.'

'Could you tell? That he was, you know . . . gay?'

336

I wince. 'Well . . . I . . . it looked kind of . . . romantic.'

'And you didn't say anything? I can't believe that, Chastity!'

'Look, Lucia,' I say in what I hope is a calming voice. 'I suspected. That was all. I don't really know you that well.'

'So you just let me go on being engaged to a fag.' She jams her fists into her hips, shaking with rage.

'It's always been my feeling that it wasn't my place to—' I attempt.

'No, Chastity! You've always hated me! Because I was engaged! And you never were, okay? And I know everything about this paper! And you're, like, some hulking Amazon from Columbia who thought you knew everything, and you made me look like a fucking idiot!'

'Okay, shut up, Lucia!' I snap back. 'I'm sorry this happened to you, but if you didn't know Teddy Bear was gay, that's because you didn't want to. Every single person at this paper knew. You wanted to be blind and you were. This has nothing to do with me.'

Her face goes white. 'What do you mean, everyone knew?' she whispers, horrified. Then, without waiting for an answer, she yanks open Penelope's door. 'Did everyone here know that Teddy Bear was gay?' she shrieks.

There's a dreadful silence. Angela, Penelope, Carl, Alan, Pete, Danielle in layout, Suki the reporter . . . They all stand there, guilt

337

and knowledge and sympathy written clearly on their faces.

Blotches of red appear on Lucia's pasty face. 'I quit.'

And with that, Lucia storms out of the office, slamming the door behind her.

We slink back to our desks. 'Staff meeting is rescheduled,' Penelope calls before closing herself in her office. As I click numbly through my e-mails, Angela slips over to me. 'How are you doing, Chastity?'

'Yick,' I reply.

'I know.' She smiles sympathetically. 'So why was she mad at you, in particular?'

'I saw Teddy Bear with a man, and I didn't tell her,' I confess.

'I wouldn't have, either.' She smiles kindly.

'Hey, Angela,' I say abruptly. 'Trevor told me you guys broke up.'

She flushes. 'Yeah. Well, we never exactly got together. He's so sweet and all that, but I don't think he was ever interested in me, to be honest. Nothing really there, if you know what I mean.'

The rest of the day passes slowly. Everyone is thinking about Lucia, yet no one wants to talk about it. Just before it's time to go, Penelope calls me into her office again.

'What do you know about peripheral vascular disease?' she asks, stretching out her hands in front of her.

'Very little,' I say.

338

'Do my hands look weird to you?'

'Maybe a little moisturizer, Pen. Otherwise, they look fine.'

'Okay, okay, I'm a hypochondriac. Listen, a little good news. Remember that piece you did on James Fennimore Cooper?'

Of course I remember. It was the one I slapped together the night I kneed Ryan at self-defense class. I pull a face. 'Yes, I do. Sorry again.'

Pen laughs. 'Listen to this.' She pulls out a piece of paper. 'Dear Ms. Constanopolous, we are pleased to inform you that Chastity O'Neill's article "The Cooper Effect—The Influence of America's First Novelist on Today's Fiction" has won first prize, blah blah blah, yadda yadda.' Penelope grins. 'Ceremony. Dinner. Five thousand dollars. For you, Chastity.'

My mouth drops open. 'Five grand?'

'Yes. Congratulations!'

'Five grand? Holy crap! This means a new furnace!' I take the proffered letter and read it myself, feeling a warm flush of pleasure travel up my neck. 'Did you enter this, Penelope?' I ask.

'Nope. Apparently, this foundation scans for articles written on great Americans, and they loved what you wrote. I had no idea.' She beams like a proud parent. 'Now don't get any ideas about going to work for the *Times*, young lady,' she warns.

'I won't,' I say, smiling.

'Seriously, Chastity. Are you happy here?'

I look up from the letter. 'Yes! Absolutely.'

'If you need room to stretch, we'll give you a column, shift responsibilities around, whatever you want. Just say the word, okay?'

'Thank you, Penelope,' I say. 'Wow. I'll keep that in mind.'

'Can I buy you a celebratory drink?'

My smile drops. 'Maybe another time. With Lucia and all, I just don't feel right about it.'

She nods. 'Sure. Good form. Okay, I'm leaving. See you tomorrow. Congratulations again.'

I'm tempted to call my brothers and parents and tell them my news, but that doesn't feel right, either. I call Ryan's cell, but it clicks immediately over to voice mail. I hang up without leaving a message. Feeling a little deflated, I leave the paper and head for home.

'Guess what, Buttercup?' I tell my dog as she pins me against the wall. 'Mommy won an award.' She slobbers in admiration, and I kiss her head. 'Thank you.'

I heat up a Stouffer's pizza, reading the nutrition panel on the side. Yikes. Angela recently offered to teach me to cook—she's doing an adult-ed class on easy French classics. Ryan mentioned last week that he wanted to have some people over for dinner, and did I think I could cook for eight or ten? When I was done laughing, he grudgingly said he'd call a caterer. I'm sure he'd approve of me learning to whip up a little coq au vin and crème brûlée.

I check the *Eaton Falls Gazette* Web site for naughty pictures and, finding none, heave a sigh of relief. Then I Google an address, clip the leash on Buttercup and head for the south end of town.

Lucia's house is even smaller than mine, a snug little place on a tree-lined street. There's only Lucia's car in the driveway, and I don't hear any noise coming from the open windows. Climbing the front steps, I knock and wait, then knock again. Buttercup flops down, exhausted. Finally, I hear the sound of footsteps. There's a pause.

'Go away, Chastity,' comes Lucia's voice.

'Nah,' I reply. 'Come on. Open up.'

'No. Just go away.'

'I'm perfectly capable of kicking in this door, you know,' I say. 'Or I might just lean on the buzzer and drive you insane.'

'I'll call the police,' she says.

'Really?' I ask.

The door opens. 'Probably not,' she admits. Her face is dull, her hair flat. Without makeup, she looks different . . . softer and definitely younger. I remember that we're about the same age, though she always strikes me as older. She's wearing pink silky pajamas, and the TV is on Mute in the background. Where are her friends, parents, sisters, brothers, dog, whatever? Where is that bitchy sister of hers

341

from the E.R. ? Why is she here alone on the worst night of her life?

'I'm so sorry,' I say, and without thinking, I put my arms around her and kiss her cheek. 'What a shitty, shitty thing to have to deal with.'

Lucia bursts into tears.

'It's okay, hon,' I say. 'It'll be okay.'

'That dog is the ugliest thing I've ever seen.' She sobs.

'Shh,' I murmur. 'You'll hurt her feelings. Can she come in?'

'Sure.'

Fifteen minutes later, Buttercup is belly-up in front of Lucia's fireplace, jowls sagging to the floor, ears spread out, paws frozen in the air. She looks like roadkill. Lu herself doesn't look much better, but I poured her a glass of wine and found a tissue box (in one of those little crocheted tissue-box-holder thingies).

'Have you talked to him?' I ask.

'Oh, of course.' She sniffles. 'He says he loves me but he can't help the way he is.' Her chest hitches as she stifles the tears.

'Have you told your family?'

She nods. 'They all suspected. Just like you.'

I bite my knuckle. I wonder if her sister or mother or whomever had ever taken her aside and asked about Teddy Bear. I know I would have, had she been in my family. 'I wish I'd said something, Lu. I just figured it wasn't my place.'

She blows her nose, then drains her wine. 'I probably would have taken your head off,' she admits. She stares sightlessly in front of her. 'I can't believe I was so dumb.' Her voice cracks.

'Oh, Lu,' I say, leaning over to pat her hand. 'We're all blind when it comes to the people we love.'

'Really?' she snaps. 'Does your doctor have a boyfriend on the side?'

'Not that I know of,' I answer. 'But you know how it is. We all shape people in our minds, one way or another.' Lucia nods. 'I'm sure I'm shaping Ryan to be . . . well. Let's not talk about me. This is your special night.'

She snorts, smiling reluctantly. 'Chastity—' She breaks off, biting her acrylic talon of a fingernail.

'Yeah?'

She looks at her lap. 'Teddy Bear was the one who put those pictures on the Web site,' she mumbles.

My mouth falls open.

'And he broke your Aragorn doll, too.'

'Why?'

'I didn't know about it!' Lucia snaps defensively. 'He just told me today. He said it was because he knew I hated you—'

'Gosh, thanks.'

'—and he wanted to make you look bad and maybe get fired so I could get your job. Because he thought I deserved it.' She swallows repeatedly, her eyes full once again.

I sigh. 'Wow.'

'Are you going to tell?' she asks, chewing her nail yet again.

'Do you want me to?' I say.

'I think he's probably suffering enough,' she whispers, the tears spilling down her cheeks.

'Okay, then. I won't say anything. It's good to know I don't have a stalker.'

'I'm sorry,' she whispers.

'It's not your fault,' I say, handing her another tissue.

'You know what, Chastity?' Lucia says, blowing her nose loudly. 'I thought you were such a bitch, but you're really not that bad.'

I can't help laughing. 'Thanks, Lu. Right back at you.'

CHAPTER TWENTY-SEVEN

I lean my head against the cool window of Ryan's Mercedes to ease its throbbing. We're headed back to his place. It's raining that soothing June rain that thrums on the car roof and against the windows. I wish we could drive all night.

'I thought that went well,' Ryan says, turning into his reserved parking place.

'Did you?' I ask, getting out of the car before he can open the door for me. 'I thought it was torture.'

344

We've just had dinner with my mother and Harry. I'm starting to worry about that.

Or maybe not. Maybe Mom just wants me to run to Dad. *Hey, Dad. Mom seems really fond of that Harry . . . better get off your ass and do something.* Maybe I should. I wonder how far Mom is going to take this Mexican standoff. Surely not much longer, because I can't imagine her letting Harry think there's actual potential there. Plus—

'What are you doing this weekend?' Ryan asks, taking out his keys and unlocking the door.

'Hm? Oh, sorry. It's my practical exam. If I pass it, I'm free and clear and an EMT.'

'I see. And it's an all-day test?' he asks.

'Yes. Saturday.' I force a smile. It's not his fault I'm feeling glum. It's not just my mom and Harry . . . it's the stupid EMT thing.

I aced my written test . . . multiple choice, come on. But the practical is the hard part, consisting of eight or so stations, each one presenting a different aspect of emergency care—cardiac arrest, poisoning, immobilization, bleeding control, shock. Volunteers will be faking a variety of injuries, from broken legs to childbirth. Chances are, I'll pass. Fake blood has not yet freaked me out, and I'm a good student. But what then? I wonder. Will I actually be able to take this knowledge and translate it to somehow being helpful?

Last week, the *Eaton Falls Gazette* did a

story about a kid who was stung by a bee at school. The kid had never had an allergic reaction before, and when he felt odd, he went to the bathroom, where he collapsed, all alone. By some miracle, another kid came upon him. This second boy had a peanut allergy. He saw the first boy's bluish face, and without waiting for direction, he yanked out his Epi-Pen and stuck it in the other kid's thigh, calling for help while he did it. Five minutes later, the bee-stung boy was sitting up, dazed and alive. The heroic little boy was modest. 'It's lucky I have a peanut allergy,' he told the cops. 'Good thing, huh?'

Then CNN carried the story of the lady who lifted the tree branch off her husband. That branch weighed almost eight hundred pounds. 'I couldn't just let him lie there,' she'd said. 'Though it was tempting.'

Ryan takes my raincoat—the manners of a prince, this guy—and goes into the kitchen. I hear the squeak of the cork and the glugging of wine as he pours.

'So, honestly, Chastity,' he says, coming in and sitting next to me on the couch. He hands me a glass of wine. 'Why are you taking this class? You don't want to be an EMT, do you?'

I take a sip of my wine. 'I don't know. I guess I'm hoping to . . . I don't know. Join the ranks of my heroic brothers. Live up to the O'Neill legacy.'

'And what is the O'Neill legacy?'

I turn disbelieving eyes on him. He gazes back innocently, waiting. 'Well, Ryan, you've been to my house. You've been to my mother's house. Didn't you see all those newspaper articles in the hall? All those pictures of my various brothers with various mayors and victims and all that? Jack has a Congressional Medal of Honor! Mark saved a kitty-cat! Trevor pulled a little girl from the river! My father alone has—'

'Okay, okay, sorry. Calm down. There's no need to yell.'

I chug Ryan's expensive pinot whatever. 'I'm calm, Ryan. I'm just surprised you hadn't noticed.'

'Obviously I knew they work in emergency services,' he says, his voice taking on that Ivy League drawl. 'I wasn't aware that they had a legacy.' He pauses. 'Jack has the Medal of Honor?'

'Yes! Which I told you on our second date. How can you forget the Medal of Honor? There's only, like, thirty-five hundred of them ever given!' Ryan continues to look blank. 'The stranded unit? Jack's helicopter? The guy with the shattered leg? Enemy fire? Afghanistan? Carrying a Marine for a mile and a half? Sound familiar?'

'Yes, now that you mention it.' He takes a wine-snobby sip of his drink, then eyeballs me again. 'So you feel that becoming an EMT will somehow elevate you to hero status?'

My mouth drops open. 'Harsh, Ryan!'

'I hate to be the one to point it out to you, but an EMT is barely a blip on the screen in the medical world.' His voice drips contempt.

Just before I'm about to slug him, it clicks. 'Are you trying to start a fight?' I ask.

He blinks. 'Um . . . well, yes,' he murmurs.

'That was really mean, Ryan.'

'Sorry. It's just . . . you know. Fighting's kind of . . . stimulating.' He grins.

I sigh. 'Ryan, maybe we . . . well, maybe it would be nice if things could be just as . . . passionate? . . . without us fighting.'

He doesn't answer for a minute. 'Right.'

He sounds so dejected that I close my eyes. 'But, sure, it is fun.'

'Oh, it's great,' he agrees instantly. 'And it does clear the air.' He reaches out and strokes my earlobe. 'I'm sorry, Chastity. Didn't mean to offend you.'

Though I wonder how that comment could be interpreted as anything but offensive, I pat his leg and forgive him. A half an hour later, we're in bed, cuddled together after twenty minutes of pretty good sex. Back to meat loaf. Too bad.

'I love you,' Ryan mutters, his voice slow with sleep.

I pause. 'Sleep tight,' I whisper.

When I'm sure that Ryan is fully asleep, I slip out of bed, grab his robe and go into the living room. In my purse, I have an emergency six pack . . . of Oreos, that is, the kind that moms put in their kids' lunchboxes. Sitting on the leather couch, the rain streaming down the sliding glass doors, I rip open the package and inhale appreciatively—is there anything that smells better than fresh Oreos? I pop one in my mouth and chew and stare and think.

Ryan has a lot of good qualities. Truthfully, I've never had a relationship quite like ours— when the guy calls when he says he will, where we have dinners and meet each other's families, talk almost every night. *Fellowship of the Ring* is one of his favorite movies. We both like to run. Honestly, I enjoy myself with Ryan. I might even love him.

Just not the way I want to. He's not the love of my life.

Only once did I feel the certainty that I was with The One. I haven't let myself think about that in a long time, not fully, because after all, it's pointless to rehash a seventy-two-hour love affair. But here in the dark, the rain beating against the roof, I can't dodge the fact that I've never loved anyone the way I loved Trevor.

When Trevor and I kissed, I felt hot and shaky and weak and strong at the same time. When he touched me, there was not just a tingle, there was a jolt. There was no meat loaf, no sir. Gourmet all the way.

For that short time, it felt like my heart had locked into the place where it was meant to be. There was that pulse of perfection, two pieces

349

fused together so it seemed that there was only one. My heart had fit with Trevor's like that.

I think back to our breakup under the chestnut tree. I think of the summer he brought Perfect Hayden home. The years that have passed without him ever indicating anything but fraternal affection for me. So much for hearts fitting.

CHAPTER TWENTY-EIGHT

Two days later, I pass my practical and become a licensed emergency medical technician. To my surprise, Jack was one of the instructors at the test, and word quickly spread throughout the realm that Chastity had aced her test. Now there is great rejoicing in the land, or at least in Emo's.

'To Lou Gehrig, pride of the Yankees,' Dad says, honoring the tradition of toasting St. Lou before anyone else. 'And to my daughter, Chastity. Good job, Porkchop.'

'To the Porkchop,' my brothers echo.

'Thanks, Daddy. Thanks, everyone.' I grin. This little impromptu party is quite a thrill. We take up two tables and our usual booth. Dad's platoon and all my brothers are here, as well as Elaina and the Starahs. And Trevor, who actually was supposed to work but arranged a swap so he could be here. He catches me looking at him and smiles. I smile back, then, feeling guilty, glance toward the door to see if Ryan has appeared. Unfortunately, one of his patients had some postoperative complications, and he's running late.

Dad, Mark, Lucky and Matt wander off to shoot some pool. Elaina is on her cell phone, talking to the babysitter. Jake and Santo go to watch the Mets game. Soon, just Jack, Sarah, Trevor and I are sitting in the Gehrig booth.

'So, Chas, what's next? Paramedic school?' Jack asks, gazing at his wife. He reaches out and strokes her cheek. Sarah closes her eyes like a cat, practically purring. The two years Jack spent in Afghanistan made them even more in love, and I smile, touched that Jack is still so smitten by his wife.

'No paramedic school, Jack,' I answer. 'I don't really know what I'm going to do with this. I'm still not really a natural. Passing the test was kind of easy, but in the real world . . .' My voice trails off.

'You'd be great,' Trevor reassures me.

'You're a loyal man, Trevor Meade,' I tell him. He grins. 'So, Sarah,' I continue, 'how are you these days?'

'Not bad, considering,' she answers. 'Jack, do you want to tell her?'

Jack straightens up and smiles. 'We're expecting another baby.'

'Aw! I thought so!' I exclaim, leaning over to kiss Sarah and punching Jack on the shoulder.

'Congratulations, guys! That's fantastic. Wow! Five kids! Holy crap!'

Somewhere in my genuine happiness for my oldest brother and his lovely wife is, I'll admit, a healthy dose of envy. They met in college, married, produced a tribe of gorgeous children and Jack still looks at her with bedroom eyes.

'If anyone can handle it, you guys can,' Trevor says, raising his beer glass to the happy couple.

'Thanks, bud,' Jack says. 'Hey, how's Hayden? You guys back together?'

'Jack! None of your business,' Sarah says. 'Excuse me, guys, I have to pee. Every ten minutes, it seems.'

I wait for Trevor to answer. He doesn't.

'What about you, Chas?' Jack asks. 'You serious with what's-his-name?'

'Ryan,' Trevor supplies.

I glance at him. 'Yeah. Sure. I met his family, did I tell you?'

'And how was that?' Jack asks.

'Freakish and bizarre,' I answer.

My brother laughs. 'Well, family's important. If you hate the in-laws, beware, kiddo.' He stands up. 'They're playing our song,' he says. 'Gotta go dance with the wife.' He ruffles my hair and goes to intercept Sarah on her way back from the loo. The strains of 'Brown-Eyed Girl' float from the jukebox. So bleeping sweet.

Which leaves Trevor and me, sitting across

from each other under the smiling eyes and dimples of St. Lou.

'So,' I say. 'Hayden.'

He nods.

'Spill, Trevor,' I order.

He grins. 'Yes, sir.' Then he stalls, taking a sip of Guinness. 'We're . . . we're trying to see if things might work out this time.'

Which could mean anything. 'I never really heard why you broke up in the first place, Trev,' I nudge.

He looks at me, his eyes so dark and serious that I feel that jolt right through my middle. I have to physically stop myself from reaching out to touch him. There's a flicker of something in his eyes, but he takes another sip of his beer and looks up. 'Speaking of relationships, here's your guy.'

'Hello,' Ryan says, sliding in next to me. He shakes Trevor's hand. 'Good to see you, Trevor.' He turns to me, sliding his arm around my shoulders. 'Well?'

'I passed,' I smile.

He smiles back. 'Of course you did. Congratulations, hon.' He kisses my cheek and takes something out of his pocket and puts it on the table in front of me. It's a slim, rectangular black velvet box. I stare at it, vaguely uneasy, and glance at Trevor, who smiles and gives a quick nod.

'Wow! This is, um, very . . . unexpected,' I babble.

'Open it,' Ryan says.

I do. Inside the box is an absolutely lovely (that is to say, expensive) pearl-and-ruby bracelet. 'Holy crap,' I breathe. 'I mean, wow. This is . . . oh, wow.' Filigree gold twines the gems together in a delicate pattern. It's the prettiest piece of jewelry imaginable, but for some reason, there's a lump in my throat, a sad lump.

'Thank you,' I manage in a strangled whisper. 'It's beautiful.'

'Not as beautiful as you,' Ryan says. He takes it out of the box and fastens it around my wrist, and as he's doing so, I tell myself not to look up at Trevor. But I do. Ryan fiddles with the clasp, and I look at Trevor and see that his smile is gone and there's a odd, blank look on his face. But then his left eyebrow bounces up and he looks impish and adorable again.

'Hi, all,' comes a voice. A body follows. Perfect Hayden slides into the booth next to Trevor and slips her arm under his. 'Hello. I'm Hayden Simms.' She smiles at Ryan.

'Ryan Darling,' he murmurs, reaching out to shake her hand.

'Hi, Hayden,' I mutter.

'What a pretty bracelet!' She cocks her head, then leans her cheek on Trevor's shoulder. Trevor doesn't exactly encourage her, but he sure as heck doesn't inch away, either.

'Yeah, very pretty,' he says. 'Nicely done,

354

Ryan.' He looks at Hayden. 'Well. Want to get a drink, Hayden? We'll see you guys later.' With that, they slip out of the booth and head for the bar. Good. I still don't like her, no matter how sunshiny cute she is.

'Nice to meet you, Hayden,' Ryan says before turning to me. 'You really like it, Chastity?'

'It's so beautiful. Ryan. Thank you. That was really sweet of you.'

He smiles. 'Is your father here? I'd like to meet him.'

'Sure! Yes! He's over there, with the boys. Come on, I'll introduce you.' We go over the pool table. 'Dad, this is Ryan Darling. Ryan, my father, Captain Mike O'Neill of the Eaton Falls Fire Department.'

'Very nice to meet you, sir,' Ryan says, shaking hands. 'Your daughter's told me a lot about you.'

Dad slings his arm around my shoulders. 'About time I met you, young man.' I elbow him sharply in the ribs. 'Nice to meet you, too. So. Are your intentions honorable?'

My brothers roar with laughter. Ryan smiles too, but says, 'Yes, sir, they are.'

'Let's sit down, then, and have a little talk.' Dad puts his hand on Ryan's shoulder and steers him back to the Gehrig booth we just vacated.

'They need to work out your dowry, Chas,' Mark comments. 'Come on, take Dad's place.'

355

I oblige, sinking the six ball with a nice bit of backspin. 'How are things with you, Mark?' I ask quietly.

'Better,' he says. 'Has Elaina said anything to you?' He glances over to his wife, who is laughing with Tara at the bar, just a few feet down from Trevor and Perfect Hayden.

'A little,' I admit. 'Four ball in the corner, brothers o' mine.'

'I'm moving back in,' Mark murmurs.

'Oh, Mark! That's great, buddy!' I give him a hug.

'Are we playing pool or reliving Dr. Phil?' Lucky asks.

'Shut up, Lucky,' I say. 'Two ball, side pocket, move your hand, Matt.' Click, clack, thunk. The ball sinks as I predicted.

'Well, you know, it'll be nice for Dylan.' Mark smiles and gives a sheepish nod. 'Thanks.'

'You're welcome,' I say.

'Can you guys hurry up and win?' Lucky asks. 'My wife is giving me the look.'

I sink the fourteen, but miss on the ten. 'Your turn,' I say. A peal of laughter comes from the general direction of Perfect Hayden, but I don't look over.

Lucky lines up his shot and misses, and Matt bemoans the fact that he got the worst pool player of our clan as his partner. Dad and Ryan are talking, laughing a little. Nice. My boyfriend and my dad are getting along great.

356

Good. Great, in fact.

Mark sinks the eight ball. 'Pay up, suckers,' he orders Matt and Lucky, who hand over their money.

Then Lucky looks up and grimaces. 'Uh-oh, guys.'

Dad is sitting like a Labrador retriever who's scented a pheasant. Ryan glances in the direction of Dad's gaze, as do we all.

Uh-oh is right. Through the French doors that divide Emo's bar from the restaurant, we can see Mom and Harry just taking their seats. And my father's face is like thunder. My heart starts to thud sickly in my throat.

Jack goes over to Dad and puts a hand on his arm. 'This is getting out of hand,' my father barks. More than a few people quiet down. Mark and Lucky walk cautiously over to join Jack. I know they won't let Dad start a fight, but they don't want to embarrass him, either.

'Back off, boys,' my father mutters. He strides over to the French doors and stands there, staring at his wife and her boyfriend.

'What's this about?' Ryan asks, coming to my side. He puts his arm around me and kisses my neck.

'Not now, Ryan,' I say, stepping away. 'My parents—'

Mom is staring back at Dad, not defiantly, not with anger or arrogance. She just looks at him through the doors. Harry is studying the wine list, looks up and sees Dad, as well. He hesitates, says something to my mom, and she looks away.

At that moment, my father seems to swell in rage. He starts forward, but Jack jerks him back. Dad wheels on his oldest son, his face furious.

'Get your hands off me, John,' he snarls, actually shoving Jack.

A lightning sheet of panic flashes through me. Oh, God, if Dad makes a scene, it'll be awful.

Then Trevor is there, Trev who has always looked up to Dad, and in recent months has looked after him, as well. He steps between Jack and my father, says something in a low voice. Dad's jaw is clenched and his eyes cut back and forth between Jack and Trev. Then he looks down, and the moment is over. Trevor nods, squeezes Dad's shoulder, and Dad walks back toward our booth.

'Dad?' I say, my voice a little shaky.

'Not now, Chastity,' he answers, not looking at me.

'Chastity, would you like a drink?' Ryan asks. As his back was to the action, he missed the whole scene. I ignore him.

'Dad?' I say as my father opens the door.

He finally turns and looks at me, and suddenly, my eternally youthful father looks old, and there's a look in his eyes, an empty, blank look. 'Daddy, are you okay?' I ask, my eyes filling.

'I'm fine,' he answers. 'I need to be alone, that's all.' And then he's gone, a rush of summer humidity filling the space where he just was.

CHAPTER TWENTY-NINE

My glum mood continues on Sunday morning. I can't shake the feeling I got when I saw that emptiness in my father's eyes. I call my mom, and she's subdued, as well.

'I'm not doing this to make a point,' Mom says quietly. 'Harry's good to me, Chastity. I care about him, we're compatible. And I'm just . . .' She sighs, and I hear years of fatigue in that sigh. 'I'm just worn out with your father. I feel like an eraser at the end of a pencil. Just worn down to nothing from years of the same thing.'

'He looked so sad, Mom,' I whisper. 'He still loves you.'

'That's not the point, sweetheart.' She's quiet for a moment. 'How are things with Ryan? Did I see him at Emo's last night?'

'Don't change the subject, Mom. What about Dad?'

'What do you want me to say, Chastity?' she snaps. 'You don't want to hear it, let me assure you.'

'What are you talking about?' I ask.

'You. You close your eyes to certain things, Chastity.' Her voice is hard.

'Okay, fine. You don't want to tell me, fine. I have some work to do, anyway.' I click End, wishing for the good old days when a person could slam down the phone.

I don't work. I go for a long, punishing row instead. It's humid, the bugs are out, sweat stings my eyes. Perfect. It matches my mood. When I return to my dock, I'm surprised to see Ernesto there. Shit. I forgot I'd promised him another lesson.

'Hey, Chastity!' he says. 'Congratulations again on passing the test.'

'Same to you, pal,' I say, climbing out of the boat. 'Sorry. I kind of forgot about you.'

'We can skip it,' he offers.

'Nah. You're here. Let's do it.'

For the next half hour, I coach Ernesto, who's actually something of a natural. We talk about the cost of single sculls and where he could keep such a vessel. He's a nice guy, Ernesto. I'll miss seeing him every week.

'So, Chas, I got a job with Ames Ambulance Service,' he says. 'They hired me two weeks ago, so long as I passed yesterday.'

'Really? That's great.'

'What about you? Are you going to apply? They're hiring, you know.'

I grimace. 'No, I won't apply. Even though I passed, Ernie, I'm not really good around blood and gore.'

360

'Fooled me,' he says.

'Fooled is the right word,' I answer.

* * *

I go to Angela's for dinner that night. Her house is half of a two-family unit, very cozy and warm. She's made spinach-and-feta phyllo triangles and marmalade-glazed shrimp and hands me a huge, fruity drink with an umbrella and a straw in it. There's mango in it, and grapefruit juice and something else, and it's absolutely fabulous.

'Will you marry me?' I ask.

'Are you talking to Legolas or to me?' she quips. Indeed, I am standing right in front of her life-size cutout of the witty elf from *Lord of the Rings.*

'Both, I guess,' I answer. She checks the oven and then asks me to have a seat in the living room. 'Listen, I wanted to talk to you about something,' she says.

'Sure,' I say, sucking down some more of the delicious drink.

'Be careful, there's alcohol in that,' she warns. 'Okay, well, remember when Trevor and I were kind of seeing each other?'

'Yeah,' I answer. She's right about the alcohol. I'm already a little buzzed. 'You know what? Tell me about that. Because I thought you guys would be cute together, and now he's with this . . . this person. And she's not very

361

nice.'

Angela pauses. 'Well, Trevor was—is—very nice. And very good-looking, of course.'

'Tell me about it,' I mutter, sucking down some more tropical yumminess.

'I guess there was just no real chemistry,' she says.

'What?' I bark. 'How can you say that? He's—' I clamp my mouth shut. 'Most women find Trevor very chemistry-ish. Crap, listen to me. What's in this drink, Ange? You trying to slip me a mickey?'

She laughs. 'Vodka and triple sec, that's all. But generous helpings of both, I admit.' She takes a phyllo triangle and bites into it. 'About Trevor . . . See, there's someone else.' Her cheeks go nuclear, and she toys with her ring. 'I met someone, and it was just . . . it's your brother, Matt.'

My eyes pop. 'Matt? What? What about Matt?' She nods. 'You're interested in Matt?'

'Yes,' she admits. 'Actually, we've been seeing each other for a couple of weeks, Chastity.'

How do I miss these things? 'That's great, Ange. Matt's great. And secretive, apparently. Why didn't you tell me? When did this start?'

'It was that day at the firehouse, when he was showing me some recipes, we just . . . clicked. And then he asked for some help about college courses, he wanted my advice, and we ended up talking for hours. But I was

362

still kind of seeing Trevor, even though we hadn't so much as kissed.'

'Really?' I blurt.

Angela smiles. 'Yes, Chastity. Honestly, the whole time we were together, I felt like Trevor was, I don't know. Not really interested. He's so nice and decent and very cute and all, and we had a really nice time together, but when I met Matt, we just . . . we both felt it. That feeling when you just know.'

'Wow.' I sigh. My glass is, alas, empty. 'So everyone's fine and happy?'

'I think so,' she says. 'I know you think the world of Trevor, and I was afraid you'd be mad.'

'No, no,' I say. 'Trevor is . . . he's great.' I glance at the ceiling. 'And I guess he's happy with Perfect Hayden.'

'Who's Perfect Hayden?' Angela asks.

'His once and future fiancée, apparently.' I sit up and smile brightly. 'So. What's for dinner? I'm starving.'

On my way home later that night, I feel inexplicably lonely. Soon, I imagine, Matt will move out. Get married. Have a few kids. Angela will go from being my friend to being yet another sister-in-law, the mother of more nieces or nephews. Not that I don't love and admire and enjoy my sisters-in-law . . . Crap. I don't know what's wrong with me. Even watching *Return of the King* doesn't cheer me up. I put on the Yankees game. We're losing,

363

ten to two, and it's the eighth inning.

Maybe I'll call Ryan, even though it's late. The uncomfortable thought dawns that I've turned first to Aragorn, then to Derek Jeter, before calling Ryan even occurred to me. Stupid, isn't it? Here I have a very real, very considerate boyfriend, and I'm checking out fictional characters and sports gods first.

With a vengeance, I stab in his number. 'Hi,' I blurt.

'Hi, hon,' he answers. 'I was just thinking of you.'

And my heart feels a little bit better.

CHAPTER THIRTY

'Where are you going, Chastity?'

Lucia is back at work, back to being bossy and a pain in the ass. Inconceivably, it's good to have her around.

'I'm covering the riverside cleanup—very exciting stuff—and then I'm going to my mother's for dinner, and then I'll probably go home and go to bed. Do I have your permission?'

She frowns. 'You're close with your family, aren't you?' It sounds like an accusation.

'Yes.' A flash of envy passes through her eyes. 'What about you, Lu? Are you close with yours?'

Her lips tighten. 'Not really. I have two sisters, both older, and they think they're better than me.' There's a lot of hurt in that adolescent sentence. 'Like my job isn't that important and I'm wasting my time here.'

'Well, for what it's worth, I thought your sister was a real bitch,' I offer.

Her face breaks into a grin. 'Thanks, Chastity.' We laugh. That's right. Lucia and I are laughing. Together and simultaneously.

'Lu—' I begin tentatively.

'What?' she asks.

'If you wanted to write a features article once in a while, I'd be willing to see how it goes.' Her face lights up under the Kabuki makeup. 'Strict parameters, though,' I continue. 'With full right to refuse to print anything. And you'd have to adhere to the word count, because I don't want to read ten thousand words on a pie-eating contest.'

Lucia is blinking rapidly against tears. 'It's about time.'

'You're welcome,' I say, rolling my eyes. 'Now I have to run. See you later.'

*   *   *

The riverside cleanup turns out to be more fun than I had anticipated, and I spend too much time chatting as I interview the director of parks and recreation and her many volunteers. By the time I get home, I'm running late, so I

365

heave Buttercup into the car and drive to Mom's house, fifteen minutes after the instructed time.

Mom is in the kitchen, fetching beers, when I come in. 'I really wish you'd been on time today, Chastity. The boys are getting impatient.'

'So? Who cares about the boys?' I say, automatically reverting to my adolescent self.

'Go into the living room,' she says soberly, and a small twinge of fear sings through my joints.

'Come on, Buttercup,' I say, and my dog follows me reluctantly, leaving the microbe she was sniffing. She flops on the carpet with a groan. My brothers and their wives are already seated, Jack and Sarah in the big chair, Lucky and Tara on the couch. Matt is reading *Sports Illustrated*, and Mark, I'm happy to see, is holding Elaina's hand. Elaina smiles at me. I sit next to Lucky, shoving his shoulder until he gives me more room.

'Where are the kids?' I ask.

'The kids are watching *The Lion King*,' Mom says. 'Now be quiet, I have to tell you something. Matt, stop reading. Questions come after I'm done. All right?'

I throw Elaina a glance of confusion. Even she, who adores my mother, looks worried.

Mom looks at the floor and folds her arms across her chest. 'Harry and I are getting married.'

The refrain from 'Hakuna Matata' drifts up from under our feet. Buttercup moans in her sleep. It's the only sound for a good fifteen seconds.

'Holy crap,' Jack breathes.

'July twenty-third,' Mom continues. 'Of course, I'd like you to be there, but if you have a problem with that, I understand.'

I feel like I've been punched in the solar plexus. She can't marry Harry. She can't. 'Mom?' I whisper. My throat is tight.

'You just met him,' Mark says.

'Three months ago, honey.'

'Does Dad know?' Matt asks.

'Not yet.' Mom's jaw is tight.

'Mamí,' Elaina says hesitantly, 'why the rush?'

'Life is too short,' Mom answers briskly.

'Mom?' I whisper again, but Lucky interrupts this time.

'Are you sure about this, Mom? I know you've been mad at Dad, but this seems a little . . . dramatic.'

'This isn't about your father, Luke. It's about Harry and me and my future.'

'Are we supposed to be happy for you, Ma?' Jack asks, an edge in his voice.

'You can be happy or not,' she says. 'It won't change anything.'

'What about Dad?' Mark asks. 'What's he supposed to do, Mom?'

She shakes her head. 'I don't know.' She

sighs. 'Listen, I know he's going to be angry. He'll need you kids.'

'When are you going to tell him?' Sarah asks.

'Tonight.' Mom looks grim. 'He's at a union meeting right now, but he's coming over later.'

My voice isn't working. And I think there's something wrong with my heart, because it's beating sickly in my chest, slow and too hard.

'Is that all?' Jack asks tightly.

'That's all.' Mom sighs. 'I know this is a bombshell, kids, but I think you should all go home. Call me tomorrow if you have anything else to say. Okay?' The boys rise obediently. 'Chastity, honey, will you stay a little while?'

I nod wordlessly.

Like ghosts, my brothers and their spouses gather their kids and trickle out the door. It's eerily quiet. I just sit on the couch in the fading light and stare at the rug. My mind is blank.

Mom comes in from waving to the last of her grandchildren and sits in her chair across from me. 'I know this is a surprise, Chastity,' she says.

A razor seems wedged in my vocal cords. 'Mom,' I say in a rough whisper, 'how can you do this? You love Daddy.'

She stares at me, then comes over and sits down next to me. 'Honey, I did. For a long time, he was . . .' She sighs. 'He was the love of my life.'

'So you can't marry Harry, Mom! Not if you

still love Daddy!' I sound like a ten-year-old, but I can't help it. Buttercup comes over to me and puts her head on my lap.

'Love gets used up, Chastity,' Mom says gently, reaching up to smooth my hair. 'If it's not returned, it gets used up.'

'He loves you, Mom!' A tear drops on Buttercup's nose, and she licks it away. 'Of course Dad loves you.'

'Not in the same way, honey.' She leans back against the couch and fiddles with her bracelet. 'Chastity, you can't spend your life loving someone more than you're loved. You know that, don't you? It makes you feel small, no matter how tall you might be.' She gives a small, sad smile.

'What . . . what are you talking about?'

'Trevor.'

I suck in a breath. 'I—I—I don't—'

'Yes, you do, honey. You love Trevor. You've loved him since you were a kid.'

My face crumples, the tears coming faster now. 'Okay, well, yes. But let's talk about you and Daddy,' I whisper.

'Okay. But I think you're being smart to find someone else, someone who thinks you light up the room.' She pauses, staring at the floor. 'Not someone who doesn't even really see you anymore.'

I don't know if she's talking about me or her or Trevor or Ryan or Dad. I wipe my eyes and try to swallow.

'I'm tired of fighting to get your father to notice me,' she says, looking so weary and wise that I have to clench my jaw shut so I don't sob. 'He spent too many years just expecting me to be there when he felt like noticing. There I was, mother of five, keeping the house, cooking, running you kids all over, taking care of you when you were sick, and I was still just as in love with him as when we first met. Meanwhile, he just kept doing whatever he felt like doing. The job, the guys, you kids when the mood struck him. It seemed like everything was more important than I was.'

Buttercup moves her head to Mom's lap now, and Mom strokes the dog's big ears.

'Do you really love Harry?' I ask around the thorn in my throat.

'Yes,' she says simply, and my heart cracks. 'I like feeling new and interesting and . . . well, adored.'

I nod, misery rising off me like a fog.

'I was hoping you'd be my maid of honor, Chastity,' she says. 'Though you don't have to answer now, of course.'

I don't want to break down in front of my mother, so I stand up. 'I have to go,' I squeak.

'Okay,' she says, standing too and hugging me. 'I love you, honey.'

'I love you, too, Mom.' I choke. 'I just have to run to my room for a sec.' With Buttercup on my heels, I escape down the hall.

370

As I was the last kid to leave for college, my room was spared from being made over into the den or sewing room, as were the two rooms that held the boys. Sitting on my old bed here in the gloom, Buttercup beside me, I look around. My basketball trophies still sit on the top shelf of the bookcase. The Goo Goo Dolls stare at me from a poster. My fuzzy lavender rug, which I thought so utterly feminine at the time, looks considerably more Rastafarian than it once did. Otherwise, not much has changed.

Tears are dripping down my cheeks. I try to take a deep breath and get a grip. I fail.

I once believed in everlasting love. I thought that, at the root of everything, beneath the irritation and impatience and bickering, my parents would always love each other. Would always be together, even when they were apart. I didn't know that someone could be the love of your life and then fade from your heart. I didn't know your heart could feel like a used-up eraser, rubbed down, grimy from neglect and overuse. It's an unbearable thought. Unbearable.

The back door slams. 'Betty?' My father's voice is laced with panic. I didn't hear his car.

'Betty, Jack just called me. Betty!' My father, who thinks nothing of tramping through burning buildings on floors weakened by flame, sounds like a frightened child. 'You can't be serious, honey. You can't do this!'

371

Their voices come to me with horrible clarity, and though I hate hearing them talk, I'm welded to the bed. Buttercup rests her head on the purple rug and watches me.

'Mike, I'm sorry, but I am. I'm marrying Harry.' There's no anger in my mom's voice, just sadness and resignation and an underlying, bleak honesty.

'Oh, Betty.' I have never heard my father cry before. I've seen tears in his eyes, yes. Quiet with grief or sharp with fear, yes, but this raw sobbing punches me right in the throat.

'I'll retire. I'll do it tomorrow! I'll call the chief right now, Betty—'

'It's not that, Mike. It's too late. I really am sorry.'

'You can't! You still love me. Please! I love you, Betty. I always have.'

Mom's voice is soothing and kind, horribly gentle—not the Father Donnelly voice, but the loving-mother voice, the one we heard when we were feverish or stomach sick or crying because we weren't popular enough or hated being tall. 'I gave you years to retire, Mike. If you do it now, it's just because you don't want me with someone else. It's not really for me.'

'Please, Betty.'

'No. I'm sorry, Mike. Part of me will always love you, and we'll always have the kids and grandkids, but it's over now.'

My father's crying breaks my heart.

Mom talks some more, but I don't hear it. After a few minutes, the kitchen door closes and I hear an engine start, then Mom's footsteps coming down the hall. She opens my door, leans against the door frame and looks at me.

'Is Daddy okay?' I whisper.

'I called Mark, and he and Luke are going over.' She looks at the floor. 'I think you should go now, honey. I want to be alone.'

*   *   *

I drive home like a zombie and feed Buttercup. Standing there, watching her devouring her kibbles, her jowls flopping against the bowl, I feel the walls closing in. I can't think about my parents—it's too sad. I have to get out of here.

Where I want to go and where I should go are different places. I shove my feet into my high-tops and run down the block, toward the place I should go.

It's full dark now, and the music of a summer night flows around me, radios playing and doors slamming, kids screaming, a baseball game down at Reilly Park. Restaurant courtyards are packed; fairy lights twinkle; people are laughing and drinking and eating and having a wonderful bleeping time. I keep running, my flat-soled high-tops slapping on the pavement.

Eaton Falls General Hospital is artificially bright and welcoming. *Hi! Glad you're here! Have a great time!* the foyer seems to shout; it's decorated with bright murals and fichus trees. *Great choice,* I think viciously.

'Can I help you?' The woman at the front desk beams.

'Which floor is the surgical floor?' I ask.

'That would be six,' she answers. 'Are you visiting a patient?'

'No,' I answer. 'I need to see Dr. Darling.'

'I can have him paged,' she offers, but I'm already loping to the elevators.

My steps are fast and hard as I stride down toward the sixth-floor nurses' station. 'Is Ryan Darling around?' I ask.

A nurse stares at me disapprovingly. 'He's with a patient.'

'Is he in surgery?'

'He's with a patient,' she repeats loudly, as if I'm hard of hearing. She looks me up and down, judgment heavy in her face 'Why don't you call his office and make an appointment?'

'Why don't you back off, okay? He's my boyfriend.' There should really be a better word than *boyfriend.* Something with dignity and solemnity. *Boyfriend* makes it sound like I'm fifteen.

'The fact remains that he's—With. A. Patient.'

'Fine! Is there somewhere I can wait?'

The nurse, who is as sweet and

compassionate as, say, Nurse Ratched, sighs dramatically. 'There's a waiting room reserved for families at the end of the hall. Please try to be sensitive to them, won't you?'

Stifling the urge to punch her in the stomach, I barrel down the hall, not daring to glance in the rooms that line either side. I'm miserable enough without seeing sad families and sick people.

The waiting room is empty, though a few Dunkin Donut cups announce recent occupancy. CNN is on the television mounted on the wall, but I don't look at that, either. My father's broken voice echoes in my head. He never believed this would happen. He just didn't listen.

Sooner than I might have expected, Ryan opens the door. He's wearing scrubs and a white doctor's coat, and if he's been dealing with human suffering, it doesn't show. He's still as icily attractive as the first time I saw him. Mr. *New York Times*. 'Chastity! What a nice surprise,' he says, giving me a kiss. 'How are you? Just here to pay me a visit?'

'Ryan, I have some bad news.' My throat clamps shut again. 'My mother is getting married.' My voice cracks on the last word.

'To Harry?' he asks, rather obtusely.

No, dumbass, I want to say. *To Barack Obama.* 'Yes, to Harry,' I snap.

'Isn't that nice,' he murmurs, then seems to see my expression for the first time. 'Or not.'

'My father is devastated, Ryan,' I announce, a hard edge in my voice.

'Sure, sure,' he placates. 'But still . . .' He thinks better of finishing and glances at his watch.

'But still *what*, Ryan?' I demand.

He tips his head and shrugs. 'Still, Chastity, you have to look at the bright side. I know you're probably sad that your mother's moving on, but your parents *are* divorced, after all. Your mom is marrying someone who thinks very highly of her, someone who's very comfortable financially. It's a good match.'

A good match. Where are we, Medieval England? Tears are welling behind my eyes. I swallow loudly, anger flickering in my stomach.

'Don't be sad, sweetheart,' he says, his eyes flicking to the clock.

'Do you have to go?'

'I have rounds,' he admits.

'Okay,' I say stiffly. 'See you later.'

'Hey, do you think we'll still go to the city this weekend?' Ryan asks, a note of concern finally tingeing his voice.

If I stay another second, I will punch him in the eye. 'I gotta go,' I blurt. 'See you.'

'Chastity,' he calls, but I'm already striding back past the bitchy nurse to the elevator. I stab the lobby button with unnecessary force, grinding my teeth as I wait for the stupid box to descend. I burst out of the door, rush past a family and back out into the sultry summer night. Running once more, a stitch in my side now, I head for downtown. To where I wanted to go in the first place. My eyes are streaming, my nose is running. So attractive.

Before I'm completely aware of it, I find myself standing in front of Trevor's building. Someone nearby plays a guitar, the gentle strumming floating easily to my ears. A baby cries. Gazing up at the windows in the northeastern corner of the building's top floor, I see lights. He's home.

Someone's just coming out of the building, so I don't have to buzz myself up, just grab the door before it swings closed. I run through the lobby and up the stairs, taking them two at a time, whipping around each landing and charging up the next flight like a Marine. When I reach the fourth floor, I burst into the hallway and skid to a halt in front of apartment 4D.

I knock sharply, my breath ragged, and when Trevor answers the door, looking more than a little surprised, I don't wait. I just throw myself into his arms.

CHAPTER THIRTY-ONE

'Chastity, what is it?' he asks, trying to pull back to see my face. I don't let him, just clench him against me, feeling the warmth of his neck against my cheek, the comforting strength of his arms around me, the smell of soap and shampoo. Oh, God, I recognize these smells, this feeling. I remember everything about him.

'My mom . . .' My voice is unrecognizable even to me.

'Is she hurt?' His voice is calm and quiet, even asking such a question.

'No!' I sob. 'She's fine.'

'Come on in, sweetheart.' Trevor disentangles himself from me, takes my hand and leads me into his apartment. I've never been here. His living room is painted a warm yellow, there's a fireplace and a lot of plants, and I can't see anymore because of the tears in my eyes. He pushes me gently onto the couch and leaves the room, returning in a second with a box of tissues, which he hands me.

'What's the matter, Chastity?' he asks as I blow my nose loudly. I need several tissues to mop up my tears. My hands are shaking, and so are my legs. I can't answer right away. 'Chas, honey, what's wrong?' Trevor kneels in front of me and takes my hands.

'She's getting married, Trevor,' I whisper, then start bawling again. 'She's getting married to Harry and my father is so . . . he sounded so . . . and I just—I never thought—they loved each other—but now . . .'

Trevor slides onto the soft brown couch and holds me, letting me cry into his neck. He strokes my hair and murmurs things I can't quite hear over the raw, seal-like barking of my sobs. He shifts so I'm closer, kisses the top of my head, and, crap, I give in.

I can't hide from myself anymore. I love Trevor. Always have, always will. I never stopped, and right now, I love him more than ever. For twelve years, I've been trying to make him just one of the guys.

He's not.

I love him. And like Mom's love for Dad, that love might be worn down by time and dejection. Someday I might look at Trevor, *my* Trevor, the way my mom now sees my father . . . the man who used up her heart.

'Trevor, I—' My voice breaks off. I pull back to look at him.

He knows. I can see it in his eyes, he feels how much I love him still, and maybe he's always known. He cups my face in one hand, his thumb sliding away my tears, stroking my cheek.

I kiss him.

It's a kiss filled with longing and heartbreak and sorrow and hurt . . . and love, of course, because it's burned in my soul, somehow, that I was meant to love Trevor, that no matter what he feels toward me, I love him with my whole heart and every molecule and muscle and fiber of me, every ounce of blood. And I don't want that to be worn away.

For a second, he doesn't move, doesn't respond, and the echo of rejection starts to

379

sound in my heart once again.

And then he kisses me back, hard and soft at the same time, his mouth desperate and hungry on mine. *Oh, thank God,* I think. *Thank God.*

His hands are on my skin, under my shirt, burning hot. I slide my hands through his thick, still-damp hair, opening my lips underneath his, and wrap my legs around him. My foot connects with the coffee table, which falls over with a thunk, but we don't stop. There's nothing that matters but us. The two of us, coming together again, at last. It's been so long, but it's like we were never apart. He feels so warm and smooth and hot and so, so good. So perfect. Absolutely right.

I yank his shirt open, tearing off a few buttons, but who cares? I've loved him for so long.

We're not gentle, and we're not graceful. We're a force of nature as we pull off clothes and kick off shoes. Something else breaks, but it's just background noise. The couch cushion slides and we roll onto the floor and don't even come up for air. I can barely hear, my heart is pounding so hard. My skin is burning, and when I feel Trevor against me, his skin just as hot as mine, I suck in a ragged breath. 'Chastity,' he says, his voice tight and rough.

'Please. Please, Trevor.' *Please don't stop. Please don't send me away. Please love me again.*

He says nothing more, his eyes dark and molten, and when we come together, I know that this is how it's meant to be. That's all. It's just the way things should be. He's my home, and I belong exactly where I am. Then my brain stops formulating thought, and only feeling is left. I love him so much my heart practically cracks in two.

It takes some time for my breathing to return to normal, for my vision to clear. Trevor is still, his heart thudding against mine, his face against my neck. His own breath is ragged, his arms still tight around me.

The couch cushions are in disarray, one of them lying partly on us, the others askew. The coffee table is on its side, and I can see a few broken shards of glass. I'm going to have a bruise on my hip, and I'm fairly sure I've left some gouge marks on Trevor's back.

I want to stay in that moment of rightness, but reality is knocking. A prickle of guilt pierces the fog of perfection, but I can't bear to let it in completely.

'Trev?' I breathe.

'Yeah.' He lifts his head and looks at me, his face serious, cheeks flushed. Then he takes a deep breath and gets up. 'Do you need a drink?' he asks, pulling on his jeans. Without waiting for an answer, he goes into the kitchen.

It's not a good sign. I put my hand to my lips, which still feel swollen and hot. I lay there for another minute, then scramble up, reaching for my shirt, my underwear, my shorts. My socks are still on. I dress hastily, glancing into the kitchen where Trevor stands in front of the sink, his hands braced on either side, the water running. The muscles in his broad shoulders are bunched and tense, and his head is hanging. He doesn't fill a glass, doesn't turn off the water. He just stands there, motionless, and I can feel the regret pouring off him in waves.

Say something, Trevor, I plead silently. *Make this be okay.* I want him to come to me, wrap me in his arms, tell me that this wasn't a mistake. He does nothing, just stands there watching the water run.

Though I want to go to him, reassure him, touch him, I don't dare. Not when he can't even look at me.

Then I'm distracted by a sudden buzzing at my feet. I look down. Trevor's cell phone, which apparently fell during our acrobatics, is vibrating on the rug. I glance again at Trevor's tense shoulders, then reach down and look at the screen.

Incoming call from Hayden.

I drop it back on the carpet and kick it under the couch. Trevor will have to find it later, won't he? He'll have to search all over and wonder, *What the heck did I do with my phone? Where could it be?*

He's still staring at the water.

I have two choices here. Leave with dignity

382

or give it all I have. And you know what? Screw dignity.

'Hey, Trev?' I say gently. 'Maybe you could come in here?'

He turns his head and nods once. Then he reaches for two glasses and fills them, finally deigning to return to the living room. He sets the glasses on the table, picks up the pieces of the glass that broke, then reaches for his shirt. He can't button it, though, since I'd ripped the thing off. Then he straightens the couch cushions and sits down.

'Chastity,' he begins, finally meeting my eyes. My stomach plummets at what I see there.

'If this is the "we shouldn't have done this" speech, can I just say something first?' I ask. My voice is rough, even a little scared.

'You're seeing someone,' he says quietly.

I look down. Of course he's right. I, who practically beat my brother Mark to a pulp when he cheated on Elaina, have just cheated on my own boyfriend. Shame burns my face. I sit in the chair adjacent to Trevor and swallow. 'I know,' I whisper.

'And so am I,' he says.

Crap. I take a deep breath. 'Trevor, you must know that I've always lov—'

'Don't, Chas,' Trevor says, staring at his knees.

'Don't what?'

'Don't say it, and don't break up with Ryan.'

I don't think there's anything else he could say that would hurt worse than that. My mouth opens, but no sound comes out. He looks up at me.

'I don't want to be the reason things don't work.' His eyes are intensely dark now, dead serious. 'He's a good guy, Chas. He can give you a lot that I never could. And he loves you.' He reaches over and takes my limp hand.

I'm not stupid. *He loves you . . . and I don't.* No translation needed. My head hurts. My heart hurts, too. It actually hurts like there's a bleeping ice pick stuck through it. I yank my hand back so hard that my elbow hits the arm of the chair with a thud. 'So, okay, Trev,' I say, trying not to cry. 'So we're just going to, what, sleep together every decade or so, and I'll be all messed up for another ten years and you'll pretend to be my big brother?' My voice grows louder. 'Huh? Is that how it's going to go?'

'No, Chastity,' he says. 'This won't happen again. I'm sorry, I'm really sorry. It shouldn't have happened at all. You know it as well as I do.'

I lurch out of my chair. 'It seems that I don't know anything, Trevor, or else I wouldn't have just shagged you senseless, now would I?'

'Chastity—' He stands, as well, holding his hands up to placate me, and I feel the strong urge to sock him a good one. 'Chas, you—' He lets his hands drop and shakes his head.

'No, go ahead, Trevor. Say it.' I point a

shaking finger at him. 'If we were together and didn't work, you'd be out your precious surrogate family. You're afraid of losing them. At least admit that, Trevor. My family means more to you than I do.'

Trevor's face changes. He takes a step closer to me. For the first time in my life, I see that he's angry. Furious, maybe. 'Wrong,' he growls in a voice I've never heard. 'Very, very wrong, Chastity. If we were together and didn't work, I'd be out *you*. You're the one I can't lose.'

My mouth opens and closes a couple of times. 'What?'

'You're the one who said we had too much to lose, remember?'

'But things are different now, Trevor. You can't—'

His voice is sharp and hard and wrong. 'You were right, that's the thing. We'll never disappoint each other this way, Chastity. We'll never break up. Never get divorced.' He takes a step back, the anger draining out of him. 'You can do better than me, Chas.'

'There is no better than you.' I say it with my whole heart, but he just shakes his head.

'You know how it would be. Firefighters make next to nothing. I'd be working two jobs, taking all the overtime I could get, and you'd start hating me after a while. Like your mom and dad.'

My eyes flood with tears. Again. He has a

point.

'If we stay apart, we won't end up like that,' he says, his voice gentle now. 'I lost Michelle, I lost my parents, I don't want to lose you, Chastity. I can't.'

'Trevor,' I whisper. 'I could never hate you. I love you. I've always loved you.'

And that's when the bleeping phone rings. Not the cell phone under the couch, but his land line. We stare at each other as it rings once, twice, three times. I can feel the blood being forced through my heart, the pulse thudding in my throat. Trevor's machine clicks on.

'Hi, babe, it's me. Just wanted to make sure we were still on for tomorrow. Call me. Love you.'

Trevor closes his eyes, and his shoulders sag. I have my answer.

'You know what, Trev?' I ask, my voice just above a whisper. 'I'm gonna go now.'

'That's not what you think,' he says.

Oh, for Christ's sake. Of all the stupid things to say! Suddenly, my temper comes crashing through, and I'm buzzing with fury. 'Really, Trev? Because what I think is that Perfect Hayden wants you back. And all that "don't want to lose you" is utter bullshit. But just in case it's true, guess what? You did lose me. Just now.'

'Don't say that, Chastity,' he warns.

'Bite me, Trevor,' I snarl. 'I'm not your

sister, I'm not your best buddy, I'm not your girlfriend. You're right. Someone out there loves me, wants me, thinks I'm great. So get the fuck out of my way and let me go to him.'

He does just that.

* * *

I walk along the feeder canal. Correction. I stomp along the feeder canal, furious. I'm so angry I'm practically levitating. Wish I had a punching bag I could lay into right about now. God! Did I learn nothing twelve years ago? Did I not remember how relieved Trevor was to break up with me? Fool me once, Elaina likes to say, shame on you. Fool me twice, I'm a bleeping idiot.

I sit down on the edge of the bank, the dew seeping into my jeans. My hands are shaking, and my cheeks are wet with angry tears. The tree branches rustle with a passing breeze, and a police siren sounds on the other side of town. I sniff, then fish a frayed tissue out of my pocket and blow my nose.

At least I know. I put it all on the line, all my love and wanting. At least I said what I've wanted to say forever. I told Trevor I loved him. There's no 'what if' anymore.

Things he said filter back into my consciousness. That he couldn't lose me. Twelve years ago, when I was eighteen, I'd said that to him. *There's too much to lose.* And I do understand what he means . . . that if we're only friends, we can stay friends forever.

But we're not only friends. I love him, and I offered him that love, and it wasn't enough to overcome that fear of his. The fear of being alone. Of losing another person in his life. Keeping things safe is what Trevor prizes most.

It's just that I thought maybe I was worth a little risk.

My breath is still hitching out of me in shocked little sobs. I can still feel Trevor's skin against mine, still taste him, but to him, it's a mistake. That hanging out at my house once in a while, watching the Yanks and shooting pool, means more than what just happened. That I'm more precious to him if I just stay one of the guys.

And then there's bleeping Perfect Hayden. He once loved Hayden enough to ask her to marry him. He loves her enough now to be, at the very least, considering that again. Hayden is worth two tries. I'm worth none.

My cell phone rings, startling me. Maybe it's Trevor. Maybe he's sorry. Maybe . . .

Nope. 'Hi, Ryan,' I say.

'Hello, sweetheart.' He pauses. 'Are you crying?'

Fresh tears spurt out of my eyes. 'A little,' I admit, guilt and shame washing over me.

'Is it your mom?' I don't deserve the concern in his voice.

388

'I—yeah.'

'Want me to come over? I'm done at the hospital.'

I wipe my eyes on my sleeve and look at the stars. 'No, thanks, Ryan. I just need to be alone, I think.'

'I understand,' he says. 'But I'll see you tomorrow, okay?'

'Ryan?'

'Yes?'

'I'm really looking forward to going away this weekend,' I say truthfully.

'Me, too.' I can hear the smile in his voice. 'Good night.'

'Good night. I love you, Ryan.' I wince as I say it. Even though it's not untrue, those words mean something very different from when I said them to Trevor a half hour ago.

CHAPTER THIRTY-TWO

Something's dead in me. Now that's a pleasant thought to have on a romantic weekend with one's gorgeous boyfriend, isn't it?

Ryan and I check into the SoHo Grand Hotel, a place so stylish and swanky that the maids are better dressed than I am. But apparently Ryan is a regular, because the concierge greets him with, 'Wonderful to see you again, Dr. Darling.'

We are shown to our painfully chic hotel room, a corner suite with minimalist furniture and stunning views of the city. 'This is beautiful, Ryan,' I say after he's tipped the bellboy/aspiring actor who is nearly as handsome as Ryan himself.

'Well, I wanted it to be special,' he acknowledges a little sheepishly. Then he kisses me and glances at the bed. 'Care to . . . ?'

'You know what, Ryan? I'm a little tired,' I say. It's not a lie. The truth is, I'm tired of comparing the two men in my life. Correction. There aren't two men in my life, are there? There's just this one.

We lie on the beautiful, sleek bed, holding hands. I tell him a little bit about where I hung out when I was a graduate student, places I ventured when I worked in Newark and came to the city for fun. He talks lovingly about his endless residency at Columbia Presbyterian, his horrible hours, the little Thai place that he frequented, the parts of Central Park where he relaxed.

Looking at Ryan, I don't feel the soul-wrenching ache I feel—felt—for Trevor. There's a lot to be said for that. If I'm not mistaken, Ryan is going to pop the question this weekend, and I'm going to accept. Enough beating of the poor proverbial already deceased horse. The dead thing in me will harden and crumble away into tiny bits. Just

390

like it did for Mom.

We have drinks in the lounge, stylish, deliciously expensive drinks (who knew a martini could cost $25?) and head up Broadway to see *Wicked*. It's wonderful. I love the show. Ryan agrees that it was excellent. Then we have a late dinner at yes, the Rainbow Room. Because my boyfriend is a wealthy surgeon, I feel no compunction about ordering filet mignon and another gold-standard martini. Later, we dance to the orchestra and, of course, Ryan is a smooth dancer.

'You're good at this,' I say, smiling up at him, since I had the sense to wear flats.

'Ballroom dancing lessons were part of my education. Seventh grade,' he confesses.

'I've never danced with a guy who really knew what he was doing.'

'You're pretty good yourself,' he says, giving me a quick kiss.

'I love you,' I tell him, more for my sake than his.

'I love you, too,' he says. 'In fact—' he releases my hand to reach into his breast pocket '—I'm hoping you'll do me the honor of being my wife.'

What song is playing? I don't recognize it. Ryan smiles beautifully and slides a chunky diamond ring onto the fourth finger of my left hand.

'It's gorgeous,' I say, and it is, platinum with

an emerald-cut stone flanked by two smaller diamonds. Stunning, like something out of the *New York Times* magazine.

'Will you marry me?' he says, more for protocol than anything else.

'Yes,' I say, and I wrap my arms around his neck and kiss him, and the people around us applaud and smile.

This will be my life, I think as we stroll a few blocks. The air is dry and clear, a light breeze swirls through my hair, the smell of bread perfumes the air. All around us, Manhattan sparkles and hums. I hold up my hand to inspect my ring, and Ryan grins. 'My parents will be very pleased,' he says.

'Really?' I say, and he laughs and squeezes my hand. Visions of Thanksgiving and Christmas with Dr. and Mrs. Darling (and Bubbles) float through my head, as surreal as a Salvador Dali painting. 'Mine will be, too.'

'Of course,' Ryan says. I try not to roll my eyes. Instead, I picture Ryan holding his own at our Thanksgiving touch-football game which, though it sounds Kennedy-esque and good-spirited, rewards creative, dirty, after-the-whistle type hits. Of course, we wouldn't want to injure Ryan's gifted hands, so he might have to excuse himself. Still. It could be fun.

We sleep in the next morning, go out for brunch and spend the afternoon shopping at Saks, mostly for Ryan, to be honest, who needed a few new suits, though he very kindly buys me some fabulous underwear and a pair of peach silk pajamas (perhaps a comment on the ancient Yankees T-shirt I usually wear to bed). We return to our hotel, where I call my mom and tell her the news.

'Oh, Chastity!' she cries. 'Honey, that's wonderful! Wonderful!' She offers to invite the boys and their families over for dinner the next day so Ryan and I can come and announce our engagement live and in person.

'Sure,' I say. 'Sounds great.'

Ryan calls his parents, too, and I talk to Mrs. over the phone. 'Please call me Libby,' she says. 'And I can recommend some very good designers for your dress, darling.'

Dr. gets on the phone, too. 'Welcome to the family,' he says heartily, and I try to forget that he's seen me naked.

Then Ryan takes the phone and fields questions about dates and locations and that kind of thing. I drift over to the window of our swanky room and gaze out at the Empire State Building.

Is this really me, I wonder? It doesn't quite feel real. I don't belong in a hotel like this one. The ring, though it sits well on my finger, looks like a prop from a movie. Though we've been gone less than twenty-four hours, I miss home. I miss Buttercup.

'I better call my dad,' I say when Ryan hangs up from his parents. I glance at my watch. It's after five, and Dad's on nights this week, so he should be at the firehouse. With Trevor, as usual. I don't think about that.

'Well, actually, your father knows,' Ryan smiles. 'I asked for his permission.'

'Oh,' I say. 'Well, that was . . . old-fashioned of you. But nice, I guess.'

I dial my father's cell. 'Are you happy, Porkchop?' Dad asks. In the background, I can hear the crackling of the radio, a few voices.

'Oh, yes,' I say. 'Definitely.'

'Trevor, guess what? Chastity's marrying her doctor,' Dad calls. I wait for the stomach pain. None comes.

'Best wishes, Chas,' I hear Trevor say after the briefest pause.

'Trevor says "best wishes,"' Dad relays.

'Thank you,' I say steadily.

'She says thanks,' Dad calls again. 'So. Put my future son-in-law on the phone, will you?'

Dad and Ryan talk a minute, Ryan ever respectful, calling Dad 'sir' and thanking him for his blessing. Finally, our families alerted to our impending nuptials, Ryan and I—my fiancé and I—look at each other.

'So. That went well,' he says. 'Any ideas on where you'd like to eat?'

I remember the little Italian restaurant on Thompson Street, where Trevor told me he was marrying Hayden. Maybe we could go there, replace that awful memory with this happy one. But I say no, no ideas. Anywhere he picks will be fine with me.

*   *   *

The boys hug me, the Starahs exclaim over the ring, my little nieces ask if they can be flower girls. 'Of course!' I say. 'Absolutely! And boys, you can be in it, too, however you want. As long as you don't hit or bite, okay?'

'That takes all the fun out of it,' Jack comments. 'Congratulations, Sis.' He envelops me in a hug, and my throat grows tight.

Elaina is waiting for her chance. When I excuse myself to go to the loo, she pounces, following me right in.

'Lainey, I really do have to pee, so—'

'Honey, are you sure about this?' she asks, sitting on the edge of the tub, nibbling her fingernail.

My breath catches. 'Are you kidding me? How can you ask me that?' My voice is bouncing off the avocado-colored tiles. 'You're the one who's been telling me what a great thing this is,' I growl in a quieter voice. "Don't mess this up, *querida*. Get over Trevor, *querida*."'

'Okay! Yes, so I said that!' she snaps. 'Big deal, you know? Chas, are you happy?'

'Yes!' I insist. 'I—definitely!' My jaw clenches. 'Elaina,' I say, and my voice is now a harsh whisper. 'This is the best I'm going to do. He's a good guy. We'll be very content together. He loves me. I love him. Okay?

395

Please don't say anything else.'

'Okay,' she says. She starts to say something, then pauses.

'What, Lainey?' I ask. My head is killing me, and we haven't had dinner, and I'm starving and just want to go home and curl up with Buttercup.

'Have you told Trevor?' she whispers.

'He knows,' I say, turning away. I pretend to fix my hair in the mirror, but I can see Elaina's worried eyes reflected back at me.

'What did he say?' she asks.

'He's all for it.' I turn back to look directly in her face. 'I told him I loved him and he said to stay with Ryan.' My face contorts.

'Shit,' she says. 'Okay, okay, I'm sorry, honey. It's okay.'

'Will you be my maid of honor?' I weep.

'Of course,' she says, her big dark eyes filling, as well.

An eternity later, filled with the goodwill of my family and my mother's freakishly good chicken piccata, Ryan and I drive back home. Buttercup comes loping sloppily toward me, and I gather her tight against me, burying my face against her cheek. 'I missed you, Miss Ugly Head,' I say.

'Aaaaroooorooroo!' she bays happily. *Right back at you,* is what she's really saying.

'My condo doesn't allow dogs,' Ryan says, stepping back to avoid a string of drool. 'She'll have to stay with your brother.'

I glare at him. 'She stays with me. And who says we're moving into your condo? Huh? I love this house. Maybe we're staying here.'

A little smile pulls at Ryan's mouth. 'Why would we stay here when we could live at my condo? This place is cute, Chastity, but it's not where I plan on living,' he says in a deliberately contemptuous tone, and before too much time has passed, we're having post-argument sex upstairs in my room.

When Ryan is sleeping, I grab my robe and pull it on, intending to go downstairs for some Oreos or a Pop-Tart or two, maybe three. But at the top of the stairs, something catches my eye. Turning in disbelief, I push the bathroom door all the way open.

It's done. My bathroom is finished. Gleaming pedestal sink, the smooth gray tiles of the floor . . . the tub! The Jacuzzi tub is in, and not only that, there's a fern sitting on one corner. And all my stuff is unpacked. The pale green towels hang from the racks that I chose so long ago, the little antique porcelain soap dish sits on the glass shelf above the sink. The pounded silver light switch cover is in place, the framed picture of the tree shrouded in mist is hung. The light fixtures are up.

It's done. It's beautiful.

I catch a glimpse of my reflection. My cheeks are flushed, and my mouth is hanging open.

The boys didn't say a word about this. They

397

must've wanted to surprise me. I can't believe it.

I hear the door being opened and a repetitive clacking noise as Buttercup's tail begins whipping some poor piece of furniture downstairs. 'Hey, gorgeous,' Matt's voice says to her.

I glance in at Ryan, who is still asleep, picturesquely sprawled on his back. I pause a second, looking at his Adonis perfection, then close the door and go downstairs. 'Matt,' I say, my voice thick with emotion, 'thank you for finishing the bathroom. It's beautiful!'

'Oh, yeah? You like it? Cool.' He opens the fridge, takes out a beer, offers it to me. I shake my head. 'Actually, I wasn't the one who did it, so I can't take any credit.'

'Oh. Lucky then?'

'Trevor, actually. Just came in here Friday morning and got to work. Didn't take that long, once he got going. It looks great doesn't it?'

'Yup,' I breathe, sitting in a kitchen chair. 'It's great.'

'So. Is the doc here?' Matt asks.

'Yes. He's staying over, if that's okay.'

Matt pulls a face. 'Sure.' He grins. 'Just don't make any unnecessary noise, okay? You're still my little sister, even if you are old enough to be engaged.'

'Ha,' I attempt. 'Right.'

'Nice chunk of jewelry he got you,' Matt

says, swigging some of his Adirondack pale ale.

'Thanks. You know what? I think I'll have a beer after all,' I say. We end up playing Scrabble until midnight, Buttercup's head in my lap, Ryan sleeping undisturbed upstairs.

CHAPTER THIRTY-THREE

Ryan wakes at five the next morning. 'What is on me?' he mutters, squinting at the bottom of the bed.

'That would be our little girl,' I say, pulling my own leg free. Buttercup sighs and moans.

'Chastity, this bed is not big enough for the three of us,' Ryan says. 'She's a very, um, pleasant dog, but she can't sleep here when I'm staying over.'

'This is her bed, Ryan. You sleep here only by the grace of Buttercup,' I smile. He doesn't smile back. 'Not a morning person, I see.'

He finally grins and sits up, kisses me on the shoulder. 'I should run back to my place. I need to shower and check my messages.'

Five minutes later, the Mercedes—*our* Mercedes, dare I call it?—has pulled away from my little house. Because I'm wide awake, I go into my new bathroom and take a shower. It's glorious. The fan works, the shower head gushes water beautifully, my soap, chosen so long ago, smells like heaven. *Thank you,*

Trevor.

But no. I can't be thinking about him, and hey, why should I? I'm engaged. He told me to stay with Ryan, and I am. If he feels guilty about shagging me, he should. If it got my bathroom finished, well, bully for me.

I dry my hair, dress and decide to go to Dad's. Since he was working last night, he should just be getting home. I stop at the bakery and get us some pastries, then head to his house. I don't even turn my head when I walk by Trevor's.

'Here's my baby girl,' Dad says, hugging me hard. When he lets me go, he takes my hand and inspects the ring. 'Very expensive,' he says, wiping his eyes.

'Oh, Daddy.'

'I can't believe you're getting married,' he says thickly. 'At least you brought pastries. Come on, I'll put on some coffee.'

Dad's apartment looks a little better than the last time I was here. The boxes are gone and he's got some curtains up. A few minutes later, we're eating amiably, drinking from matching coffee mugs. 'You happy, Porkchop?' Dad asks.

I'm getting a little tired of everyone asking me that. Isn't it obvious? 'Yes, Dad. Very happy.'

'He seems like a good guy.' I nod. 'And it's good to have a doctor in the family, I guess.'

'Jack would say it's better to have a

paramedic,' I smile.

Dad laughs automatically. 'Yes. Well.' He swallows. 'Did your mother tell you she's set a date?' he asks, not meeting my eyes.

'Yes.' I put down my chocolate croissant. Mom's wedding is looming large, though Ryan had provided a nice distraction. Three weeks, for God's sake. 'What are you going to do, Dad?'

My father takes a long sip of coffee. 'Nothing, Chastity.'

'You're not going to even try? What about retiring? Maybe if she saw that you were really out, she'd take you back.'

Dad sighs. 'She's going through with this, honey. It's not . . . I'm too late.'

'She told me you were the love of her life.' My throat is tight. The parallels between my mother and me are certainly not lost. Both of us marrying someone who is not the love of our lives. Crap. I seem to be crying.

'Being a fireman is who I am,' Dad says quietly. 'I won't give that up, not until I can't do the job anymore. I'll always love your mother, honey. And we have you five wonderful kids, and God knows how many grandkids, right? We've agreed to be very civil about this. I'm happy for her.'

'Liar,' I say wetly.

He smiles sadly. 'Yeah, well it's my own fault.' He clears his throat. 'But that's yesterday's news. Tell me about how your man

401

popped the question.'

I tell, Dad approves, we manage a few laughs. Finally, I glance at my watch. 'I have to go to work, Dad,' I say. 'Will you be okay?'

'Sure,' he says. 'Of course. Off you go. Out with you. Shoo.'

I head into work, where much fuss is made over my Tiffany engagement ring. ' "Embrace the power of the Ring, or embrace your own destruction," ' I say to Angela, who laughs merrily. 'Hey, Ange,' I say to her when the others have drifted away. 'Matt was talking about you last night.'

Her face lights up. 'He's fantastic, Chastity,' she says breathlessly. 'I'm . . . well, I'm head over heels. I can't stop thinking about him.'

'It seems mutual,' I murmur.

'Well, you know what it's like when you've met that perfect match,' she sighs.

'Yes. Yes, I do.' And I picture Ryan. Not Jeter, not Aragorn, and certainly not Trevor.

*　　*　　*

My mother calls that afternoon, and I agree to be maid of honor, no matter how awful it feels. 'Just don't make me wear one of those hideous dresses, Mom,' I say.

'Wear whatever you want, sweetheart,' she answers blithely. 'Wear a Yankees uniform. Wear your brother's turnout gear. I don't care. I'm getting married, we're going to Norway for our honeymoon—'

'Norway!'

'—and we're going to have a lot of fun. And so are you and Ryan. Aren't you? Where are you going on your honeymoon?'

'We haven't even talked about it, Mom. We're not at the planning stage just yet.'

'Don't dawdle,' she advises. 'Being married is wonderful.'

'Not by your account,' I mutter.

'I heard that.'

'So?'

'So say what you mean, young lady.' Her voice is thorny.

'So are you sure you want to marry someone you don't love as much as you love Dad?' I ask, just as thornily.

'Are you sure you want to marry someone you don't love as much as you love Trevor?'

It's like a punch in the throat. 'Mom!'

'Sorry, sorry,' she backpedals. 'I'm trying to make a point. That the man who's the most suitable husband might not be the one who makes your toes curl in bed, all right?'

My face blanches. 'Let's change the subject,' I mutter.

'But there are other qualities that make a life partnership work. Ryan has them. So does Harry. So why don't you back off, okay, honey?'

'Wow. You're . . . ouch. I think you've . . . yes, I'm actually bleeding here.'

'Love you!' she calls. 'Please don't wear blue to the wedding.'

'You said you didn't care what I wore.'

'I was lying. Think pink. Bye, honey.'

*　　　*　　　*

The next week passes more or less normally. Mrs. Darling—Libby—e-mails me daily with news of bridal fairs in New York City—would champagne be all right for her dress color?— asks me how many people I'm envisioning for my half of the guest list, informs me that her preliminary calculations have a number around two hundred and seventy-three for their side, of course Ryan's sister (the famous Wendy Darling) would like to be a bridesmaid, would that be all right? I e-mail back, telling her that everything sounds fine with me, that wedding planning is not my thing, and I'd be happy to turn it over to her.

Ryan and I go out for dinner with two other couples one night. Both husbands are surgeons, both wives are very fit, very polished, very pleasant.

'Are there any women surgeons at the hospital?' I ask as the men discuss who's who.

'Of course,' Ryan says. 'Dr. Thrift, Dr. Escobar and Dr. Adams.'

The other men nod silently. The wives smile. Or they don't stop smiling, having been Botoxed into perma-smile.

'I'd love to meet them, too,' I say.

'Of course,' Ryan answers. 'All in good time.'

'Do you work, Susan?' I ask one of the wives.

'Oh, no,' she says around her teeth. 'I'm a sahm.'

'A what?' I ask.

'A sahm. S-A-H-M. Stay-at-home mom.'

'Lovely,' I say. 'Two of my sisters-in-law are also, uh, sahms. And you, Liza?'

'The same! Sahm!' she croons. They regale me with reports of their children's activities: karate, violin, piano, basketball, baseball, lacrosse, soccer, voice lessons, French club, chess club, drama club. I vow to make sure my kids have time to just play, the way I did. I played and read and wandered the neighborhood with my brothers. And Trevor.

Speaking of Trevor, he e-mailed me four days ago. *Dear Chastity, I hope you're doing well. Just wanted to say congratulations again. Hope to see you around Emo's one day soon.—Trevor*

I haven't written back because I just don't know what to say. And I haven't seen him around Emo's because I haven't gone to Emo's. I'm avoiding him.

CHAPTER THIRTY-FOUR

Several days later, I'm forced to cover a budget meeting of the city council. If there's a cure for insomnia, I've found it.

In order not to fall asleep and possibly drool on my shirt, I sit in the front row on a punishing metal chair and take notes, silently cursing Suki, who usually covers these things, while making a mental note to buy some chocolate for her, since she usually has to cover these things. The endless construction project has gone over budget. Again. The school board is asking for more money. Again. The senior citizen council wants . . . shocker . . . more money. Again. Town crew . . . more money. I pinch myself to keep from dozing off.

After several months have passed—okay, okay, it was just several hours—I am finally released from the hell of the budget meeting and find myself blinking in the bright light of a glorious summer afternoon. The leaves of the trees that line Main Street are lush and green and just about edible. The air is sparkling clean and dry, the sky shimmers with a blue so pure it makes your heart ache with joy. Birdsong fights with the noise of rush-hour traffic as commuters try to disentangle themselves from the closed-off streets and cross the bridge over to Jurgenskill. The

Hudson runs clear and deep along River Road. I can't wait to get home and go for a row.

Suddenly, there's a screech of brakes and horrible bang. A car has crashed into one of the Jersey barriers along the edge of the construction site. As I watch in horror, another car smashes into the first. The blare of horns pierces the air.

Racing down the street, I'm not quite aware that I've called 911 until I hear the dispatcher's voice. 'Two-car MVA at the corner of River and Langdon streets,' I say, leaping over a bundle of newspapers someone left on the sidewalk. 'Car versus barrier, then got rear-ended. Might be injuries.'

'I'm dispatching the fire department right now,' the operator says.

I shove my phone in my pocket as I reach the intersection. Traffic is stopped now, people are getting out of their cars to look. The driver of the second car, which rear-ended the first, gets out. Already, his cell phone is pressed to his ear.

No one has gotten out of the first car.

Shattered bits of glass are everywhere. The first car looks like a soda can that's been crushed. The driver, a woman, is unconscious. I walk up to the car door.

'Ma'am?' I say, my voice shaking. There's blood on her face, coming from her head. 'Ma'am? Can you hear me?' She lifts her head and blinks.

'Try not to move,' I say. 'You've been in an accident. Um, um, I'm an EMT. My name's Chastity.' The back door of the car is dented, but I give it a good tug and it opens. 'I'm just going to hold your head still, okay?'

'What happened?' she asks groggily.

'You hit the barrier,' I say. 'Can you tell me your name?'

'Mary,' she answers. 'Mary Dillon.'

Blood, warm and sticky, is dripping onto my hands as I hold her head so that she's facing forward. My mouth is as dry as sand and my legs are trembling. 'Do you have any pain, Mary?'

'A little,' she says. 'My head stings.'

'How about your stomach? Any pain or tenderness?'

'No. My shoulder kind of hurts. The left one.'

'Okay,' I say. 'That's probably from the seat belt. How about your neck?'

'Um, a little.' She tries to look around, but I keep her head still.

'Don't move your neck, okay, Mary? Just stay looking straight ahead.' My voice sounds more normal. The blood trickle seems to have slowed, but I can't risk taking a good look. 'The ambulance is on its way, okay? Help is coming.' I think for a second. 'Do you know what day it is?'

'Uh, Thursday. July eleventh?'

'Great. How old are you?'

'Thirty-five,' she tells me. 'Am I in bad shape?' she asks, fear thick in her voice. 'Is something wrong with my neck?'

'You've been in an accident, so we always check the neck and back. But you seem pretty good to me,' I tell her. 'The fire department is on its way. They'll take good care of you.'

A crowd has formed around us. A man, the driver of the second car, peers in the window. 'Can I help?' he asks.

'Are there any doctors or paramedics around?' I ask him.

'I'll check,' he says, backing away. I hear him asking the crowd. No one steps forward.

I try to remember what else I should do. God! There seems to be so much! 'Mary, do you remember what happened? Did you black out?'

'Oh, shit,' she says. 'I was reaching for my cell phone. Stupid.'

'Gotcha. Um, how about any medications?'

'Just vitamins.'

'Any medical history? High blood pressure, fainting, anything like that? Diabetes?'

'No,' she says. 'Nothing.'

'Any chance you could be pregnant?'

'Not unless it's immaculate conception,' she says. I can see a smile in the rearview mirror.

'Well, your name *is* Mary,' I say, smiling back.

I can see the fire truck up ahead, and

the EFFD ambulance, lights flashing. Unfortunately, the traffic snarl and the construction are making it hard for them to get here. My arms are starting to shake from not moving them . . . and from fear, too, heck.

'You're an EMT?' Mary asks.

'Yup,' I answer.

'Lucky for me.'

The sirens are louder now. 'How's the pain?' I ask.

'Not that bad. Mostly my head and shoulder. Am I okay?'

'Nothing else?'

'No.' She sighs. 'I just bought this car.'

I smile. 'At least you seem to be okay.'

At last, a fire truck and the department's ambulance arrive on the scene. The guys swarm off the truck like efficient, gear-clad bees. One leans down to me. It's Trevor. For some reason, I knew it would be. We haven't seen each other since the big night, since we fought.

'Hey, Chastity,' he says, sounding mildly surprised. 'What've we got?'

'Hey, Trev. Um, well, this is Mary, age thirty-five. She was reaching for her cell phone, right, Mary? And then she hit the barrier, then bam! She got hit from behind.' Trevor nods, and my voice picks up speed and confidence. 'I witnessed the accident. She's got a laceration on her head, some shoulder and neck pain, so I've been holding the C-spine.

She remembers what happened, is alert and oriented. Positive LOC for less than a minute.'

Trevor nods. 'Hi, there,' he says to Mary. 'I'm Trevor. I'm a firefighter and a paramedic. We're going to get you out of there and take you to the hospital to get checked out. Sound good?'

'Okay,' Mary says. 'Can she stay with me?'

Trevor glances at me, smiling. 'You bet.' Helen comes over, talks to Trev for a second, goes back to the truck. I stay in the back of the car, holding Mary's head, my heart still thumping.

Santo approaches with a cervical collar and gets in the back with me. 'Hold her steady, Chas . . . good girl.' He snaps the collar into place. 'We're all set, Chas,' he says. 'You can get out now.'

'Good luck, Mary,' I say, patting her shoulder gingerly.

'Thank you so much,' she says, reaching up to grip my hand.

My legs still wobble when I get out. I take a few steps away from the car and watch Eaton Falls's bravest do their work. Trev seems to be running the scene— I guess my father is back at the firehouse, not on this detail. Trevor talks into the radio, then goes to the ambulance and opens the back doors. He and Paul take out the stretcher. Santo checks Mary's abdomen and shoulder, and they slip a vest over her to further stabilize her spine. Jake has the Hurst

411

tool and starts cutting through her door, which is apparently stuck shut.

When Jake is through, Trevor moves in and guides Mary onto the backboard. He says something to her and takes her hand, his face so warm and reassuring that I know she'll feel better just because he's there. Then he and Paul lift her carefully and load her onto the stretcher, strapping her in. He's talking to her the whole time, smiling at her, doing what he does so well.

I love him. I'll always love him and I realize I'd rather be alone than with someone who's not him. No matter what Trevor says, no matter who he's with, no one else will do. My heart is so raw and unguarded at that moment, the truth is so unbearably stark, that my knees buckle, and I have to sit down on the curb.

Trevor bends down to listen to Mary, then looks up. His eyes find mine. He gestures to Mary, and her hand lifts up in a wave. Then she's loaded into the ambulance, and Paul climbs in with her. Jake gets in the driver's seat, and a second later, the lights are flashing, the siren is blipping and off they go.

Trevor comes over and kneels in front of me. 'Are you all right, Chastity?' he says, his voice scraping my swollen heart. He takes my hand and puts his fingers on my wrist, checking my pulse.

'I'm fine,' I say, not looking at him. I'm still shaking. Trevor peers into my face, his beautiful eyes worried. 'I'm not going to faint,' I assure him, glancing at those chocolate pools for just a second. I manage a smile, and he squeezes my hand.

'You did it, Chas,' he smiles. 'You looked like a true O'Neill out there.'

'Thanks,' I whisper, my chest tight.

'Are you sure you're okay?' he asks, letting go of my hand.

'Yes,' I say in a more normal voice. 'It was just a little . . . overwhelming.'

He nods, then glances at the engine. Santo is talking to a little kid, her eyes starry in that classic 'I love firefighters' look. Helen climbs into the engine. Trevor looks back at me. 'That's a beautiful ring you've got there,' he says quietly.

Despite my thudding heart, I keep my voice light. 'Thanks. Ryan has great taste.'

'In more than just rings.' His gaze drops to the pavement. 'I should go.'

'Okay,' I say numbly. 'Thank you, Trevor.'

The light catches the reflective letters on the back of his gear as he walks away. His hair ruffles in the breeze off the river, but the rest of him looks heavy and tired. Santo climbs into the driver's seat, gives the horn a little blast and waves at me. I wave back and watch them leave.

The police are still milling around, talking to the driver of the second car. They ask me a few questions. A tow truck comes. When I'm

413

finally allowed to go, I call the office and tell Pen I won't be back today. Then I go home, change into shorts and a tank top to row in. While I'm at it, I slide my engagement ring off my finger and put it carefully in my jewelry box.

CHAPTER THIRTY-FIVE

Rowing is a great way to empty the mind. There's nothing but the swish of my oars and the rippling from the bow as I cut upriver. Feather and square, catch and drive, feather and square. The breeze dries the sweat on my back, the sun beats hot on my legs. I can hear the laughter of kids from the park. A golden retriever catches a Frisbee. Then I'm past the park and there are no people to look at anymore, just the trees and the Adirondacks rising all around me, green and majestic, as solid as a castle wall.

Trevor's words echo in my head. *You did it, Chas. You looked like a true O'Neill out there.*

He's right. I helped. I didn't save someone's life or anything, didn't push them from harm's way, didn't run into a burning building, but I helped someone in a time of need. Funny, after all these years of wanting so much to join the club, of wondering what it would be like to be the one who had the knowledge or the skill or the guts, the feeling is oddly hollow. Sure, I'm glad I was there for Mary, but as far as my own ego and self-image go, well, who really cares?

When I get home, Buttercup is lying as if dead on the lawn.

'Come here, girl,' I call. She raises her massive head and obeys, lumbering over to me, tail whipping, then flops at my feet. I stroke her ears and plant a kiss on her bony head. 'You like it being just us girls, don't you, honey?' I ask. Her tail whips back and forth. 'Me, too.'

That night, around eight o'clock, Matt and Angela are cuddled up on the couch watching *The Fellowship of the Ring*. I come downstairs, freshly showered, and watch as Arwen summons the river spirits to sweep away the Ring Wraiths and saves little Frodo's life.

'She rocks,' I murmur.

'You said it, sister,' Angela agrees.

'You going out, Chas?' Matt asks, glancing back at me.

'Yup. I'm going over to Ryan's.' I pause a casual beat or two. 'Hey, do you know if Trev is working tonight?'

'I don't think so. He was on today,' Matt says, not taking his eyes off the screen.

'Yeah, right. I just didn't know if there was overtime or whatever, since Hoser's still . . .' *Too much, Chastity.* 'Okay, guys. See you around.'

415

'Bye, Chastity,' Angela calls, smiling. Matt looks at her and touches her hair with smitten adoration. She blushes and returns his gaze with equal sappiness. I give them five minutes before they're unclothed and going at it like ferrets.

'Young love,' I sigh. They don't even hear me.

I drive to Trevor's so that I won't have time to chicken out. 'It's Chastity,' I say, when he answers his buzzer. 'Got a sec?'

'Sure.' He buzzes me in.

I leap up the stairs. When I burst through the hallway door, Trevor's waiting in the doorway for me, unbearably appealing in jeans and a plain white T-shirt. The smell of garlic wafts out of his apartment. 'Hey,' he says.

'Hi,' I say, feeling my face grow hot, and not because I just ran up four flights. He looks a little nervous, and hell, who can blame him? 'I'm not here to maul you,' I blurt.

He gives a little laugh, then steps into the hallway and closes the door behind him. 'What's up, Chastity?'

'Here,' I answer, thrusting a piece of paper at him. 'It's just easier like this.'

It's a note. I had to write one because I didn't think I could say all I needed to without crying. Trevor takes it carefully. 'Read it,' I order.

His eyebrow raises questioningly, but he unfolds the paper and reads silently. I already

416

have it memorized. The dang thing took me five drafts.

Dear Trevor,
    I want to apologize for coming over that night a couple of weeks ago. I was upset and emotional, and throwing myself at you the way I did was ill-advised at best and breathtakingly stupid at worst. I said things that I deeply regret now. Trev, you will always, always be my friend and part of my family. You have a special place in my heart and you always will. I'm sorry I put you on the spot the way I did. I hope you'll forgive me.
—Chastity

He reads it a couple of times before looking up at me again, his eyes dark and serious. 'Chastity . . .'

At that moment, Trevor's door opens and a blond head sticks out. 'Hey, Chastity!'

'Hi, Hayden,' I murmur. I'm not really surprised.

'What are you guys doing in the hall? Come on in!' Her perfect smile doesn't reach her eyes.

'I'm actually on my way out,' I say, glancing at Trevor. 'I just had to, um, drop something off.'

'Oh,' she says, her fake smile dropping a notch. 'Well, take care! Trev, honey, I think those veggies are just about to burn, and you know how I am in the kitchen.' She doesn't move from the doorway.

'Okay, well, I should be on my way,' I say, taking a step down the hall. 'Trev, you . . . I guess that's it. Take care. Enjoy your dinner.'

'I'll talk to you soon, Chastity,' he says. He looks back at my note, folds it carefully and puts it in his jeans pocket.

'Hon? The squash?' Perfect Hayden gives Trevor's arm a tug.

I'm down the hall and into the stairwell in record time. About halfway down the stairs, I stop and sit. I still have a lot to do tonight, and I need a clear head.

'Chastity?'

My head jerks up. 'Hayden.'

She glides down the stairs and stands above me. Well. I can't have that, so I get up and tower over her. Sometimes being a quarter inch shy of six feet has its benefits, and this moment is definitely one of them.

To her credit, Hayden is not cowed. She puts her manicured hands on her hips and stares at me. 'It's time to let him go, Chastity.'

Ouch. 'Trevor?'

'Of course, Trevor. Stop guilt-tripping him all the time.'

'Excuse me?'

'You know exactly what I'm talking about. You drifting in and out of his life, reminding him of the one time you were together, way

418

back in college.' I see he told her about that. Crap. 'You're still mooning after him, and it's really getting pathetic.'

Two times, Hayden. We were together two times. Guess he didn't tell you about time numero dos. Aloud, I don't say anything, just look down upon Hayden (literally and figuratively).

'Well?' she asks, swishing her long blond hair back over her shoulder.

'I'm not guilt-tripping anyone, Hayden. Trevor and I are connected, whether you like it or not.' I raise an eyebrow.

'He loves me, you know.'

'Sure.'

'We're probably going to get married.'

'Sure.'

'So just back off.'

'Sure.'

It's an old O'Neill sibling trick—to incite the most rage, simply agree endlessly. It works yet again.

Hayden's face grows blotchy, but her chin goes up. 'If he really wanted you,' she hisses, 'don't you think he would have done something about it by now? Do you think he'd be with me? Where's your pride, Chastity?'

With that, she spins on her tiny little heel and flounces back up the stairs, back to Trevor.

* * *

419

When I get to Ryan's place, he's watching CNN. 'Chastity! We didn't have plans, did we?' he asks.

'No,' I say. 'Ryan . . . I need to tell you something.'

He clicks off his plasma screen TV, Anderson Cooper's face disappearing in a blink. He leans in to kiss me, then stops. 'What is it, honey?' he asks, his voice gentle.

I can't answer. My throat hurts and my mouth is dry and tears spurt into my eyes.

Ryan studies my face. 'I see,' he murmurs.

My tears spill over. 'I'm sorry,' I whisper. 'I'm sorry.'

He leads me to the couch and passes me a box of tissues. The scene is so reminiscent of the night at Trevor's, but I'm in no mood for irony. 'You're breaking it off?' he asks.

My ragged inhale answers for me.

Ryan sits next to me, sighing, then scrubs his hand through his McDreamy hair. 'Well, what the hell happened?'

'Nothing, not anything in particular. Ryan, I think you're a wonderful man,' I blubber. 'You have so many nice qualities. And I do care about you. You're very thoughtful and—'

'Please, Chastity,' he says dryly. 'I don't need you to bolster my ego.'

'Okay. Sorry,' I say, my face scrunching with tears. I dig in my pocket and hand him back the ring. He looks at it, frowning.

'I thought things were going so well,' he says. He looks irked, and confused.

'They were. Nothing went wrong, nothing really happened, Ryan, it's just . . .' My voice trails off. What am I supposed to say here? There's no good answer.

'It's Trevor, isn't it?' Ryan asks.

I bow my head. Harvard/Yale taught the man more than how to cut into people, I guess. 'Yes,' I whisper.

Ryan swallows. 'I hope he . . . I hope he's good to you,' he says magnanimously. He gives his head a little shake.

'We're not together,' I say, fiddling with the hem of my shorts.

Ryan's gaze snaps back to me. 'Then why are you breaking up with me?'

I swallow. 'Because, Ryan, I think you deserve someone who loves you with her whole heart.'

'Well, that's a noble sentiment, if a bit sappy,' he replies. 'Are you sure, Chastity? I think we're really well-suited for each other.'

I shift on the couch to face him more directly. 'Ryan,' I say softly, 'I'm in love with another man. I care about you, and I like spending time with you . . . but not like . . . It's just not enough.'

'It's enough for me,' he says softly, and I can see that it's true.

'Not for me,' I whisper, the tears dripping off my cheeks. 'I'm sorry. I hope you find what

421

you're looking for.'

He pauses. 'I'll miss you, Chastity. You're a lot of fun.' For a minute, I think he might get mushy, but no. 'Well. Good luck.'

'Same to you,' I say, and with that, my engagement is officially over and done with.

What next, I have no idea.

CHAPTER THIRTY-SIX

Work is incredibly busy the next day, mercifully, so I don't have time to think about Ryan or Trevor or Perfect Hayden. Instead, I'm immersed in editing, assigning stories, talking to Alan about various and sundry issues, running things by Pen. Lucia gives me her piece for the month—seventeen column inches on making a wreath for your front door. 'Looks fantastic, Lu,' I say, flying past her in order to avoid discussing it. Suddenly, I lurch to a stop and take a closer look at her.

'Lucia,' I ask hesitantly, 'how are you doing about Teddy Bear and all that?'

'Fine!' she snaps. 'I'm fine, okay?'

'Are you ready to start dating again, do you think?'

She hesitates, her frown evaporating. 'Why?'

'Let me put it this way. Do you want to have kids?'

'Two,' she whispers back, catching my drift. 'A boy and a girl. Hopefully in that order.'

Holy crap. I smile. 'Mind if I fix you up with a surgeon?'

Because let's face it. I didn't exactly break Ryan Darling's heart. I have a feeling that Lucia and Ryan meeting could be the beginning of a beautiful friendship.

I decide not to tell anyone in my family about breaking it off with Ryan until after Mom's wedding. In truth, I'm lying low. If Matt suspects something, he's keeping his mouth shut. Or he just doesn't notice, too wrapped up in Angela and planning his college courses to notice his sister's love life (or lack thereof). I cover by going out with the gang from work a couple of times, switching Ernesto's rowing lessons to the evening, seeing a couple of movies by myself, with only a silo of popcorn for company. I take my dad out to dinner, but we go up to Lake Champlain so I don't have to run into anyone from town.

Oddly enough, now that I'm single once again with no prospects for husband in sight, I feel more relaxed. Happier, even, for some reason. I guess I've found that I'd rather be alone than with the wrong person. Even if the right person is with someone else.

I avoid Emo's. I avoid the firehouse. I really don't want to see Trevor just yet.

I ask my mother if she'd like me to stay with her the last few days before the big day.

'Oh, honey, that would be great.' She smiles. 'I've hardly seen you! Yes, by all means.'

And so, two nights before her wedding, she and I are sitting in the living room of my childhood, drinking cheap pinot grigio and having a rather wonderful time. Buttercup is asleep on my old bed; even from down the hall, we can hear her snoring.

'You really love that dog, don't you?' Mom asks.

'Someone has to,' I answer. I study the living room walls . . . there are dozens of pictures of us, the O'Neill kids and grandkids, front teeth missing, christenings, first communions, graduations, baseball, basketball, crew, hiking, skiing, camping, action shots ordered from the paper, Matt and the little old couple he helped rescue from a house fire. Jack getting the Medal of Honor. Lucky and his fellow bomb squaddies when they defused a homemade and very powerful bomb from a high school. Mark and the kitty-cat montage.

And Dad. He's everywhere, smiling, blue eyes gleaming, abundantly happy in every single picture.

'Where's your wedding picture?' I ask, noting a blank spot on the wall.

Mom sighs. 'In the closet.'

I swallow. 'Can I have it?' I ask quietly.

'Of course.' She says no more, just takes another sip of her wine.

'Mom?' I venture.

424

'Not another lecture, honey,' she says, gazing out the window at the dark street.

'No, no.' I pause. 'Ryan and I called it off, Mom.'

Her eyes flick back to me, unsurprised. 'I thought so. You haven't mentioned him for days. Why, honey?'

'Well, I just . . . we didn't . . . Trevor. That's why.'

She sets her wine glass on the table next to her chair. 'What did he do?' she says, an ominous hint of Holy Roman Inquisitor in her voice.

'Not a thing,' I lie. My eyes fill, however, and Mom doesn't miss it. 'I just love him, Mom. Even if he doesn't quite feel the same way.'

'Quite?'

'Well, I know he cares about me and all that crap, but he doesn't want a relationship. With me, anyway. Too much to lose.'

'So you tossed over a perfectly good fiancé for nothing, honey?'

I snort. 'Yes. I'd rather be alone than with someone who didn't . . . measure up.' I wipe my eyes. 'Don't say anything to anyone just yet, okay?'

She nods, then goes into the kitchen and returns with the wine bottle. 'Well, whatever. I think you're brave, Chastity, forging out on your own. All or nothing. Do or die. By the way, I heard about that car accident when you were so calm. Good for you, honey! I'm so proud of you.'

'Thanks, Mom.' I take a slug of wine, and maybe the alcohol gives me the courage to say something once more, just for the record. 'You don't have to marry Harry, you know. Dad will love you till the day he dies.'

'In his own way, yes,' she says bitterly, then she starts to cry, too. 'Oh, isn't this fun? I'm so glad you came over,' she sobs, and I laugh wetly and go over to hug her.

'Let's run off to Vegas, just us girls,' I suggest, and she gives me an affectionate swat.

'I'm going to be very happy with Harry,' she proclaims. 'Guess what I'm giving him for a wedding present?'

'A new prostate?' I suggest.

'No, you bad girl. *The Joy of Sex.*'

I blanch. 'Now who's the bad girl, hm? Let's change the subject! Isn't *The Office* on tonight?'

* * *

I awaken the next morning with my dog draped over my torso and no blood at all in my extremities. 'Off!' I mumble, shoving Buttercup with my lifeless limbs. 'Breakfast time.' She ignores me and remains corpse-like. I pet her ears and stare at the ceiling.

Mercifully, there is no official rehearsal dinner tonight. Instead, we're going to Harry's

426

to meet his daughters and grandchildren and have pizza. 'Okay, dog. Up and at 'em.'

My dog and I roll out of bed and careen down the hall, my legs still prickling. Water's running in the kitchen, so that means Mom's making coffee, thank God. I may be a little hungover.

The back door opens and closes, and I hear familiar footsteps. I grab Buttercup's collar and lurch to a stop just outside the kitchen.

'What are you doing here, Mike?' my mother asks.

My breath catches. *At last!*

'Chastity, we know you're there,' Dad says. 'Come on in here, Porkchop.'

'Morning,' I mutter, obeying. Dad raises an eyebrow and doesn't smile, making me feel like I'm in sixth grade again. I slink over to the coffeepot and pour myself a cup.

'What is it, Mike?' Mom asks, smoothing her hair down. She's dressed already, looking very cute in her sweater set and beaded necklace.

'Betty—' he begins.

'Don't start!' she barks. 'You can't do this to me the day before my wedding. I won't—'

'Quiet, woman!' Dad snaps. 'Listen. It's not what you think.' He glances at me.

'I'll just take my coffee down to the rec room, where I won't eavesdrop at all,' I offer.

'No. Stay, sweetheart.' He looks at Mom again, then takes her hand, very gently, and

427

looks down at her from the ten-inch difference in their height. 'Betty,' he says softly, 'you were a wonderful wife and an extraordinary mother. Thank you.'

A sob bursts out of me, causing coffee to splatter down my front. 'Sorry,' I say, covering my eyes. Buttercup licks up the spilled coffee, then lies at my feet. Tears drip down my cheeks.

Dad doesn't even glance at me. 'I hope you and Harry will be very happy together, honey, and I'm sorry for every time I disappointed you,' he tells my mother.

She's crying, too. 'I'll always love you, Mike,' she whispers.

'I'll always love you, too. I wish I could've given you what you wanted.'

I press my arm against my mouth to stifle my crying. Dad leans down and kisses Mom on the forehead, then hugs her. His eyes glow with tears, but he's smiling, too.

'Mike?' my mom says. 'Will you do something for me?'

'Anything,' he answers, and in this moment, he means it.

'Will you give me away tomorrow?'

Dad wipes his eyes, then pulls back to look into Mom's eyes. 'It would be an honor,' he says.

CHAPTER THIRTY-SEVEN

The next day at one-thirty in the afternoon, I give my dress a final tug. 'Do I look ridiculous?'

Elaina steps back and examines me critically. 'You look hot, *bambino*. This is your color.'

'Pink?' I ask incredulously. *'Pink?'*

Olivia bursts through the bedroom door. 'Oh, Auntie, you look so pretty!' she breathes. 'Like Cruella DeVille!'

I shoot my niece a sharp look. 'Thanks, Livvie. That's definitely what I was going for.'

'It's your hair,' Olivia explains. 'It's black-and-white, like Cruella's.'

'It's *not* black-and-white,' I tell my six-year-old niece with thinly veiled patience. 'I have one or two gray hairs. My hair is black.'

'Actually, you do have kind of a streak going on here,' Elaina says, examining my head.

I slap her hand away. 'Where are the rest of the girls?'

All of us bridesmaids—that is, my nieces and me—are wearing pink. A deep rose for me, pale pink for the girls. Mom, to my surprise, is wearing a red dress. She looks fabulous. Her cheeks glow, her blue eyes snap with excitement, and any bitterness or sorrow she's been hiding seems to have evaporated

429

with my father's grand gesture.

No males are allowed at the house; it's just us womenfolk as we dress and curl and spray and brush. The Starahs are in charge of their daughters, and I help buckle little shoes and zip little zippers. My brothers, father and nephews—and of course, Harry—will meet us at the church.

After the photographer torments us with an hour and a half of picture-taking, we spend several years (or so it seems) discussing who will ride with whom to the Unitarian church. 'I'm just gonna walk,' I threaten. 'It'll be faster than this conversation.'

But it's raining out, so my threats are empty.

Finally, we clamber into the minivans and cars and head off. Mom, Elaina and I are alone in Mom's Chrysler, me chauffeuring while the two of them sit in the back.

'You look beautiful, Mamí,' Elaina says, fixing a stray curl behind Mom's ear.

'Did Chastity tell you she dumped Ryan?' Mom says mildly.

Elaina sighs. 'Yes. Too bad about that ring. Could've sent my baby through college.'

I grin in the rearview mirror. 'Well, you could always finish divorcing Mark and marry Ryan yourself, Lainey.'

'You know very well I'm not divorcing Mark,' she says. 'In fact, I might as well tell you, I'm pregnant.'

The car swerves to the right as Mom and I

430

shriek. 'Lainey! That's wonderful!'

She blushes. 'Yeah, well, he's a new man and all that, you know? So maybe a girl this time.'

Mom is dabbing tears. 'I'm so happy, Elaina, sweetheart,' she says, hugging Lainey tight.

I am, too, and if a flame of envy is dancing in my heart, well, I'm pretty used to it.

'Oh, look, there's the church!' Mom exclaims. 'This is so exciting! I barely remember marrying Mike, I was so sick with Jack.'

'Jack's a bastard? I knew it,' I comment. Sure, we kids did the math, but Mom and Dad never admitted it. They insisted that Jack (weighing in at nine pounds, twelve ounces) came two months early.

Men in suits wait for us, faces obscured in a sea of umbrellas. Some, no doubt, are my brothers. And Trevor. And Dad.

Jack helps me out of the car, as I am awkward in my long dress. 'Lucky, why are you wearing a dress?' he asks. I flip him off cheerfully. 'Sorry, Chas,' he amends, ushering me inside. 'You clean up nice.'

'Thanks, Jack. How's Dad?' I glance around. Dad is talking to Matt. Angela waves to me from a pew.

'Dad is eerily fine,' Jack answers.

'Chas, can you load this film for me?' Lucky asks. 'I'm all thumbs.'

'Yet you defuse bombs for a living. How reassuring.' I take the proffered camera and do as I'm told.

Lucky laughs. 'Put a dress on her and she's all high and mighty. I like you better when you're one of the guys.'

'Join the club,' I murmur, handing his camera back to him. 'Here.'

'Hey, Chastity.'

I turn around. 'Hi, Trevor.' I bite my lip. 'You look very handsome.' And tired, and a little sad.

He smiles, but his eyes don't join in. 'You . . . that's a nice dress.' He closes his eyes briefly, acknowledging the lameness of his compliment.

'Thanks,' I say, forgiving him.

He clears his throat. 'Chastity, what's your dad doing here?'

'Oh, you didn't hear? He's giving away the bride,' I say, forcing a smile.

His eyebrows bounce up in surprise. 'Are you kidding me?' he asks too loudly.

'Trev! Over here, bud,' Mark calls from a front pew. Trevor hesitates.

'Go ahead,' I say. 'I have bridesmaidy things to do.'

Still looking stunned, he walks toward the front of the church, glancing back at me. I shrug.

Mom bustles in behind me. 'There you are!' she says, as if I were hiding. 'Where's your father?'

'Right here, Betty. Can I be the first to kiss the bride?' Dad smooches her cheek. 'Don't you look gorgeous,' he says, and he seems to mean it. He's all Cary Grant today, smiling and debonair, good grace and manners. Mom grins up at him.

Seeing them smiling moonily at each other, I wait. Wait for Mom's smile to fade in abrupt realization. Wait for her to make the announcement. To call it off. Wait for her to glance down the aisle at Harry, five foot seven—too old for her, too chubby—and then stare at my tall and handsome, strong and heroic father and realize that no one will ever fill Mike O'Neill's shoes. To declare to everyone that true love has conquered, and she and Dad will stay together, happier than ever, till the day they die.

But she doesn't. Instead, she adjusts my dad's pin, a Maltese cross, the symbol of firefighters. Then she checks to see that all her granddaughters are in place, and they are, a shimmering mob of creamy pink satin. Sarah nods at the choir loft and walks down the aisle to where Jack and their boys are sitting. The organ starts playing, and the girls begin their march. First Sophie, strewing pink rose petals, then Olivia, her coppery curls bouncing. Then comes Annie, who is scowling at Luke as he tries to take her picture. Claire, holding baby Jenny, comes last. When they're all seated in the front pews with their brothers and parents, it's my turn.

I take one more look at my parents, together for the last time, arm in arm, smiling. *Do it, Mom,* I will her. She smiles at me as if she's reading my mind. Being Mom, she probably is.

'Go on, honey,' she whispers.

So I do. Heart aching, I do.

Trevor is watching me as I make my way down the aisle. I hope I'm smiling, but I bet I'm not. I can't seem to feel my face, actually. Trev looks . . . odd. Bleak. The way I feel.

Then I'm past him, already at the plain little altar.

'You look lovely, Chastity,' Harry whispers.

How can my mom be marrying a man I've only met four times? How can this guy be the one who will sit in my father's chair?

Mom and Dad are right behind me. Dad kisses Mom's cheek, shakes Harry's hand, and I surreptitiously wipe away a tear. Dad turns away, and my throat slams shut. *No, Daddy! Fight for her!*

But Mom is beaming. Harry is beaming. Dad sits in the second row with Mark and Elaina, picks up Dylan and kisses his cheek, possibly, I think, to hide the tears in his eyes.

And then, without a lot of pomp or circumstance, my mother turns to Harold H. Thomaston and becomes his wife.

*   *   *

434

The church hall is decorated with pink streamers and pink flowers. Pink balloons are tied in bundles to the concrete posts, and the DJ is setting up in the corner. It looks more like a seven-year-old girl's birthday party than the wedding of two senior citizens. The Starahs cleverly hired a couple of high school girls to keep an eye on their broods, and the kids are running around, stuffing deviled eggs in their mouths and getting sugared up on Shirley Temples and root beer.

My plan is to have a large glass of wine as promptly as possible, but Mom forcibly introduces me to each and every one of Harry's relatives and friends. By the time I sit down, my cheeks ache from fake smiling and my feet are killing me, encased in tombs of size-eleven kitten heels invented by a man whose mother must have beaten him daily to inspire such misogyny.

'How are you doing?' Angela asks, sliding next to me.

'Not that great,' I admit. 'How about you?'

'Matt's telling your father he's leaving the fire department,' she murmurs, toying with a napkin.

'Kicking him when he's down?' I suggest, looking over to where Matt and Dad sit, head to head, faces serious.

'Well, to be honest, Chastity,' Angela says gently, 'your father doesn't seem that unhappy.'

She's right. That's probably the most depressing thing of all. That, or Trevor's face. He's sitting in the corner table with Jack and Lucky and their many children, staring at the saltshaker, clearly lost in thought. Unhappy thought. At least he had the grace not to bring Perfect bleeping Hayden.

'Your brother wants to be a teacher,' Dad announces, thumping into the chair next to me. Matt sits down more gracefully next to Angela.

'And how do you feel about that, Dad?' I ask.

He eyes Matt. 'I'm surprised, that's all, son,' he says. 'I thought you loved the fire department.'

'I do, Dad. But I want to try this, too.'

'Fine, fine,' he mutters. 'If I've learned anything, it's that you can't keep a man away from the work he loves. Right, Chas?'

I roll my eyes and chug a little wine.

'Well, Matthew, you'll be a great teacher. And a husband one day soon, if I'm not mistaken,' Dad announces heartily. I sputter some wine—so graceful, really; I should've been a princess.

'Excuse me?' I ask.

Angela's face is bright red. Matt grins. 'Well, we're planning to get married. Nothing official yet, since I don't have a ring and all that, but, well, I'm giving notice, Chas. Angie and I are moving in together.'

'Great!' I bark. 'That's just great. That's just bleeping wonderful. So happy and all that crap.'

Angela's face falls, and I'm immediately repentant. 'Shit. Sorry, Ange. I *am* happy and all . . .' To my horror, I start to cry. 'It's just that . . . I'll miss you, Mattie. So will Buttercup.'

'We'll be two blocks away, Chas,' Matt says, putting his arm around Angela. 'And I couldn't do better than this girl, could I? Just think. Another sister-in-law.'

All four of my brothers, married. Everyone except me. Boohoohoo. I get up, hug them both, mess up Matt's hair and give him a smack, then go to the bathroom to cry a little. There's no respite, though, because my father bangs on the door. 'Chastity! Your mother's going to dance with my replacement,' he calls. 'She wants you there.'

'Great,' I mutter at my reflection. Reaching into the bodice of my dress, I yank up my strapless bra and stomp out of the bathroom.

All the guests are gathered round the little dance-floor area. 'Ladies and gentlemen,' the DJ says, and I resist the strong urge to stick a finger in my mouth and make a gacking sound. 'Appearing for the first time as man and wife, Mr. and Mrs. Harry Thomaston!'

Everyone claps—even sulky little old me— as they take to the floor. The song is Norah

Jones's cover of the beautiful Hoagy Carmichael song, 'The Nearness of You.'

Harry is smiling besottedly at my mother, and she grins back, and suddenly, her happiness breaks through my thorny, sulking heart. She deserves this. She really does, and my eyes fill with tears—again—at the sight of her face.

'And now the bride and groom would like to invite the members of their families to join in,' the DJ oozes smarmily.

Of course, I don't have a mate, I think as JacknSarah, LuckynTara, MarknElaina and MattnAngela drift out onto the floor. Jack leans down and kisses Sarah's tummy, Lucky is making Tara laugh. Elaina and Mark are doing that hot staring thing they do with each other, looking like they're about to burst into a pasa doblé or something. Matt has his cheek against Angela's blond hair. *What a gorgeous family,* I admit. Harry's two daughters are there somewhere, too, but I have to say our genetics are quite superior. What a great job Mom and Dad did!

'Come on, Porkchop,' Dad says, and leads me out to join them.

The familiar smell of my dad envelops me, Johnson's baby shampoo and Old Spice, and I lean my cheek on his shoulder. 'Are you okay, baby?' Dad asks. 'Your mother told me about Ryan.'

'So much for her vow of silence,' I mutter.

'Are you?'

'I'm fine,' I say.

'What happened with you two, anyway?'

'He just wasn't the one, Dad. Blah, blah, bleeping blah. You know how it is.'

Dad chuckles and kisses my hair. Then he stops dancing and looks up.

'Can I cut in, Mike?'

It's an emotional day, sure. But the sight of Trevor standing there, asking my dad if he can dance with me . . . It does something to me. My heart surges toward him—the man I've loved since I was ten, the man I'll always love—and for one second, I feel as exposed as a baby mouse in a room full of feral cats. Dad looks at Trevor, smiles and steps back, winking at me, and Trevor takes me in his arms.

His hand is warm and firm on mine, and the heat of his body shimmers into me, even though we're keeping the proper distance. My cheek grazes his, just enough to feel that he's clean-shaven today, and heat wiggles through me. I'm actually dizzy with the nearness of him.

Then the song fades, Trevor pauses—the Chicken Dance is sure to follow—but no, the fates decide to be kind, and the DJ sticks with Nora. 'Come Away with Me.' Oh, God. I can hardly breathe. We start dancing again.

'Hi,' I whisper.

'I didn't tell you how beautiful you look,' he says, and it's hard to look into his chocolate

439

eyes with words like that.

'Thank you.' My voice isn't working properly. My hand is on the back of his neck, my fingers just brushing against his hair, wanting to slide into the richness there. I can see the pulse in his neck, and maybe it's a little fast. We don't say anything for a minute. My heart is pounding so fast I feel a little faint. I try to absorb every sensation—his heat, his hands on me, the clean soapy smell of him.

'Where's your fiancé?' Trevor asks casually.

I stiffen slightly, and Trevor steps back a little. 'Well,' I breathe. 'Um, we sort of broke up.'

Trevor's eyes widen a fraction, an eyebrow raising in surprise. He stops dancing, but none of the other couples seem to notice, too caught up in being in love. 'Why?' Trevor whispers, still holding my hand, his arm still around me.

My heart thumps harder, slower, each beat waiting for my answer as I stare into Trevor's eyes. I open my mouth to give some answer, some casual *it-didn't-work-out* kind of thing. But instead, I hear myself say something else entirely.

'Because he wasn't you.'

Trevor's lips part ever so slightly. He blinks twice. He doesn't say anything. The song ends.

'How about that, folks?' the DJ bleats. 'And now to change the pace a little. Anyone here know the Macarena?' Everyone claps and cheers, and I feel my dress being tugged.

'Auntie! Auntie! I know the Macarena!' Claire shouts. 'Come on! It's fun! "Hey . . . Macarena!"'

I put my hand on her head, and Trevor takes a step back. Without saying a word, he walks off the dance floor and out of the church hall.

*   *   *

My mind is blank for the rest of the reception. My heart is blank, too. It can only take so much, I surmise. Maybe it's getting used to being in this state of brokenness, of incompleteness. Who knows? *Hey, you did all you could,* my heart whispers. *Thanks for trying.*

I dance with my nieces and nephews. I pick them up and twirl them and pretend I'm going to drop them, and they shriek and jump and wait impatiently for their turns with their beloved Auntie. I wave to my mom and smile at my brothers. When Mark asks where Trevor went, I just shake my head and shrug. Then I dance with Harry, towering five inches above him.

'I want you to know how lucky I feel,' he says. 'Your mother is a splendid woman. I'll take good care of her.'

'You better,' I mutter, then correct myself. 'I know you will, Harry. Sorry.' He smiles his forgiveness.

Just as I'm about to sit down with various

441

and sundry family members for our rubber chicken, my mother approaches. 'Will you make a toast, honey?' she asks. 'Harry's brother is very shy.'

'Sure,' I say automatically. Dad, who's sitting across from me, gives a nod. Mom flutters across to the DJ, then zips back to Harry.

'And now,' says the DJ, who really should work for Barnum & Bailey, 'the daughter of the bride, Chastity O'Neill, will say a few words for the happy couple.' I make my way over to the dance floor and take the microphone, then turn to the guests.

My mind goes completely blank.

'So,' I say. 'Well.' I swallow. 'Hello.'

Lucky, always the first to start misbehaving, covers his face with his hand. Tara shoots him a look but immediately looks down as her own laughter rises. Then Mark, then Elaina and Matt, then a few of the kids. I grin, and my heart seems to approve. *We'll be okay,* it says.

'Shut up, boys. Sorry, Mom.' I grin, then take a deep breath. 'I guess there are a lot of kinds of love,' I begin.

'Chastity.'

I freeze.

Trevor is standing at the back of the hall.

'Chastity,' he says again, and starts walking toward me.

It's silent in here now; the only sound, that of the caterers clattering in the adjoining

442

kitchen. Something's wrong with me, I think distantly, watching Trevor come closer and closer. My legs start shaking, my eyes sting, my heart races. I may throw up.

'Chastity,' he says quietly. 'I can't live without you another minute.'

The mike falls to the dance floor with a thunk as I cover my mouth with both hands. Tears spill out of my eyes, and I can't seem to draw a breath. The room is absolutely silent.

'I've loved you my whole life, Chas, from that first day you took me home after Michelle died. And I'm terrified you'll leave me or you'll stop loving me or even worse, something will happen to you. But I can't be without you anymore.' He takes my hands, which are shaking wildly, and swallows. 'Today I watched Mike give away the woman he loves. I can't do that, Chas. I thought I could, I thought it would be better if you were with someone else, but I was wrong. And I swear to you, I will love you the rest of my life and nothing will ever come before you. Please, Chastity. Forgive me and marry me and have a bunch of babies with me, and I'll—'

The rest of his words are cut off, because I'm kissing him. And crying, bawling, really, and Trevor hugs me hard and long. His arms are shaking, and his eyes are wet. Then he pries me off him and slides a ring onto my finger. 'I had to go to Jurgenskill for this,' he says, grinning. 'Nothing in town was open.' I

443

just wrap my arms around him again, because really, I don't even care what the ring looks like; it could be a piece of string as far as I'm concerned. All I can do is cling to Trevor and weep, apparently.

'Well, holy crap!' my father blurts in the silence. 'Where the hell did this come from?'

'About time,' Mark declares.

'Here, here,' Jack seconds.

'You're telling me,' Matt says. 'Try living with her.'

'Did you guys know?' Lucky asks. 'I've known for years.'

'Can I be your flower girl?' Claire asks.

But I hardly hear anyone, because Trevor is kissing me and whispering, over and over, 'I love you, Chas. I love you, I love you, I love you.'

EPILOGUE

Eight months later, I have to pee so badly I may die.

'I know, it's uncomfortable,' Sally the tech says, squeezing warm goo onto my stomach. 'But just you wait. It's worth it. How far along are you?'

'Fourteen weeks,' I answer.

Trevor takes my hand and squeezes it hard, grinning, those beautiful brown eyes dancing.

We got married a month after my mom's wedding. We had no flower girls or limos. I wore a cute little white dress and my red high-tops. Buttercup waited outside, baying mournfully, and Matt sneaked her in just before the ceremony started, distracting the clerk with his movie-star good looks.

City Hall was packed with O'Neills, C Platoon, A Platoon and D Platoon (B Platoon had to work), Bev Ludevoorsk, Ernesto and his wife and the whole staff of the *Eaton Falls Gazette*, minus Lucia, who quit the day after her first date with Ryan Darling, M.D.

Nothing fancy, just Elaina as my matron of honor and my father as best man. I was bawling by the time Trevor took my hand and told me he'd love me and cherish me all the days of his life. In fact, there wasn't a dry eye

445

in the house. Dad was crying, Mom was crying, Elaina was hiccupping away, the Starahs . . . even Harry, still mostly a stranger to me, was crying! We went to Emo's for the reception. It was the most beautiful wedding ever.

If you're wondering about Perfect Hayden, well, guess what? Trevor dumped her the night I went over with the note. When I asked him why, he just said, 'Why do you think, dummy?' And then he kissed me, and we ended up doing it on the stair landing, not able to wait till we got to our bed upstairs.

'So do you guys want to know the sex?' the tech asks, staring at the screen.

'Sure,' Trevor answers. I concentrate on the blurry, other-worldly images on the screen.

Suddenly, we can see a profile . . . a little nose, forehead, lips, a tiny, ghostly hand. My heart bucks, and Trevor sucks in a breath.

'There's your baby.' Sally smiles.

Our baby. That's our baby. I look at my husband, unable to speak. His eyes are full of tears. I smile wobbly, and he kisses my hand.

'Oh, hey, what's this?' Sally says, frowning at the screen.

My stomach drops, and an ice-cold wave of fear sucks the joy out of my heart.

'What is it?' Trevor asks, his hand gripping mine.

'Huh,' she murmurs. 'Did you guys know you were having twins?'

It takes a minute for those words to register.

'Holy crap,' I breathe, a huge smile bursting over my face.

Trevor's shoulders are shaking, his hand covering his face. Laughing, crying, some of both. 'Oh, Chastity, I love you,' he whispers.

'They're identical,' Sally says. 'See that? One placenta, one sac. How wonderful!'

'Can you tell what they are?' I ask, turning back to look at my babies. My *babies!*

'I sure can,' she says. 'Congratulations. You're having boys.'

'Holy crap!' Trevor blurts, laughing. 'Oh, my God. You're amazing, Chastity. Wait till your father hears.'

Smiling, crying from the sheer joy of it, I reach down and touch my slightly rounded stomach. My boys. My sons. Four brothers, the Eaton Falls Fire Department, Trevor and now twin sons.

Looks like I'll always be one of the guys.

And you know what? That's fine with me.